Struggling
Free

A first novel by Margaret Penfold, Undiscovered Authors Regional Fiction Winner.

Acknowledgements

So many people have given me so much of their time and expertise during the years this novel developed that I found it difficult knowing where to start with my thanks. In the end I adopted the strictly chronological approach.

My first thanks then goes to Jean Chapman, who persuaded me to start this novel way back in 1983 and has been unfailing in her support ever since. Never has it been truer of anyone that if you want a favour doing, you ask a busy person.

I could not have managed without the initial help of two people, who do not wish to be named, but who provided me with insider help on Arabic and Jewish political attitudes and customs during the mandate period.

I bless the day I stumbled on the web page of the Palestine Police Old Comrades Association. The help of their forum members has been invaluable. I must thank them for being such good friends over the past nine years and answering all my questions so enthusiastically

I am grateful to my family too for providing me with loving care and not teasing me too much over my prolonged unpublished status. My son John has gone even further and provided literary critique and artwork suggestions.

Margaret Kaine, a friend from the time we were in creative writing classes together, has been constantly supportive, urging me to keep going despite all those rejection letters, diligently pestering literary agents and hunting out publishing opportunities on my behalf.

That brings me to the time I joined Leicester Writers club. I must thank all members who had given me such wonderful support. In particular, I would like to thank Bead Roberts, Dave Martin, and Biddy Nelson, all extremely busy people who have made the time to wade through my manuscripts and provide most positive and useful critiques.

Lastly, in chronological terms, I must say Thank you to 'Discovered Authors', who have shown sufficient faith in my work to publish it, and particularly to Natalie who has been so patient with me through the ups and downs in the complex process of getting the work into print and between covers.

Struggling
Free

By
Margaret Penfold

Penford, Margar   iamond

Struggling free   s
/ by Margaret
Penfold

ISBN13 978-1-905108-40-4

Printed in the UK by BookForce

BookForce UK's policy is to use papers that are natural, renewable and
recyclable products and made from wood grown in sustainable forests
where ever possible

BookForce UK Ltd.
50 Albemarle Street
London W1S 4BD
www.bookforce.co.uk
www.discoveredauthors.co.uk

Granny Hadad marched over to the Bay bush and held up one of the failed eggs.

'See this hole at the side? The chick started to crack the egg but was unable to struggle free.'

'Couldn't you have broken the shell for it, Gran?'

'No, Suzanna, chicks have to break out themselves. If someone does it for them, they never survive.'

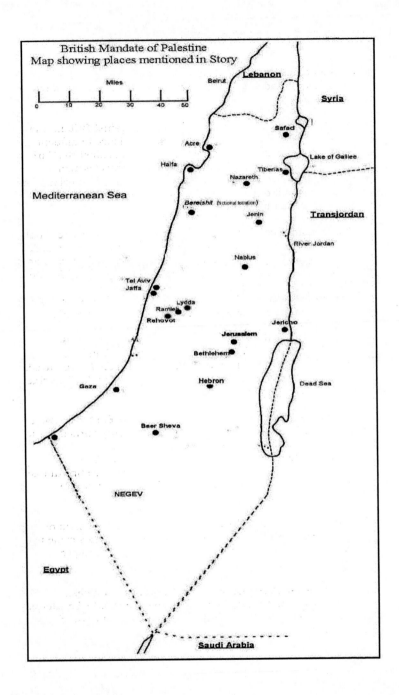

Background History and Introduction

In 1938, when this story starts, Palestine as a country was only sixteen years old; it had previously been part of Syria and ruled by the Turks.

During WW1, when Turkey sided with Germany against Britain, the British Embassy in Cairo offered political independence to influential Arab sheiks in the Turkish Empire, if they rebelled against the Turks. Back in England, Balfour, the British foreign Secretary, issued a declaration saying it would favour Palestine becoming a homeland for the Jews, so long as it did not prejudice the civil and religious rights of the non-Jewish communities.

These two, seemingly contradictory promises, might have worked out, if it had not been for the presence of oil in the neighbouring lands of the Middle East. Energy hungry France and Britain needed ports on the East Mediterranean coast to which oil could be piped. While the British foreign secretary and British ambassadors were making promises to both Arabs and Jews, the British government was conspiring with the French to carve up the Turkish Empire.

In 1922, the League of Nations granted a mandate to France to administer what is now Syria and Lebanon and gave Britain a mandate for Iraq, Transjordan and Palestine. The Arabs felt betrayed. The League of Nations stipulation that Britain should make Palestine a national home for Jews added to their grievances.

Britain speedily built an oil pipeline from the Middle East to Haifa, a previously insignificant village on the bay of Acre. They turned it into a modern town, with a large harbour and oil refinery. Goal achieved, Britain handed Iraq and Jordan over to Arab leadership, but found itself still having to administer Palestine due to the difficulty of creating a Jewish homeland in a country where most inhabitants were Arabs.

The situation might have resolved itself, since, in the 1920s, more Jews left Palestine than entered it. In 1933, however, Nazis came to power in Germany. To the dismay of the Arabs, Jewish refugees flooded into Palestine.

In 1936, the Arabs in Palestine rebelled. They cut the oil pipe, sabotaged transport and communication systems and attacked Jewish settlements. By October 1938, Arabs were in control of most of Eastern Palestine.

'This is the situation when the story's first fictional character Patsy Quigley, a seventeen year old British woman of Irish extraction, enters Palestine. Patsy's family belongs to a fictional fundamentalist group, The Second Chosen. In that era Palestine acted as a magnet for fundamentalists from all three major religions that traced their history back to the patriarch Abraham - Judaism, Christianity and Islam. Although fictional the Second Chosen are typical of the many fundamentalist Christian groups in Palestine'

Please refer to the glossary at the back of this book for explanations and definitions of unfamiliar terms.

Part 1

Shell-bound

Chapter 1

October 1938

Patsy knew nothing except that she was unhappy. When more fully awake, she felt her clothes soaked in sweat and wondered why she was wearing a dress, not pyjamas. Her nostrils complained of fusty air. She opened her eyes to darkness. Her body, swaying to a rhythm of metallic clattering, told her she was on a train. A chorus of snores brought her up-to-date. She was with her parents and assorted missionaries 2000 miles from where she wanted to be, and she had a problem that she could not share.

She needed a wash and wanted a cigarette. She fumbled in her overnight bag, found her flashlight, and shone it briefly on her watch. Seven am. If the train were on schedule, they would be in the Negev by now.

She picked up her bag, groped her way past her parents, and slid open the carriage door, blinking at the brightness of electric bulbs that had seemed so dim the previous night. Quickly she stepped into the corridor and pushed the door shut behind her. She scowled at a notice pasted across a steel shutter.

Do not attempt to open by order of the Palestinian Government

Some wag had scribbled beneath, 'Unless you enjoy being shot at.'

She remembered a chorus she used to sing in Sunday School.

We're all aboard on the Hallelujah train.
On the holy gospel line.
When God calls 'Who's for Heaven?'
We answer -'Us, we're saved'.

This Hallelujah train, though, felt as if someone had diverted it to hell.

She headed for the lavatory at the end of the coach. Struggling in the confined space, and thankful to be slim, she stripped off her clothes and sponged off sweat and grime accumulated since leaving Port Said. She powdered her face to disguise faint freckles on her forehead, brushed her shoulder length fair hair, and rolled end curls round her fingers. She checked that her eyebrows needed no further plucking and applied mascara to her lashes but didn't dare use her lipstick. Her father would notice that. She donned fresh underwear, shook out a clean linen dress.

Leaving the lavatory, she contemplated smoking in the corridor but realised that her father could emerge at any time. She trod across shaking plates that joined the first class carriage to the restaurant car. No one else was there so she sat at the nearest dining table and drew her bag of smoking apparatus out of the secret pocket in her bag.

She contemplated her gold lighter, a parting present from Tim. Not seeing him for a whole year was unbearable. She remembered the thrill running all the way up her arm when they had first held hands, walking by the lakeside in his country home and the ecstasy when, two days later, he had kissed her so gently.

She fitted a Craven-A into a holder, lit it and practised blowing perfect smoke circles. A waiter wearing a long white tunic, scarlet fez, and crimson cummerbund emerged from the galley, coffee pot and menu in his hands. She was hungry but conscious that she had spent almost all her month's allowance in Port Said, confined herself to ordering a café au lait. After the waiter left, she returned her lighter and silver cigarette case to her bag and wallowed in the misery of missed opportunities. Why hadn't she run off and found herself a job while she had the chance? She inhaled deeply, heaped two spoonfuls of sugar into her coffee and considered that question along with the related ones. Why had she never had the guts to stand up to her father? Why did she always give in to him in the end?

She closed her eyes and relived the scene when she had met up with her mother after her parents had returned from a tour of Ireland. Freshly in love, she had been so happy that afternoon. She had babbled away about her plans to read archaeology at Oxford, working her way up to mentioning Tim. She only noticed the lack of response, when her mother stretched up from the case she was unpacking, and said, 'Your father wants to talk to you. You're to meet him in the park across the road.'

Patsy took another drag on her cigarette. Somewhere within that scene in the park lay the answers to her questions.

She recalled setting out, certain that now she was this new grown-up, in-love, sort of person, she could deal with whatever torrent of verbal penitence her father was about to pour over her that day.

It hadn't happened that way. He had greeted her with the bald statement that he had booked her a passage to Haifa.

Patsy replaced the coffee cup on its saucer, and stared at a gloomy monochrome poster of the Garden of Gethsemane, while fighting off an earlier memory that rode on this one's back. She forced that earlier memory to recede by focussing on the present.

Being here in Palestine did not mean she had to fulfil all her father's expectations. She need not be born again in the blood of the lamb, nor give up mixing with unbelievers. To start as she meant to go on, she would refuse to attend Morning Service on Sunday. That would show him.

A British Palestine Police sergeant entered the restaurant car. She recognised him as the good-looking constable a friend's big sister had brought to Good News services when she was ten. How he had escaped conversion, despite everyone praying for his soul, had greatly puzzled her at the time.

'Good morning, Sergeant Monteith,' she said, holding her cigarette holder above her shoulder, Bette Davis style.

Pausing, the sergeant raised his eyebrows, obviously puzzled that she could greet him by name. Then he smiled.   'You must be the Quigley girl. I saw your parents at Kantara. Well, well, little Patsy, all grown up! Sent to school in England, weren't you?'

'Yes, five years of it.'

The sergeant surveyed the empty carriage. 'May I join you?'

This was more of an adventure than she had expected. 'Of course.'

He slid into the seat opposite.   She leant back and blew a smoke ring; she was Margaret Lockwood playing opposite a fuller-lipped Ronald Coleman. If only she had had the courage to put on lipstick. Not that she would be unfaithful to Tim, not now she had almost promised to marry him. Besides the sergeant was too old for romance, he must be nearly thirty.

The waiter returned with menus.

'I-I'm eating with my family,' she stuttered in embarrassment.

Sergeant Monteith raised a hand. 'Please, Miss Quigley, do be my guest.'

She pictured her father's annoyance when he found her breakfasting with an unbeliever. It was too good an opportunity to miss, but she didn't want to sponge on a stranger. 'Thank you, Sergeant Monteith. Maybe just a coffee and roll.'

The waiter refilled her cup. The sergeant leaned back. 'My friends call me Peter, Miss Quigley.'

'And my name is still Patsy.'

Peter pulled a starched napkin from its ring and immersed himself in the menu. The coffee lapped at the sides of the cup. He looked up; 'I'm having the full breakfast, Patsy and will feel uncomfortable eating it opposite someone nibbling a roll.'

The aroma of coffee had brought on hunger pangs. She gave in to temptation gracefully.

Once the waiter had gone, Peter leaned forward. 'Strange time to be visiting Palestine, at the end of the school holidays?'

'I-I'm home for a year, t-to get practical archaeological experience,' that stammer again, as if she were lying, but it was true, even if she had only thought about going on a dig after her father had forced her return.

Peter frowned, his fingers drumming the table. 'Where?'

He sounded as if she had said something out of place or perhaps her uncustomary stammer had put him off. She watched his face as she replied, 'In Samaria.'

He laced his fingers. 'But Patsy, Samaria is Oozelbart territory.'

'Oozelbart?' a word new to her.

'Terrorist, bandit, what you will - Oozlebarts have completely taken over that part of Palestine. There'll be no digs there this year.'

She sat back, disappointed. She had so wanted to work with the famous archaeologist, Kathleen Kenyon. She tried another site that had fired her imagination. 'What about the Jezreel Valley and Megiddo?'

Peter shook his head. 'The American team that comes out every year hire local villagers to do the donkeywork. They will let you look around, but that's all. If you just want to visit ancient sites, you could do worse than take a look at the caves at Wadi Mughara. They are not too far from Haifa.'

'The Neanderthal Caves? Yes, I read about them.'

The waiter brought bowls of steaming porridge. She poured cold milk on hers as she enthused, 'The way they got out that whole skeleton, completely encased in about a ton of earth, to England. It was like a miracle. I...'

Then everything changed.

A metallic explosion. A gigantic jolt. A screech of wheels.

Patsy felt herself thrown back against the seat, and then bounced forward. Her porridge dish slid towards her, and lifted from the table. Someone screamed. Peter's hands slid across the table, pushing his cutlery. She thudded back again.

Darkness. She wondered if she had died.

Her hands gripped the arms of her chair. Her fingers rubbed woven fabric beneath the velvet. Dead people couldn't do that - could they? She lifted wet fingers to her nose. Not blood, coffee. She slid her feet forward. The floor was solid. Why couldn't she see? Her back twisted in fear until she remembered the closed shutters.

'Patsy, are you OK?' Peter's voice from a distance.

'My parents?' she panicked. 'Are they all right?'

'Wait here. I'll find out.'

She detected an underlying tremor in his voice, and for some reason the tremor reassured. The table shook; she heard his feet moving from under the table, then his footsteps crunching as they moved up the aisle.

Blinding radiance forced her eye shut. She jerked her head away from the source of light and cautiously opened her eyelids. She saw, as if through a sheet of water, the waiter sitting motionless on a table, a large coffee stain marring the white of his tunic, a mess of broken crockery and liquid on the floor. She turned, able to bear the light now. Peter stood in the open doorway, revolver in hand, staring out. He swivelled his head and his voice skated across stillness. 'The first class carriage is fine, Patsy. Your parents will be OK.'

She watched his mouth move, almost in slow motion, as he spoke to the waiter, 'You have water in the galley?'

The waiter sprang to his feet. 'Sir, I will see to it now, sir.'

More crunching of glass.

Peter climbed down until only his head remained visible. He called out, 'Patsy, you're sure you're all right?'

'I told you.' She was immediately ashamed of the unnecessary snap in her voice. She felt her feet trembling; her attempt to control them failed.

'In that case, if there is water, tell the man to fetch it. Then gather up clean tea towels and carbolic soap. Bring them outside unless you hear shooting.'

He dropped out of sight.

She hauled herself to her feet, swaying dizzily. Her mother burst into the carriage. 'Oh Patsy, praise the Lord, you are all right.'

'Um Pat!' Patsy ran towards her mother and hugged her tight. 'Um Pat, I'm so glad you're OK. I was so worried.'

'Things may be worse further down the line,' her mother warned, 'Your father's gone to see what he can do. Now that I know you aren't injured, I'll join him.'

'I am collecting cloths and soap,' Patsy said, 'The waiter is fetching water.'

'I'll see you outside then.' Her mother left.

Patsy made her way down the aisle, kicking aside broken crockery. She could hear distant screams, mixed with a louder, incongruous bleating of sheep, but no gunshots. Pushing through the swing doors of the galley, she discovered the cook, eyes glazed, holding up blistered hands. Fat, frying pans, porridge, and sausages littered the floor; only the screwed-down water boiler remained upright.

She had to help him. She tried the cold tap. It worked. Hoping she was doing the right thing, she pressed a wet cloth round his hands. In Arabic, rusty from years of disuse, she said,

'You must keep the cloths on.' He managed a faint 'Kataherek,' in respectful thanks.

The waiter returned, filled a bucket, showed her, when asked, where he kept the linen cloths and bars of red carbolic soap. She hated leaving the cook in agony, but could think of nothing further she could do.

She carried the cloths and soap to the carriage door. Outside, beyond the parallel line of telegraph posts, an expanse of seemingly flat grey rock stretched to the horizon, yet when she looked to her left, the railway line curved round a scarp high enough to hide the front of the train. A goat bolted past, out beyond the guard's van, into the wilderness. Sheep were jumping through a ventilation gap in the overturned cattle truck. The luggage van had cracked open, spilling trunks and suitcases. Closer, four second-class carriages, still intact, tilted at increasingly awkward angles. Soldiers with Tommy guns stood alert at the doors. Other soldiers, flat on their stomachs, lay on the ground, eyes to their rifle sights.

She dropped what she was carrying to the ground, before stepping onto an iron ladder that ended halfway down. She reached the bottom rung, took a deep breath, and jumped. Clinker grazed her knees, laddered her silk stockings.

'Patsy!' Her mother stood in the doorway of the first class carriage, holding her fashionable cloche. 'You'll get sunstroke before you know it. You must wear your hat.' She threw it down.

Tugging it on, Patsy looked up. Her mother was holding the canvas bag that accompanied every journey they made. It contained water, primus, metal teapot, evaporated milk, sugar, and a first aid box.

Patsy stretched up to take the bag and then helped her mother down.

'The cook burnt his hands,' she told her, 'I wrapped them in wet cloths. Is there anything else I should have done?'

Her mother shook her head. 'No, I don't think so. I'll check him later. I'm afraid we'll see worse before the day is out.'

They passed the guard perched on one of the telegraph poles that marched parallel to the track. He held a phone to his ear.

'Let's hope that the Arabs haven't cut the wires in both directions,' her mother said, 'We don't want to be stuck here.'

Rounding the bend, they discovered the extent of the disaster. All third class carriages, apart from one that had slid over the tender, lay on their sides. Smoke poured from the cabin of the overturned engine.

Patsy gritted her teeth. Her mother said quietly. 'Wallowing in emotion will help no one.'

Her father, along with Peter Monteith and several other men, was already wrenching off shutters. A woman in a black scarf, blood pouring from her face, pushed a baby through shattered glass. A boy of about four, his face covered in blood, tugged at her father's legs, attempting to drag him to another window.

'Um, um,' he screamed.

'Ann,' her father shouted, over his shoulder, 'See to this child. He's getting in the way,' but her mother was in the middle of lighting the primus.

'I'll go,' Patsy offered and clambered up. As gently as she could, she prised the struggling boy from her father. Blood poured from a gash in the child's cheek. She was overcome with pity. What could she do to show she was only meaning to help? She tried, 'I must mend your face,' hoping it sounded better in Arabic, then carried him, screaming, and kicking, down to ground level.

When she straightened, the child wrenched free. She caught him as he tried to climb back, held him firmly while she cleaned his face, flinching at the sight of exposed bone.

Her mother handed her a bottle of iodine. 'That cut really needs stitches – but you'll have to do your best.'

She didn't want to use the iodine, knowing how much it hurt but if she didn't the cut would turn septic. She steeled herself, trying to ignore the boy screams. She applied a plaster and let him go. He raced back to another carriage window beneath which her father and Peter Monteith were now panting in their efforts to extricate a woman whose hands still gripped the legs of a pair of chickens. The little boy wriggled himself through the window and buried his head in the woman's wide sleeve.

She saw Peter wipe a filthy hand over his sweating forehead. 'We can't free her, Seamus,' she heard him say; 'We'll have to leave her.'

Patsy raised her arms. 'Peter, can you pass the child to me?'

Peter shook his head. 'Let him stay. His mother will worry less knowing where he is.'

From the next carriage down, a voice, with a strong Cambridge accent, shouted, 'If anyone has water bring it here.'

She took over a jug, but whoever had called for water was no longer there, only Arabs struggling to push back a caved-in roof crushing a blood-covered youth. She handed the jug to a man taller than the rest who had a scar cutting across an eyebrow.

'Shukra.' He muttered his thanks in colloquial Arabic, as if they were equals, and poured water into the mouth of the trapped youth.

The next few hours passed in a blur as she bathed wounds, gave out drinks, and pulled out people trapped under wreckage.

The sun grew hotter. She helped build a ramp out of wreckage so they could drag the worst of the wounded into the shade of the intact first and second-class carriages. Her mother handed her a cup of heavily sugared tea. She sat on the ground to sip it and became conscious of the foul odour of blood and excrement mingling with her own stink of dried sweat, porridge, and coal dust. Screams from the wounded punctuated a continuous buzzing from flies circling unbound wounds. Where, she wondered, did flies come from in this seemingly lifeless wilderness? She slapped at them as they swarmed round her and put her hands to eyes smarting from heat and salt.

'Pull yourself together, Patsy,' her father ordered as he passed by and she stood up to start over again.

At the end of eternity, and just before the water ran out, an engine chugged in from the North drawing wagons of repair equipment, carriages filled with rail workers, doctors, and nurses. Professionals took over. The guard ushered unwounded passengers onto the relief train.

One hundred miles to the North of the Negev, in the fertile Sharon Valley, another seventeen year old, Dalia Leitner, from a German Jewish family, was hurrying down concrete steps to her school's soundproof basement.

Chapter 2

For the second time that week, Dalia knew she was going to be late home, and she had run out of excuses. If her best friend, Ruth, had been with her, she could have pleaded an impromptu hockey practice, but Ruth didn't belong to the club's firearms section.

The Youth Leader explained the extra rifle practice. 'In the current situation, you lot will be using arms in earnest before the year is out.'

'But we've no weapons,' Dalia pointed out.

'Hagana are busy persuading all settlements to invest in firearms,' the Youth Leader told her.

'Our kibbutz already has a large stock,' drawled a boy who's Hebrew had retained much of his parents' Yankee accent.

Amos, the arrogant little schmuck. He had tried it on only last week in the bike shed. She'd soon had his hand out of her blouse and back where it belonged. Dalia hoped his crotch was still sore. She envied him access to arms though. The oh-so-respectable grown-ups of Bereishit would never agree to anything illegal. The only firearms in her settlement were the licensed shotguns the night guards carried.

By the time practice had finished, and she had pedalled home, she still hadn't concocted a credible pretext for being late.

Itzack Wollheim, the settlement's blacksmith was on gate duty that evening.

'There's someone at your house, came on a motorbike,' he told her, as he unlocked the heavy padlock.

She hoped a stranger might divert her mother's attention and wondered what kind of visitor had come by motorbike.

It wasn't just any old motorbike, she realised, as she reached the house and saw the Record machine next to the kitchen wall. Only one person she knew owned a top model like that. Bubbles of excitement streamed out from her chest along the length of her body. She flung her cycle to the ground, took a deep breath, straightened her back, cooed a Shalom, and made an elegant entrance.

As she had anticipated, Cousin Elsa's youngest son, Shimon Mabovitch, motorcycle champion of the Maccabean games was there, lolling at the kitchen table next to her father who was still wearing his muddy work-clothes.

Shimon's eyebrows arched as he rose to shake hands. 'Is this the lanky girl with ginger pigtails I used to know?'

Dalia gave a complacent pat to her auburn curls, and tilted back her head in Myrna Loy fashion. 'I've grown up since then.'

Her mother entered from the yard. 'Ai-ee Dalia, late again? Who is this boy who makes you keep the goats waiting?'

Dalia's cheeks flamed.

'Are you so ashamed of him,' her mother carried on, 'that you can't bring him to meet us? He's a kibbutznik, yet? Shimon, these children of mine, they have no respect for their parents. They tell us nothing. You would not treat your mother so.'

Shimon glanced at his watch. 'Cousin Trudi, I need to look round Bereishit before it gets dark.'

'Dalia, can show you round,' her mother replied.

Dalia looked at her mother in surprise, while her heart knocked against her chest.

'But, Eema, the goats...'

'You should thank your father, busy though he is; he milked them for you, and showed Shimon the animal sheds at the same time.'

Her father winked, and she guessed he had used the excuse to have a session with Shimon on his own.

Dalia could scarcely look at Shimon as they left the house. The more she tried to force her face into fashionable pallor, the worse it burned. Her nose must be shining like a Hanukah candle. She was bursting to tell him that she had no boyfriend.

'I was at firearms practice,' she said, 'but don't tell my parents. They would kill me.'

'Understood,' he assured her, and added, 'I hear you're a reasonable shot.'

Her body pulsated in delight but she pulled herself together, remembering her duty as his guide. She pointed to the oval of neat bungalows.

'Everyone lived in two-room wooden huts before we came. Now most people have used my father's designs to build larger houses of cob and red tiles that suit the climate better.'

Shimon displayed little interest in her father's architectural skills. He seemed more interested in the stone synagogue at the heart of the oval.

'A good strong building that,' he approved, 'It could keep you safe if you get raided. Now show me this perimeter fence your brother Uri spoke of so proudly.'

Dalia led him up the track at the side of their house, past the animal sheds into the fields beyond the buildings. She waved to the fan shaped fields on her immediate right. 'That is my father's land.'

Shimon looked surprised. 'I thought your community owned everything in common?'

'No, Bereishit is a moshav not a kibbutz. We market cooperatively, club together to buy expensive equipment, and the whole community decides on what crops to grow each year, but every family takes the profit from their own two fields and orchard.'

'So everyone farms?'

'Every family, but some family members earn money in other ways. For instance, Frieda Alterman is a midwife, Thelma Goldstein runs our bakery, and Itzack Wollheim has set up an ironworks on his father's land and markets goods to people outside the moshav.'

A pleasant perfume of orange blossom wafted from beyond the top field. Dalia watched Shimon give an appreciative sniff and reflected how much he would miss the orange groves of Rehovot now he worked for the water company. When they reached her family's grove though, Shimon marched past the citrus trees, pausing only to ask about the pyramids of fist-sized stones standing close to some of the trunks.

'We collected them to defend ourselves in case of an Arab attack,' she told him.

He nodded and moved to the boundary to examine the eight-foot stout wire fence with its formidable overhang. 'Not as impregnable as your brother suggested,' he commented. 'Wouldn't keep off a determined attack.'

He studied the outlying houses of the nearby Arab village, then walked back to lean on the orchard gate and gaze across the harvested cornfields where the setting sun highlighted tethered Billy goats nibbling at the stubble. He studied the quilt of vegetable patches, and beyond them the geometrical eclipse of neat houses with windows glowing gold in the sunset. Dalia leaned on the gate beside him.

'Everything is so orderly,' Shimon commented, 'It would drive my father insane. He would especially hate that perimeter fence cutting you off from your neighbours.'

'But our neighbours are inside the fence.'

Shimon straightened. 'Nu? Those people from the Arab village? They are not neighbours?'

Dalia thumped the gatepost. 'No!' Memory accompanied the denial. She and her parents, fresh from Germany, on their hotel balcony near the station in Haifa, unable to travel further because of a riot. Arabs, on the street below, throwing stones at policemen. Her mother sobbing 'Oh, Albert, it's out of the frying pan into the fire.' Her father comforting, 'Once we settle at Bereishit, Trudi, you won't have to know Arabs are here.'

She turned to face Shimon. 'We have nothing to do with them.'

Shimon shook his head. 'That fence!'

'What's the matter with it?'

'It's a challenge to the young men - Arabs who haven't had a chance to get to know you as people growing oranges, vegetables, owning a few sheep and goats, a cow or two, just like themselves. We have no fence round Rehovot. We have no trouble.'

'Not yet, you haven't,' she snapped, and then hated herself. Here she was alone with Shimon, her ultimate dream come true, and all she could do was quarrel.

Shimon shrugged. 'If you keep the fence, then you must arm properly. Hagana can find you weapons.' He leaned back on the gate.

His stance reminded her of his father, Uncle Moshe, although, of course, Shimon was taller and far better looking.

Another flash of memory. Uncle Moshe, short-legged, bushy-bearded, fetching them in his mule-cart from Lydda station after the riot in Haifa had died down. The mule cart catching up with an Arab shepherd wearing a live lamb round his neck. Uncle Moshe slowing the cart, greeting the Arab unintelligibly. The shepherd, noticing her gazing at the lamb, bending down to stroke a woolly sheep, whispering in its ear, waiting a few seconds, then gently lifting the lamb from his shoulders, holding it out to her.

She relived that moment of thrilled awe when she'd said, 'May I, really?'

And a smiling Uncle Moshe replying, 'B'Seder. Mahmoud, here, has asked the mother's permission.'

The first time she had touched live fur. The lamb nestling in her lap. Uncle Moshe telling her father, 'This man's grandsons help me with my orange harvest when they are not busy in their uncle's groves.'

Her shock at hearing that statement; her father's raised eyebrows; Uncle Moshe's response, 'I know, I know, Alfred. The Agency says we should employ only Jews but, in Rehovot, we believe we should work hand-in-hand with Arabs. Of course we give precedence to Jews, but at harvest there is work for all.'

Yes, she thought now, Shimon has inherited his father's maverick outlook but how can he combine that with his position in Hagana?

She probed, 'You don't approve of moshav villages?'

'But I do,' he assured her, 'I want to found a moshav in the Negev but in the right way, cooperating with the Arabs already there. We need to solve the irrigation problems first, of course.'

He straightened and gave a devastating smile. She experienced a frightening quivering between her thighs.

'And what do you want to do when you grow up, Dalia?'

A slap in the face, that. She drew herself erect, threw back her permed head. 'I am grown-up now.'

He nodded. 'I am sorry. I could have framed that better. I meant, what career are you intending to follow when you leave school?'

She tossed her head. 'Pioneering farming.'

'Why?'

'It's the only way to serve Eretz Israel.' She heard the smugness behind her words and hid her cheeks in her hands. If only she had been born a blonde. A blush might look fetching beneath fair hair, but under red?

She watched Shimon's smile fade. 'There are other ways to serve Eretz Israel, Dalia. I will be speaking to you about them soon.'

He must mean he would invite her to join Hagana! She walked back in the deepening dusk bubbling with excitement.

During supper, she mulled over their conversation. Her elation abated as she remembered what a balagan she had made of the unprecedented opportunity.

Shimon and her father left after supper to discuss security with Rav Cohen, the moshav's unofficial leader, who lived next door. Dalia had only just finished helping her mother wash up and was putting her homework on the kitchen table, when Ruth came over carrying her homework in a satchel. The two of them retired to Dalia's minute bedroom. Sitting on the bed, her exercise book propped on a board on her knees, Dalia regaled Ruth with most of the conversation she had had with Shimon. She asked her what Ruth's father would think about the moshav buying illegal arms.

'He'll never let us have them.' Ruth said, 'You're doing all that training with Youth Club for nothing. How did your mother take to you being late home?'

'She thinks I have a secret boyfriend.'

'Doesn't she know how you feel about Shimon?'

'She doesn't think of him as boyfriend material.'

'But you're not related by blood, you said.'

'I think my mother forgets that sometimes.'

They stopped talking to concentrate on their homework. At least, Dalia supposed, Ruth was concentrating. She herself had one ear open, listening for Shimon's return. She wanted to cry when she heard his motorbike rev up and roar off.

Up in the Judaean hills, a third woman, Suzanna Khader, from a Christian Arabic family, walked to work on the outskirts of Jerusalem. A woman, this undersized child of fourteen? In Palestine, in 1938 many Arabic women, both Muslim and Christian married at fourteen.

Chapter 3

With every step, the bags in Suzanna's hands grew heavier and her worries burrowed deeper. She wished she had listened to her Aunt and stayed in Beirut. What should she do if Rebels had occupied the house?

As she trudged up the potholed drive between two dusty fallow fields, she watched anxiously for movement in the belt of pine trees surrounding her employers' isolated home. Resting the bags on the ground, she fingered the white scarf covering her hair, remembering her mother's words when they had met, all too briefly, at Lydda bus station.

'For once, and I never thought I'd live to say this, Suzanna dear, I agree with your Aunt Julie. You should have stayed in Beirut. If you insist on coming back to Palestine you must get yourself a black scarf.'

She wished she had walked on further this morning and found a shop selling the black scarves worn to demonstrate support for the Rebellion, but the vegetables had been so heavy.

At the fork in the drive Suzanna started towards the kitchen courtyard, until she realised that going round the back of the house would expose her to anyone hiding in the pine trees. It would be safer to use the front door.

Her legs didn't want to cross the stone slabs of the veranda but she forced them on. Outside the door, she pulled a bunch of keys from one of the bags, then hesitated, and instead tugged at a chain beside the door. A camel bell above the lintel clanged loudly. When, after a whole minute, she heard nothing, she unlocked the door, cautiously pushed it open onto the whitewashed hall, and sniffed. The air smelt reassuringly stale. She took the vegetables into the kitchen and carried her bags of schoolbooks and clothes up to the bedroom she shared with Renshaw. A warm glow came over her at the thought of seeing him, Evie and little Clare again.

She inspected the rest of the house. No signs of disturbance, so she threw back shutters and returned to the kitchen to peel potatoes.

A knock on the back door startled her. She peered through the window and saw the deliveryman with the groceries Mrs Shepard had ordered before leaving for England. The butcher's boy was not far behind.

She had stew and potatoes simmering on the electric stove and was making Renshaw's bed, when the doorbell clanged.

Thinking that the Shepards had returned early, she raced downstairs, and flung open the front door, only to find a uniformed messenger boy outside. He thrust out a telegram with her name on it. Her body went still as her mind raced from one disaster to the next:

Her mother had taken a turn for the worse?

Rebels had assassinated her uncle?

The British had arrested her brother?

Conscious of the boy's impatient shuffle, she forced trembling fingers to open the flimsy envelope.

'DELAYED EGYPT STOP BACK LUNCH TOMORROW STOP JAMES SHEPARD'

Her relief so great, she could only shake her head when the boy asked if there was a reply, but even before his bike had bounced down the drive, she had another worry. That night she would be alone in the house.

She stood in the hall tugging at a broken fingernail, then shrugged, and returned to the kitchen, now sweltering under its corrugated iron roof. She gazed at the steaming saucepans and thought of Mary from the workers' quarters, a woman only a year older than herself but married with a small baby. Mary was not a close friend but they talked whenever they met in the grounds. She might welcome a portion of stew.

Suzanna walked through the kitchen yard, skirted a ruined mosaic-lined pool, and took a path leading to the estate workers communal courtyard, marked out by a single row of rocks. To her embarrassment, Mary was sitting with other women, all embroidering tablecloths for the tourist trade. Babies slept under their chairs; small children raced round the courtyard and young girls minded the cooking fires.

The women saw her and stopped sewing; the young girls left their posts, the small children forgot their games. Flustered, Suzanna kept her gaze fixed on her friend.

'Mary, I have made beef stew but Mr and Mrs Shepard are not coming until tomorrow.'

A woman she recognised as the supervisor's domineering wife asked, 'And you do not wish to waste this food?'

Too embarrassed to reply, Suzanna could only jerk an Arabic negative.

The supervisor's wife revealed her prized gold tooth. 'Then we will come to help you out. We will be over, as soon as we have fed our men.'

Suzanna gave an involuntary gasp – a dozen or so women and twice that number of children, for a meal intended for five?

She, hurried back, certain that the women were laughing at her. There was nothing she could do now except boil rice to supplement the potatoes and extend the stew with onions.

Two hours later, all the women and children were sitting on the ground outside the Shepards' kitchen eating, not only the stew and potatoes, but olives, tomatoes and freshly baked flat bread that they had brought with them.

The women chatted companionably while the children played. When they had discussed the Rebels' progress long enough, the conversation switched to the peculiar habits of the British.

'Why do Inglisi cook indoors, even in the height of summer?'

'Why do they deliberately expose their skins to salt water and burning sun?'

She confessed her ignorance on these subjects but when the supervisor's wife asked, 'And why do they wear red coats when they ride horses to hunt jackals?' She remembered something Mr Shepard had once said.

'I have heard it is the unspeakable in pursuit of the inedible.'

The women pondered this riddle - the inedible was easy. 'That is the jackal,' they agreed.

Mary hazarded, 'The unspeakable that must be the dogs they take with them.'

'No,' the supervisor's wife contradicted, 'Inglisi love dogs. There is a hidden message in this saying that only the Inglisi can understand.'

More at ease now, Suzanna confided her fear of spending the night alone, 'Last evening, when I was staying near the Bethlehem Road, I heard shooting that sounded as if it came from our olive groves.'

The women giggled.

'No one gets hurt,' one woman said, tossing her head and causing her dowry to jingle.

'You have nothing to worry about,' the supervisor's wife observed.

Mary alone responded sympathetically, 'Suzanna, you can sleep in my house tonight. My husband would not wish any woman to remain alone, unprotected.'

The supervisor's wife looked thoughtful. 'That could prove useful. The Rebels have told my husband they will stay here tonight. The British blew up houses in the village that sheltered them.'

'The British do that in all villages helping Rebels,' put in an old woman. 'We are in danger.'

The supervisor's wife ignored her, and continued, 'Suzanna, if you stay with Mary, the Rebels can sleep in the Inglisi house.'

The women all laughed but Suzanna hesitated. She knew she should be proud of a chance to help the Rebels, but what would Mrs Shepard say if she returned home to find her house wrecked.

'The Rebels must take nothing,' she insisted, 'must leave no mark of their presence. If they do the Police dogs will track them.'

The old woman backed her up, 'I have heard of these dogs from South Africa. A witchdoctor gave them the gift to track even through water and fire.'

'I will warn my husband about the dogs,' the supervisor's wife promised, 'The Rebels will listen to him.'

The women left. Suzanna tidied the courtyard. She checked that she had enough birthday money left to buy more meat, and unpacked her schoolbooks and clothes. A plain wrapped parcel of sanitary towels reminded her of Aunt Julie's hissed instruction when she had handed them to her so furtively on Beirut station. 'If you need these before Christmas, write to me, and I will contact the marriage broker.'

She sat at the desk between her bed and Renshaw's and wrote to her mother.

Dearest Um,
I hope you are feeling better now. I should have told you something yesterday but I was upset at seeing you looking so unwell. Aunt Julie is trying to find me a husband. If you want me to marry then, of course, I will, but if you still want me to carry on studying for matriculation here with Mrs Shepard, could you write to Aunt Julie and tell her,
Your loving daughter,
Suzanna

Having written one letter, she remembered she hadn't yet written her monthly letter to Mrs Quigley, who had befriended her after her mother had sent her to school in Nazareth.

Dear Mrs Quigley,
Thank you for your card. Ireland looks a very beautiful place. I hope you had a good holiday in England too. I am so happy for you that your daughter has come back with you. I know how much you have missed her.
I too am back in Palestine. While I was in Beirut, I went to school with my cousin. The teachers there said I was doing very well for my age and that Mrs Shepard must be a good teacher.
Again, thank you very much for all you have done for me,
With lots of love,
From

She sealed both letters, ready to take them to the Post Office when she went shopping in the morning.

With dusk approaching and the men's evening bonfire already lighting up the top terrace, Suzanna gathered up blankets and her knitting bag and set out, careful to leave the back door unlocked. She had never been inside Mary's house. She imagined it similar to the dark, cockroach-infested room that her family had rented in Jaffa, when her father started up his taxi business.

Mary's room, though, was more like the village home where she had been born. Decorated clay food bins stood in one corner next to gaily-dyed baskets, woven from coils of wheat stalks. A black and white goat-hair rug lay on the floor; a white crocheted cloth covered a low table on which stood gilded icons of the Holy Mother and St George; plus a card from Mrs Shepard congratulating Mary on her recent fifteenth birthday.

In this modern house, though, an electric bulb hung from the ceiling, a walnut sideboard took pride of place at the back of the room and gaz tins replaced pottery water jars.

Suzanna settled comfortably on a sheepskin next to the baby while Mary placed a glass of tea and a sesame cake by her side. When Mary took up her embroidery, Suzanna brought out her knitting.

They were chatting about the afternoon's unexpected feast when Mary's husband, Abu George, came in. He greeted Suzanna courteously before picking up his son, throwing him playfully in the air and catching him. Then, handing the baby to Mary, he retrieved a rusty rifle from under his son's blankets.

While Mary calmed the excited child, Suzanna watched Abu George swagger out to the bonfire around which the other workers, all similarly armed, had gathered. She recognised a handsome young man from Bethlehem who had turned his head and smiled when she had wheeled Renshaw past him during last year's olive thrashing. She had thought a lot about that smile ever since.

Some men she failed to recognise. The Landlord must have taken them on while she was in Beirut. One in particular caught her attention, tall, with bullet-filled bandoleers criss-crossed over his chest.

'He's not one of us,' Mary told her, 'but we are honoured to have him as a guest. He is a Syrian friend of the Grand Mufti.'

'What is he doing here?'

'He wants to see for himself how well our men shoot.'

The baby began crying. 'I'll have to feed him before I put him down again,' Mary apologised, and shut the outside door.

'Doesn't it worry you, your husband keeping a gun in the house?' Suzanna asked, as Mary unbuttoned the front of her dress, 'If the police find it they will hang him.'

Mary shrugged, and put the baby to her breast. 'All men have guns nowadays. The police will not trouble themselves unless someone is killed.'

'But the Shepards are coming home tomorrow. If Mr Shepard hears men shooting in our grounds he will make trouble.'

'I will tell my husband, but you know men. They never listen.'

'That is true, so I will keep an eye on Mr Shepard for you,' Suzanna promised.

Mary looked up, a sly smile in her eyes. 'Did you see that Daoud Naser out there, next to my husband?'

Suzanna cast her eyes down. 'I don't know any of their names,' but she was certain that Mary was talking about the young man from Nazareth.

'No, of course not,' Mary replied, 'but he asked my husband to find out the name of your father.'

Suzanna's heart thumped. Someone really did fancy her.

'My father's dead,' she replied.

'So who is your guardian?'

'My Uncle George in Jenin – but,' she added reluctantly, 'my mother does not want me to marry until I have been through university. That will be in seven years.'

'Seven years?' Mary exclaimed, 'But who will want to marry you then?'

Certainly not Daoud Naser. Suzanna wanted to cry. She told herself that it did not matter anyway, because Uncle George would never accept a common fellah into the family.

Looking longingly at the baby, she asked, 'May I hold him when you've fed him?'

Gunshots sounded from the direction of the railway.

Mary smiled. 'You are missing your Inglisi children?' Her face grew grave. 'I pray every night to the Holy Mother that the doctors in England will cure your Renshaw so that he will be able to walk.'

She handed the baby over. Suzanna cuddled him, and wished she had a child of her own.

Suzanna Khader, Dalia Leitner, and Patsy Quigley were strangers in October 1938, but the decisions and choices they made during the following months determined the fate of two men. Suzanna was the first to involve herself in the developing tragedy.

Chapter 4

Suzanna retrieved her overnight bag from the washhouse where she had left it before shopping for more meat and a black scarf. There was a muddy puddle round the courtyard pump. She stepped carefully round it to enter the kitchen. Her heart sank when she saw a trail of muddy footprints leading into the hall.

As soon as she had the meal on the stove, she scurried round the house washing floors, straightening chair covers and picking up discarded melon seeds until she was satisfied that she had destroyed the last vestige of the Rebels' overnight occupation.

The Shepards arrived later than she had expected. It was almost dark before the taxi grumbled up the rutted drive. Her heavy plait bumped against her back as she ran across the flag-stoned veranda.

A small bundle of energy pushed its way out of the taxi, came hurtling over and hugged her. Suzanna laughed in relief. Five-year old Evie Shepard had not forgotten her.

Mrs Shepard stepped out at a more sedate pace, three-year-old Claire clinging to her skirts. Suzanna released Evie and stood respectfully erect. Mrs Shepard stooped to kiss her cheek.

'My Suzanna, how you've grown. It's lovely to see you again. I am so sorry we are late, but we must thank the Good Lord for his protection. Do you know, if I hadn't had to take Renshaw to the doctor's in Port Said, we would have been on that train the Oozelbarts attacked yesterday. As it was, we had to wait in the Negev until they cleared the wreckage.' She paused and looked around. 'They told us in England that the whole country had gone to pot, but things look peaceful enough here.'

Suzanna closed her fingers round the blue amulet under her bodice 'Oh, so much trouble while you were away, Mrs Shepard, but not for this house.'

'Good, but first things first. We must get Renshaw cleaned, fed and into bed. Eve, you help your father bring in the luggage.'

Suzanna smiled down at flaxen-haired little Clare but the child buried her head further into her mother's skirt. Suzanna bit her lip. If Clare could not remember her, then there was little chance of Renshaw doing so. Apprehensively, she followed Mrs Shepard to the taxi.

Mr Shepard, who was supervising the driver carrying in the luggage, gave her an appraising glance through his thick spectacles. 'My, Suzanna, how you've grown.'

'Suzanna,' Mrs Shepard's voice, suddenly curt, 'Get Renshaw out.'

Suzanna poked her head into the taxi, bracing herself but to her delight, Renshaw raised his oversized head and beamed. He even managed a strangled 'Su-su,' while lifting his arms. She heaved him out of the taxi, and into the large wheel chair that Mrs Shepard had unfolded. He had grown so much while he was away. He must be twice Evie's weight now; even though he was only two year's older. Indoors, she struggled to carry him up the narrow stairs.

Mrs Shepard and Clare trailed after her.

'Am I glad to have you to help again,' Mrs Shepard exclaimed as she sank onto Suzanna's bed to cuddle a sleepy Clare.

Suzanna went to the bathroom, thankful she had remembered to light the geyser earlier, and brought towels, flannel, soap and a bowl of warm water from the bathroom. She removed Renshaw's outsize nappy, a difficult task because he wouldn't stop wriggling.

'Did the English doctors do anything?' she asked while washing him, 'Did they say when he would be able to walk?'

Mrs Shepard sighed, 'The specialist wanted me to keep him in England, but I couldn't allow Jimmy to return alone.'

Suzanna left Renshaw's mother to coax him into pyjamas while she checked on the lamb stew. She noticed she had left her overnight bag in the kitchen. She picked it up, and found a huge muddy footprint beneath it. Mrs Shepard chose that moment to come into the kitchen.

'What's been going on here?' she demanded.

Suzanna wanted to crawl under the kitchen sink. 'I-it must have been the butcher yesterday. He brought in the meat while the floor was still wet.'

'And you haven't washed the floor since. Really Suzanna, you are going to have to do better than that.'

Mrs Shepard poured some water into a glass and left.

Suzanna let out a sigh of relief.

Half an hour later Evie was telling her, 'Suzanna that's the bestest tea I've had since we went away. Can I have some more?'

Suzanna was refilling Evie's plate in the kitchen when heavy footsteps tramped down the drive. She was removing the greaseproof paper from Evie's favourite golden syrup pudding when shots rang out by the railway. Peering round the kitchen door, she saw Mr Shepard jumping up, wiping his mouth, preparing for action.

She hurried into the dining room. 'See, Mrs Shepard, the shooting does not concern us. It is just the Rebels who come from Bethlehem.'

Her mistress tugged at her husband's jacket. 'Sit down and finish your meal, Jimmy. You handed in your revolver before you left, remember?'

'No need to go, anyway,' Suzanna put in, 'the Rebels do not stay.'

While she was serving coffee, the men pounded back along the drive, with loud-mouthed Abu George boasting that he had hit every target.

Mr Shepard, a hand cupped to his ear, listened intently. 'I'll visit the supervisor first thing tomorrow.'

That threat gave Suzanna a restless night.

Rising before dawn, she risked a quick dash to the workers' quarters. Mary, already outside and kneading dough, looked up in surprise.

'Mr Shepard will be coming soon, Mary. Everyone must bury their guns.'

Her friend jumped up, wiping floury hands on her skirt. 'I will wake Abu George.'

'When you have spoken to him, you must go to the supervisor's wife. She must ask her husband to tell Mr Shepard that the guns the workers used last night belonged to Rebels from Bethlehem who forced everyone to practise.'

Suzanna went back to light a fire under the boiler in the washhouse, worried that the workers would not listen to their women. Her sense of anxiety increased when Mr Shepard strolled across the courtyard with Evie.

While serving breakfast, she noticed Evie rolling a spent cartridge case round her mug of warm milk. 'Daddy found lots of bullets,' Evie told her proudly. 'He gave me one to keep.'

After prayers, Suzanna trembled as she watched Mr Shepard walk over to the supervisor's house. When he returned, she pressed her ear to the lounge door and heard him telling his wife, 'No need to make a song and dance about it, Addy. With the rent we owe, we can't afford to antagonise the landlord, but there will be no more trouble. I warned the supervisor. "Any more shooting occurs in these grounds, and I'll pick up the phone and speak to the police."

Suzanna offered a prayer of thanks to the Holy Mother. Mary's husband was safe for the moment.

Chapter 5

Suzanna knew the Rebels were losing when Mrs Shepard mentioned that the line from Jerusalem to Lydda was to re-open. She heard nothing about the British using hostages to ensure the trains' safety, until Mary told her.

'The supervisor's wife says the British are tying patriotic effendi to trolleys and sending them in front of the trains. We're going to watch. Do you want to come?'

Mrs Shepard had gone off to a coffee morning and left Suzanna in charge of Clare and Renshaw, so she pushed Renshaw's wheel chair, with Clare clinging to the handle, up the bumpy path to the vineyard. The women, carrying baskets to harvest the last of the grapes, stood at the edge of the terrace from where they had a clear view of the line.

A trolley, worked by fellahin prisoners in ankle chains, rounded the curve. In its centre, tied to a chair and guarded by police, sat a dignified effendi, wearing the currently obligatory keffiyah, but one tied with an elaborate golden iqal.

Suzanna recognised him as a friend of her uncle. At the same time, the supervisor's wife gave a cackle of sarcastic laughter.

'Look everyone, look!' the supervisor's wife shouted, 'The British have made a mistake. That effendi is no patriot. He's a moderate who sold land to Jews.'

The women shouted ribald remarks. Renshaw joined in the laughter but the noise frightened Clare who started to cry and clung to Suzanna. Suzanna picked the child up to comfort her, seething with indignation. Her father had sold his olive trees to Jews to buy his taxi. These women could have been jeering at him, if he had been alive.

She rounded on them. 'For St George's sake! What if the British had arrested your husbands and had forced them to work that trolley? Would you be laughing then?'

The supervisor's wife lifted her nose in the air, most of the others pretended not to hear. Mary's face glowed red but she kept silent. Suzanna swung the wheel chair round and left.

****

Mary slipped into the Shepards' kitchen courtyard a few days later, glancing nervously to left and right.

'It's all right, Mary,' Suzanna reassured her, 'I have calmed down, and the Inglisi are still in bed. But what has brought you? Is the baby all right?'

'He is well, praise be to the Holy Mother. My husband told me to come. Two Rebels stayed in the supervisor's house last night. One asked to see you alone in the vineyard. He says he is your brother.'

Her brother? It was almost two years since she had seen Habib. His band were based in Northern Palestine, and were keeping themselves busy setting the oil line from Iraq on fire. What would he be doing in Jerusalem? She sensed a trap.

'Mary, I must be sure it is my brother.'

'Yes,' her friend agreed, 'You cannot meet a stranger alone.'

Suzanna bit her thumb. Just supposing this really was her brother, and he needed her help?

'If I write this man a note, will your husband take it?'

'Yes, but what if he cannot read?'

Suzanna laughed. 'Then I will know he is not my brother.'

Renshaw was still asleep when she slipped upstairs. She tore a page from her history exercise book and scribbled, 'How did my father die? Give the answer to Abu George.'

Renshaw stirred, his lips puckered. She kissed his forehead. 'Not now, Renshaw, please, I will be back soon. Please, please, don't cry and wake your mother.'

She raced downstairs. 'I have to see to Renshaw,' she told Mary as she handed over the note and a pencil, 'but I will come to your house after I have taken Evie to school.'

She hurried back, attended to Renshaw and managed to display a calm face while serving breakfast but hustled Evie to school and rushed back to the workers' quarters. The reply had come. 'My idiot of a step-father wrote off his taxi when he drove it into a wadi.'

Suzanna laid her head back and laughed. Habib had never forgiven her father for wrecking the taxi he had bought with the proceeds from the sale of his olive trees.

'It is my brother,' she told Mary and raced to the vineyard. The leaves of the fig tree at the centre of the vineyard rustled, and a man stepped through its canopy. A bushy beard hid the lower part of his face and a voluminous white keffiyah overshadowed the rest.

She turned to run.

'Little Suzanna,' the man called, 'You look so grown-up.'

She stopped, 'Habib, y-you look like a fellah,' she stammered.

'To look like a fellah is a sign of honour, Suzanna. Fellahin are the only ones brave enough to drive out the oppressors...'

Afraid that he was about to embark on one of his long, political lectures, she cut in, although still addressing him with the formality due to his gender and seven years seniority. 'I am pleased to see you again, dear brother, but I cannot stay long. Mrs Shepard will be angry. What are you doing in Jerusalem?'

Habib leaned against the dry-stone wall surrounding the vineyard. 'Our band came south to help take El Quds. We stayed at a village on our way. When we left, British soldiers burnt the homes of the people who had sheltered us and imposed a fine on the village. Many babies will starve this winter. When we reached Jerusalem our men fought valiantly and we took control of El Quds until yesterday when the British brought more soldiers and drove us out, but,' Habib straightened his back, raised his voice to declaim, 'we are not permanently defeated. We will rise again.' He slumped to speak normally, 'For the time being, however, the strike will end.'

'You will go back to work for Uncle George?'

'Will he have me?'

'Of course he will. Family is more important than politics. I know Uncle George was angry when you joined the Rebels but he has kept your things safe and has told his friends that you have taken advantage of the strike to study abroad. Go and see him in Beirut.'

'How is Um?'

'She did not look at all well when I last saw her.'

'Then I will visit her first.'

'Good. She will be so relieved to see you safe and well. Now I must go.'

Habib straightened. 'Wait. Although we are all returning to civilian life, our commander, Ahmed al-Zeid, my best friend, my blood brother, promised to write when he judges the time is ripe to fight again. I told him he could write to me through you, and gave him your employers' Mail Box address.'

Suzanna stared at him in horror, her mind in turmoil. Did Habib realise he was risking everything she had worked so hard for? She struggled to speak politely.

'I don't think your friend should send me your letters, Habib. Mr Shepard fetches the post. He could become suspicious. Our mother would be furious if Mrs Shepard sacked me and I couldn't take my exams.'

'Surely the success of the Arab nation is worth more than your chance to sit exams?' Habib replied, 'Our mother should be proud of you.'

Suzanna was sure he was wrong, but said nothing.

'Suzanna,' her brother continued, 'do you really want us to give in to the British and hand our country over to the Jews?'

Suzanna didn't have the time to stand round arguing. Against her better judgement, she lifted her head, and said, 'If it means so much to you, I will do it.' She turned and rushed back to the house.

'Where on earth have you been, Suzanna? I can't trust you an inch,' Mrs Shepard called from the landing when she entered the house. 'Come up here at once.'

She found Mrs Shepard dabbing a damp flannel to Renshaw's still face. She took the flannel Mrs Shepard held out, dropped onto her knees, and pressed it to dear Renshaw's forehead, biting back tears of guilt, while Mrs Shepard sat on her bed absentmindedly rolling Clare's hair into golden ringlets.

If she had been at home instead of talking with her brother, Suzanna told herself, she would have noticed Renshaw turning faint and could have applied the flannel before he became unconscious.

The doorbell rang. Mrs Shepard took back the flannel. 'That'll be the doctor. Go and make yourself useful, for once, and let him in.'

While the doctor examined Renshaw, Suzanna hovered outside the bedroom, duster in hand.

'He'll pull through this time,' she heard the doctor's gruff voice, 'but, from now on, it will be all downhill. You shouldn't have brought him back, Mrs Shepard. A specialist could have done something. No chance of you returning to England?'

'Not for another three years,' she heard Mrs Shepard reply, 'My husband and I put our trust in the Lord. We have prayed this through and feel it right to stay together.'

Suzanna flung her duster against the wall. How could a mother deliberately put her own son's life at risk? She should have stones instead of children.

Chapter 6

Suzanna stared at the unfamiliar handwriting on the envelope, certain it was from Habib's friend. She was conscious of the whole Shepard family watching as she tore it open and tried to look nonchalant, but her stomach thrummed. She felt quite dizzy with relief when it turned out to be a Christmas card, one of those pretty ones with pasted flower petals that tourists had loved before the war.

'It's from the headmistress of my old school in Nazareth,' she told Mrs Shepard.

'Does she say anything?'

Suzanna read the message aloud wondering what she would have done if the card had been from Habib's friend.

Suzanna dear, I do hope you are keeping well. All the teachers here wish you a Merry Christmas. Your good friend, Mrs Quigley told us she had visited The Middle East Bible Society H.Q. on your behalf while in England and asked the director to get in touch with me. Now be prepared to hold your breath. The Society can offer you a scholarship to Bible College in England, provided you pass matriculation. Mrs Quigley and I have found sponsors for your travelling expenses. You can tell Mrs Shepard that I will be writing to give her the details. You will be such an asset to the mission work here, dear child, when you qualify.

'But that's wonderful,' Mrs Shepard commented, 'how kind of Ann Quigley to do all that, especially when she has her own daughter to cope with. Quite a handful too, I gather. You must work extra hard to justify her faith.'

Suzanna realised Mrs Shepard expected her to look grateful but she didn't feel grateful. She did not want to go to England and be a missionary. She wanted go to the university in Beirut and be a teacher at Haifa High School. Everyone looked up to teachers at Haifa High.

'I will have to discuss this with my mother,' she evaded.

She wrote to her mother that evening, telling her about Mrs Quigley's proposal and saying how unhappy she felt about it. She received a reply by return of post.

Suzanna, my dearest daughter, what wonderful news. You will get the best education in the world in England. Hearing this has almost made up for my bitter disappointment in not being able to get

*to Jenin this Christmas. I have to stay in Jaffa to organise a
wedding reception for my employer's daughter.*

Suzanna bit her finger to stop herself crying. She had always
spent Christmas Day with her mother. Even last Christmas, when
Uncle George and Aunt Julie were in Beirut, her mother had come
up to Jerusalem and taken her to Lebanon on the train.
She carried on reading.

*Talking about weddings I would have thought Habib would have
found the right girl for himself by this time, but he told me, if you
please, that he wants to do things the traditional way, have Aunt
Julie go to a marriage broker. Takes after his father, of course. I
hope you show more initiative. However, it is his life, so, very much
against my principles I have written to your Uncle George. I want to
talk to Habib again though so I have asked him to bring you down to
Jaffa with him for a day, during your holiday.*

Suzanna put the letter down. At least her mother still wanted
to see her, even if only as an afterthought. It's always Habib first
and me second, she thought, and why can't Um understand about
me not wanting to go to England?
She wrote back,

Dearest Um,
*Please don't make me go to England. I'd rather stay with Aunt
Julie and get married. I don't want to live in England on my own.*

Her mother replied,
Suzanna dearest,
*I know the thought of living in England on your own may seem
frightening while you are still so young, but it will be different when
you are old enough to go. Meanwhile you really must try to
appreciate all Mrs Quigley is doing for you.*

Suzanna knew further pleading would be useless. So no Beirut
University, no High School teaching job, and when she returned
from England, she would be too old to marry, and would have to
live as an old maid all her life. She sobbed herself to sleep.

Chapter 7

Western Christians celebrated Christmas a fortnight earlier than the Greek Orthodox, so once New Year was over and the house cleaned properly, Mrs Shepard allowed Suzanna to set off on her week's annual holiday.

Suzanna clambered onto the decrepit bus already crowded with villagers carrying goods back from the suq. Mrs Shepard and Evie called out their farewells and Clare made her doll wave its hand. Suzanna couldn't answer because the man behind was using his bulky roll of carpet to ram her down the aisle. She jammed against a pair of well-feathered live chickens that a woman was holding upside down by their legs. When the woman found a place, the carpet pushed her onto the long seat at the rear of the bus, next to a man wearing an evil-smelling sheepskin coat. The carpet man squashed into a space on her other side. When no more passengers could cram into the aisle, the bus left.

Odours of sweat, spices, and chicken dung recalled childhood shopping in Haifa, when she had been little and had lived in a village near Jenin. In those days village women were freer than townswomen, so no one had raised an eyebrow at her mother travelling to the suq without her husband.

However, Suzanna had not lived in a village since she was seven. It bothered her having men in such close proximity. One or other of the men on each side of her squashed closely against her as the bus zigzagged across steep hills shimmering in coats of freshly sprouted winter grass. She drew her scarf over her cheeks and held tightly onto the seat in front.

At Ramallah, half the passengers left the bus but even more squashed on. A wrinkled old woman, in widow's white, rammed a basket of eggs against Suzanna's knees. The man with the smelly coat stood and courteously offered the widow his seat. The old woman peered up suspiciously before sidling past him. Suzanna risked a quick glance at the man who had behaved in so eccentric a fashion but a bulky keffiyah obscured much of his face. She guessed he was a Rebel from an ultra-liberal family, returning home in disguise.

The bus coasted down to the fertile Jezreel Valley and stopped in Jenin's town square. Stiff and weary, Suzanna picked up her bag, grateful to be behind the carpet man who cleared a way to the exit.

She stood on the packed dirt of the square waiting for someone to meet her and was about to risk Aunt Julie's wrath by walking home unchaperoned, when a plump, black-scarved woman in an expensive mink coat threw her arms round her. Over the woman's shoulder, she saw another black-scarved woman, younger and more shapely.

'Aunt Julie, Cousin Marie!' Suzanna exclaimed, 'I didn't recognise you.'

'Oh, ma cherie, have we changed so much since the summer?' Aunt Julie pinched her cheek and looked her up and down. 'But you, you have changed. We were looking for someone much smaller. You are filling out well. We could make it a double wedding?'

Marie kissed her. 'Take no notice of Um, Suzanna; she has weddings on the brain. Your mother has written to tell her you are not to marry until you have been to college.'

Aunt Julie shrugged. 'Such stupidity. Wadia will be sorry when she finds herself with no grandchildren.'

A house servant relieved Suzanna of her bag, and they walked the short distance to Uncle George's house. Aunt Julie tapped on the ornately carved door, set in a surround of sculpted pink and white stone that Suzanna had always admired. A porter opened up. A servant came running to serve cakes and hot coffee; another ran her a bath. Suzanna relaxed into her annual week of luxurious living, wishing her mother would allow her to stay at Aunt Julie's permanently even if it did mean early marriage and no college.

****

January 6th, Christmas Day, Suzanna woke in a feather-mattressed bed, nostalgic for the village Christmases of her childhood. She remembered rolling up bedding by the light of a single clay oil lamp; wrapping warmly to walk to the cemetery at the end of the village, picnicking in the graveyard at dawn on dried apricots, figs, raisins, olives and goats' cheese. The grown-ups would offer cups of coffee to great-great grandpa staring down from a sepia photo in the glass fronted marble niche at the head of his tomb. Grandma would polish his antique wineglass before handing it to grandpa to fill with the first of that year's wine. After the visit to the dead, came the joyous tour of the living.

She stepped out of bed thinking this would be the first Christmas she had spent apart from her mother and wished her mother had loved her enough to insist on being here today. Without her mother, there would be nothing special about this Christmas in town although, even here in Jenin, just as they had done for the previous two years in Beirut, Uncle George and Aunt

Julie maintained the traditional custom of visiting and being visited. This year everyone was to finish up at Aunt Melia's house.

Aunt Melia pounced on her when they arrived. 'How is your dear mother? I wish she lived nearer.'

'She wasn't looking too good when I saw her in October, Auntie.'

Aunt Julie flung up her head. 'Melia, you know our Wadia, still working every hour the good lord sends, all for a pittance. No wonder her health is suffering.'

'As soon as I have learnt to drive, I will visit her,' Aunt Melia responded.

Aunt Julie looked horrified. 'You won't drive to Jaffa by yourself?'

'Why not? If little Suzanna can travel on a bus all the way from Jerusalem, then I should manage it to Jaffa sealed in the privacy of my own car.'

Aunt Julie obviously regarded this as a criticism of the way she performed her role as Guardian, because she drew herself up tall and retorted, 'Suzanna travelling on her own was not my idea, Melia. Left to me, she would never have gone to Jerusalem in the first place.'

Suzanna watched Aunt Melia roll her eyes at Great Aunt Candice, another stalwart of the Women's Movement. 'How can we persuade other women to become independent when my own sister is so conservative?' she asked, but threw an arm round Aunt Julie's shoulders. 'There are some things we agree on, though. Come and sign our petition asking the government to release the prisoners they are detaining without trial.'

As the older women went off, Suzanna slipped over to the corner where Marie was already chatting to Aunt Melia's two youngest daughters, home on holiday from boarding school.

'You don't mean it! She travelled to university in England alone?' Marie was exclaiming in horror.

'Who did?' Suzanna asked, feeling this was a conversation, in which she could take a personal interest.

'My friend Sa'ida Jarralah,' Cousin Nadia, the elder of the two sisters, answered, 'you must have heard me talk of her, Suzanna.'

'But she's Muslim,' Marie exclaimed, 'and her father's a senior judge.'

'Jerusalem isn't like Jenin, Marie.' Nadia's face had that irritatingly superior look Suzanna hated. 'It's a sophisticated place. Big city Muslims make their own rules.'

For once Suzanna felt she could hold her own against the elegant Nadia. 'Did I mention,' she said oh so casually, 'that I have been offered a scholarship to an English university.'

Nadia and Marie stared incredulously, but Aunt Melia's youngest daughter, who had not been bothering to follow the conversation, gave an excited squeal. 'Look whose just walked in.'

The three oldest girls hardly moved their heads, although their eyes swivelled sideways, but Suzanna could not keep up the sophisticated pose. 'Habib!'

In complete disregard of the niceties, she ran across to where the men congregated. 'Habib, I am so pleased you have come.'

'And I am glad to see you too, sister dear.' Habib, dressed impeccably in a smart lounge suit, with no trace of a beard, smiled down. 'I have a present for you from our mother.'

He held out a beautifully wrapped package.

Suzanna tore off the paper and discovered the icon of the Holy Virgin that her mother had always kept on a special shelf. When she was little, she had been impressed that the halo round St Mary's head and the stars on Her forehead and shoulders were painted in real gold. She knew how much this icon, passed down the family from one generation to another, meant to her mother.

'Um said she is giving it to you to show you how sorry she is for not being here today,' Habib said.

Tears welled in Suzanna's eyes. Her mother must really have wanted to see her. This Christmas was becoming special after all.

Habib held out another parcel. 'And here is something from me.'

'I am not a child now,' she protested, 'you don't have to bring me presents any longer.'

'I am giving you this because I know you are no longer a child.'

So she unwrapped it, and found a hand-written book, containing a selection of poems by Ibrahim Tuqan, all in exquisite calligraphy and decorated with patterns in coloured inks.

'It's magnificent,' she exclaimed, 'did you copy all those poems yourself? Where did you find them?'

'In newspapers. They meant so much to me and to my friend here while we were campaigning. We used to read them to each other in the evenings.'

The man beside Habib spoke up, 'I am sorry your brother has forgotten to introduce us properly.'

Suzanna clapped her hand to her mouth. So excited at seeing her brother, she had ignored the tall stranger beside him. Habib's face too, flushed crimson. 'Oh, Ya Ahmed, a thousand apologies. Suzanna, meet the brother of my heart, Ahmed al-Zeid. Ahmed, my brother, meet my sister, Suzanna. This is the man, Suzanna, whose letters you will be passing on.'

'Any sister of my brother is my sister,' Habib's friend bowed his head courteously.

She dipped her head in acknowledgment before concentrating on Habib's present. 'This is the first book in Arabic I've ever owned, Habib - apart from the bible Mrs Quigley gave me. Please recite one of the poems.'

Habib took the book back and chose a poem called *The Broker* that condemned landowners who secretly sold part of their estates to Jews. At the last line, he raised his voice, '*Although the newspapers shield them we know the truth.*'

Uncle George appeared from behind. 'Hush, Habib, some things are better thought than uttered. Now Suzanna, you must join the other girls.'

She crossed the room and showed off her presents.

'I love your icon,' Marie exclaimed.

'Those poems,' Nadia said, 'you must learn them by heart. My mother will want to hear them. Look, here she comes. Show them to her.'

But Aunt Melia had something to tell them that caused them to forget everything else. She had booked two taxis and a whole row in the best cinema in Haifa, especially for the women of the family.

Suzanna had never been to the cinema. The Shepards regarded picture palaces as Devil's playgrounds so she stared in awe at the auditorium with its statues, velvet-covered seats, and ceiling-to-floor length gold tasselled curtains. The film was an outrageously comic story, starring Fred Astaire and Ginger Rogers. The musical score set her feet dancing and she loved the songs. In the taxi home, she and her cousins all sang *Change Partners* and *I used to be colour blind* in English.

'Just remember,' Aunt Julie warned when they reached home, 'we may enjoy the antics of these Yanks but we live with the dignity of Arabs.'

Maybe, but that did not prevent Suzanna and Marie practising dance routines for half an hour before they climbed into bed.

Chapter 8

Suzanna pulled the washing out of the boiler and gasped in horror. Everything, sheets, towels, pillowslips and, worst of all, Mr Shepard's best Egyptian cotton shirts had turned bright pink. She found the culprit tucked into a pillowcase of Renshaw's, a once red slipper now shrunk to half its size and transformed to a delicate shade of rose.

Mrs Shepard chose that moment to enter the washhouse. At first, she stared in disbelief and then ranted. 'You idiot child. It's going to cost a month of my husband's salary to replace that lot. Why ever did I take you on? Just what are you going to do about it?'

The words hit like strokes of a cane. Suzanna shouted, 'I'm giving in my notice, that's what.'

She raced out of the washhouse up to the bedroom she shared with Renshaw until her temper had subsided, then went downstairs determined, this time, not to retract her notice.

She found it hard to stick to her resolve though when Renshaw woke while she was praying in front of the icon her mother had given her. He put up his arms, and when she bent down, he gave her one of his slobbery kisses. She hugged him tight so that he wouldn't see her tears.

Renshaw pointed at the icon. 'Pic-pic.'

'I am saying my prayers like you do with your Mummy,' she explained.

Next morning Mrs Shepard said that she had managed to save most of the whites by dipping them in Milton and asked Suzanna if she still wanted to leave. Suzanna recognised that this was the nearest Mrs Shepard would get to an apology and agreed.

That evening Mr Shepard handed her a letter with a Jenin postmark. She recognised the handwriting. 'It's from my cousin Marie,' she told Mrs Shepard. Her spirits soared as she read it aloud.

Suzanna, I now have a fiancé, Antonius. You should see his photograph! He is so handsome! You will be a bridesmaid, won't you? Your mother has promised to come to the wedding so you will be sleeping at Aunt Melia's house.

Antonius is sending Granny Hadad two lengths of material for you, red silk for the wedding day, blue linen for the bride's night. Granny Hadad has the patterns.

'You're going to be busy,' Mrs Shepard said.

****

When Suzanna walked over to Katamon on Saturday evening to spend her day off with Granny Hadad, the parcel had arrived. Ever since her family had returned from Beirut, Suzanna had spent her day off at Granny Hadad's. Strictly speaking, Granny Hadad was Great Grandmother Hadad, and, even more strictly speaking, was Nadia and Samira's great grandmother, not hers.

That Saturday and Sunday, her cousins had gone to Jenin with Great Aunt Candice to celebrate their father's birthday, so she had Granny Hadad to herself. They spent Sunday morning cutting out the two dresses, a traditional North Palestinian tunic, and a Parisian bridesmaid's dress.

After lunch, Suzanna sewed seams. At one point, to rest her eyes she gazed round the room, first at the tiny figure opposite, enveloped in a large leather armchair, and swathed in a voluminous white scarf that almost hid the embroidered village dress underneath.

Granny Hadad's dark brown, deeply wrinkled face was bent over the tablecloth she was embroidering. Because she was going through an Indian phase in honour of a man called Mahatma Gandhi, instead of using Palestinian cross-stitch, she was creating a magnificent tapestry peacock with a tail all colours of the spectrum.

Beyond Granny Hadad, Suzanna saw bookshelves filled with volumes written in both French and Arabic. Glass doors opened onto a garden guarded by a tall, dry stone wall. The almond trees, shading hives, had already lost their blossom. Mahmoud, the chief gardener, was hoeing a bed of plants with velvet, patterned leaves. One day when she was rich, Suzanna promised herself, she would have a dress made of material like those leaves, and live in a house like this with servants to look after everything.

Granny Hadad cut a thread, chose another vibrant colour, and then looked up. 'And what sort of week did you have, little one?'

'Terrible, Granny, I handed in my notice again.'

Suzanna noticed Granny having difficulty rethreading her needle. She held out her hand. 'Here let me do that.'

Granny Hadad meekly handed over thread and needle. 'So what will you do now?'

'Oh. It's all right, Gran; I took my notice back. I couldn't leave Renshaw, could I?'

She gave back the threaded needle but the old lady kept her head up. 'You are staying on with the Inglisi only because you want to look after Renshaw? Not because your mother wants you to get your matriculation?'

'A bit of both, I suppose, Granny. Sometimes though I wish my mother wasn't set on my going to Bible College in England.'

'If you could do what you wanted, what would that be?'

'You know, Granny, I think now that even more than teaching I would like to be a nurse. I do so enjoy looking after Renshaw.'

That was the first time she had voiced the ambition. Saying it aloud made it seem more possible.

Granny Hadad bent over her sewing. 'Suzanna, don't get too involved with that "child of God". They never last long on this earth. They are only lent.'

Suzanna did not want to think about that, so asked, 'Do you think it would upset my mother too much if I became a nurse?'

Granny Hadad looked up again. 'You are old enough now to take charge of your own life.'

The grandfather clock in the corner of the room chimed five. Granny Hadad put down her embroidery. 'Time to collect the eggs.'

They went out through a kitchen full of the latest modern appliances, including an electric toaster and vacuum cleaner. Granny Hadad handed Suzanna a basket. While they searched the yard, a broody hen came out from behind a bay tree escorting three fluffy chicks.

'You let Tutu sit on five eggs, Gran. Why has she only three chicks?'

'Two haven't hatched.'

Suzanna stared down at the eggs they had collected. 'How do chicks get inside eggs?'

Granny Hadad gave a snort. 'Biology is obviously not your strongest subject.'

'No, Mrs Shepard said it was unsuitable for a young girl.'

Granny Hadad gave another snort, of disgust this time. 'Well Suzanna, an egg, when it starts out inside a hen's body, has no shell. It has no shell so that the cockerel can fertilise it. Once a cockerel fertilises an egg, a chick starts growing inside it and the hen makes a shell round it.'

'Why does the chick need a shell?'

'To stop it dehydrating. Unfortunately some chicks are too weak to hammer their way out.'

Granny Hadad marched over and reached beneath a bay bush. She took out one of the failed eggs. 'See this bulge at the side? The chick started to crack the egg but was unable to struggle free.'

'Couldn't you have broken the shell for it, Gran?'

'No, Suzanna, chicks have to break out themselves. If someone does it for them, they never survive.'

Chapter 9

Mrs Shepard came up to say prayers with Renshaw, so Suzanna retreated to the kitchen to finish her essay on the role of ghosts in Macbeth. She was struggling with the banquet scene, when her mistress entered. From her heightened colour, Suzanna could tell something was wrong.

'Suzanna, do you know why Renshaw keeps asking for a pic-pic when we say prayers?' Mrs Shepard began, 'He keeps saying, "Like Su-su".'

'He means my icon of the Holy Mother, Mrs Shepard. I keep it in my drawer so he won't break it, but you can borrow it.'

'You take out a picture of Mary when you pray? Why?' Mrs Shepard's tone exuded hostility.

Suzanna hesitated. She wished she knew why her mistress was angry. The answer seemed so obvious, that it couldn't be the right one.

'Well?' Mrs Shepard demanded.

The obvious would have to do. 'So I can pray to her.'

Mrs Shepard straightened her back and glared. 'You pray to a picture? Why?'

'To ask the Holy Mother to pray for me.'

Mrs Shepard's compressed lips looked almost ugly. 'There is only one mediator between God and man; Suzanna, that is the Lord Jesus. In this household we do not pray to graven images.'

'It's not a graven image!' Suzanna protested, but Mrs Shepard, was already on her knees on the kitchen floor, leaning against the table leg.

'Let us both pray,' she commanded, and, without waiting to see if Suzanna had joined her, began, 'Dear Lord Jesus, hearken to my prayer. Enter the heart of my dear sister-in-the lord, Suzanna, that she may heed thy divine commands.'

Anger welled up inside Suzanna. She was not having her mother's beautiful icon called a graven image, 'I am handing in my notice,' she said and flounced out of the room, leaving Mrs Shepard alone on the floor.

She walked round the grounds until bedtime, telling herself that this time she really would not withdraw her resignation.

Next morning Mrs Shepard did not ask her to change her mind about leaving as she usually did.

The days of working out her notice dragged by. Every time Evie hugged her at the school gates, tears sprang to her eyes. At night after she put Renshaw to bed, she sat sobbing in the kitchen, gazing at her schoolbooks and worrying about her mother's disappointment.

She was in the kitchen, paper, pen, and ink on the table, ready to write to Aunt Julie asking if she could stay with her in Jenin, when Mrs Shepard called her into the lounge. Mr Shepard was there too.

'Suzanna,' he started, 'my wife and I have prayed together about this matter of your icon. My wife realises now that she may have been wrong to force our beliefs on you, so we will not insist that you give up your habit, although of course we will pray that you come soon to obey our Lord's command. All we ask is that you do not let Renshaw see you praying to your icon. Now do you still want to leave?'

She accepted the olive branch.

After she had undressed for bed that night, Suzanna took out her icon as usual but dropped it into her dressing gown pocket, and made her way to the bathroom. There, she sat on the edge of the bath, as far away from the toilet bowl as possible, and said her prayers.

Chapter 10

Marie was now writing weekly:

You should see the picture of my Parisian wedding dress!

I have sewn enough sheets and pillowcases to last my lifetime!

I am in the middle of an extra large tablecloth in red and black cross-stitch. It looks rather fine even though I say so myself.

Slaving at housework all day, bending dog-tired over her schoolwork in the evenings, working at her bridesmaid's dresses into the small hours, Suzanna begrudged Marie a life with nothing to do but prepare her trousseau for a marriage where she could hand over all unpleasant work to servants.

She worried about getting her dresses finished on time. Mrs Shepard found her sewing in the kitchen late one evening. She thought her mistress would be cross but instead she proved sympathetic. 'That's far too much to do by hand,' she said, 'I'll teach you to use my sewing machine.'

Not only did Mrs Shepard let her use her machine but even ran up some of the seams herself, leaving Suzanna free to concentrate on the elaborate embroidery needed on the bodice of the traditional dress.

The dresses were finished the evening before Suzanna climbed into Great Uncle Hadad's overcrowded car. Speeding along at thirty miles an hour, the journey to Jenin only took three hours, but she could hear the drum already pounding a beat in the wedding hall two streets away. She knew she could not spend long with her mother.

She handed her baggage to one servant and tripped excitedly behind another into the living room, but only Aunt Melia was there to greet her.

Suzanna's high spirits evaporated. 'Where's Um, Auntie? I thought you were fetching her yesterday?'

Aunt Melia put her arms round her. 'She is here, Suzanna, even though I didn't want to bring her when I realised how ill she was, but she insisted, said she must not disappoint you again. As soon as we arrived, though, your uncle ordered her off to bed.'

'Where is she now?'

'In the best guest room. You may go up, but remember not to overexcite her.'

Suzanna walked upstairs heavy footed and opened the bedroom door. Her mother propped up against pillows looked so old, so fragile. An outsider would never have guessed that she was the same age as robust Aunt Melia and bustling Aunt Julie.

Her mother gave a faint smile. 'Don't look so worried. I am only resting. I'll be all right tomorrow. I'm coming to the celebrations later tonight.'

Suzanna moved inside, and lifted her mother's worn hand to her mouth. 'Oh, Um, it's been so long since I saw you.'

A fit of coughing pushed her mother forwards. Blood stained the handkerchief she placed in front of her mouth. When she could speak again, she said, 'You have no time to stand round here chatting, darling.' She paused, panting, before continuing 'The drumming started sometime ago. Now go off and make yourself beautiful so I can be proud of you.'

Reluctantly, Suzanna left and ran to the bedroom where Nadia, the chief bridesmaid and the other bridesmaids had already changed into their traditional North Palestinian costumes.

To her delighted surprise, her best friend from her schooldays, Angelique ran over and hugged her. 'Oh, Suzy, I have been so looking forward to seeing you again.'

'I can't believe you're here. I am so pleased,' Suzanna said.

'Now you're here at last, Suzanna,' Nadia said, 'I want to see your dance.'

Suzanna's stomach turned over. She had forgotten that every bridesmaid had to create and perform an individual dance.

'Come on, then,' Nadia said sharply, 'We haven't got all night.'

Suzanna stood on one foot, ready to improvise, but could think of nothing. She had never felt so ashamed. What would Angelique think of her? She put her hands to her face.

'I didn't do one,' she whispered. 'I thought with so many bridesmaids I wouldn't have to.'

'By the Holy Mother,' Nadia swore, 'Whatever possessed Marie to ask you to be a bridesmaid. We'll just have to miss your dance out. Now hurry and get dressed. Make sure you do nothing else to let us down.'

Suzanna managed not to cry as she changed into the blue dress, which a servant had placed ready for her. She was brushing her hair when the door opened and Aunt Melia entered. 'Suzanna,' she said, 'May I have a word?'

'What else can I have done wrong,' Suzanna thought as she followed Aunt Melia outside.

'Suzanna, I am very sorry about this,' her aunt said, as soon as she had shut the door behind them, 'but we have to take your mother to hospital in Haifa. I thought you would like to say goodbye to her before she goes.'

Suzanna raced to her mother's bedroom.

Aunt Melia's husband, Dr. Hannay, was sitting beside her mother, checking her pulse. Aunt Melia's personal maid, Maada, was packing her mother's bag.

Suzanna knelt down. 'Um.'

Her mother's eyes fluttered open a fraction. 'Suzanna,' she whispered, 'I am so sorry about this. Please don't let it spoil your enjoyment.'

'Um, I am coming with you!' Suzanna said.

'No, Suzanna,' her mother whispered, and closed her eyes.

'No Suzanna...' Aunt Melia started, but Dr Hannay interrupted, 'Melia, Suzanna accompanying her mother makes a lot of sense. It will help Wadia, having her daughter with her, and you shouldn't leave Julie to cope with this wedding alone. You know what she's like.'

Aunt Melia looked as if she were going to argue but thought better of it. 'You're right, I suppose, Anton, but you must take Suzanna to the flat over the Haifa shop after you leave the hospital. Maada will look after her. Maada has the Beirut phone number so she can get hold of us if we are needed.'

She turned to her maid. 'Maada, ask someone to bring down Suzanna's things and then run over to George Hadad to fetch the keys to the Haifa flat. Suzanna, do you want to let Nadia know that you are not going to the wedding, or shall I pass on the message?'

Suzanna couldn't face telling Nadia that she was abandoning bridesmaid duties altogether. 'Could you do it, please, Auntie?'

She held her mother's hand until the ambulance men arrived with a stretcher and then sat in the back of the ambulance.

Her mother opened her eyes. 'Suzanna you shouldn't be here.'

'I want to be with you, Um.'

Her mother gave a faint smile and closed her eyes again.

Aunt Melia ordered Maada to sit beside the driver. 'Make sure you look after Suzanna well.'

At the hospital, the ward sister made Suzanna wear a mask but allowed her to remain even while the hospital doctor was examining her mother. 'You did right to bring her in,' he told Dr Hannay.

Her uncle then wanted to take her back to Uncle Georges flat but Suzanna felt her mother would disappear forever if she abandoned her. So Maada brought her in chicken sandwiches, a flask of coffee, and the book she had found while unpacking Suzanna's bag.

Suzanna sat dozing in a chair beside her mother all night.

The next day her mother, although still obviously ill, was in a talkative mood. 'If anything happens to me, Suzanna, don't let your Aunt Julie force you into marriage. You must go on and get your degree in England. Your aunt means well but she doesn't understand. Promise?'

Suzanna hesitated. She did not want to upset her mother but needed to know. 'Um, why is it so important to you that I take a degree in England?'

'English degrees are recognised throughout the world. You will be able to earn your own living any time, anywhere. Listen to your Aunt Melia rather than Aunt Julie in this matter.' Her mother stopped to cough again, and fought for air, but insisted on carrying on talking once the bout had subsided. 'Women should be economically independent, Suzanna, capable of keeping their children and themselves if they have to. It shames me that I cannot give you a home myself.'

'Why did you not go on to college like Aunt Melia, Um?'

'I wanted to, so much I wanted to. I envied your Aunt Melia. However, my mother insisted I marry a husband her sister had found for me. Abu Kadin Hadad was a good man, the whole village respected him, but he was fifty and I was fourteen.'

'But couldn't you have continued studying when Abu Kadin died?'

Her mother laughed, which led to another prolonged bout of coughing. When she recovered, she said, 'You don't do things like that when you are a widow with a small child to look after, and there is famine in the land.' She turned over and slept again.

The book Suzanna had brought with her was one of her set books, *Vanity Fair*. With nothing to do, while her mother slept, but read, Suzanna was surprised at how much she enjoyed it. Perhaps this was what studying in England would be like.

Her mother woke in nostalgic mood. 'You were asking about life after Abu Kadin, Suzanna. I went to live with your Uncle George and Aunt Julie when I was first widowed, but grew bored. I horrified your Aunt Julie when I accepted your father's proposal without consulting my brother. He owned nothing but a few olive trees, but he had big ideas and wanted me to be part of them. I was lucky. Your Aunt Melia supported me. She has always believed a woman should choose her own husband. Between us we persuaded your Aunt Julie and your Uncle George not to disown me.'

Her mother dozed off for a while. When she opened her eyes again, she said, 'Your father was a fine man. If he had lived, we would have finished up with our own nation-wide car hire business. Do you remember him?'

'Of course, especially from when I was little and we lived in the village. I didn't see him so much when we moved to Jaffa because then he was always driving his taxi or quarrelling with Habib.'

'Yes, he and Habib never got on, but he did try to be a good stepfather. I can't tell you how much I miss him, even after all these years.'

Her mother fell silent, and a few minutes later, was asleep again. She woke briefly while Suzanna was reading.

'I am glad you are keeping up with your studies. Don't ever let yourself be confined to a luxurious prison like your Aunt Julie.'

'But Aunt Julie is not in prison,' Suzanna protested.

'No, I suppose if she does not see it that way, she isn't,' her mother conceded, 'but for you it would be.' Her eyes closed again. Suzanna looked at the clock by the ward sister's desk. The wedding service would be over now and everyone on the way to the reception in Beirut.

A porter pushed in a trolley to take her mother away to undergo a battery of tests.

Suzanna slept at the hospital a second night.

She and her mother talked some more before her mother had to go for more checks.

Aunt Melia and Aunt Julie arrived at the hospital soon after Maada had brought Suzanna some hot lamb stew in an enamel lunch pot. Aunt Julie told her that Uncle George had phoned Mr Shepard and explained that she would not be returning for a few days.

That night she slept in the large flat over Uncle George's Haifa shop on the Nazareth road, not far from the oil refinery.

'This will be Habib's home when the broker gets round to finding him a wife,' Aunt Julie said.

They met Uncle George at the hospital and waited anxiously for the doctor's verdict. When it came, it was what they had all feared. Her mother had tuberculosis.

Uncle George had a long session alone with his sister before Suzanna went in to see her again.

Her mother addressed her in a listless tone. 'Your uncle is sending me to a sanatorium in the hills, Suzanna. It will cost a lot of money, but I am too tired now to fight. I am leaving it to him.'

More than anything else that showed Suzanna just how ill her mother was. 'I'll find a job near you, Um,' she promised.

'No!' Her mother sat up in bed abruptly, and another fit of coughing wracked her... 'You must go back to Jerusalem,' she said eventually.

The nurse came in and shooed Suzanna out.

So Suzanna went back to Jerusalem. She worried about her mother every day. She wanted to visit her at the sanatorium in Safad. Uncle George offered to pay her bus fare, but the return journey would take more than a single day.

'Your mother is in the Lord's hands,' Mrs Shepard said, whenever Suzanna asked for extra time off, 'You must trust Him. You can go later when she will be a better state to appreciate your visit.'

By the end of August Mrs Shepard was still refusing to let her visit her mother, but on different grounds.

'No Suzanna, I can't spare you while the Lord is using me to help the German Christians. You know, don't you, that Haifa is now a strategic zone and all Germans have to move out. Can you imagine old Mrs Engelhard setting out to blow up a refinery? Yet she has to leave the home she has lived in all her life. The whole world's gone mad.'

Chapter 11

The hottest day of the year and Mr and Mrs Shepard had gone off yet again to find accommodation for their German friends. Suzanna sent the children out to play under the shade of the tall pines before struggling to clean the kitchen, roasting under its corrugated iron roof. When she went into the courtyard, the sunlight was so intense it seemed dark and the deep blue of the overhead sky, too close for safety, more menacing than a thundercloud.

The Shepards returned, late in the afternoon, pleased with their negotiations. The two girls went rummaging to find materials for a kite, while Renshaw dozed in the kitchen courtyard. Suzanna was cooking in the kitchen when she heard Evie scream in the hall. She ran out and found her pulling one of the dining room chairs through the front door. While Suzanna shouted, 'Evie, what are you doing with that chair?' someone outside slammed the door shut. Evie buried her head in Suzanna's apron. She felt the child trembling.

'Whatever is the matter, Evie?'

'There's a snake Suzanna, a big black one. It put up its head and tried to bite me.'

Suzanna's village grandmother had insisted snakes near a house were a portent of evil to come. She clutched the blue amulet hidden beneath the material of her dress.

Mrs Shepard came running downstairs, Clare trailing behind. 'What's all the fuss about, Suzanna?'

Evie continued to cling to Suzanna's apron while turning her head to answer, 'A snake, Mummy. I thought it was a telephone cable but it wasn't. It put its head up when I put the chair on it. Daddy told me to go back inside.'

'Where's your father?'

'Outside with the snake.'

They heard a thud on the veranda.

Evie cried, 'Daddy.'

'Jimmy!' Mrs Shepard screamed and flung open the door.

Mr Shepard, a spade in one hand, held the body of a large black snake high in the air. Its tail swept the ground next to its severed head.

'An Egyptian cobra by the look of it,' Mr Shepard commented.

'Goodness knows what it's doing here,' Mrs Shepard exclaimed.

Suzanna's grip on her amulet grew tighter. The snake's message must be urgent if it had travelled so far to deliver it. She worried that it concerned her mother. Would killing the snake make the omen more or less powerful?

Patsy Quigley thrashes about more wildly than Suzanna as she struggles to break through the prison walls erected by her father and the Second Chosen. Her struggles are a key element in the fate of one of the men.

Chapter 12

Leaving Haifa Central Station, after the most memorable journey of her life, Patsy looked at Kingsway with interest. Its former raw modernity had mellowed. Trees, mere saplings when she had left, now dappled pavements with shade. Shop windows flaunted sophisticated displays of Parisian fashions. In the street traffic flowed faster, more cars, fewer camels.

Her father engaged a taxi. Within minutes, they had left behind the red-roofed houses of the original German colony and were zigzagging up Mt Carmel; the view refreshing Patsy's faded memories of the blue expanse of curved bay, and distant white-capped Mt Hermon. She felt saddened by the new refinery, which had daubed the previously rural Northern plain with work sheds, factories, clutches of oil storage tanks and two prominent cooling towers.

Beyond the green suburban gardens at the summit of the mountain, where young pine trees smoothed a wadi's former craggy grandeur, Patsy leaned forward in anticipation. Nearly home, now. The taxi lurched up the gravelled drive between cypresses standing to attention, towards the stone strength of the two-storey house. Her eyes watered, and she realised how much she still loved her childhood home despite all that had happened the last time she had visited. Blinking back tears, she recalled the innocent years when in their imagination she and her father had turned the house into Richard the Lionheart's castle and re-enacted the Crusades in their grounds. That loving, inventive father had been the person she had adored above everyone else in the universe.

The taxi stopped. Her mother squeezed her hand. 'Welcome home, darling.'

Patsy jumped out of the car. Her father brushed past, followed by the taxi driver carrying her parent's bulky hand luggage. A servant she did not recognise ran out to greet her mother. Patsy stood alone on the drive, a stranger to her own home.

Then Cook, even broader in the rump than she had remembered, stepped majestically across the stone-slabbed veranda. Patsy moved towards her tentatively and Cook, abandoning stately dignity, ran forward, to pinch her cheek affectionately. 'Little one but you have grown. See you are taller than me. And what has happened to you, today? You should have been here for lunch. Now it is almost supper. We have been worrying.'

'Our train was blown up,' her mother explained, 'but the Lord looks after his own.'

Typical, Patsy thought, always the Lord, no mention of the Railway Company's special regard for first class passengers.

Her mother handed the new servant the bundle of ruined clothes they had removed in the washroom on Gaza station.

'Dewya, when you have taken hot water up to the bedrooms, can you deal with these? My daughter will need that dress tomorrow morning.'

Patsy picked up her case, walked indoors, and mounted tiled stairs to the bedroom whose whitewashed walls now held such bitter memories of her last visit.

She removed a paper bag from the case, tipped the contents onto her bed, and spent the next ten minutes screwing a bolt to the top of her bedroom door.

****

Two days later Patsy was on the veranda immersed in her father's copy of *The Megiddo Water System*, when she heard a car draw smoothly to a halt beside her deck chair. She looked up at a red Tatra T87 that Tim would have died for.

A young man, sporting a red fez, a black sports blazer and immaculately pressed grey trousers, jumped out in one fluid movement. Patsy assumed this was the Syrian property owner who had phoned earlier although she had been expecting a much older man. As he approached, she studied his face. An eyebrow-dividing scar added an extra *je ne sais quoi* to its classical beauty. She'd mark this man on her dance card any evening.

Hey, steady the buffs, she told herself. He's an Arab.

The young man offered a 'Good morning' with hardly a trace of foreign accent. His accompanying smile created havoc in her nether regions. She succeeded in rising from her deck chair with all the languorous grace that she had admired in Tim's mother.

'Mr al-Zeid? My father is expecting you.'

She ushered him to her father's study, but could think of no excuse to accompany him inside.

In the kitchen, where she went to order coffee, Cook proved a mine of information.

'The al-Zeid family used to be big all over this part of the world, Miss Patsy, but when the Inglisi and French put up boundaries and called "here" Palestine and "there" Syria and "that" Lebanon, the al-Zeids chose to be Syrian. They didn't sell their Palestinian property to the Jews, though, like so many did. This young man here today must be the second son of the old Mr al-Zeid who used to visit your father. I heard from a cousin that he had put this son in charge of his Palestinian affairs.'

'But Cook, I thought Syrian Arabs spoke French. How is it Mr al-Zeid speaks English so well?'

'His father sent him to school in England.'

'Why?'

Cook gave a shrug, 'Everyone knows English is now necessary for big business, and the al-Zeids are big business.' She straightened biscuits on a plate.

'Do some Muslim sects cut a scar through the eyebrows of their young men?'

Cook looked puzzled 'I've never heard that.'

A loud knock on the back door interrupted Patsy's interrogation. Two men in railway uniform stood in the courtyard.

'The Inglisi luggage has been saved by the will of Allah,' one of them informed Cook, 'but someone must check all pieces are present.'

Cook, looking flustered, whispered, 'Miss Patsy, your mother has not yet left out the baksheesh box.'

'I'm spent out, Cook. I'll have to disturb my father.' Patsy experienced a frisson of pleasure at the excuse to see Mr al-Zeid again. She took the tray of coffee with her and knocked on the study door. Her father's face softened. 'Mr al-Zeid, may I introduce my daughter, Patricia?'

The young man rose politely, gave a dazzling smile as he held out his hand. She put down the tray to clasp it. To her surprise, although his nails were immaculately clean and manicured he had a worker's callused palm and thumb.

'This will interest you, Patsy,' her father said, 'Mr al-Zeid studied archaeology when he was at Cambridge. He could give you a hint or two for when you go up.'

Archaeology! That accounted for the rough skin - all that digging and keeping the sides of a trench straight. She explained about the luggage and the porters to her father.

He pulled a sheet of paper from a drawer. 'I'll go myself, and check against my list.'

She felt awkward when her father left. Somewhere she had read that in Arabic Society, a young man and young woman should never be alone in the same room. However, this Muslim seemed perfectly at ease. He spoke of his time at Cambridge with affection while she poured coffee.

'What made you study in England?' she asked as she held out the plate of biscuits.

He regarded her with amusement; 'It is always good to know the enemy, Miss Quigley.'

She stared. 'Enemy, Mr al-Zeid?'

Was that confusion on his face as he busied himself choosing a biscuit? Perhaps not, because he laughed again.

'By enemy, I meant those European archaeologists who steal my country's heritage.'

She challenged that. 'British archaeologists keep immaculate records, Mr al-Zeid. They do not steal, well not nowadays, anyway.'

Amusement again in his eyes as he answered solemnly, 'Of course, Miss Quigley. I intended no offence. I was making a joke.'

'It's no joke to impugn professionals,' she snapped, thinking of those models of probity, Dr Garrod and Kathleen Kenyon, and immediately wished she had kept her mouth shut. How could she be so insensitive? What would British archaeologists feel if Arabs had excavated the best sites in England, and an Arabic government had kept the artefacts?

Mr al-Zeid ate his biscuit in silence. Her father returned.

'I must go now,' she blurted, and almost ran from the room.

Hot-cheeked she fled the house and raced across the grounds. Dusty heat rose from the remnants of parched grass. She felt the sun beat down on her head and sought out her childhood shelter, the fig tree in the vineyard. Its stout branches still curved to form a circle at ground level. She pushed her way through a curtain of leathery leaves. Standing with eyes shut to erase sunlight dazzle, she breathed in the moist aroma reminiscent of spiced coconut, then opened her eyes, sat on the ground and prepared to stay leaning against the fig tree's pimply trunk until she heard Mr al-Zeid drive off. How could she have made such a fool of herself? She didn't do things like that with men in England. Tim's face sprang to her mind. Why couldn't she be there with him? Why had she allowed her father to drag her out here? Why did she always give in to her father?

Unbidden the memory she hated most in the world rose to the surface. Herself in bed, one arm protecting her breasts from the slavering mouth; one hand clenched over her genitals; that purple thing frantically sawing through her thighs; a hateful desire to draw that ugly thing in fighting her determination to let it come no further; the shouted words above her head, 'I shouldn't be doing this, Patsy. I shouldn't be doing this. You mustn't let me in.'

She pushed the nightmare away and concentrated on why she had given in to her father, when he had first told her he had booked her a passage to Palestine. She had fought robustly at first, although as they were in the middle of St James' Park in London she couldn't yell at him as loudly as she had wanted.

She closed her eyes to relive the scene.

****

'No, Popeye! I'm not going. No, no!'

'Don't call me by that stupid name.'

She would though. He had forfeited the name Dad long ago.

'You're coming back with us, Patsy, like it or not.'

'But I am sitting the Oxford Scholarship this year.'

'You can manage without a scholarship. If, and when, your mother and I decide that you are ready to go to university, we will pay your fees, but first we want to see you give your life to the Lord before you venture out into the world with all its temptations. Just look at you now, painted like a whore.'

****

Picking a leathery fig leaf, Patsy rolled it round a finger as she recalled her continued attempt at rebellion.

****

'I'll find a job; support myself. I won't go back with you, Popeye and you know why!'

Only then did her father behave as she had expected earlier. He slumped onto a park bench. Tears welled in his eyes. She knew, though, that despite her seeming victory, he would defeat her in the end. He always did.

'Patsy it was wrong, what I did to you, when you came back to Haifa. The way you lead your life now is my punishment, but I am still your father and I must not let my sins cost you your soul.'

He looked up, the tears now rolling down his cheeks.

Feeling both ashamed, and disgusted, she focussed on the mottled bark of a London plane tree, placing her hands on its trunk while her father continued.

Patsy, you know the pressure I was under with your mother in hospital; the doctors saying she might be an invalid for life, the new baby dying, all the projects I had to complete on time, but at least I kept you a virgin. You know I kept you a virgin. You must forgive me.'

You must forgive me

There it was, the reason she could never win against her father. She shook her head, breaking free of the memory now it had achieved its purpose. She lifted the crushed fig leaves to her nose, inhaling the scent. The Lord's Prayer pounded in her skull. 'Our father which art in heaven, forgive us our trespasses as we forgive others.'

Every time her father begged her forgiveness, she recalled her own sins, every unkind word she had ever spoken, every childhood quarrel, and worst of all, the thirty piastres she had stolen from her mother's purse when she was nine. How could her sins be forgiven, if she refused to forgive? It had nothing to do with her father's God, in whom she no longer believed, more a law of pendulums.

The words of forgiveness always crept grudgingly from her mouth, losing her the battle because forgiveness entailed reinstating her father's rights to her obedience except, she was no longer a child. The way she ran her life was now her responsibility.

Chapter 13

Patsy woke desperate to recall the dream that had left behind a foreboding of impending disaster. She sat up and reviewed her action plan. She would say nothing to her parents about boycotting Sunday morning service until her father took the Austin out of the garage, then she would saunter back to the house. Her father would shout. She would pause in the doorway and fling her words nonchalantly over her shoulder, 'Oh, Popeye, whatever made you think I was going to Sharing?'

Satisfied she had rehearsed sufficiently; she dressed and crept downstairs. No servants. She remembered this terrifying Sunday emptiness from childhood, as if, overnight, God had called the righteous to glory, leaving her orphaned. In those days, she had always run back upstairs to peek round her parent's bedroom door, to check they were still there.

She climbed the steep step to the balcony girdling the top of the watchtower, emerged under a sky of pink-edged translucent eau-de-nil and gazed over parched ground waiting for the first rains. Athlit Castle pierced the horizon, only a mile or so from where Dr Garrod had found the Neanderthals. One morning she would catch the train to Athlit, visit the caves, and hike back along Carmel ridge.

The sky above strengthened to a truer blue; the pink, fading to white mist, withdrew to the horizon. Her mother called her down to breakfast.

Anticipation of imminent triumph grew during her father's lengthy grace, expanded throughout the consumption of Sunday boiled eggs, and grew full blown by the end of family prayers. Her mother innocently applied the deflating pin, 'I am so looking forward to having you with us this morning, Patsy. Everyone I've phoned has asked after you.'

She felt her heart bang its way almost into her throat, as she rethought her strategy. She succeeded in bringing out the words, 'Actually, Um Pat, I thought I would stay behind, this morning; see to the dinner.'

Her mother rolled her napkin slowly and placed it in its ring, but her father's hand slammed hard on his bible, jingling the empty cups. She wasn't scared of him, she told herself, tensing to run if he rose from his chair.

Her mother spoke, voice high, 'There's no need, love, things are easier now I have a refrigerator and electric stove. Cook prepares everything before she goes off. All I do is put meat and potatoes into the oven before we leave and boil vegetables when we return. Please come. It means so much to me.'

Patsy gathered up used crockery while wondering how to reply. She could see that sticking to her guns would upset her mother. Facing up to defeat, she muttered, 'Very well, I was only trying to help.'

An hour later, she climbed into the back seat of the Austin. After all her planning, her sole token of protest had been to don her most frivolous hat.

Her father parked the car in front of the New Covenant Hall - still the same rusty corrugated iron hut.   Several Saints, in dignified Sunday best, came up to welcome back her parents. They expressed their greetings to her in cooler terms. Perhaps her hat, with its Hollywood veil over one eye and a jaunty feather at the side, was not such a good idea.

Mr Manners, the chief Spiritual Guide, approached, strutting in front of his dumpy wife. Patsy had half-hoped to find their daughter Joanne with them although, at Easter, Joanne hadn't mentioned that she was spending the summer in Haifa. On the other hand, no one had seen her in London recently.

Patsy waited for a lull in conversation and asked, 'Mrs Manners, did Joanne get over this summer?'

Mrs Manners stared at her in consternation.   Her mother glared at her. Mrs Manners stuttered at last, 'W-well no, she and her husband have been too busy settling into their new home.'

Patsy could not believe she was hearing this. Joanne married and settling down before she had sat her degree?   Only last Christmas she had been extolling the delights of college life. 'I am making the most of it all,' she had gloated. 'Free and single. The only time I'll be able to live just for me.'

Mr Manners turned from her father and faced her.   'Sister Patricia, if you let me have the letter of introduction from your last Assembly of Saints, I will pass it on to the Spiritual Guides.'

Letter of introduction? What was the man talking about? He knew perfectly well who she was. She scrutinised her parents. Her mother was biting her lip. Her father's hooded eyes, and his casual turn of his head, signalled anxiety, as he answered on her behalf, ' Brother Frederick, you know as well as I do that there is no Assembly near that ungodly school to which we both entrusted our daughters. I withdrew Patsy expressly so she could worship with the saints here.'

Mr Manners compressed his lips.   'Patricia, have you been received into Fellowship?'

She stared him straight in the eyes, hoping to shock him. 'No.' His look of disapproval delighted her.

'Have you been baptised by total immersion?'

'No!' but now beneath the censure, she detected a gleam of triumph as he replied smoothly, 'Then, my dear, you do realise you may not sit in fellowship, although you are, of course, welcome to occupy the strangers' bench.'

Her mother stiffened. Mrs Manners looked as if she wanted to argue, but was too frightened.

'Brother Frederick.'

She heard the repressed fury in her father's voice. Much as she enjoyed his humiliation, she would rather not witness it at the hands of that arch hypocrite, Mr Manners. On impulse, she gave her mother a swift kiss on the cheek, swivelled on her heel and marched to the pavement. A bus, on its way to town, drew up. She jumped on it. From the step, she shouted, 'See you at lunchtime.'

The bus driver held out his hand for the fare. She broke into her collection money, slumped into a seat, fighting a need to burst into tears, stared ahead, and concentrated on the episode's positive aspect. She had accomplished what she set out to do; she had missed Sharing.

By the time she had jumped off the bus at the far end of Kingsway, she was experiencing an almost overwhelming sense of freedom.

She stood still to take her bearings. If she remembered correctly, the terminus was near the suq. She took a right turn and there was the maze of overhanging buildings and dark, narrow streets that had been her childhood Mecca. Here, clutching her weekly pocket money piastre, she had agonised over which of the myriad exotic treasures on offer she should buy.

She paused to breathe in the dominant smells, - donkey, camel, falafel, and somewhere beneath a whiff of sewage, a hint of rosewater. The odours, the cave-like shop fronts exactly as she remembered; but the people looked different. Every woman wore a plain black headscarf; a few even had the full veil. Shopkeepers and coffee shop customers had replaced their crimson, black-tasselled fez for white keffiyahs kept in place with black iqals. Only the cut of their expensive European suits distinguished them from the fellahin guiding loaded donkeys and camels through narrow alleys.

Everyone was watching her - not exactly in hostility, more in surprise. A tall man, wearing the ubiquitous keffiyah, barred her way. 'Miss Quigley?'

She recognised him as the man to whom she had given a bucket of water; but how did he know her name?

'Miss Quigley, I suggest you head back to Kingsway. The suq is not the safest place for a British lady.'

'Mr al-Zeid!'

She recovered from her surprise quickly enough to protest, 'But I've been here often....'

Mr al-Zeid gave his devastating smile. 'Now, if you really want to be adventurous, come and have coffee with me,' and he had his hand under her elbow and was steering her away.

'Where are we going?'

'The Technion, where Arabs, Jews and even the British can still mix freely.'

They had reached his red Tatra. Mr al-Zeid gave a piastre to the urchin guarding it, before holding open the passenger door for her to get in. He then swung the starting handle and took his place behind the wheel where he exchanged his keffiyah for a fez.

This amused her. 'And what did you wear in England?'

He produced a trilby from under the dashboard.

'But why were you wearing a keffiyah?' she asked, when her giggles had subsided.

'Politics. The Grand Mullah has declared that if everyone wears a keffiyah it will confuse the police.'

They drew up in front of the classical façade of the Technion, walked into the student café, and joined a group of men, most of them somewhat older than the average student, who were conversing in Hebrew. Mr al-Zeid introduced her, in English, as Miss Quigley, an archaeology student from Oxford. He introduced the men by their forenames.

'You must call me Patsy,' she told them.

Mr al-Zeid smiled approvingly 'My name is Ahmed.'

The students switched to English and continued a discussion of the British proposal to partition Palestine between Jews and Arabs.

'Not the ideal solution but we would be willing to accept it for the sake of peace,' a good-looking young Jew named Shimon commented, 'but we don't need political boundaries. All we want from governments is that they organise the water supply and build roads.'

Someone laughed. 'Shimon, you should join the communist cuckoo party.'

'What's wrong with partition?' Patsy asked.

'It didn't work in England,' Ahmed commented, 'Neither the Danes nor Angles liked it, if I remember rightly.'

'That was because the Danes were the invaders,' she retorted.

'Exactly,' Ahmed commented.

She felt herself going hot, falling into that trap so easily. She gulped her coffee and checked her watch. 'I must get back. Is there a bus stop handy?'

'I will give you a lift,' Ahmed stated.

They were silent in the car until her house came into view. 'I miss Mt Carmel,' Ahmed commented, 'as a child, this was my favourite home.' He jumped out to open the passenger door. 'I pray Allah that he will grant us another meeting.'

'I trust so too,' she replied with equal formality.

She let herself into the house and busied herself in the kitchen, alternating between reliving her morning adventures and worrying about the scene to come.

She heard the Austin drive up, moved to the kitchen door, and peeped out. Her father stalked into his study, but her mother joined her in the kitchen and slumped on to Cook's chair. Patsy poured her a cup of tea.

'I'm sorry.' Her mother stared into her cup as she stirred in sugar. 'I should have warned you about Joanne Manners. I'd assumed you'd heard.'

'No, last I knew she was enjoying life at college.'

'So, she was, but - she had to get married. The baby is expected next month.'

Patsy felt hot all over. How could Joanne have done something like that? No wonder, Mr Manners had turned on her. 'Is that why you wouldn't let me stay on at school?'

Her mother nodded. 'We were so worried. Suppose you went... well... wild, like Joanne? Cut off from believers; living in that atmosphere. Suppose you never came through to the Lord?'

'Um Pat,' Patsy spoke as gently as she could, 'I won't ever belong to the Second Chosen. It's not right for me but that doesn't mean...,' she hesitated, too embarrassed to come out with - I'll get myself pregnant, not to Um Pat. 'Well - you know,' and despised her own feebleness.

Her mother's tongue licked her lower lip, but her eyes smiled. 'You prefer the Methodists? I thought you might. Both your Uncle Tom and Aunt Helen are happier with them. Well, in my Father's house are many mansions. Accepting Jesus is all that matters, and I know you have done that.'

Patsy bit off her denial and poured her own tea. She concentrated on refilling the kettle as she said, 'I'm not going to the Good News Service this evening.' .

'Perhaps best not,' she heard her mother reply, 'I don't think I will either - not tonight. Next week, though, we will all go together.'

'No!' she blurted out, then twisted round, and saw her mother's stricken face. 'Oh Um Pat, I am sorry.'

She went up to her and hugged her, while reconsidering her position. After all why shouldn't she go? It might provoke her father even more, to watch her "not being converted".

Chapter 14

At morning prayers, her father pleaded with the Lord to save his daughter from burning and return her to the fold. Patsy concentrated on picturing Tim, not so easy when Ahmed's compelling face pushed itself to the fore.

Her father left for work. Patsy picked up another slice of now cold toast and added butter and marmalade. In the hall, the phone rang.

Her mother opened the dining room door. 'For you, Patsy.'

'It can't be. I don't know anybody.'

'An Aileen Doyle. She asked for Patsy Quigley.'

'I don't know anyone called Aileen.' Puzzled, Patsy dropped her toast and went to the phone.

'Hello,' a voice with a strong Irish brogue; 'Is that Patsy? For sure, you won't know me but I am Aileen Doyle. I nurse at the government hospital. Peter Monteith mentioned to my Mick that he had met you on the train. He thought you might want to join the tennis club. Are you any good?'

'I was in the school team.'

'Grand. We're short of women who can hit a ball over the net. Would you be after a game, tomorrow about ten? I'm off duty then.'

Patsy's allowance didn't run to Tennis Club subscriptions. Caution prevailed. 'That's really kind of you, Aileen. I'll just check my diary. If you give me your number I'll ring back.'

After she had hung up, she went to look for her mother 'One of the nurses at the hospital. She wants to know if I'm joining the tennis club. Do you and Popeye still belong?'

Her mother looked at the floor. 'No, we left when our membership proved a stumbling block to some of the Saints.'

Patsy felt the prison bars grow tighter. Her mother raised her eyes. 'But a young girl like you needs healthy exercise.' She pursed her lips and tapped a foot. 'I'll fork up your membership fee, Patsy. Just one thing, though, don't make a song and dance about the tennis club when you talk to the Saints. Your father is a Spiritual Guide, remember.'

She threw one arm round her mother and went back to the phone.

****

A muscular young woman, slightly older than herself, in a cream broderie anglais tennis frock stood in the hotel foyer. The woman's eyes crinkled. 'Patsy Quigley? I am Aileen Doyle. I thought you might be after coming through this door. The changing rooms are at the back.'

'Proper changing rooms? We dressed in the jon-jons when I was here last.'

'My Mick has been telling me how tough it was when he came out. I've only been a year here myself and to tell the truth of it, am still missing home. It will be grand having another Irish girl to talk to.'

Patsy shook her head in apology. 'I don't think I count as Irish. I have never been to Ireland. My father left before I was born.'

'Your father, was he in the RIC now?'

Patsy laughed. 'No, my uncle was, though and he was a wild one by all accounts. When he joined the Palestine Police, my grandma Quigley ordered my father to apply for an engineering job in the Holy Land to keep an eye on him, but Uncle foiled Grandma by applying for a transfer to Kenya two years later. My father stayed on though.'

After Patsy had donned her school tennis whites in a luxurious changing room of polished marble, Aileen led her through a spacious bar to sloping lawns at the rear. Patsy stood still to take in the long vista of craggy slopes running down to green orchards and the white frilled Mediterranean.

One court was still free so they could play straight away. Aileen proved a strong opponent. The sets dragged on evenly, neither woman losing a service.

Although it was early November, the day was warmer than most English summers. Patsy's starched tennis frock soon lost its crispness and clung to her back. Just when she thought she could go on no longer, Aileen called out, 'For sure that was grand, but there's no need to go killing ourselves while other people are waiting for a court.'

'Mick,' Aileen shouted over to a sturdy young man sitting at a table next to Peter Monteith, 'Will you order drinks for Patsy and me while we change?'

Patsy came back still hot and exhausted, even after a cold shower. Peter pulled out a cane chair. She sank into soft cushions in front of a glass of 7-up, half-full of ice. The smile Peter gave her was the sort that usually had her squirming in her cinema seat but she remained pre-occupied with the cool liquid. Anyway, that smile, good as it was, was nothing compared to Mr al-Zeid's.

Peter introduced her to his friend Mick Murphy. She let the subsequent conversation wash round her, while soaking up the group atmosphere so similar to that of the house party where she had first met Tim.

'Mick,' Aileen asked, at one point, 'what makes you and Peter friends?'

Mick chuckled and leaned towards Aileen. 'For sure, I only hang around with Peter, because he's opted out of the competition. He's getting married this year, would you know?'

'Mick will be my best man,' Peter added.

'But Mick, you've only been back from furlough six months. For sure they won't let you go to England, so soon?'

'I'm marrying out here in Haifa, Aileen,' Peter said.

Patsy waited to hear more about this wedding, but Peter picked up his and Mick's glasses and went into the bar.

The canvas of the sheltering umbrella ballooned. The light lost its intensity. Empty glasses rolled off the table. No more sunshine. Chilly sweat on her back. Patsy looked behind. A black bank of cloud, sweeping in from the north, had blotted out the sun.

Five minutes later they were in the bar watching water cascade down the windows. Waiters ran outside, and lifted their arms in the air, cheering. Patsy remembered doing that as a child when the first rains came.

Chapter 15

Patsy stared at the olive wood fire in the living room, her book neglected.

'Patsy, is something wrong?'

She breathed out loudly. 'Nothing, Um Pat, except I'm frittering away a whole year of my life. I still can't forgive those Yanks at Megiddo for not taking me on.'

'If only you would accept it as the Lord saying that you should be doing His work, dear.'

Patsy made no reply, just fiddled with a wooden camel.

'Tell you what,' her mother said at last, 'I'll pay for you to take a shorthand/typing course, always a useful string to your bow.'

Not the most thrilling offer she had ever received. She remained silent, studying the carving marks on the camel.

Exasperation shrilled her mother's voice. 'It will help you with record keeping. All archaeologists have to keep decipherable records.'

Patsy laid the camel on its side. Her mother was right. She might as well accept the offer.

****

So the New Year found Patsy in a large upper room in central Haifa in front of a masked typewriter, the only British woman amongst a collection of Armenians, Arabs, Jews, and Greeks. How strange, she reflected, that we should be here, learning together, when, outside, Arabs and Jews do not even use the same buses and Jews are throwing bombs at Arabs in the suq.

Her fingers missed the keys again. She promised herself that when she got home, she would practice on her father's portable.

By the end of her third typing lesson, Patsy had stopped scowling at the typewriter. As she rose to leave the classroom, she smiled at the people close by. An Arabic woman with marcelled hair, long, curling eyelashes and a Parisian styled dress, approached her.

'Hello' the woman said, in a voice made even more attractive by its foreign accent, 'My name is Maftur Naoud. Most of us go on to Edmonds after the lesson. Would you like to join us?'

'Never give foreigners the impression that you consider yourself superior,' her father had warned long ago.

'It is not their fault the Lord did not make them British,' her mother had drummed into her.

Patsy accepted the invitation gracefully, but with considerable inward trepidation.

At first, she sat in the café in awkward silence, waiting in dread for the subject matter to turn foreign, but the conversation continued in the lingua franca of Hollywood English; the topics – boyfriends, American film stars and plots of the current films. The comments the other women passed on the male stars of their fancy were as immodest as those of her former schoolmates. The Jewish women talked about their dates; the Arab women, who, in dress and appearance, could be mistaken for Parisians, listened avidly. Maftur even contributed to part of that conversation. She mentioned in a whisper, after a nervous look behind, that she had, not exactly a liaison, but a desire to marry a local boy, a friend of her eldest brother.

'It is always marrying cousins in our family,' she complained, 'If only Ismail were my cousin, my parents would be delighted to have him as a son-in-law, instead of this Syrian cousin they have chosen.'

Most of the others nodded in sympathy, but a Jewish woman, Golda, spoke impatiently, 'It's your life, Maftur, you just tell your parents you are not marrying the Syrian guy.'

Another woman, Miriam, whom Patsy had assumed was an Arab until she noticed the silver Star of David dangling from her necklace, rounded on Golda. 'Oh, you are so European. You do not understand our Palestinian ways.'

Patsy's curiosity overcame her shyness. 'Miriam, how long has your family lived in Palestine?'

Miriam held up her head. 'On my father's side only 200 years but on my mother's side 300.'

That turned some of Patsy's ideas upside down. She had assumed no Jews had lived in Palestine before the end of the nineteenth century.

Patsy gradually grew more comfortable with the group and even told them about Tim, 'I like him very much, but I want to be free to follow a career.'

Maftur exclaimed at that, 'But you British have so much freedom, already. Not like me.'

She fumbled in her bag and pulled out a photograph. 'This is the man my parents want me to marry. I have never even met him.'

Golda put out her hand, took the photograph, and immediately changed her tune about Maftur standing up to her parents. 'Wow! That guy looks like Adonis. I'd grab him if I were you.'

The woman, sharing the photograph with Golda, added, 'If he were handed to me on a plate I'd be over the moon. I take it he's got money?'

Maftur shrugged elegant silk clad shoulders. 'Oh, he is well enough heeled, but he lives in Damascus. I know no one there. Ismail, on the other hand,' her eyes softened, 'he lives in Haifa, and his family is not exactly poor either.'

As the photo passed from hand to hand, everyone declared this prospective husband to be as handsome as men came. Patsy waited nervously for the photo to reach her. What would she say if she found the man ugly? When she saw the photo, she nearly dropped it. She was looking at Ahmed al-Zeid.

'Handsome is as handsome does,' she muttered before passing it on, 'you go for what you want.'

Maftur pulled a face. 'It would be easier if I could only discover something about this man that would displease my parents.'

Chapter 16

The maid had taken two days off, so Patsy had volunteered to feed the hens. She held a clay bowl in one hand, throwing grain from left to right with the other, doing her best to side-step birds flapping round her feet. While she worked, she planned.

'I'm going for a picnic with Aileen and Mick next Sunday, Um Pat. After church,' she checked the wording of that phrase, to make sure she was not saying that she was actually going to church, 'we will get together with some more of Aileen's friends. Mick and Aileen will bring me home.'

Word perfect by the time the bowl was empty, she found her mother in the morning room and came out with her rehearsed speech.

Her mother shook her head. 'Not on a Sunday, dear.'

Patsy brought herself close to an outright lie. 'Um Pat, Aileen needs me. She doesn't think it right to picnic alone with Mick.' She straightened her back, the embodiment of a respectable chaperone.

'All right,' her mother conceded, 'I'll speak to your father and explain the situation, but don't make a habit of it. Ask cook to bake some fairy cakes to take to the picnic. If Nurses' Homes are anything like they were in my day, your friend will have no proper cooking facilities.'

She tried to stop her father driving her to the Nurses' Home but he insisted. Fear that he would search her bag caused her feet to judder on the car floor.

'Don't be late back,' her father ordered as he drew up the car next to Mick's battered Ford.

'Mick and Aileen will give me a lift home. Um Pat has lent me a key. There's no need for you to wait up.'

Her father made no comment but sat in the car with the engine running, watching until Aileen met her at the door.

Mick and Peter were already in the lobby, lounging beneath a large notice.

NO MALE VISITORS IN NURSE'S ROOMS AT ANY TIME

Aileen led her up to her room to unpack her evening clothes. Patsy hung up her Sunday best as well.

'How did you manage to sneak all that past your father?' Aileen exclaimed.

She grinned. 'He knew about the Sunday best. I wrapped them round my evening dress, and my dancing shoes are not much bulkier than my bible.'

They ran downstairs and Mick drove along the coast road almost as far as Khayet Beach. He turned left up a dirt road through orange groves and parked in a small quarry. A goat track led up to a miniature gorge dividing miniature cliffs. They carried the picnic bags through the gorge.

The air was fresh but warm, the hillside still red with anemones, although they were beginning to drop their petals and age had elongated their dark centres. Anemones, Patsy remembered, sprang from the blood of Adonis as he lay dying. One of the women at secretarial college had compared Ahmed to Adonis. This picnic, she thought, would have been even more fun if he had been here.

Aileen spread a cloth on a flat rock and set out cucumber and cream cheese sandwiches, plus the cooked chicken and local wine Mick and Peter had supplied. Patsy had tasted wine before but still felt guilty drinking it, especially on a Sunday. The guilt added an agreeable edge to the flavour.

After the main course they sprawled on smooth grass lazily nibbling at Cook's moist fairy cakes and talking about Aileen and Mick's wedding the following December, a wedding at which she was to be a bridesmaid.

'For sure you will love Newtown Barry,' Aileen told her, 'and the cottage we are renting, just down the road from my Mam, that's grand. While you are in Ireland, why don't you cycle round and visit where your Da was born.'

The subject changed to Peter's wedding. Aileen commented, 'A shame that your Penelope didn't manage to bring your mother round to the idea. When is she leaving?'

'She has one last town to play. Then she's on the boat. I'll just have time to finish painting the flat.'

They fell silent watching the sun drop low in the sky, creating a golden path across the Mediterranean. Patsy looked down on the bathing huts of Khayet Beach.

'The water will be warm enough for swimming, soon,' Patsy said, 'I wish Khayet Beach wasn't so far from Haifa.'

'You can come to Police Beach with us any time we go,' Aileen said, 'and for sure you won't find it difficult to get an off duty constable to invite you when we're on duty.'

They packed the picnic things away and carried them back to the car.

Mick drove them back to the Nurses' Home and the two men went off for a beer in the NAAFI bar.

In her room, Aileen fetched out a navy blue silk dress trimmed with downy white feathers.

'That's beautiful!' Patsy exclaimed.

Aileen pulled a face. 'Seen the night lights rather too often, and that's the truth of it, but I can't afford anything new, not while we're saving for the wedding.'

Patsy twisted herself into her jet beaded black dress and ran a hand down her smooth sides. Now it was Aileen's turn for admiration. 'That's grand, Patsy. For sure your parents didn't buy it you.'

'No, I bought it with money my aunt gave me for my birthday. Not quite what she had in mind but she had to agree it suited me. I'll have to change into my Sunday best before I go home, though.'

'That's no problem. Peter's already moved into a flat. It's on your way home so you can change there.'

While Patsy was applying scarlet nail varnish, she thanked Aileen for asking Mick to give her a lift back.

'For sure it was nothing.' Aileen waved her hands gently to let her darker polish dry. 'And you needn't start fretting while we are out. I'll make sure Mick runs you home in good time.'

The men returned. Patsy quivered with happiness at their appreciative wolf whistles before they walked the short distance to the nightclub.

Electric bulbs in tinted glass shades lit gleaming tables set round a polished dance floor. A band in evening dress played on a platform, while a woman crooned loudly in a Southern American accent. At the other end of the room, green shaded ceiling lights shone down on gaming tables. Patsy contrasted the club's glitter with the dismal brown paint and flat lighting of her normal Sunday evenings.

Mick brought over gin cocktails sporting purple parasols. Her father would have a fit if he could see her now. Happiness rippled through every nerve.

A handsome man, in an immaculately pressed green uniform, approached and, in broken English, asked her to dance. His dancing proved more polished than his English.

'Have you lived here long?' she asked.

The man laughed. 'I am from Italia. I fly here every week. My name is Guissepe. You come here from Germany, I think. What is your name?'

'From Germany?' she pushed away from his tight embrace. 'I am British.'

'No, you are too beautiful to be British,' Guissepe squeezed her more firmly against his chest.

Unsure whether to be flattered or insulted, she pushed away again.

'Ah, you are cold like an English Meess,' the airman admitted, 'but I will warm you, yes?'

She drew herself up ramrod straight. The airman said nothing more until he thanked her stiffly at the end of the dance. Aileen laughed when she saw Patsy's face. 'So you are not as overwhelmed as most by the charm of our Green Mice?'

'Green Mice?'

'The Al Italia pilots who make the twice weekly run from Rhodes. Most women fancy them, and that's the truth of it.'

'Well I don't. Where are Peter and Mick?'

Aileen pointed behind her. 'He's after having a small flutter on the gaming tables.'

The band started a quickstep. A British Signals lieutenant asked her to dance. Although a trifle dull, he was infinitely preferable to her first partner. After that, she had a partner every dance and felt completely desirable. She wanted to stay dancing forever. When the band paused for a rest, Peter brought her another cocktail, with the wonderfully decadent name, *Devil's Claw*.

'Did you win?' she asked.

He gave a satisfied grin. 'Enough for another pot or two of paint.'

She had barely taken the first sip from her cocktail when Aileen nudged her and whispered, 'Time for Cinderella to leave the ball. Peter says you can change at his flat.'

She didn't want to leave but laughed and chatted with the others in Mick's car and up the stairs of the new block of flats half way along Stella Maris Road. She giggled while Peter blocked the entrance to pick up a telegram. She floated, full of her magical evening, into a lobby smelling strongly of turps while Peter switched on the light.

A sound half way between a moan and a scream cut through her bubble of happiness. She heard Peter shout, 'No, no, no,' watched Mick remove the slip of paper from Peter's hand and read it, stiffen before handing it wordlessly to Aileen. Aileen read the telegram, gasped and took hold of Peter's free elbow. Mick put his arm round his friend, half-supporting him. He and Aileen led Peter through a doorway and shut the door.

Patsy stood alone in the bare lobby holding her case, wondering what calamity had overtaken her friends, ashamed because, while they were so upset about something that must be important, she was worrying about changing her dress and getting home on time. She opened a door hoping it led into a bathroom but found a broom closet so packed with paint tins that there was no room to stand. She opened another. It led into a kitchen with a second door at the end. She crossed the floor, cautiously tried the handle, and found herself looking at Aileen and Mick on a settee facing Peter. Aileen, tears streaming from her eyes, was holding Peter's hand.

No one saw her. She closed the door. She couldn't change here in the kitchen – Mick or Peter might come in while she had her dress off. The same thing applied to the lobby.

Aileen came into the kitchen, mopping her eyes with a handkerchief. She stopped, startled. 'I am sorry, Patsy. I had forgotten you were here. Can you help me make a pot of tea, now? If you could get the cups out of the press.'

'What happened?'

'Penelope passed away.' Aileen filled a kettle.

Patsy did not know Peter's fiancée, had not even seen her photo, but a numbness spread outwards from her chest. 'How?'

'We don't know.'

Patsy found four cups and saucers, set them out on a tray. Aileen placed the kettle on the electric stove. Patsy fiddled successfully with the knobs. Aileen elaborated, 'The telegram from Peter's mother, just said 'Penelope died yesterday. Funeral on Wednesday. Letter following.' Now where's the tea and sugar? Peter will need a lot of sugar. He's in shock and that's the truth of it.'

Patsy hunted through the cupboard again and found both tea and sugar. Milk she took from the icebox. When the kettle had boiled, she filled the teapot and said, 'I'll carry in the tray.' She knew that was really only an excuse to enter the lounge and become part of the group, however sad the occasion. She set the tray on a side table and poured. Aileen picked up a cup and tried to get Peter to drink. Mick aided her efforts.

Patsy glanced at her watch. Nearly 1 o'clock. She ought to phone home. Mick looked up, frowned. 'Patsy, you still here?'

'Mick,' Aileen reminded him, 'we promised to take Patsy home.'

'I can't leave Peter like this.'

Aileen looked down at Peter, who seemed oblivious of their presence. 'Mick, I'll stay in case he wants anything, but you must take Patsy home.'

Mick strode silently out of the room, beckoning Patsy to follow. She didn't dare mention that she hadn't changed. Mick made no conversation on the journey. She felt herself pinned to the side of the car as he rounded the bend in Stella Maris Road faster than she had deemed possible. He skidded the car to a halt on the road outside her house. Light, from an unshuttered window, streamed down the drive, throwing ruts into relief.

'You'll be all right from here.' A statement not a question. 'I must get back.'

The car screeched off almost before Patsy's shoes had touched the gravel. She ducked behind the nearest cypress, scrambled out of her black dress and dance shoes, pulled on her Sunday best. She walked up the drive, her feet, clumsy with fear, stumbling on every stone. She reached the porch, groped for the key in her bag, but the front door opened before she could find it. The dark silhouette of her father filled the frame and the light filtering past him highlighted her crimson nails. She hid her hands behind her back, pressed her painted lips together but too late. Her father roared, 'Harlot, Scarlet Woman,' flung out his hand, and slapped her left cheek. Her own hands jerked up too late to protect her face. She felt him snatch her bag so roughly from her shoulder that he ripped her Sunday best. She watched helplessly as he snapped the bag open, yanked out her beautiful dress, and deliberately ripped it apart. Jet beads pinged as they bounced on the stone slabs.

The torn dress hurt far more than her slapped cheek. Her face would heal but no amount of invisible mending would right her precious dress. Her father flung her dance shoes at the nearest cypress and hurled her bag after them. As she swivelled to retrieve them, he seized her by her hair, spun her round, thrust his face into hers, sniffed, then roared again, 'You have been drinking too.'

His free fist bounced off her right cheek. Still gripping her hair, he dragged her inside and across the hall, shaking her head from side to side, while repeating the words 'Harlot' and 'Scarlet woman.'

She glimpsed her mother running down the stairs still tying the belt of her dressing gown, heard her scream, 'No, Seamus, no.'

Her father twisted her hair further round his hand so that the top of her head arched back almost to her shoulder blades. He hit her again, this time across the ridge of her nose. Warm liquid gushed from her nostrils.

'That's enough, Seamus,' her mother shouted the words almost in her ear, 'enough.'

Her father let go of her hair. She fell and banged her head on the quarry tiles. When she opened her eyes, her mother was leaning over her, shielding her from her father. Her father shouted, 'You want to protect this precious daughter of yours, who has spent the Sabbath drinking, smoking and whoring?'

Patsy sprang up, raced upstairs, locked herself in the bathroom, and ran the tap, thankful for the new electric pump. She dipped her face under the flow, turning the water scarlet, then cautiously opened the bathroom door, and peered out. The landing was empty. She crept to her room, and reached up to draw the bolt on the door, but couldn't feel it, so switched on the light. Screw holes showed where the bolt had been. She wedged a chair under the door handle hoping it would win her enough time to jump out of bed and place her weight against the door should her father try to get in. She kept on her bra when changing into pyjamas, tied her trouser belt in a double knot, switched off the light and climbed painfully into bed but kept her head above the blankets, so she could hear if her father renewed his attack.

Footsteps sounded in the corridor. She slipped out of bed, picked up her hockey stick, placed her knees against the chair and yelled, 'Go away, you bloody hypocrite.'

She waited for the handle to turn. Instead, she heard something boring into the wood, an odd squeaking, followed by the clang of a bolt sliding into place. Seesawing emotions of fear and anger created an urgent need to wee. She looked hopefully under the bed. Thank goodness, the po was still there.

She must have fallen asleep after getting back into bed because by the time she had registered the crash of a falling chair, the door had opened. She lay stiff with terror, pretending to be asleep as she heard the click of a light switch.

A hand, not her father's shook her. She opened aching eyes; saw her mother examining her face and lifted her hands to her sore nose. The action hurt her neck.

'Not as bad as it might have been,' her mother commented, 'a couple of black eyes and a few other bruises but nothing that won't mend. Your father has calmed down. I'll speak to you in the morning.'

Grey daylight filtered through slits in the shutters when she woke again. Her mother was there once more.

'Are you in a fit state to talk?'

Patsy struggled to push her aching body into a sitting position. Her mother continued, her face stern, 'Patsy, why did you lie to me?'

Guilt overwhelmed her. 'I'm sorry. I just wanted an evening with my friends. Sunday was the only time we could get together.'

To her self-disgust, she burst into tears. 'It all ended so terribly,' she said between sobs, 'even before I came home.'

Her mother's eyes widened from shutters of reproach to circles of fear. 'What do you mean, "It all ended terribly"?'

Patsy fumbled in her bedside drawer for a handkerchief and dabbed her eyes. She wriggled sore shoulders against the pillows. 'One of our crowd - Peter Monteith - you know him.'

Her mother compressed her lips, folded her arms, straightened her back. 'Go on.'

'He got a telegram just before Mick was supposed to bring me home.'

Her mother frowned. 'So?'

'Um Pat, it said his fiancée was dead.'

Her mother sank onto the bed. After a pause, she whispered, 'How terrible,' – but, despite her words, she exuded relief.

'That's why I was so late, Um Pat. Mick had to look after Peter before he could take me home.'

Her mother lifted herself off the bed. 'Well, I suppose you have been punished enough. Your father has gone to work, so it won't hurt for you to come downstairs. I'll get you some breakfast.'

Patsy could not leave it there. 'Um Pat, I am sorry I lied to you. I shouldn't have done that, but,' she sat up straighter, wincing with pains that ran from her nose through her shoulders and all the way down her back, 'my father should not have hit me. If he does it again, I am going to leave home, find a job in Jerusalem or Cairo and tell everyone why.'

'No Patsy. Admittedly, your father went too far but he does have a right to correct you. Spreading gossip like that could prove an obstacle to sinners seeking the Lord.'

'I don't care.'

Her mother sat back on the bed. 'Then here is something that you may care about. Your father is in line for promotion. We are counting on the extra salary to pay your university fees. Gossip will ruin his chances.'

'That's blackmail, Um Pat.'

'And what have you just been doing, Patsy?'

She shut her eyes, acknowledging the response. 'I'm sorry. I just wanted to say that my father must not beat me again. I will have it out with him.'

'Don't provoke him, Patsy. He is under considerable strain.'

When her mother left, Patsy peered at herself in the mirror. She couldn't meet people looking like this.

Downstairs, her mother fetched a bowl of porridge but she shook her head; 'I'm not hungry.'

'Just try one spoonful.'

The one spoonful brought a miraculous return of appetite. She cleared her bowl and was ready for the bacon and her eggs her mother brought a few minutes later, along with a haversack. 'You could do with a walk, dear, to clear your head. There will be no one about on the mountain. I've put in a pair of sunglasses just in case and packed a few sandwiches. When your father returns for lunch I'll tell him that I sent you out.'

Before she set out, Patsy slipped a notebook and pencil into the haversack.

Her face still ached but the sunshine was pleasant as she walked along the mountain ridge where she used to pick spring flowers when young. The bright scarlet of dwarf tulips gleamed invitingly today. She reached an outcrop of boulders, where she had often played on Sunday afternoons, while her parents sat reading their bibles. She had intended to spend the day here until she saw pegs dividing the area into small plots and felt saddened that her childhood playground would soon disappear. She walked on until pegs were no longer in evidence.

Finding a smooth rock to sit on, she took out her notebook, scribbled, erased, and scribbled until she was satisfied with what she was going to say to her father that evening. Then she took out her packed lunch.

As she ate, she looked around. Athlit castle looked a lot nearer now. If she had set out early enough, she could have walked to the Neanderthal caves and back before dark.

On the walk home, she rehearsed the speech she had prepared.

Her stomach muscles tightened when she entered the lounge where her father was reading the Palestine Post. In an effort to steady her voice, she spoke formally, 'Father, may I have a word with you in your study?'

He looked up, folded his paper, and nodded briefly before standing and moving along the corridor. He took his seat at his desk and raised his eyebrows; 'I am listening.'

The rat was expecting an apology? She clenched her fists and recited her speech, 'Father, our views on morality differ, but that is not what I want to talk to you about.'

She noticed her father's air of confidence waver. He opened his mouth but she hurried on. 'I am too old for corporal punishment, father. If you lay one finger on me again I will tell Um Pat what you did when she was in hospital.' She saw his face crumple but carried on, 'and I will lay a serious charge against you with the police.' She hoped he would not guess she would be too ashamed ever to carry out those threats.

He did what she had expected. He dissolved into tears that turned into sobs. He hunched over his desk. Gulping he begged her forgiveness but she would not fall into that trap again. 'I am not going to discuss this, father. I just want you to know where you stand.'

She walked out of the room.

Chapter 17

Patsy was enjoying the weekly get together at Edmonds, listening to Golda describing the new house her parents were building on the outskirts of Tel Aviv, when there was a loud crash. The café's large glass window shattered, the heavy curtains blew open, a blast of air rocked the table, spilling the coffee, crashing crockery to the floor and sending her flying back against her seat.

Before the curtains closed, she saw a Union Jack, lift slowly into the air from the first floor of the Police HQ next door, and fall onto a pile of rubble erupting from the ground floor of the Khayet building.

She loosened her grip on the table and checked that she was still all in one piece. She looked round at her visibly shaken companions. None appeared injured, although shards of glass from the broken window littered the floor.

'Al ham du lillah'!' Maftur exclaimed beside her.

'If the curtains had been open it would have been a different story,' Patsy replied. She stepped high over the shards to draw back the slashed curtains and peer out.

No mutilated body parts, for which she was thankful. She wondered who was responsible for this outrage - Arabs or Jews? More likely the Jews this time, she thought, furious with the government for cutting back on immigration.

A waiter approached their table and replaced the stained tablecloth. He brought clean cups and poured more coffee.

A loud clanging announced the arrival of a fire engine. The women crowded round the window. Two ambulances rolled up. Patsy, uncomfortable. It seemed so unfeeling to go on drinking coffee next to a building where people she knew might be hurt, or even dead.

Three neatly bandaged police officers emerged, one of them Peter Monteith, his arm in a sling. Both ambulances drove off. Other police came out and press-ganged smartly dressed Arabic businessmen into clearing debris.

Maftur waxed indignant. 'The police shouldn't force effendi to work as labourers. The bombs are not their fault.'

Patsy felt ashamed of the high-handed tactics of her countrymen, hunted for a change of subject. 'How are the marriage plans going?'

Maftur waved her hands and smiled smugly. 'Negotiations have begun with Ismail's parents.'

'What happened to that good-looking man whose photo you showed us?' Golda put in.

Maftur grinned. 'That Ahmed al-Zeid? He went off the list.'

Miriam gave Maftur an admiring glance. 'How did you wangle that?'

'My father discovered something about him he considered unsuitable.'

Patsy felt oddly pleased but disturbed at the same time. 'What made him unsuitable?'

Maftur was disappointingly vague. 'Politics, perhaps.'

Chapter 18

In the suffocating heat of mid August, Patsy lounged on a deckchair at the Police Beach Club. The club consisted of a tacky pavilion and a rather ramshackle pier on a short stretch of rocky shore squashed between the harbour breakwater and the hospital. The government had originally acquired the land before the new harbour existed to accommodate the police launch. For Patsy the Club was the nearest place on earth to Paradise. She had spent much of the summer here as a guest of one young British policeman, or another.

This morning she was mulling over the loving letter she had received from Tim. Recalling the pain of kissing him goodbye outside Southampton docks, almost a year ago, she reminded herself that it was now just over a month before she saw him again. She wanted to see him, of course, but would really miss the club when she left Palestine.

She picked up her glass of ice-cold 7-up and glanced at her escort of the day, immersed in the political pages of the Palestine Post. He was a pleasant enough young man, good looking too. She had met so many attractive men this year, but no one she liked as much as Tim. The image of Ahmed al-Zeid flashed across her mind. She dismissed it as irrelevant. Ahmed was Arabic and Muslim.

If Tim really felt the same about her as his letter suggested, becoming engaged to him as soon as possible might be her best option. Her father would have to treat her differently if she was engaged, but then, she reflected, he probably would refuse to pay for her to go through college. Anyway, engagements turned into marriages eventually and she wasn't sure about marriage. It would interfere with her career.

She set her empty glass back on the tabletop, and gazed at the British children diving from the pier. She might go in for another swim herself soon; make the most of the Med while she could. No, need to decide about Tim until she reached England.

Mick walked across the sand and woke Aileen by kissing the top of her head. He flopped into the fourth chair at the table. 'Have you heard the latest?'

They looked at him expectantly.

'Hitler's giving up Poland?' Aileen asked.

Patsy's escort gave a cynical chuckle.

'No something a bit nearer home. Peter's been promoted.'

Aileen smiled. 'That's grand.'

Mick shook his head. 'Not if promotion turns him into a contrary auld fecker like Inspector Sutton. What Peter really needs is to have fun again.'

Aileen's face turned grave. 'I guess all our fun days are ending, Mick. If this war starts soon, we won't be home for our wedding.'

Patsy broke in. 'The war, it can't really be as close as that?'

Her escort looked up from the paper and laughed. 'Really, Patsy, where have you been these last few weeks?'

The answer to that was down here on the beach, perfecting her diving skills from the end of the pier, practising her crawl. 'I try not to think about things I can't affect,' she replied loftily.

Mick looked grave. 'You can't affect it, but sure to goodness it can affect you, Patsy.'

'Now isn't that the truth,' Aileen put in. 'Patsy, we're not wanting you going sooner than you have to, but you should be after getting an early berth home if you want to get to college.'

'It's only three weeks until I leave.'

'That may be too late,' her escort said.

'OK.' Patsy said, 'I'll talk to my father about changing my ticket.'

Her father, however, refused. 'Out of the question, Patsy. People are fighting for places on the boats. If the Lord wants you to return to England, he'll delay the war until you are home.'

The arrogance of it, Patsy thought. Her father couldn't seriously believe his God would hold up a war on her behalf. This, though, wasn't the time for entering into a theological argument. If only she had an income of her own.

The next day an Arabic land mine killed her father's boss while he was inspecting the construction of a new road.

'Seamus, it could have been you, in that vehicle.' Her mother exclaimed. 'It's dangerous keeping Patsy in Palestine. We ought to send her home now, if we possibly can.'

'The mine wasn't intended for Toulif Bey,' her father said, 'The Oozelbarts even tried to prevent him driving over it.'

'I don't care who it was intended for, the man died,' her mother retorted.

'He wasn't saved,' her father said 'The Lord protects his own.'

Four days later, the Union Jack on the beach clubhouse flew at half mast after a Jewish landmine in Jerusalem killed two British inspectors walking home after a shift.

Once more Patsy's mother pressed her father to buy her an earlier ticket.

'The Troubles won't last once war is declared,' he said.

Listening to the wireless daily now, Patsy realised preparations for war were speeding to a crescendo. On Thursday, the British government evacuated more than one and a half million children from major English towns. On Friday, Hitler invaded Poland. On Saturday, the British Parliament passed a National Service Act.

There was now less than a week before she sailed.

Dalia had fewer domestic issues than Suzanna and Patsy. Idealism fuelled her adolescent rebellion.

Chapter 19

November 1938 The Sharon Valley

A single low wattage bulb lit the basement. Fighting panic, Dalia Leitner faced three hooded figures.

Each, in muffled tones, had interrogated her on her loyalty to Eretz Israel, her attitude to discipline, her willingness to suffer discomfort during training, all much as expected and she had regurgitated well-rehearsed answers. Now, though, the examiners had fallen into unnerving silence. Running trembling hands through her hair, she envisaged her whole future disintegrating if Hagana rejected her. A dripping tap sounded louder, the smell of damp concrete grew more pervasive. Her palms felt moist.

The light went out.

Her chair swivelled.

Unseen hands pulled her up; pushed her forward.

She envisaged her nose crashing into a wall, her feet stumbling over machinery, her body toppling into a pit.

Here, she told herself, was the real test, the previous question and answer session mere ritual. She drew a deep breath, forced a leaden left foot forward, did the same with her right, then walked steadily forward, chin tilted high, until hands halted her.

A door opened to reveal two lighted candles in the centre of a table, covered by blue cloth. At one end of the table lay a leather-bound bible, at the other an ancient pistol, both reassuringly familiar symbols.

A light beamed into her eyes, blinding her again.

A deep voice ordered, 'Place one hand on the bible, the other on the pistol.'

She groped forward, the light still dazzling, until her hands felt the edge of the table and the smell of hot wax filled her nostrils. Careful not to ruck the cloth, she fumbled sideways until the fingers of her left hand touched grained leather. Her right hand found the pistol's cold muzzle.

'The bible and the gun, the two principles by which we of Eretz Israel defend our homes,' the voice intoned, 'lift your hands and turn round.'

From dazzling light, back to profound darkness.

'Walk forward seven paces.'

No hands guided her this time. Sweat dropped from her face as she took each step.

'Now, by the Supreme Conscience of Zionism make your allegiance.'

With swollen tongue filling her mouth, she blundered through the familiar vow. 'I will remember always that our purpose is to provide security for those who work for Eretz Israel. I will regard Hagana as the servant of this purpose and not its master. I promise to beat off attacks but will not let the smell of blood go to my head.'

She finished, drained of energy.

The voice boomed, 'I now declare you one of us.'

Dalia's shoulders sagged in relief.

A door opened onto a well-lit room filled with a cheering crowd. Amongst them, she recognised fellow sixth formers, mostly kibbutzniks. She wiped the sweat trickling into her eyes as her interrogators removed their hoods. Two were members of the upper sixth - but the third, and her overworked heart thumped even faster, was Shimon Mabovitch.

Shimon stepped forward. She felt him kiss her cheek and, in ecstasy, heard him say, 'You are already an impressive shot, young Dalia. Now we will train you in earnest.'

On reflection though, she was not so happy with that epithet 'young'.

As she cycled home at dusk, she mentally replayed the nerve-racking Hagana initiation. She put her hand to her cheek where Shimon's lips had been and dreamed her way home until she shalomed herself into the kitchen.

'Ai-ee, madam - here at last. What excuse this time? This boy, when are we going to see him? That's what I want to know.'

If only she could tell her mother what she had really been doing that afternoon. Dalia raced into her room without speaking, put on her farm clothes and ran outside to milk the goats.

An hour later, she was back in the kitchen more ready now to face her mother.

'Nu, those lads on sentry duty are trigger happy tonight,' her mother grumbled as shots sounded beyond the perimeter fence, 'Don't they understand bullets cost money, yet? They will hit a stray sheep and...'

A loud clanging of the village's emergency gong drowned her words.

'Ai-ee!' her mother grumbled. 'Not at supper time again!' She rose to switch off the lights. Dalia snatched up a flashlight, grabbed her stopwatch and set it. Her father, still wearing his kippa, raced through the back door.

Dalia pulled open the seldom-used front door. Although already pitch dark outside, a flickering lamp across the green marked the stone synagogue. Little Johnny Goldstein, silhouetted against the glow of an interior coal fire, stood obediently in the neighbouring doorway.

'Got him,' she called to the child's mother. The door closed behind them. She used her flashlight to race the child to the synagogue entrance where Ruth stood, holding the crèche register.

Dalia pressed her stopwatch and angled the flashlight onto it. 'Three minutes, four seconds, my best so far,' she announced triumphantly, but when she looked up, her friend was not smiling. 'Ruth, what's the matter?'

'It's not a practice, Dalia. This is for real. My brother has been shot.'

Dalia clutched her friend as she imagined the worst. 'Josh! He's not...?'

Ruth shook her head and managed a slight smile. 'Only a flesh wound, thank goodness, but you can imagine the fuss Eema is making.'

'Where...?' she began, then broke off as beautiful but terrifying orange flames leapt high in the citrus grove behind her house. Yells and tattoos of gunfire followed. Fear contracted her stomach muscles.

'My father's out there,' she shouted and bolted back across the common, pausing only to call over her shoulder, 'Ruth, you'll have to manage without me.'

She dashed up the track between her house and the Goldsteins', past the animal sheds, wondering how her father, with only stones for weapons, could repulse a horde of armed invaders. She reached the open vegetable fields still listening to gunfire and crouched to take stock. Her mother, a dark figure against the flames, raced across the cereal field beyond the vegetables.

She shouted, 'Get down, Eema,' and watched her mother drop on all fours and crawl on. Dalia did the same even when, in the next field, barley stalks speared her knees and palms.

The flames were dying now, although black smoke still swirled from the grove, and gasoline fumes masked the perfume of orange blossom. She joined her mother at the top of the field. The two women crouched, arms around each other, peering through the railings. Rags smouldered where flames had been; intermittent flares from stray clumps of dried grass revealed little damage. Dalia detected a dark form stretched prone on the ground next to a pile of the stones and shrieked. Her own danger forgotten, she raced her mother into the orchard.

Without lifting his head, her father hissed, 'Idiots. Keep down.'

In relief rather than obedience, Dalia collapsed to the ground. Her father raised an arm, hurled a stone towards the fence, causing an outburst of excited cries beyond. A spate of gunshots whizzed past on both sides. If only she had her own rifle, she thought, she could have shown these Arabs a thing or two. She began to crawl towards the stones.

'Keep your head down. Haven't you the sense you were born with?' Her father angry now.

Dalia buried her face in raked soil, breathing in the dusty smell. More shots tore by. Fresh shouts, then sounds of receding feet. Silence, a long silence. The sandy soil irritated her face.

Rav Cohen, Ruth's father, walked into the grove. 'Are you all right there, Albert? Nurse Schwartz called the police. They should be here soon.'

They all sat up in relief. 'I'll keep watch until the police arrive,' her father decided.

Two hours later Rav Cohen escorted a British Policeman to their house and, in slow English, introduced him to her mother as Sergeant Monteith.

'Ai-ee,' her mother retorted in swift Hebrew, 'he comes now when all is finished. He would have been here in half the time yet if Arabs had attacked British property.' In halting English, she added, 'Now that you have hurried here would you like a cup of tea?'

While her mother was pouring, Dalia stared at this police officer in his starched khaki uniform, not a Brylcreemed hair out of place, holding his head so high his neck must ache. A gleaming revolver hung from his polished belt.

Her hands crept to her face as shameful memories of other uniforms flooded her mind. Twelve years old in Munich, kept behind by a teacher, leaving the school gates. A crowd of her friends on the sidewalk, jeering, throwing stones. Herself jumping up at the back, only to find her own nanny, Christine, at the centre of the disturbance. Christine held up by brawny men in Brownshirt uniform. Round her neck, a placard,

I AM A SOW. I WORK FOR JEWS

Christine shouting, 'Get on that tram, Dalia. Go straight home.'

Dalia's cheeks flushed as she remembered how she had jumped onto the tram leaving Christine at the mercy of the Brownshirts.

'You acted sensibly for once,' Christine had reassured her later, 'Going home to summon help.'

Why then did she always feel guilty when she saw brown or khaki uniform?

'Dalia,' her mother said, 'take the sergeant to your father.'

Pulling herself together, she led the police officer to the citrus grove. He questioned her father in fluent Hebrew to Dalia's embarrassment as she remembered her mother's caustic remarks.

The Sergeant examined the scene. 'Spur of the moment stuff,' he concluded, 'the end of a wedding party, some youngsters showing off to their elders. A recurrence is unlikely, but we will search their village. I will check with the Muhktar that Oozlebarts have not been around stirring up the youngsters.'

After the police officer had left, Ruth came over.

'How's your brother?' Dalia asked.

'Fine, but tell me what happened here?'

Sitting with her friend on her narrow bed, Dalia described the attack.

Ruth, looking suitably horrified, told her, 'Abba has phoned Hagana. He says it is time we bought extra firearms.'

Dalia opened her eyes wide. 'Your father did that? But I thought...'

'He says he had no choice. We can no longer trust the British to defend us.'

Ruth mentioning Hagana, reminded Dalia of her secret, the first she had ever kept from her friend.

'Ruth, what would you do if Hagana asked you to join them?'

'They wouldn't.' Ruth lowered her voice; the wall was thin between Dalia's bedroom and the kitchen. 'You know what a rotten shot I am. Besides, I'll be away in Haifa next year, remember?'

Ruth looked up at the ceiling. 'If ever Hagana asked you to join, though, I'd understand that you couldn't tell me about it. It wouldn't spoil our friendship, would it?'

Dalia flung her arms round Ruth and hugged her. 'Oh, I am so lucky to have you as my friend.'

Chapter 20

To Dalia's disappointment, Hagana sent her brother Uri, not Shimon, to conduct firearm negotiations at Bereishit.

She came away from the moshav meeting, seething. Having voted to buy rifles from Hagana, the fuddy-duddy oldies had spoilt everything by adding a proviso that only people over the age of eighteen should use them. She marched straight into the milking shed rather than risk quarrelling with her parents who had voted for that stupid amendment.

Uri entered the shed when she was on the third cow. He patted the rump of the nearest, which stamped its foot, narrowly missing his toes.

'What brings you here?' she asked, 'You haven't come to help by any chance?'

Uri shook his head. 'There's something I must tell you, Dalia.' He hesitated and then burst out, 'I'm not going to the Technion next term.'

Dalia jumped up and stared at her brother in amazement. 'But you promised Abba you would, after you finished your three years at that kibbutz.'

The cow, that she had been milking, mooed. She resumed her place on the stool, her hair resting against the animal's flank.

'I only agreed to go Technion to become a more efficient farmer. Now Abba wants me to study architecture. I know bobkesh about architecture, and that's the way I want to keep it. Before we made Aliyah, remember, in the kitchen at Munich, the day the Brownshirts raided his office, he agreed to put architecture behind him. You heard him. Now, if you please, he wants me to partner him in a rural architectural business.'

'Well he's good at architecture,' Dalia pointed out, 'It's not as if either of you will be giving up farming.' She stood up to swap buckets and moved on to the next cow. 'With so many refugees, Abba says people have to live somewhere and that somewhere might as well be somewhere suitable.'

Milk tinged against the metal base of the bucket. Uri kicked a post.

'Uri,' Dalia went on, 'studying local materials has been Abba's hobby for four years. You wouldn't want his research wasted?'

Uri folded his arms. 'It's not just Abba and architecture that's getting to me. It's Eema too. She's been going on about marriage again.'

Dalia thought of Ruth, who had made no secret of her three-year-old crush on her brother.

'There's plenty of women not a million miles from here who wouldn't turn you down.'

Uri stamped his foot. It landed on a cowpat.

'I don't need a girlfriend,' he snarled as he scrubbed at his shoe with a bunch of hay, 'I already have one and she believes marriage is a system of slavery imposed by men on women.'

Poor Ruth, Dalia thought. Aloud she asked, 'What's your girlfriend's name? What's she like?'

'Zia, and she's wonderful,' Uri replied, 'And you're not to tell Eema about her either, you hear? Zia and Eema would just hate each other, so I couldn't bring her back here, marriage or no marriage.'

Uri picked a clean straw from the bale above his head and placed the end in his mouth.

'How can I tell Abba and Eema tactfully that I'm not going to the Technion and won't be coming back here to live?'

'You can't,' Dalia answered, 'they will be upset whatever you say, but the longer you leave it the worse it will get.'

Uri straightened and walked out.

Dalia had finished milking, and was changing for the evening meal when she heard her father shouting, her mother crying. She tried blocking her ears, and felt, rather than heard the back door slam. She ran outside.

Uri recognised her footsteps and shouted over his shoulder. 'I won't be coming home again in a hurry, Dalia,' then stormed off to the bus stop.

****

The firearms arrived three weeks later, hidden in a delivery of building stone. Dalia helped her father wrap the two consigned to their family in a well-greased tarpaulin while her mother watched.

'Let us pray we never need to use them,' her father said as they buried them in the vegetable field.

'Ai-ee!' her mother responded, 'and even if we did, one could stay buried forever yet, with the son, who should be using it, refusing to come home.'

'Uri's bound to be full of chutzpah at his age' her father said, 'He'll come round when the time's right.'

'Ai-ee! That gives him the right to go breaking our hearts?'

'Nu, Trudi, you want a son with no spirit? Come now and let's have supper.'

In her bedroom after supper, Dalia lifted the cover off her typewriter, pausing as usual, to remember the accusing face of the teddy bear she had left behind in Munich to make room for the Remington.

'*Dear Uri,*' she wrote.

It is potato harvest holiday so I have time to write. Tomorrow Ruth and I are going potato picking at the farm school, our last potato harvest before Ruth starts a nursing course in Haifa. I shall miss her so much, but not as much as Eema misses you. Have you told her about Zia? I have said nothing, but I think you should.

Abba is so proud of you. To listen to his boasting you would think you had founded a new kibbutz all on your own. He really does need you home though. You do realise that he is nearly forty-five, don't you? It won't be long before he is too old to manage without you. I hope you will visit soon even if Eema does nag about it being time you got married.

Großvater has promised that he and Großmutter will come for a long visit when he retires. Abba wants them to settle for good, but can you see them leaving Lübech for ever, the way Großvater loves his town. Remember how every time we visited he would take us all round the old part, and knew a story about every building.

Please if you do nothing else, please come home for Hanukah,
Your loving sister, Dalia

****

Dalia and Ruth cycled over to the Farm School. They had no sooner registered than a brisk young woman whisked Dalia away along with a group of kibbutzniks she recognised from her Hagana initiation. The woman took them to a secluded area behind the poultry houses and told them to wait. The kibbutzniks huddled together giggling and gossiping. Feeling excluded, Dalia wandered off to sit out of sight on the step of a hen house, wishing more than ever that Ruth were a member of Hagana.

A whiff of tobacco smoke and a masculine voice at the side of the hen house broke through her reverie. 'Did you see? The Ice Queens are separated at last. Here's your chance, Yossi.'

'Ice Queens' had been the Kibbutzniks' nickname for her and Ruth ever since she had been stupid enough to tell some girls at school that they had vowed to stay virgins until their wedding day. How naïve she and Ruth had been when they were young. It certainly wasn't a vow she intended to keep if she found someone exciting enough, someone like Shimon, say.

'Naw,' drawled a familiar Yankee voice, 'You'll get nowhere. Frigid as an ice block, that Dalia. Anyway, what do you want with her when you could take your pick from any number of proper sabras.'

Amos! That piece of dreck. The cheek of him now to pretend to turn up his nose at her, and was it her fault she had been born in Germany?

She jumped up, ready to tell the lads that she was the equal of any stuck-up Palestinian-born kibbutznik, when she heard the leader return with another group and went to join them.

'A long schlep to weapon practice, today, so we need to get moving,' the woman told them.

With no close friend to confide in, Dalia's anger simmered during the march over rocks and thorn bushes, under a sun that soon became uncomfortably warm, even though it was already November.

After three hours, the squad arrived at a remote wadi ready to flop, but the Hagana instructor waiting for them allowed no rest. He handed out potatoes stuffed with detonators and tutored them in the art of tossing hand grenades. Dalia made sure her 'grenades' landed closer to the target than those of any kibbutznik sabra, but would have relished her victory more if Ruth had witnessed it, or Shimon had been the instructor.

Rifle practice came next. Dalia was taking aim, when a motorbike roared along the top of the wadi. She turned to see Shimon dismounting. With an effort, she steadied her arm, retrained her eye, and kept her shot true.

After she had handed back the gun, Shimon beckoned and walked her out of earshot. 'Dalia, your mother has been telling mine how well you speak and write English and what a waste of talent it is that you are leaving school early.'

'My mother has sent you to talk me out of farm-college?'

Shimon laughed. 'Not your mother! But Hagana needs all the well-educated English speakers it can get. Tell me, have you ever thought of becoming a typist?'

'No. I plan to do something exciting with my life.'

'Excitement is for children. Have you heard of Mossad el Aliyah Beth?'

She shook her head.

Shimon tapped the side of his nose. 'A new organisation devoted to helping all Jews enter Palestine, but especially those from Germany. They desperately need typists in Tel Aviv and Haifa.'

Shimon smiled, causing instability in her legs, contractions in her stomach and a strong desire to rush into his arms. 'Dalia, I admit being a typist is not the most glamorous job in the world but a loyal Hagana member always sacrifices personal preferences for the good of Eretz Israel.'

He brought a hand down, placed it under her chin, tilted her face and gazed straight into her eyes. While waiting expectantly for him to kiss her, she tossed aside pioneering plans that had taken four years and many hours of argument to complete. His lips came no nearer and she realised he was waiting for her to say something.

She heard her voice, unnaturally high, say, 'B'Seder. I'll withdraw my application to farm-college, stay on at school, and make shorthand and typing the subjects I work hardest at.' She thought of Ruth. 'But I'd like to work in Haifa not Tel Aviv.'

'That's the girl. Anyone would take you for a sabra!' Shimon gave her another searing smile. How much longer before he kissed her? 'But remember to keep the reason for your career change secret.'

'Of course.' No one would hear a word from her, whatever methods of torture they might use for interrogation - except, 'may I just tell my friend, Ruth?'

'No, no one at all.'

She nodded. 'B'Seder.'

Shimon took his hand from her chin and glanced at his watch. 'I must hurry. I promised my mother I'll be in Rehovot for supper.'

He jumped on his bike.

She stood watching the bike career off along the ridge, wondering what difference it would have made if she had seized the initiative and kissed him.

Only half way on the long weary walk home, did she start worrying that she would have to confess to her parents that she had changed her mind about what she wanted to do with her life yet again.

Chapter 21

Dalia entered the kitchen carrying the mail she had picked up on her way home and found Uri sitting on a kitchen chair as if he had never been away.

'Ai-ee Dalia,' her mother greeted her in an ecstatic tone, 'your brother has come to his senses at last.'

Dalia glanced at her brother, puzzled. No mention of a girlfriend or wedding? She handed her father the letter from her grandparents. He tore it open and thumped the table in excitement. 'You won't believe this, but that obstinate old man has given in at last. They are coming over.'

'Nu, read the letter out then,' her mother looked ready to snatch it from his hands.

'Dear Albert, Trudi, Werner and Dalia,' her father read.

Strange hearing German spoken again, even stranger to hear Uri called by his German name.

'The situation, even here in my beloved Lübech, has deteriorated to such an extent, that, I fear for your mother's safety. As you say, we shall have no trouble with a visa since you are now Palestinian citizens. Our doctor has advised that we should either leave straight away or else wait until the end of your summer. Straight away is, of course, impossible, with all the arrangements that have to be made, so we will be coming, with all our affairs set in order, next October.'

Dalia felt a surge of nostalgic happiness. How wonderful to see her grandparents again. She could almost smell Großmutter's wonderful cakes baking in the kitchen.

Her father folded the letter and placed it back in the envelope. 'It gives us time to add on a new bedroom, but I wish they were already on their way.'

'Why does Großpapa think Großmutter is in more danger than he is?'

'Because your Grandmother is Jewish,' her father said.

'But so's Großpapa!'

'No, he's a gentile and so were his parents and grandparents before him. Surely you knew that, Dalia?' her mother cut in.

'Großpapa, not Jewish?' The statement sounded ridiculous. 'Großpapa, pure German?' The word 'German' sounded ugly now, not the proud word it had been when she was little.

'Yes, but that doesn't stop him being a good man,' her father replied.

Around her, Dalia's world re-ordered itself. Dear kind Großpapa all German, her beloved father half German, she herself quarter German. She pushed the uncomfortable thoughts from her head and concentrated on why Uri was coming home.

The opportunity to find out came when he helped her with the milking.

'Uri,' she asked as she passed him with a full bucket, 'has your girlfriend decided it's all right to get married after all?'

Uri shook his head. 'We've split up.'

She prepared to expend sympathy. 'Oh, I am sorry. Are you very upset?'

'No. She turned into a nagging bitch. Kept on that I was spending too much time on Hagana. She wasn't what I thought.'

If he wasn't upset, she wasn't.

'Ah well, there's other oranges on the tree, and talking of Hagana, you know about Aliyah Beth?' she paused, suddenly remembering Shimon had told her to talk to no one about it, but he couldn't mean Uri, who was so high up in Hagana, could he?

Uri nodded. 'Yes, but Großpapa and Großmutter won't need them. They can come in legally.'

Dalia's turn to be impatient. 'I know that. It's not what I am talking about. You've heard I've joined Aliyah Beth?'

'You've what? When? Why?'

So Shimon hadn't told him! She couldn't take back her words. There was no recourse but to continue.

'Aliyah Beth wants to infiltrate typists where they can pick up useful information. That's why I am working so hard at typing and shorthand at school, but how do I tell Eema and Abba that I'm not going to university, that I am going to be a typist when I leave school?'

Uri gave a roar of laughter. 'Sis, remember the advice you gave me? Just go ahead and tell them, you said. My advice to you is to leave telling them until you have to, and then choose your moment carefully.'

She thought that over. There was no hurry. After withdrawing her application for farm-college, her mother had already assumed that she was agreeing to go to university. She could wait until the end of the school year to tell her different.

Chapter 22

Dalia paid Thelma Goldstein for the loaf of bread and reached over to pick up the self-addressed brown envelope from the counter, where the postman left all Bereishit mail. She felt nervous opening it, certain she hadn't done as well as she could in the exams but gave a squeal of delight when she read the results.

'I've passed. I've passed,' she shouted at Thelma and rushed home, determined to confront her parents with her new career plans.

Her mother screamed predictably, 'Ai-ee! A typist yet? First farm-college, now this? Nu, when do you know your own mind? You listen to me. You go to university, my girl. You get proper qualifications.'

Dalia had her arguments ready. 'Eema, I need to find out what it is like in the real world. Please, let me work in Haifa for a year first.'

As she had hoped, her father supported her. 'Dalia's right, Trudi. Cocooned here in the Sharon Valley, she has had no experience of the outside world. A year working in a cosmopolitan port like Haifa can only do her good.'

Eema snorted. 'A port yet. Ai-ee! She will be a sailor next, you see.'

Dalia wrote to Shimon the same evening, boasting that she was now a qualified typist and would prefer to work in Haifa.

A week later, when she returned from school, her mother, up to her elbows in flour, greeted her with the news that Shimon was coming to supper. 'So I haven't had time to grade the eggs. You can do them.'

Dalia had already sorted the first basket of eggs, and was starting on the second, when the door of the tiny shed opened and Shimon squashed himself inside, closing the door behind him. She could feel his warmth against her back and had to twist her neck to see his face.

'Congratulations on your typing and shorthand successes. Now when are you coming to Haifa?' Shimon's lips were almost touching her face. 'I can't wait to take you to cafés and concerts.'

She felt her knees weaken at the thought of going to a concert with him.

'When term finishes. I still have the ordinary exams to take.'

'That shouldn't stop you contacting an agency now.' He pulled a scrap of paper from the top pocket of his shirt. 'XL is the one you must contact, no other agency, just that one.'

While accepting the paper, her fingers touched Shimon's hand and a weakening shock travelled up her arm. Shimon bent towards her. She lifted her face to encourage him. Their lips were almost touching.

The shed door swung open, hitting Shimon and pushing his leg against the egg basket. The top layer of eggs tumbled to the floor.

'Dalia, Shimon,' Uri said, 'Eema says supper's ready.' He looked at the egg yolk on Shimon's trouser leg and laughed. 'Come on, Shimon, my mother will get that off for you.'

Dalia glared at her brother and pushed the note into her pocket before bending down to mop up broken egg.

At supper, her mother seized the opportunity to berate Shimon over Uri's frequent absences.

'Ai-ee, you people from Hagana, so often you call him away. Always in the middle of a harvest or when a cow goes sick. We are supposed to manage? And now here is Dalia ready to leave too.'

'I know a Rumanian immigrant who could help with the farm, Aunt Trudi.'

'And where would we sleep him?'

Her father placed an arm round her mother's shoulders. 'Until October he can use the room we have built for my parents. If he needs to stay I can build another room over the cow sheds.'

Shimon opened the door leading to the new room and peered in. 'You have room for two immigrants there, Uncle Albert.'

'Two it is now?' her mother said.

Her father interposed, 'Nu, Trudi, remember how Cousin Elsa squashed us all in when we first came over?'

Her mother held up her hands in surrender.

'Shimon,' her father said, 'I am right in thinking these two Rumanians will have no visas?'

Shimon looked at the ceiling. 'Hagana have provided them with papers.'

As soon as Shimon's motorbike had screeched off, Dalia rushed over to Ruth's house.

'Guess what,' she burst out, 'Shimon has promised to take me out to cafés and the theatre when I go to Haifa.'

Ruth hugged her. 'I hope I will still see you.'

'Oh, Ruth,' Dalia exclaimed, 'Nothing and no one will ever come between you and me. Being near you is the main reason I want to work in Haifa.'

Her father was studying the Palestine Post when she returned home.

'Trudi, there's an advert here for an Austin7, a real bargain.'

'Nu, what would we do with a car?' her mother retorted, 'You are planning to run Dalia into to Haifa each day and fetch her home every night?'

'No, but I could fetch her on Friday afternoon and return her Saturday night or even early Sunday morning.'

'Ai-ee, you have forgotten they have invented buses?'

'Buses take too long. If you want Dalia home for Shabbat, I am going to have to fetch her.'

Her mother read the advert. 'You will get this car looked at by a garagenik before you buy?'

The Rumanians arrived before the car did, one tall, dark bearded, gaunt, and taciturn, the other short, smooth shaven and volatile. They spent their leisure time together playing cards except when Uri tutored them in Hebrew.

Dalia was not used to two young men so indifferent to her presence and felt slightly put out. They were hard-working men though which was just as well, as her mother could hardly prise her father from the driver's seat of the Austin once it arrived.

Chapter 23

A letter arrived from the XL Agency inviting Dalia to an interview. Her mother insisted on accompanying her into Haifa so her father drove them both in on the way to the research station.

With difficulty, Dalia persuaded her mother to wait at a nearby café. A printed notice on the Agency's door boasted:

XL, Palestine's most prestigious job agency. Please walk up.

The door opened onto a narrow flight of stairs.

On the landing, a frosted glass door bore a hand-written notice, 'Enter.' Trying to breathe normally, she let herself into an airy office where a sleek grey-haired woman banged furiously on a typewriter. Without stopping work, the woman looked up with a brief smile. 'Dalia Leitner?'

Dalia managed a nod. The woman took her fingers off the keys long enough to point to a door behind her. 'Max is expecting you.'

She knocked. A gruff voice shouted, 'Come in.'

She entered a windowless cupboard of a room containing a short, bald man in kibbutz khaki sitting behind a small wooden table that almost filled the room. A desk lamp spotlighted the hair on the back of his fingers.

'Close the door,' he ordered.

She had to squash against the table to obey.

'I am Max Zeidner, but call me Max. Don't look so worried, girl. We're not turning you into Mata Hari overnight. When you earn good references then we may move you somewhere useful.'

He handed her a swathe of papers. 'Two application forms for a post in the typing pool at the port authority's cargo section, one already filled in for you to copy onto the other, in your best handwriting, please. You do that here.'

He stood. She breathed in to give him room to leave, took his chair and read the completed application form first. Its accuracy made her slightly uncomfortable. How did Aliyah Beth get to know so much about her?

Max returned, glanced approvingly at the completed form. 'OK, the rest is up to you. You will have no trouble with the firm's speed and accuracy tests at the level we are placing you.' His fingers tapped the table. 'You will enrol for an advanced secretarial course, though, once you are in Haifa.'

'But...'

'Nu, we will pay. Tell your parents you have won a scholarship.'

He passed over a slip of paper. 'Here is the address of the secretarial college. Make friends there with girls who are not Jews. Such contacts can prove useful, and while you are there, check how the other girls dress. You can learn a lot from the daughters of Arab effendi. Your frock is about three years out of date.

'Now about the job. Your aim is to obtain a good reference, so no taking sides in office quarrels, always be punctual and tidy, and keep your private life impeccable. In the unlikely event that you find anything useful, pass it on to Shimon Mabovitch. Have you found lodgings in Haifa, yet?'

Dizzy with trying to remember everything, and upset about the comment on her brand new dress, Dalia just shook her head.

'Then I recommend Giza Barat's premises. She's not part of our organisation, but all the more valuable for that. I happen to know she has a vacancy so you must call straight away. Giza will be an excellent character reference when we slot you in somewhere sensitive, so treat her with respect.'

He took the paper back and scribbled the address of the lodging house.

'Oh, one other thing,' he said as he returned the paper and she squeezed past him to leave, 'no more weapons training, right? We want your record clean.'

No weapons training? No making friends at work? Tied to a desk nine hours a day? Spending what little leisure time she had at secretarial college, and turning herself into a clothes dummy? Dalia wanted to say that she had changed her mind and was going to university after all. Only visualising the disappointment in Shimon's beautiful eyes prevented her doing so.

She told her mother she had applied for a job, and the owner of the agency had recommended digs.

Her mother insisted on inspecting the lodging house with her and discovered she had already met Giza at a meeting of the tree-planting charity they both supported. She came away approving both the accommodation and the owner.

'A good sensible woman, that Giza Barat, a friend of Cousin Elsa's, yet. You will be in safe hands.'

'But it costs so much.'

'So!' her mother retorted, 'You have the profits from your citrus groves.'

'I don't have to save them any more?'

'Nu, at eighteen you are old enough to manage your own affairs. Your father is arranging right now to transfer the el-Tirah account into your name. But spend as little as possible. Put the rest by, for when you start a proper career.'

Next morning, still smarting from Max's remarks, Dalia took the bus into Tel Aviv by herself, withdrew a substantial sum from her new bank account, and spent the whole day choosing high-heeled shoes, a pillbox toque, the latest Coats patterns and materials.

'Ai-ee,' her mother said, when she showed her the purchases, 'this is Haifa you are going to work in, not Paris.'

****

Dalia, in her new clothes, sailed through her interview.

The day after leaving school, she started work at the Export/Import Company close to the harbour, full of enthusiasm for Aliyah Beth and dreams of Shimon.

The job in Haifa, typing bills of lading, proved not exactly stimulating. Every lunchtime, mindful of Max's orders to refrain from office politics, she marched off to a shady niche between two huge rocks at the end of the harbour breakwater. There she sat, munching her sandwiches, and observing the goings on at the British Police Beach club.

Beautiful women, in decorous costumes, lay on towels, gossiping and sipping drinks while keeping an eye on their equally beautiful babies. Young children splashed in a paddling pool or roamed the short stretch of beach rummaging in rock pools. Older children dived off a rickety wooden pier that stretched beyond the wave line and swam daringly close to men playing energetic games of water polo. The men, when they emerged from the water, were as bronzed, and muscular as kibbutzniks.

One man in particular caught her eye, more serious looking than most, with an air of sadness about him. There was something familiar about him.

To Dalia's profound disappointment, Shimon did not keep his promise to take her to concerts. He merely summoned her to an occasional brief meeting in a café to check all was going well.

'I would like to see more of you,' he apologised, 'but we are working flat out bringing in immigrants. Things are bad in Germany.'

So, life in Haifa would have been dull if it had not been for Ruth and, surprisingly, the women on her secretarial course.

She met Ruth at least once a week at the milk bar where they spent their time filling each other in on gossip gleaned from their respective visits to Bereishit. On several occasions, Ruth mentioned, with some satisfaction, that Uri had come up to Haifa and taken her to the pictures. Dalia made as little comment as possible, but hoped that Uri would not let her friend down.

The women at the secretarial college invited her to their weekly coffee evenings at a café in Kingsway. Many were Arabs and, as Max had said, they dressed in the height of European fashion. They were so different from the Arab women in the village next to Bereishit; she would not have recognised them as Arabs if she had passed them in the street.

She made a particular effort to talk to two women, one a British woman who turned out to be nothing like the arrogant bitch she had expected, and the other an outstandingly beautiful Arabic woman. She even ended up liking them both.

She lived, though, for the Friday evenings and Saturdays that she spent with her family. Everyone in Bereishit kept Friday evenings in the observant way, but dispensed with orthodox Shabbat rules for Saturdays.

Every Saturday that summer, her father squashed her, her mother and Uri into the tiny Austin7 and they spent the mornings on Nathanya, Tel Aviv, or Khayet Beaches. When Ruth was off duty, she came too, sitting on Uri's knee.

By August, life in the export office was hectic.

'I'm putting in so much overtime, you wouldn't believe it,' Dalia grumbled to Ruth, 'All these war rumours and what is happening in Poland. Everyone wants their orders processed the day before yesterday.'

Back home, her father worried about his parents. 'I hope they have the sense to get away before war starts.'

'They'll be all right, Albert, even if they stay,' her mother put her arm round her father's shoulders, laid her cheek against his. 'The Nazis will be too busy fighting off the French and British to worry about Jews anymore. We are lucky to be here though, out of the fighting.'

'So long as the British win,' Abba commented.

War

Chapter 24

Sunday 3rd September 1939

As soon as her parents left for Sharing, Patsy switched on the wireless. Parliament was meeting again. (Parliament meeting on a Sunday?) The Prime Minister had issued an ultimatum. Unless Hitler had assured him by 11 am GMT that he would withdraw his forces from Poland, the British would declare war. She went on listening to commentators until she heard the Austin return unexpectedly early, and then hastily switched off the wireless and retreated to the kitchen.

Her father marched straight into the lounge, and switched the wireless back on. (Her father listening to the wireless on a Sunday?)

Her mother joined her in the kitchen.

'It's an emergency, darling. Inspector Sutton came by the hall with a message, even though he had been called back on duty.'

During lunch, they kept the lounge door open and the wireless turned up to full volume but it was well into the afternoon before they heard that war had been officially declared.

Listening to the Prime Minister's short speech, Patsy felt her priorities flip. The thought, 'What will happen to me now?' transformed into, 'What can I do to help my country?'

****

Dalia was at work when she heard the news. Customers went into panic, laying siege to the warehouse, checking that goods bound for Germany on allied ships had not yet shipped. To make matters worse, the banks had closed to prevent a run on them. Despite the rushed chaos during the Prime Minister's speech, broadcast in the office, she had time to worry about her grandparents locked inside a Germany that had disowned them.

****

Susanna was phoning the sanatorium on Granny Hadad's telephone when Mr Chamberlain declared war on Germany.

Granny Hadad insisted the whole household gather round her wireless to listen to the British Prime Minister.

'One good thing about this,' Granny Hadad stated afterwards, 'The Jews will stop making trouble now. They would rather have the British in Palestine than the Germans.'

Chapter 25

On the way to Bereishit on the first Friday of the war, Dalia's father told her that Uri was talking of joining up.

'Your mother is not happy.'

A slight understatement - she had scarcely stepped into the house before her mother started. 'Ai-ee, Dalia, Uri will get himself killed; all for these British who think nothing of us, will not even let us have our own brigade. No, off he goes, doing what he likes best, away from home, fighting. Nu, the farm does not matter. He will see the world. He will be a big hero, so.'

Uri attempted to damn the stream. 'I would have thought you'd have been pleased, me fighting Hitler, Eema.'

Her mother ignored the interruption. 'While you are away, your father is growing younger? The fields no longer need ploughing?'

Uri sighed, the ultra patient, dealing-with-Eema sigh he had developed to perfection. 'Josh has already gone down to the recruiting office.'

'Nu and Miriam is not kibitzn? Louder than I am, she is.'

'She has more to complain about. At least you have the Romanians to help on the farm. No reason for them to move on, now Großpapa and Großmutter can't come.'

'Ha! You need to remind me of this? Strangers now, where my family should be.'

Later, while they were watering the goats, Dalia had her say. 'You do not have to do this, Uri. Let the British do their own fighting.'

'I didn't want to join up,' Uri admitted, 'especially now I am going out with Ruth, but Hagana insists.'

'Hagana? Why?'

'We'll need trained soldiers after the war. Might as well let the British pay for the training.' He clapped Dalia on the back. 'Hey, don't you think I'll look good in uniform.'

She shuddered but didn't mention her aversion to khaki and brown uniforms.

'You disapprove, Sis?'

'Disapprove is not the right word. Your place is in Eretz Israel.'

'I won't be enlisting until the spring,' Uri, said, 'I have to train a new bunch of Hagana recruits first, but I thought I might as well get Eema used to the idea.'

'Give her more hours of worry than she needs, you mean.'

After work on Sunday, Dalia made a special journey up to the Nurses' Home where Ruth lived.

'Your mother says can you ring Bereishit tonight to let her know when you are off duty. Your brother wants to come to Haifa tomorrow to say good-bye.'

'I wish Josh hadn't joined up. I don't know how my father will manage. At least your brother is not leaving yet. Let's hope the war ends before he goes.'

'Ruth, how is it with you and Uri? Is it getting serious?'

Ruth hesitated. 'Y-es' she answered slowly, 'but he's not ready to settle yet, is he?'

Dalia didn't know how to answer that. She thought Ruth was right, but did her friend really want her agreement?

'Just as well,' Ruth added, without waiting for a response. 'I have three years' training to do before I qualify, so I guess I'm not ready either.'

Dalia laughed in relief. 'You'd be my ideal sister-in-law, Ruth, but I'm glad you are not rushing to turn into a staid, married woman.'

****

In the middle of October, Patsy received a five-week-old letter from Tim.

We are expecting raids any day here. Everyone is going round with gas masks. I am so thankful that you are tucked safely away in Palestine. Of course, I miss you, my darling, I miss you more than I can say, but even if you had been here, I would not have had been at Oxford with you. The Yeomanry has called me up. My father has lent me his best horse for the duration. You never know. I might even get posted to Palestine.

At the bottom of the letter, Tim had added a postscript –

I may never return once I get sent to the front so I cannot ask you to wait. If you meet someone else, you must feel yourself free.
"I could not love thee dear, so much, Loved I not Honour more."

Strange, she reflected, how attitudes change so quickly. We all used to laugh at that quotation by the 17th century poet Richard Lovelace, before the war.

She wrote a cheerful informative letter back about the people she had met at a First Aid course and told him that in a week's time, she would be clerking full time at the local police headquarters.

It's my way of doing my bit. The police are absolutely inundated with new regulations on food, fuel, and water. You would think this war was being fought with paper.

****

In the Shepards' household, war took a temporary back seat, as Renshaw's fits of unconsciousness became more frequent. Suzanna's prayers had no effect. She suspected that she had offended the Holy Mother by dragging her into the bathroom every night.

Chapter 26

Tomorrow, Patsy started her war work. This day though was hers and she was using it to hike to Wad' el-Mughara.

The Carmel range was clothed in mist when she set out and the silvered sun aped a full moon. A few miles into the walk along the ridge, the sun had won through and light sparkled on the rippling sea. She removed first her scarf, then her jacket. A wadi interrupted her path forward, so she followed a goat track down the mountain to level soil and citrus groves.

She walked through orchards of ripening oranges, to the accompaniment of clacking jars on irrigation pumps, and then took the main coast road as far as the village of El Mazra'a. At a local shop, she bought lemonade and asked the Arab shopkeeper the way to the caves. It turned out that the woman had been part of Dr. Garrod's renowned all-female workforce. She talked nostalgically about her time working in the caves, before giving detailed directions.

A mile or so further on, Patsy found the campsite, now just a herringbone pattern of paths. The site faced a wadi that cut deep into the mountain. Limestone crags lined both sides. Piles of boulders showed where quarry workers had blasted for harbour stone before making their discovery.

She took a precipitous path up to the largest of the three visible caves. As she climbed, she felt her head grow heavy. Colours changed in quality. She stopped halfway up to stare around. From this angle, the boulders on the wadi floor hid all traces of civilisation, but she had the feeling that even if she could see past the rocks, there would be no main road, no traffic.

Noticing movement in a bush clinging to a crevice, she bent down, carefully selected a rounded pebble, and then threw it. A bird fled from the bush, squawking but unhurt. A clumsy throw, she thought, another meal missed. She scurried on up the steep path almost on all fours. As she drew nearer the cave, instinct urged her to slow down, keep silent, and choose her footholds with care. She hugged the rock face and peered inside. A bulky, hairy shape hulked down, scratching in the dirt floor. She screamed, more in territorial fury than fright.

The shape leapt up. A hand, flourishing a revolver, protruded from a flurry of sheepskin cloak and crashed her back into the twentieth century AD.

The hand lowered the firearm. A familiar voice said, 'Patsy, I am so sorry if I frightened you.'

She blurted, 'Ahmed! What are you doing here? Why the gun?'

'I was just checking the back fill had been done properly.' Ahmed looked down at his revolver and tucked it back into its holster. 'There are brigands in Palestine. You shouldn't be roaming Carmel alone.'

'Why not? The police have cleared out the Oozlebarts. I had to visit the site while I could. I'm starting work tomorrow. Anyway, why are you here? I thought Syria was your domain.'

Ahmed extended his hands, and shrugged, Arab style. 'Properly speaking, this is Syria. But I had not realised that you were interested in Palaeontology. Your father spoke only of biblical archaeology.'

At the word 'palaeontology', she experienced what Saul must have felt on his way to Damascus. Up to that moment, she had had no thought of studying anything more ancient than the walls of Jericho and then only because she wanted to refute her father's belief in Joshua's miraculous victory. Proving the existence of Pre-Adam humans, though, would annoy her father even more. She now passionately wanted to study palaeontology.

'I want to follow on from Dr Garrod's work,' she said, 'I haven't mentioned the matter to my father yet.'

'Ah, you English women, you are so independent. But this site has been most efficiently back-filled. If you want to study Neanderthals then you must come to Syria.'

Ahmed pushed aside his sheepskin cloak, put his hand into the breast pocket of a perfectly respectable jacket, pulled out a card. 'If you are serious about palaeontology, contact me. I may be able to find you a dig.'

The irony of this opportunity arriving when her time was no longer her own! All the same, she tucked the card into her haversack.

Ahmed moved out of the cave. 'Now if you will excuse me, I must say my prayers.' He pointed to a dangerously narrow path edging its way along the cliff face. 'You will find walking home a lot quicker going that way.'

He removed his cloak, spread it so it blocked the path leading down to the wadi floor, took a bottle of water from a pocket, and proceeded to wash his feet and hands. He then prostrated himself on the cloak, bowing up and down and stretching his arms.

She could hardly walk across him, so had no choice, but to take the route he had suggested. She kept one hand firmly on the rock face and tried not to look down the precipice on the other side. As she walked, her mind dwelt on her strange experience on the way to the excavated cave. Would she have remembered those strange feelings, she wondered, if she hadn't come across Ahmed in his sheepskin coat. Was her sudden decision to study Neanderthals a co-incidence, or was it 'meant,' as her mother would say. If it was 'meant', would she have to re-arrange her beliefs yet again?

At the tip of the wadi, the path widened into a miniature paddock in front of a small cave. Judging by the carpet of dung both inside and outside, wandering shepherds often used this cave as a sheepfold. Patsy took advantage of its cool interior to rest on a rock and drink her lemonade, while staring through the entrance at cars, lorries, and trucks speeding along the main Haifa to Tel Aviv road.

She noticed a string of three donkeys leave the road and make their way into the wadi, two donkeys so loaded with fodder that they resembled mobile hillocks. Taking out her cheese and cucumber sandwiches, she positioned herself so that she could see the large cave. The sight provoked no odd feelings.

Ahmed had finished praying and was making his way down the path, still wearing the voluminous coat. He had put on a keffiyah too.

The donkey train halted in the shade provided by the rocks. The rider dismounted, hobbled his donkeys, and settled on a large boulder. Ahmed reached the wadi floor, salaamed the donkey owner, and sat next to him.

Patsy ate a piece of seed cake while watching the two men talk. As she was about to leave, she noticed Ahmed hand a package to the man before walking off towards the main road.

Chapter 27

The Arabic constable guarded the entrance to the Police HQ as if it were Buckingham Palace. Patsy showed him her pass. He scrutinised it closely before letting her in. A British constable she recognised from the beach club escorted her beyond the front desk, led her along a corridor past a canteen and up some stairs. He opened a door with a brass plaque engraved 'Office' and ushered her into a high ceilinged room lined with shelves of office supplies. A slim, professionally dressed woman with olive skin and wavy black hair raced her fingers over the keys of a substantial typewriter.

'Miss Boutaji, your new colleague, Miss Quigley,' the constable announced and gave Patsy a wink before withdrawing.

Miss Boutaji gave a friendly smile, and rose from her chair in a single fluid movement.

'I hope you will call me Leila.'

For the duration of the war, Patsy realised, the quality of her life would depend on this woman.

'Thank you, Leila. My name is Patsy.'

'I am glad to have your help, Patsy. This war has made so much extra work. A friend of mine, Maftur Naoud told me that your typing and shorthand skills are excellent.'

'You know Maftur?'

'She was in my younger sister's class at Haifa High.'

'You went to Haifa High! I was in the Prep department. We had Miss Norman in Transition. Did you know her?'

Leila grinned. 'Miss Norman? Strict but fair, I remember her OK,' she said, picking up a pile of handwritten papers and walking over to a small table that held a portable typewriter, a ream of typing paper and a pile of flimsies.

'This is your desk.'

Leila placed the pile of papers on the table. 'Here is something to start you off - inventories from German houses. The government decides the police should guard German household goods so we get the job of typing the inventories in triplicate. Will you be all right doing them without help? I have to get on now or I will have Inspector Sutton moaning at me.'

'I can imagine,' Patsy said, who knew the inspector as a strict spiritual guide and a close friend of her father. 'I should be OK.'

'If not, just shout,' Leila said.

The door opened and there stood Inspector Sutton himself, straight backed as ever and frowning. 'I have come for my reports, Miss Boutaji.'

'They'll be ready by lunchtime, sir.'

'Lunch time is not good enough, Miss Boutaji. I need them for 11.30.'

He swivelled in what only just missed being a parade turn, and left.

Leila pulled a face and slid behind her typewriter, her fingers moving over the keys almost before her skirt touched the chair seat.

Patsy sat at her desk and skimmed through her material – just boring lists of household effects. The name, Engelhard, caught her eye. She remembered their furniture from childhood, polished cherry wood inlaid with mother of pearl. 'Not my cup of tea,' her mother had said 'But nevertheless, horrendously expensive.'

She wondered if the government had interned the Engelhards, and checked their current address, - Jerusalem, the Russian Compound – so they were living in reasonable comfort. She took extra care to copy this inventory accurately, not fancying having to apologise to a steely-faced Mrs Engelhard if anything went missing.

'I'll just wander down to the Canteen to get a bottle of 7-up to drink with my sandwiches,' she told Leila at lunchtime.

Leila shook her head. 'Sorry, Patsy. The canteen is off-limits. We are not allowed to fraternise.'

It was strange, sitting in the office, munching her sandwiches with Leila. It made her realise just how different her social life would be from now on.

Chapter 28

Suzanna took her concern about Renshaw to Grandma Hadad who listened in silence, screwing her walnut face into even deeper wrinkles.

'Animals can often help sick children,' she observed at last. 'That man, who lives in the hut beside the railway, breeds rabbits. You suggest it to Mrs Shepard.'

'Any straw in a storm,' Mrs Shepard said and mentioned it to Mr Shepard, who went off with Evie and came back with a tiny rabbit, white with black spots on its rear. Evie had already named it Specklebottom.

When Renshaw saw the rabbit, his face broke into his first smile for a long while.

'Nice, nice,' he extended his arm to stroke the animal that Evie held out.

Suzanna found an orange box. Evie and Clare lined it with hay and placed it on Renshaw's bedside table. Renshaw kept his gaze fixed on the rabbit, gurgling appreciation, and stroking it while Suzanna stood by to protect the baby animal from his clumsier movements.

Watching him, she hoped Specklebottom would keep him alive long enough to return to England and the specialists.

Mr Shepard came in after she had put Renshaw into clean pyjamas.

'Say goodnight to Specklebottom, Renshaw,' he ordered and picked up the orange box.

He allowed Renshaw one more stroke before removing the rabbit. Renshaw screamed continuously but Mr Shepard was relentless.

'The child has to learn.'

Eventually Renshaw's screams diminished to rasping sobs. Mrs Shepard urged her husband to return the rabbit but he overrode his wife's protest; 'He'll soon get into the routine.'

The sobs died out. Renshaw lay rigid but open-eyed. Mrs Shepard brought her husband in again. He stared at Renshaw, then said, 'Suzanna, would you mind if the animal stays in your bedroom tonight?'

As if she were the one who had wanted it taken out!

Mr Shepard brought the rabbit back in a hutch he must have spent the whole evening making, and deposited it on a table in the far corner. Renshaw stirred, gazed at the rabbit's nose twitching through the chicken wire, but didn't smile.

'Don't let the rabbit out, Suzanna,' Mr Shepard ordered, 'Renshaw will only work himself up into another fury when you return it.'

After Mr Shepard had left Suzanna tried to work at a history essay on the repeal of the Corn Laws, but was too conscious of Renshaw' distress to concentrate. Every time he saw her glance at him, he held out his hands begging to have the rabbit. Against her instincts, she remained firm.

'Specklebottom needs to sleep like you do, Renshaw.'

Renshaw was still awake by the time she was ready for bed. She kissed him on the forehead before surreptitiously removing the icon from her drawer and slipping into the bathroom. A heavy crash disturbed her before she had even begun to pray. She heard no accompanying bellow, but all the same, tucked her icon into her dressing gown pocket and raced back to the bedroom.

Renshaw lay sprawled on the floor, one arm outstretched towards the rabbit, his blue eyes open but unseeing. She heaved him onto his bed, receiving no response other than a rattling snore. Terrified, she shouted down the stairs. Mr and Mrs Shepard raced up.

Mrs Shepard yelled, 'What have you done to him, Suzanna?'

Mr Shepard ran downstairs to the telephone.

Mrs Shepard threw her arms round Renshaw and screamed, 'Suzanna, you good for nothing, go downstairs and boil a saucepan of water.'

Mr Shepard, grey faced, stopped her as she crossed the hall.

'We will be taking Renshaw to hospital when the ambulance arrives. Please look after the girls until we return.'

Five minutes later the ambulance men banged on the door. Suzanna watched as they carried out a stretcher with her Renshaw on it, still unmoving, still wide-eyed but no longer snoring.

The front door closed. She took out her icon to plead for Renshaw's recovery but her prayers ricocheted into emptiness. Mrs Shepard's disapproval had created a barrier between Renshaw and the Holy Mother.

She climbed into bed and sobbed herself to sleep.

Next morning, when Suzanna surfaced, a soft scratching and a slight barnyard odour had replaced the usual stench of soiled nappy. Renshaw's bed was still empty, and so was Mr and Mrs Shepard's when she went to look.

Her stomach twisting with anxiety, she picked up the cage, carried it out to the yard, and refilled the rabbit's water container before getting on with her daily chores. She tried to forget how ill Renshaw had looked on the stretcher.

Evie came down extra early. 'Suzanna, where's Daddy? He promised to help me pick rabbit food before school.'

Suzanna's throat constricted; tears sprang to her eyes. Turning her back to fetch cereal dishes, she mumbled, 'Renshaw has had to go into hospital again.'

Evie accepted the answer without comment and picked up a raffia basket.

No sooner had Evie gone outside, than Clare wailed her way down stairs, terrified at finding herself alone. Suzanna put her arms around the child. The act of comforting provided comfort.

She was giving the girls breakfast, when a car drew up outside. She ran into the hall to see Mrs Shepard, hatless, hair all over the place, bursting in, shouting wildly, 'Your fault, Jim! All your fault, he was conceived in sin.'

Suzanna retreated to the dining room where Clare was crying again. 'Finish your breakfast, girls,' she said as gently as she could. She went into the kitchen, shut the door, leant against the sink, in an agony of despair.

The door swung open. Mrs Shepard barged in, eyes red and swollen. 'He's gone to glory, Suzanna,' she shouted and slumped into a chair.

Suzanna felt an internal scream tearing her stomach while she watched herself make a pot of tea for Mrs Shepard and collect dirty dishes.

Time to take Evie to school. She wondered whether she should take Clare with her. She found the two girls in the lounge listening to their father. Mr Shepard waved her away.

She returned to the kitchen to perform her usual chores while circumnavigating Mrs Shepard, observing, as if from outside, both herself being busy and Mrs Shepard sitting still, hands interlocked, eyes wide, repeating non-stop, 'Where's Renshaw?'

Not knowing how to answer Mrs Shepard's question, she ignored it.

The bell above the front door clanged. Suzanna let in Mrs McKinnon, Mrs Shepard's closest friend, and led her to the kitchen. Mrs McKinnon took one look at Mrs Shepard, and ordered Mr Shepard to call the doctor. She then took over Clare and Evie.

'Suzanna, these children will go with me. Will you help them pack overnight bags, please?'

'Can we take Specklebottom with us?' Evie asked, 'Renshaw won't want her anymore now he's in heaven.'

As she accompanied the girls to their bedroom, Suzanna heard Mrs McKinnon coaxing Mrs Shepard upstairs.

When the doctor had left, and Mrs McKinnon had removed Evie, Clare and the rabbit, Suzanna felt free to go to her room. She buried her face in her pillow and sobbed. Granny Hadad had warned her that Renshaw would die but she had not expected it to hurt quite so much.

There was a knock on the bedroom door. She opened it. Mr Shepard, his face shrivelled, stood outside.

'Suzanna, I am sorry to disturb you. I know how much you must miss Renshaw but we should console ourselves with the knowledge that the Lord in his mercy has removed him from his earthly suffering. Now please will you make a bowl of soup for Mrs Shepard and take it to her room.'

She did that, but Mrs Shepard would not look at her when she placed it beside her bed. Suzanna plodded through the rest of her duties, but could not stop herself crying.

Even next morning, in the kitchen, while wondering if she should start cooking breakfast, she found herself bursting into tears.

She heard the door open, and turned to see Mr Shepard enter the kitchen. She felt terrified. He knew she must not be alone in the same room as a man. He had promised Habib that she would be chaperoned at all times. She clutched the blue amulet beneath her dress hoping its powers of protection covered this situation.

Mr Shepard stood by the table and took off his glasses. The red rims round his eyes emphasised the pale gold of his strange irises. Suzanna squeezed her blue amulet tighter to ward off the evil eye. As she did, tears splashed from her chin onto the back of her hand.

Mr Shepard stepped towards her, put an arm round her shoulders, and drew her close. Terrified, she pushed him away, ran to the back of the kitchen, and huddled over the sink. 'I want to go home,' she shouted, 'I want to go home.'

Nothing happened. She peeked round. Mr Shepard was standing still, wiping his glasses with his tie.

'Yes, I think you should,' he said slowly as he replaced his glasses, 'you're no good to Mrs Shepard while you're in this state. Take a week's holiday to pull yourself together. I'll send a telegram to your people.'

Chapter 29

Dalia and Ruth spent part of the evening of Simchat Torah that year, dancing outside the synagogue nearest the hospital. Not for long, because Ruth was on early shift next morning. It had been fun though. They went back to the Nurses' Home feet tapping on the pavement.

Home Sister met them as they entered. 'Nurse Cohen, your mother phoned and left a message. If you have a Miss Leitner with you, will you ask her to phone Bereishit?'

Dalia frowned as she hurried to the phone, then waited while the moshav nurse, who still owned the only phone, fetched her mother.

'My Dalia, my Dalia, you have rung. Ai-ee. Such dreadful news.' Her mother broke into sobs.

Dalia clenched her free fist, her stomach rolling over, willing her mother to continue, and yet not wanting to know the worst. 'Has something happened to Abba?'

'No Uri,' her mother managed.

'Uri?'

Ruth pulled at her arm. 'Dalia, what's happened?'

Dalia placed an arm round her friend's shoulder.

Her mother was speaking again. 'The British - they arrested Uri.'

'What?'

'They have taken him to prison, Acre prison where they do the executions yet.'

'Why?'

Just another burst of weeping.

Dalia concentrated on being strong for her mother. 'Eema, I will come home. I will hitch a lift.'

'Dalia,' her father's voice now, calm. 'There is no need to panic.'

She visualised him, stroking her mother's hair while he talked.

'I will fetch you home at the end of the week as usual. The British arrested forty-two of our boys on their way home from rifle practice and took them to Acre, the only prison that can hold so many. We wanted to tell you ourselves rather than have you read it in a newspaper.'

Once she had laid down the phone, Dalia told Ruth what had happened.

'Ai-ee. They'll all be hanged for carrying firearms,' Ruth wailed.

Dalia laid her cheek against her friend's face. 'It won't come to hanging, Ruth. The British know we're on the same side as them against the Nazis.'

Ruth put her hands to her eyes. Dalia held her close and wished she didn't have to leave, as much for her own sake as Ruth's, but the Nurses' Home had strict rules. A notice on the wall insisted, no visitors after ten at night. The wall clock read five to ten.

Ruth pulled away. 'Wait there, Dalia, I'll be back,' and ran off.

Dalia waited preparing to stand her ground when Home Sister came to lock up.

Ruth returned. 'Home Sister has excused me from early shift. I am going back with you, Dalia.'

Giza was a gush of sympathy when she heard the news. 'Of course you must stay, Ruth. What are the British thinking of?' She sprang into action, producing a camp bed and blankets.

Before going to bed, Dalia and Ruth stood by the window, staring over the refinery to Acre. Dalia thought of Uri imprisoned in the gloomy dungeons there.

'I know one thing,' Ruth said, 'Uri and Josh wouldn't have been in such a rush to join up if they had known this was going to happen.'

'Hagana should form a squad to raid that castle,' Dalia burst out.

Ruth put out her hands. 'No, Dalia, we may be angry, but violence is not the way. Besides, it would take more than a squad to storm that castle. We must leave it to the solicitors.'

Chapter 30

While at work, Dalia tried to push the knowledge that her brother was facing charges, which could bring the death penalty, to the back of her mind.

In the evenings when Ruth was off duty, she and her friend talked to each other trying to find what comfort they could from the efforts of the Jewish Agency.

On her day off, Dalia attempted to comfort her mother but without much success.

'Ai-ee, Dalia. We didn't catch a single glimpse of Uri,' her mother wailed when Dalia saw her on the Friday after the trial started. 'The British, they allow no relatives at the trial, except for the wives of the two married men.'

'Perhaps it will be different when they announce the verdict.'

'Perhaps' her mother shrugged. 'Nu, I wish you could be there.'

On Saturday night after Abba had dropped her outside her digs, Shimon Mabovitch emerged from the shadows. He pointed to the pillion of his motorbike parked in an alleyway between two buildings. 'Climb on.'

'Where are we going?' she asked, even as she was hitching her skirt to swing her leg over the back of the bike.

'Mt Carmel.'

She clung tightly to his shoulders as the bike lurched forward, roared up Stella Maris Road, and tilted at an acute angle round the hairpin bend. Any other time she would have been in seventh heaven, but not now, while Uri was in such danger. Shimon slowed the bike to a halt outside a row of small shops. He held out his hand to help her dismount.

'Uri has sent a message asking me to make sure you and Ruth are with your mother when the British announce the verdict,' he said as he led her into a stylish modern coffee shop.

She gasped in surprise. 'But how did Uri send that message out?'

Simon tapped the side of his nose. 'No need for you to know the mechanics. I will take you in a car I am borrowing from an Arabic friend.'

'You're so close to an Arab you can borrow his car? But you're in Hagana.'

Immediately she was angry with herself for throwing up this negative stuff when she should have been expressing her gratitude. Why did she have to be so prickly?

Shimon merely smiled gently and pulled out her chair.

'This particular Arab and I were at the Technion together. We both want Independence from the British and both believe Arabs and Jews can live cooperatively in a shared Palestine.'

'There's no room for both in such a small country!' Dalia exclaimed.

'When I was little I read a story,' Shimon replied, 'about refugees from Persia who fled to India.'

A waitress, in a starched frilled apron over a black dress, interrupted to take their order.

'Their spokesman visited a local ruler to ask if they could stay in his kingdom,' Shimon continued when the waitress had left, 'The king received him courteously, and served coffee.'

Dalia wondered what Shimon was going on about, but at least it was a change from talking about the trial.

'The king waved his hand at the densely populated countryside around his palace. "As you can see, there is scarcely room for my own people," he apologised. "We have no space for strangers." The Persian spokesman said nothing, just poured coffee into his cup until it reached the brim, then took a spoonful of sugar and trickled it into the full cup. Not a drop overflowed. "See," he told the king, "the sugar has entered the full cup without displacing the coffee; it merely tastes richer. In the same way, by combining the talents of our two peoples you could create a more prosperous kingdom and still have room for all." The ruler was impressed and the two peoples have lived together in harmony ever since.'

Dalia frowned. 'Our science teacher taught us about dissolving sugar, but it doesn't work in practice. Whenever I tried, the coffee always splashed into my saucer.'

The waitress returned with a silver coffeepot, china cups, milk, sugar, and petit fours on a lace-covered tray. Shimon poured the coffee, filling his own to the brim. 'Now watch my party trick.'

She had to smile when he trickled in sugar without slopping a drop.

'It just takes persistence,' he said with a grin. His face grew serious. 'About tomorrow, we've heard from a reliable source that the British will be handing out harsh sentences.'

Dalia covered her face with her hands. 'The British will hang Uri for practising fighting against Germans?'

'Dalia, it won't be the death sentence.' Shimon put his hand on her arm. 'The British cannot afford to upset the American Jews to that extent, but the verdict will be worse than most people expect.'

'I hate the British.'

He raised his eyebrows. 'And how many British do you know?'

She stopped to think. She couldn't count the Goldsteins from next door since they were also Jewish, so no one except Patsy Quigley from Secretarial School whom she rather liked.

'You don't hate the British,' Shimon observed quietly, 'You hate the system they run. Now drink up and I'll walk you over to the Park.'

They stood side by side, leaning over the wall at the bottom of Allenby Park looking across the moonlit bay. Dalia concentrated on Acre, sandwiched between majestic mountains and broad sea.

'So many have been imprisoned and died in that castle,' she said, 'but how many remember them?'

'Prisoners aren't always forgotten,' Shimon answered, 'Look over the wall.'

She saw a moon silvered stone building standing in a large garden.

'That is a memorial to a prisoner, killed by a firing squad a century ago. Today, all over the world, people remember him.'

The evening breeze on the mountaintop blew chilly. She shivered and Shimon put an arm round her, just as she had so often dreamt he would do.

Angry with herself for indulging in such fantasies while Uri was in danger, she shook off Shimon's arm, and then saw his hurt look. 'It's only... Oh, I didn't mean...' She burst into tears. Why did everything always have to happen at the wrong place or the wrong time?

'B'Seder,' Shimon muttered, 'I'll take you back.'

He dropped her at her digs, saying he would collect her outside the Hadassah hospital at 7.30 am.

Shimon was still not in a talkative mood when she and Ruth climbed into a flashy red Tatra. She stared miserably out of the car windows as they crossed the Kasson River, drove past the airfield and over the railway, and skirted the refinery with its huge workers' settlement of tiny box houses. Leaving the main road, the car headed inland through sparsely cultivated country.

They rounded a bend to find hundreds of people barring the road, all jostling for position in front of large, heavily guarded gates. Shimon drove the car into an olive grove unofficially transformed into a park for coaches, mule carts, and cars. He handed ten piastres to the strongest of the boys fighting to guard the Tatra, promising another ten if the car was intact when he returned. They walked out of the grove. Dalia and Ruth looked round the crowds in despair.

Car horns sent people scuttling. A convoy of camouflaged trucks nosed its way towards the gates. Dalia hoped for a glimpse of Uri but saw only British soldiers, rifles at the ready, standing outside tightly tied canvas. Sentries opened the gates. The convoy drove between rows of wooden huts and turned a corner.

'Show's over, folks,' one sentry called in English, banging the mesh gates shut before the crowd could surge through.

Dalia caught a glimpse of her parents with Miriam and Rav Cohen. She nudged Ruth and they ran, pushing through the crowd. Her mother clung to her. 'Ai-ee, Dalia, you have come. The trucks have been. I thought this day we'd see Uri, to wish him good luck.'

'Nu, I warned you, Trudi,' Miriam Cohen said. 'Why should today be different? We haven't seen our boys once, yet. That woman, the one married to that uppity boy from Nahalal, she went through with a British officer. She has promised to give us the verdict. I hope she will be up to it. If it's left to the British we will have to wait and read it in the Palestine Post.'

Shimon tapped Dalia's arm. 'Meet me by the car after the verdict has been announced, OK?'

He walked off.

It was a long, empty morning. She and Ruth stood silently side by side. At 1 o'clock the convoy returned, canvas still drawn across the tailgates. Ruth gripped her hand. Dalia glanced at her mother who had turned pale and was hanging on to her father's arm. Beyond the mesh gates, a solitary female figure walked slowly down the road. Everyone looked at the slightly built young woman. The sentry opened the gates.

The woman stood still, her eyes filling with tears, her mouth working, 'Ten years,' she managed at last. 'Ten years with hard labour.'

Her mother yelped like a wounded dog. Dalia rushed to take her free arm. Miriam Cohen fetched out a bottle of smelling salts.

Dalia fumed. What sort of people were the British who could steal ten years from the lives of 43 young men practising to defend the country against a common enemy? She was angry, with not only the British, but also herself, unable to say or do anything to comfort her parents and Ruth.

She helped her father manoeuvre her mother to the side of the road. Once her mother had sufficiently recovered, they walked to the car park where Shimon approached her parents.

'Today is not the end,' he told them quietly, 'The Agency will fight on.'

On the journey back, Dalia held Ruth's hand, but they said nothing. At the hospital, Shimon brushed his lips against Dalia's cheek.

'Dalia, we'll get those sentences reduced. I am going straight on to a Hagana committee meeting.'

Dalia climbed the hospital steps with Ruth in a whirl of mixed emotions - grief for Uri's lost years, yet also hope that Shimon would somehow get the sentence cut. With her fingertips, she touched her cheek, the place where Shimon's lips had been, then slid them round to her lips.

That night she lingered in front of her bedroom window staring at the lights of Acre, where the British had now locked up Uri and the other boys with common criminals. The Germans and the British, she thought, was there anything to choose between them?

Chapter 31

All the way to Jenin, Suzanna saw eyes, not only Mr Shepard's weird tawny ones, but also Renshaw's as she had seen them last, blue and unseeing.

Aunt Julie welcomed her enthusiastically. 'The house is so empty now all my girls have gone,' she confided, as she chaperoned her along Jenin's bustling streets. 'You can stay with me as long as you like. You don't have to earn your own living, you know. My husband is honour bound to support both you and your mother. It is not charity.'

'My mother doesn't see it that way.'

Aunt Julie frowned. 'Why? She signed her inheritance over to her brother when she married so he owes her his support.'

Suzanna stared at her aunt, who echoed her own surprise, 'You did not know? But women always do that. In return, our brothers are responsible for us if our husbands die.'

Lying in bed that night, trying not to think about eyes, Suzanna realised she could stay in Jenin with a clear conscience for as long as she liked.

At first, Suzanna welcomed the orderly, undemanding pace, the spacious house, the pampering servants, with Aunt Julie teaching her how to run a large household, keeping accounts, checking references, monitoring the cleaning and laundry, writing grocery and butchery lists. Gradually though, she understood what her mother had meant by calling Aunt Julie's house a luxurious prison.

No women of any genteel family in Jenin, with the exception of Aunt Melia, ventured anywhere unchaperoned. No popping over the road to fetch a loaf of bread, or have a neighbourly chat. If they needed something urgently, they dispatched a servant. Gossip they passed on by telephone.

Suzanna missed not only Renshaw but also shopping and having children dependent on her. She longed for Evie's loving hugs and enthusiastic chatter.

Not that she was short on chatter in Jenin. Aunt Julie and the servants chattered all day but, unless Aunt Melia was present, the content was dull. She would have liked to retire early to bed to read but if she kept the light on in the bedroom for longer than a quarter of an hour, her aunt sent in a servant to turn it off.

In the past, she had studied to please others, first her teachers, then her mother, and more recently Mrs Shepard, but now she found learning interesting in itself. She even enjoyed working through Euclid's geometry theorems after the light was out.

Being in Jenin had one big advantage. She was nearer her mother.

Aunt Melia promised that as soon as she mastered her double-declutch, she would drive her and Aunt Julie to the sanatorium.

****

Aunt Melia chose a chilly day in November to declare herself a competent driver. She arrived unannounced, complete with large picnic hamper. Aunt Julie climbed nervously into the front of the open leather-upholstered car. Suzanna sat alone in the wide rear seat.

Leaving Jenin, they crossed the Jezreel Valley and climbed into the winter green hills of Galilee from where Suzanna gazed down at the blue lake.

The road then corkscrewed downhill, with Aunt Julie squealing every time Aunt Melia allowed the car wheels to skim the edge of a wadi. The temperature rose as they descended, so by the time they reached Tiberias it felt like summer again. They passed neighbourhoods where wealthy Arabs and Jews lived side by side, and women walked confidently in the streets, holding little lapdogs at the ends of leads. How much freer a place, she reflected, than Jenin. If she were ever rich, this was where she would live.

They sped on to the northern end of the lake to where the road zigzagged uphill to bracingly cold Safad; another mixed Arabic and Jewish community. The sanatorium, though, was uncompromisingly Jewish, with nurses and doctors all talking Hebrew.

'It's like being in a foreign country,' Aunt Julie whispered.

Aunt Melia, who knew some Hebrew, tackled the receptionist.

'No more than two visitors at a time,' she translated, 'Julie and I will go first, Suzanna, and prepare your mother for your visit.'

A young nurse came through after her aunts had left, and addressed Suzanna in Hebrew.

'I am sorry I don't speak Hebrew,' she replied in English.

The nurse gave a broad smile. 'You speak English? Oh good. I come from Manchester. I was asking who you're visiting.'

'My mother, Mrs Hadad.'

'Ah, yes. We are worried about her. She tells us she is going back to work as soon as she leaves. I hope your family can persuade her that she will need to rest for a long time.'

'We will try,' Suzanna replied, 'but we won't succeed.'

The aunts returned.

'I'll show you where to go,' the nurse said, and led her to an open-air balcony.

Her mother was propped up in one of a long row of beds.

'Surely my mother is too ill to be outside in this weather.'

'Fresh air is an essential part of the cure,' the nurse replied, 'It's not as bad as it looks. Your mother has plenty of blankets. I'll leave you now.'

Suzanna was shocked to see her mother's face so deadly pale, apart from two bright red patches on her cheeks.

'Well, Suzanna, how is life in the harem?' her mother greeted her, accompanying her words with a wry smile.

'A little boring,' Suzanna admitted.

'Yes,' her mother agreed, after a fit of coughing, 'and if your Aunt Julie has her way, you'll remain bored for the rest of your life. Why did you leave the Shepards?'

Suzanna didn't want to upset her mother by telling her about Mr Shepard.

'I didn't want to stay after Renshaw died.'

'But you knew Renshaw wouldn't be on earth long.'

'Yes,' Suzanna admitted, 'but I didn't realise how I would feel about it when he died.'

'You probably needed time to get over it, but you should be all right by now. You must go back to the Shepards and keep up your studies. They are your passport to a life of your own. I just wish I had had your opportunities.'

'I'll go back soon,' Suzanna said, but she didn't mean it, not while she remembered Mr Shepard's disturbing eyes, and his arm round her shoulders.

All the same, she thought on the drive back, I don't want to live my life like Aunt Julie.

They stopped at a warm picnic spot near Tiberias to feast on cold roast chicken, olives and pickled cucumbers and Suzanna listened to Aunt Melia boasting about her older daughters, all well qualified, all gainfully employed, all respected by other women, and by men as well. Aunt Julie, rehearsing her daughters' housekeeping skills, did not impress her nearly as much.

A servant handed her a letter from Mrs Shepard on their return to Jenin.

'Eve is missing you so much,' Mrs Shepard wrote, *'Please come back soon. I cannot cope with her tantrums much longer.'*

She handed the letter to Aunt Julie who skimmed it, and dismissed it with a flourish. 'Let her sort out her own problems.'

'I take it Suzanna's ex-employers are asking her to return?' Aunt Melia said.

Aunt Julie waved a hand. 'They know when they are on to a good thing, but I am keeping Suzanna here.'

Aunt Melia transferred her gaze. 'And how do you feel about that, Suzanna?'

Suzanna glanced apologetically at Aunt Julie before replying, 'I want to get back to my studies, but I don't want...' she hesitated.

Aunt Melia cut in. 'Julie, you have every right to bring up your own children in the outdated way you prefer, but I owe it to Wadia, to speak up. If Suzanna is willing to persevere with her studies, we should support her.'

Suzanna knew she had to tell her aunts about Mr Shepard. 'Just one thing worries me.' She stopped. The aunts willed her to continue.

'Before I left Jerusalem M-Mr Shepard was alone with me in the kitchen. H-he put his arm round my shoulders.' She did not mention his eyes. Her aunts would not understand how frightening those eyes were.

Aunt Julie sat up straight and glared at her sister. 'That settles it, Melia. Of course you cannot go back, Suzanna.' She leaned forward, and lowered her voice, 'What else did he do?'

Suzanna shook her head. 'Nothing.'

Aunt Melia frowned. 'He just put his arm round your shoulders? Were you upset before he did that?'

'I was crying,' Suzanna admitted, 'because of Renshaw, you know.'

'Habib told them,' Aunt Julie protested, banging her knuckles together, 'when she first went, he told them, you must never allow Suzanna to be in a room alone with a man.'

Aunt Melia ignored her sister. 'And he had just lost a child.' She tapped her chin thoughtfully. 'To the Inglisi, a woman of fifteen is still a child. Suzanna where were Mrs Shepard and the other children, when this happened?'

'Mrs Shepard was in bed, she was so upset about Renshaw. Her friend had taken the girls back with her.'

'I will write to Mrs Shepard, telling her about this,' Aunt Julie said.

Aunt Melia snapped, 'Julie, stop making an unnecessary fuss. Consider the circumstances. The poor man had no choice but to be alone with our Suzanna. He was only trying to comfort her as he would one of his own daughters. If she goes back now, Mrs Shepard will be in control of the household; her children will be back. Suzanna will have no trouble.'

Now that Aunt Melia put it like that, Suzanna realised she had let her imagination run away with her. After all Mr Shepard could not help the colour of his eyes.

'Melia, we should take no risks,' Aunt Julie started, but formidable though she might be, she was no match for her sister.

Two days later, Suzanna was on her way back to Jerusalem.

Chapter 32

In the middle of December, Mrs Jones poked her head round the office door. 'Miss Boutaji, the superintendent would like to borrow Miss Quigley for a while.'

Patsy picked up her shorthand notebook and pencil but, when she entered the superintendent's room, there were two seats in front of his desk, one of them occupied by Mrs Jones, who motioned her to the other.

'Miss Quigley,' the superintendent began, 'You have been here several weeks now, and Miss Boutaji reports well on your work. How do you feel you are settling in?'

'I am very happy here, sir,' she answered cautiously, 'Miss Boutaji has been most kind and helpful.'

'The station is lucky to have such an excellent office manager,' Mrs Jones put in.

'Of course! Of course!' The superintendent twirled his fountain pen between his fingers and looked up. 'Miss Quigley, I have a delicate matter to put to you.'

He placed his fountain pen on its marble holder, and laid his hands flat on the desk. 'What I am about to say must on no account be perceived as a criticism of Miss Boutaji, who, as Mrs Jones has just said, is an excellent Office Manager.'

Mrs Jones nodded in vigorous agreement.

'However,' the superintendent continued, 'I am under considerable pressure from the powers-that-be to keep sensitive material away from non-British personnel. So far, Mrs Jones has been able to skim off top-secret documents and deal with them herself. The CID, though, is now setting up a new top-secret project. We were hoping to recruit another British lady but that has proved impossible.'

'Everyone is involved in war work already,' Mrs Jones said defensively, as if the superintendent were accusing British women of slacking.

Patsy suspected the superintendent was working up to asking her to move into his office. She didn't fancy spending her day working with two old people.

The superintendent continued, 'So, Miss Quigley, I want you to work here for an hour a day - Mrs Jones will set up the arrangements with Miss Boutaji. I must emphasise, however, that nothing you see or hear here should be discussed outside these walls.'

Patsy felt relieved. An hour a day would make a welcome break in routine.

On her new desk next day, she found a miscellaneous pile of handwritten reports and newspaper cuttings, every page stamped 'Top Secret.'

Everybody already knew that the British had appointed the Jewish Agency to recruit Jews into the armed forces, that Hagana had promised not to fight the government for the duration of the war and that the Grand Mufti of Jerusalem was anti-British.

She was shocked though to discover that the Jewish Stern Gang was offering the Germans a deal, support for the Axis against the Allies if all European Jews were allowed to migrate to Palestine, and that the Grand Mufti was recruitiing Axis agents throughout the Middle East.

Spending just one hour a day at the task, it took her until the week before Christmas to type and underline her way through the pile.

The day after she finished, Peter Monteith entered the superintendent's office holding a box containing punched and tabbed cardboard strips, a pair of scissors, and a tub of glue. He asked her to paste a cardboard strip onto each page and a set of vertical keywords on each strip. Mrs Jones looked over from her desk. 'It's all right, Miss Quigley, I have asked Miss Boutaji if you can work here all day.'

Later Peter returned with a carrier bag, from which he took a large bundle of knitting needles and ten 18-inch high slotted wooden stands. 'Welcome to Operation Knitting needle.'

By the end of the afternoon, working on the floor, they had created a device, which allowed anyone to search through the documents on key words. The superintendent was impressed when they demonstrated how he could search the documents for instances of several words at once merely by pulling out the right knitting needles. He ordered two constables to fetch a ping-pong table from the canteen for the new device.

Patsy left for home wishing the project wasn't top secret. She wanted to tell her mother about her day. Her mother, though, had urgent news of her own.

'Patsy, your father rang at lunchtime. He has his promotion. We'll be moving to Jerusalem before Easter. You'll have to give in your notice.'

Patsy, one arm still in her coat, took a deep breath. 'Why?'

Her mother puffed in exasperation. 'Because it's only good manners. Even if you decide on a transfer, you should let the superintendent know, a.s.a.p. He'll have difficulty finding a replacement here.'

'Um Pat, I don't want to leave Haifa.'

'I know dear, nor do I. I have too many friends here but there's no help for it. One good thing, Cook has agreed to come with us. You do realise, don't you that this means your father is now only two steps from receiving a knighthood when he retires? The Lord honours his own.'

'I thought Second Chosen are supposed to be in this world but not of it.'

'True, Patsy but on the other hand, the more honour you have in this world, the more the Lord can work through you. This is the Lord's doing, and we should not question it.'

Patsy needed to think her position through. She pulled on a warm cardigan and went up to the tower.

No moon, tonight, but the stars in the hollow black sky were brighter than she had ever known. There could be a frost later. She leaned over the balustrade and imagined herself living in Haifa free of her parents' supervision. She wondered what would happen to this house when her parents left. Ahmed had said it was his favourite home. She wished she could afford to rent it herself but her wages were too meagre for even a bed-sit. There had to be a way to make staying in Haifa possible. Her first step must be to speak to the superintendent.

'Of course we need you here,' the superintendent told her, 'I'll have a word with your father and tell him how much you are doing for the war effort. We'll find you lodgings. One of the young marrieds might be glad to make a bit extra. You can't cough up too much from your pay, can you? I'll find a way round that, probably billet you on them officially, find something in the war regs to cover that, eh?'

When she arrived home that evening, her father has already told her mother that the superintendent had informed him his daughter's work was vital to the war effort so he had agreed to her staying behind.

'Patsy, I don't know why you are doing this,' her mother said in an accusing voice, 'The Jerusalem Police would have found you a similar job.'

The stricken look on her mother's face shamed her. She attempted to make matters right by saying, 'I'd tell you why only it's hush-hush.'

'This war!' her mother exclaimed.

The superintendent called her in a week later, 'Good news. I spoke to Sergeant Raven from traffic. He and his wife have a young son; can never get out together, not good for their morale, eh?'

Patsy clamped her lips to prevent a smile - she had heard all about Sergeant Raven and his penchant for chasing pretty nurses.

'I suggested he ask his wife to take you in as a lodger on condition that you do at least one night's baby sitting a week. How does that suit?'

She had met the Raven child, Roger, on Police Beach. He seemed no more of a handful than any other active nine-year old. Roger-sitting would be a small price to pay for independence.

'Fine, sir. Thank you, sir.'

She walked out hardly able to believe freeing herself from her father's supervision could be this easy.

Chapter 33

Three days after the saddest Western Christmas Suzanna had known, Mrs Shepard burst into the kitchen, straight from morning prayers, unable to contain her fury.

'That husband of mine, Suzanna,' she ranted, taking no notice of her two children huddled by the sink. 'Did he tell me to my face that he was going to join up? No-o-o. He had to mention it in a prayer, first. You know what he's doing now?' She did not wait for Suzanna's reply. 'He's only marched down to the recruitment office. I told him that he should wait for a sign from the Lord and you know what he said? "You can't be given a much bigger sign than a world war." I just hope the girls and I can get a passage back to England.'

Suzanna gripped the side of the stone sink to prevent herself yelling. For St. George's sake, didn't she count for anything? How could Mrs Shepard talk so casually of returning to England, after she had promised to tutor her for matric?

In the end, the recruitment office turned Mr Shepard down. For hush-hush reasons, he claimed, as he stalked round the house making everyone's life a misery.

Suzanna realised she had made a mistake in returning to Jerusalem.

****

On the first day of her Christmas holiday in Jenin, Suzanna learnt that:

Everyone could wear proper hats again.
Marie was pregnant.
Aunt Melia's eldest daughter was engaged to an army doctor.
Nadia had applied to be a nurse in the Red Cross.

The aunts kept the best news until last. At the end of January, Habib would marry her old school friend Angelique, who had requested that Suzanna be her chief bridesmaid.

Suzanna couldn't believe it. After Angelique had watched her make a hash of Marie's wedding, she still trusted her?

The big question was, would her mother be fit enough to attend the wedding. Aunt Melia promised to take them to Safad to find out.

****

So here was Suzanna, with Uncle George, Aunts Julie and Melia, and Habib thawing out in the foyer of the sanatorium after being frozen by the icy wind, horrified to learn that her mother was still on a balcony.

Aunt Julie and Aunt Melia took first turn to speak to her mother, while Uncle George went off to speak to a doctor. She and Habib were left on opposite sides of a comfortably warm waiting room.

Almost in a whisper Habib asked, 'This girl I am to marry, I can see from her photograph that she's pretty. Apart from that, all I know about her is that she is good at accounts and will be an asset in the shop. What is she really like?'

'Really good fun, Habib. We were best friends at school even though she was a daygirl. She is very clever too. I am so proud to be her chief bridesmaid.'

Uncle George returned and flung up his hands. 'The doctor won't say when your mother will be cured so we will just have to go ahead and name a date.'

Aunt Julie and Aunt Melia came back from the balcony, frozen. Uncle George told them his decision and then went to see her mother. The aunts poured coffee from a thermos, and settled to serious wedding talk.

Uncle George did not stay on the balcony long and Habib allowed her to go next. Her mother's face, apart from the two vivid patches on her cheeks, almost matched the surrounding snow - topped mountains. Despite her coat, Suzanna shivered and wondered how her mother would ever get better.

Uncle George's visit had obviously left her mother unhappy. 'My only son marrying, and they are stopping me going to his wedding!' she burst out before Suzanna had time to greet her, 'These doctors, once they've got you they won't let you go.'

'I am sure you will be well enough to attend the wedding, Um, but Uncle George had to set a date, otherwise it would look bad to Angelique's parents.'

Her mother sat up straight. 'They've kept some patients here two years, you know. Still let's talk of happier things. Now tell me, Suzanna, how are you getting on with your studies? Your Aunt Julie was upset that you went back to the Shepards but I am glad you did. Just think, only two more years now, and you'll be in university.'

Suzanna realised that she would have to wait until her mother was out of hospital before she left the Shepards.

****

Back in Jerusalem, after her annual holiday, Suzanna could not believe the difference in the Shepard household.

'Great news,' Mrs Shepard told her, all smiles, when she met her at the bus station, 'We are moving to Haifa and we want you to come with us.'

Suzanna could scarcely stop herself jumping for joy. 'My brother lives in Haifa now, Mrs Shepard. He works in a shop on the Nazareth Road and he is getting married soon. I will be able to visit him every week when he is married. Which part of Haifa will you live in?'

'The Lord has looked after his own again, Suzanna. The Engelhards, remember them? They are letting us rent their place on Mt Carmel until the government sees fit to let them return. There's a small cottage in the grounds just right for you.'

Chapter 34

Suzanna found the next few weeks hard work - scrubbing, dusting, and packing things into tea chests. She was grateful that her brother had employed the dressmaker from her native village to make and embroider the pre-wedding dress, and an Armenian seamstress in Haifa to run up her European-style bridesmaid's dress. It allowed her time to practice her dances. She was determined to dance well for Angelique. On Sundays, Granny Hadad and her daughter Great Aunt Candice took it in turns to coach her in the group dances and supervise her solo.

'You will never reach the standard of girls who have practised every week for the past ten years,' Granny Hadad told her, 'but what you lack in technique you make up for in imagination.'

Great Aunt Candice was more critical. 'A solo is meant to follow tradition,' she rebuked as she watched Suzanna's dance that owed more to Ginger Rogers than Palestinian tradition.

'But Angelique will like it,' Suzanna retorted, 'and she is the one I am dancing for.'

****

Angelique, taller, but otherwise hardly changed from the skinny twelve year old she had shared all her secrets with three years earlier, came running out to greet her as Suzanna jumped out of Aunt Melia's car two days before the wedding. After much mutual hugging and cries of delight, Angelique dragged her upstairs to join the other bridesmaids, all friends who had known each other at school, except for two cousins from Haifa. It was more like an end of term party for boarders and daygirls than a serious wedding event. Suzanna found it hard to believe that in only two days time boisterous Angelique would be a responsible married woman.

That evening when the bridesmaids and bride sat gossiping on the largest bed in the room, it was hardly surprising that Habib was the centre of conversation. Suzanna spoke of Habib's kindness when, as a child, she had scraped her knees, or couldn't manage her homework; she extolled his love of poetry; qualities that she considered would make him a particularly suitable husband for Angelique. Later, the others interrogated her about her employers. What was it like living with the British? Did they behave as scandalously as everyone said they did?

She had to laugh. 'Not my family. They spend their time reading the bible and praying. Mrs Shepard never wears makeup, does not even go to the hairdresser. Mr Shepard doesn't drink or smoke.'

The focus switched to Leila, the oldest cousin, who worked as an office manager at Haifa Police HQ.

'Do you really work with men?' Angelique asked.

'No,' Leila replied, 'the only other person in my office is a woman but men come in occasionally. One British policeman even asked me to a party last New Year.' The other girls looked half-shocked, half-envious until Leila added, 'but my mother wouldn't let me go, of course.'

'I am training to be a secretary, too,' another bridesmaid offered, 'My father said he might as well get a return on the money he forked out sending me to school.'

Suzanna sat there wondering why she was slaving away for the Shepards in exchange for tuition, when she could get a good job after a short secretarial course.

****

Next day Suzanna donned the traditional long tunic of finest white Egyptian cotton, uniquely embroidered with brick red and blue embroidery in the circle, hoop, and triangle patterns of her native village. She then joined the rest of the bridesmaids, all wearing similar tunics embroidered with the patterns traditional in their own villages. They dressed Angelique in an even more heavily embroidered Nazarene coat. Angelique's mother came in carrying her great-great-great grandmother's smadeh, a cloth skullcap with a padded horseshoe rim sewn with golden coins, and two long golden chains. The bridesmaids decorated Angelique's hands and feet with traditional henna patterns before they placed this heirloom on her head, escorted her to the hired hall and sat her on a throne.

With all Angelique's other unmarried female relatives and school friends, the bridesmaids lined up in front of the throne and faced a table laden with wedding presents where a white pearl-decked Parisian wedding dress took pride of place behind Habib's huge, multicoloured basket of gifts.

The drumming quickened now. Suzanna stepped forward and undulated upwards, stretching gracefully, as she ordered her toes and heels to tap the floor in time to the music. Then she swooped low in traditional obeisance to the bride.

Angelique smiled in appreciation, and suddenly Suzanna's legs and hands took control. They improvised further than she had in practice. Her feet moved faster, tapping and kicking, her arms whirled in rhythmic movement, her trunk twisted and turned as it obeyed the instructions of her legs and arms, until eventually she sank to a finish amidst an astonished round of applause.

Afterwards, she immersed herself in the communal dances, swept up in the totality of female comradeship.

The dancing lasted until well past midnight but Suzanna bounced up early next morning to put on the European dress in blue silk. With the other bridesmaids, all wearing dresses made from the same pattern and material, she attired Angelique in her white Parisian dress with its magnificent ten-foot long trailing skirt.

While a hairdresser worked on Angelique's head, and set the long Nottingham lace veil in place, the bridesmaids once again decorated the bride's feet in traditional henna patterns.

The rest of the bridesmaids escorted Angelique back to the hall holding her train well above dusty ground level. Suzanna followed them carrying a large canvas bag. The bridesmaids sat Angelique on her throne again and Suzanna arranged Angelique's skirt round her feet to disguise the fact that she was wearing sensible running shoes. Then she and the other bridesmaids crowded in front of the bride to sing traditional songs.

Outside, car horns blared. The doors burst open. Her brother, accompanied by all his friends and male relatives, strode into the hall, ritually pushing the women aside. He stood in front of Angelique, bowed, and held out his hand. Angelique put her hand into his and Habib swept her off her feet to carry her down the steps of the platform.

Then Angelique's father rushed into the building, reclaimed his daughter, and hustled her outside. Habib gave chase. Suzanna clutching her bag followed the rest of the bridesmaids outside and watched while Angelique and her father climbed into a waiting car. The driver, with much hooting, drove off.

Habib's henchmen joined Habib and the bridesmaids as they ran after the car, laughing and shouting, until it stopped outside the church. There the priest negotiated with Angelique's father and Habib while Suzanna removed Angelique's running shoes from her feet, put them into her bag, and replaced them with white court shoes decorated with mother-of-pearl. The priest invited the bride and groom, plus their attendants, to follow him to the far end of the church. There they congregated on a carpet square round a table bearing a bible and a cross. The priest blessed two rings. Angelique and Habib placed them on their fingers. Now Suzanna took a carton of candles from her bag and a box of matches. She lit two and gave them to Angelique and Habib, before handing a candle to each bridesmaid. After lighting her own candle, she used it to light the candle of the nearest bridesmaid who then lighted the candle of the next bridesmaid. Once all candles were lit, the priest placed crowns on the heads of the bridal couple and explained that they were symbolic of the roles Angelique and Habib would play in their new family. Appropriate the symbolism for this pair, Suzanna thought. Habib and Angelique would have their own flat, unlike poor Marie who was already complaining that life in her mother-in-law's household was not worth living and that she hardly ever saw her husband.

While Angelique and Habib shared a common cup of wine, the priest told the story of the Lord Jesus turning water to wine at a wedding in nearby Canaan. Then the newly married couple followed the priest in a circle round the table, and the service finished with a blessing from the priest.

The religious rites over, the bridesmaids, now officially designated 'Handmaidens-of-the-bedchamber,' helped the bride into a curtained partition at the front of the first of two buses taking everyone to Haifa. Suzanna joined the rest in teasing Angelique about the final part of the ceremony.

In Haifa, a huge four-tier iced wedding cake stood on a table. European guests arrived and both sexes mingled and danced to a band playing waltzes and foxtrots, just as in the films.

Suzanna went to get something to eat from tables loaded with canapés, tiny sandwiches, and petit fours. Habib, who had his friend Ahmed al-Zeid with him, called her over, and whispered, 'Great news for Arabic Independence, ya Suzanna. Ahmed has been telling me that the Grand Mufti is negotiating with the Germans, who have asked him to recruit agents in Palestine.'

Suzanna wanted to shout, 'This is your Wedding Day, Habib. Why are you going on about politics?' but she couldn't shame her brother in front of his friend.

Ahmed al-Zeid smiled and said, 'Habib says you know my tenants on Mt. Carmel, Suzanna, a Mr and Mrs Quigley and their charming daughter.'

Grateful for the change of subject, she replied, 'I have known Mrs Quigley for several years but her daughter was at school when my employers lived in Haifa.'

Angelique's mother came up, tapped her on the shoulder, and whispered, 'Time you took Angelique away.'

Suzanna noticed Habib tense and Ahmed al-Zeid place a reassuring hand on his arm.

She rounded up the other maidens-of-the-bedchamber. They surrounded Angelique who had been gaily showing off wedding presents, but lost her merry smile as they led her away.

Suzanna had the key to the flat, and led the women upstairs where they set to work bathing and perfuming Angelique. They clothed her in a white silk nightdress, and propped her up on huge lace-frilled pillows in a double bed. Sunk into the pillows Angelique looked small, frightened, and far younger than her sixteen years.

'You'll be all right, Angelique,' Suzanna whispered, 'Habib won't be rough. He doesn't enjoy hurting people.'

Then she joined the other bridesmaids standing round the bed, laughing, and joking to keep up Angelique's spirits.

When a flushed Habib arrived, pushed through the door by the groom's companions, he looked no more confident than Angelique. Suddenly, it was her brother Suzanna wanted to reassure, but that was not her role.

The maidens-of-the-bedchamber waited, their eyes downcast, until the raucous companions had retreated, then they loudly wished the bridal pair every happiness and raced back to the wedding feast.

The European guests had departed. The women were dancing modestly in one half of the room while the men pranced energetically in the other half. As Suzanna joined in the dancing, she wondered how Angelique and Habib were getting on.

Before she dropped into bed in Jenin in the early hours of the morning, she took out her icon and prayed that Angelique and Habib would like each other. The Holy Mother smiled.

Part 2

Chipping Through

Chapter 35

'There's been a hiccup, Suzanna,' Mrs Shepard announced, two days before the move to Haifa, 'We no longer have the cottage in the grounds so we don't know where to sleep you. Could you stay at your brother's until we've got things sorted?'

Suzanna attempted to hide her excitement, as she agreed to pick up the phone and consult Habib. She heard Angelique, in the background, clapping her hands.

The Shepards dropped her outside Habib's shop on the way down from Jerusalem.

Marriage suited Angelique, Suzanna thought when she walked through the shop door and saw her friend flying down the stairs to meet her. Dressed in a stylish crepe de chine frock and with shoulder-length marcel-waved hair replacing her schoolgirl plaits, Angelique looked years older than the frightened child she had last seen shivering in the marriage bed.

Angelique, playing the attentive housewife to perfection, showed her into a small-whitewashed room with a desk, a comfortable cushioned chair, an oval mirror and a bed made up with starched sheets and a predominantly blue patchwork quilt, then stayed to help her unpack.

When Habib came bounding up from the shop, they moved to the living room. Angelique smiled at her husband before hurrying off into a modern kitchenette, leaving the door open. Suzanna watched her serving up the evening meal, something with lots of cumin judging by the smell.

'How's business?' Suzanna asked her brother.

Habib raised his arms and extended them wide. 'Booming, booming. Running the shop is so much easier now I am married to an expert accountant.'

'This European War is doing us a good turn,' Angelique said, as she entered bearing a steaming tray piled high with spiced rice and lamb stuffed with dried apricots, 'People who once would never have eaten Palestinian food are queuing to buy it.'

Habib smiled affectionately at his wife. Angelique dimpled back as she placed the tray on a low table in the middle of the lounge. Suzanna noticed she looked Habib in the eyes when she smiled at him. Love had obviously entered this marriage at an early stage.

They took their places, sitting on hand-embroidered cushions laid out on the floor. Angelique's cooking tasted every bit as good as it had smelt. Suzanna felt so comfortably full by the time

Angelique fetched the finger bowls, that she would willingly have sat there chatting idly for the rest of the evening.

Angelique, though, persuaded Habib to take them to the pictures, and the three of them set off to the local cinema. How different this building was from the palatial palace where she had seen her first film. Empty melon seeds carpeted the floor, rowdy British Tommies puffed pungent fumes of local tobacco. The shabby wooden chairs, though, were more comfortable than they looked and what did surroundings matter, once the film started?

Suzanna felt strange stirrings as she squirmed in her seat, watching glamorous Gary Cooper battle against the sadistic commander of the French Legion.

'Did you enjoy it?' Angelique asked, when they stumbled into the chilly February night.

'Wonderful,' Suzanna gave a contented sigh, 'and all this too,' she waved her hand round the noisy, night street, 'very different from dull Jenin. I thank the Holy Mother every night that Habib married you.'

'And,' Angelique responded, 'I, too, thank the Holy Mother that you are my sister-in-law. We are going to have such fun.'

Chapter 36

It was the middle of February before Mrs Shepard phoned to say she had sorted out somewhere for Suzanna to sleep.

Suzanna caught the earliest bus, and dismounted by the small but prosperous shopping centre on the summit of Carmel. Consulting the sketch map Mrs Shepard had drawn in Jerusalem, she walked past smart shops and cafes, and took the right fork along a road that skirted a recently forested wadi. Opening the first gate, she walked up a path beneath iron arches, towards a stone house resembling a Turkish fort. Evie raced down the path towards her, shouting, 'She's here. She's here.'

Mrs Shepard and Clare were waiting under a wooden canopy at the end of the long veranda.

'Am I glad to see you?' Mrs Shepard exclaimed, as she planted a kiss on Suzanna's cheek, 'I have been going crazy having to do everything myself. I have enrolled both girls at Haifa High but haven't yet had the time to take them there.'

They moved into a large flag-stoned chamber lit by one small window and furnished with the Shepard's oak dining table and chairs. One corner of it was partitioned off with thick brown curtains.

'This is your bedroom,' Mrs Shepard said, drawing aside the curtains to reveal a truckle bed.

Mrs Shepard then proudly pointed to a new refrigerator, which broke into a piercing hum when she opened its door. Evie whispered reverentially, 'It even makes ice cream.'

'I've put it in the dining room,' Mrs Shepard said, 'Because it isn't safe to bring electric power into the kitchen. I've had to get rid of my electric stove. I'll show you how to work the paraffin one. It's rather like a set of primuses, but not so noisy.'

She opened a door next to the refrigerator and they moved into a dingy kitchen built entirely from sheets of corrugated iron. A five-foot tall iron pump dominated the central area.

Suzanna looked at the archaic stone sink. 'Where are the taps?'

Mrs Shepard grimaced. 'We don't have mains water. We have to pump water from an underground cistern.'

She pointed to two large narrow-necked terracotta jars protected by net circles weighted down with sewn-on blue beads. 'That's where we store the drinking water. So, Suzanna, your first job each morning will be to pump up and boil the drinking water.'

'What about washing-up water?'

'You pump that too and heat it - and bath water, shaving water all other water except for the jon-jon which flushes from a rain tank on the roof. There's a second pump in the yard for the wash house.'

Suzanna realised her workload was going to be even heavier than it had been in Jerusalem, without the pleasure of having the children around her during the day.

She wasn't happy with her sleeping accommodation. She brought Habib back with her on Sunday evening to argue against it, only to find that in her absence Mr Shepard had placed a bedside table, bookshelf, and wardrobe inside the partition to form solid walls against the blankets. Mrs Shepard had placed a standard lamp and cane armchair in front of the desk to add a touch of luxury. Habib gave the improvised room his approval on the understanding that no one but his sister would have access to it.

That night, reassured by the Shepards' promise to respect her privacy, Suzanna took out her icon and placed it on her desk.

'Please let me pass matric first time so I need only stay here a year,' she prayed.

****

'What subjects will I be taking for matric?' Suzanna asked Mrs Shepard next day.

'I will write off for the exam syllabus and then we will talk about it,' Mrs Shepard promised. It was weeks, however, before she fulfilled that promise.

'Right,' Mrs Shepard said when at last she had the syllabus in her hand. 'This is how it stands. There's no chance of you being ready to sit the exams next year, so we'll aim for the summer of '42. We'll enter you for English Lit. and Grammar, Mathematics, French, Latin, General Science and Religious Studies. Let's hope we can still get the set books. I will supervise most of your studies but Jimmy will mark your science exercises as he knows more about that side of things.'

'He'll teach me?' Suzanna did not like the sound of that.

Mrs Shepard gave her a sharp look. 'No, I'll go through things with him, and then explain them to you. Now let's get straight what happens if you pass.'

'I want to go to the American University in Beirut,' Suzanna replied.

'Nonsense, my girl, after all Mrs Quigley has done for you? You take up that scholarship she found for you.'

'But what if the war is still on? I won't be able to go to England.'

Mrs Shepard shook her head vigorously. 'Oh, it will be over long before then.'

Chapter 37

On a wet, chilly day in March 1940, Patsy waved good-bye to Cook and her parents. She returned, damp and miserable, to the bare interior of what was no longer home, waiting for an agent to collect the key.

The bell rang. Ahmed, in a red fez, smiled when she opened the door. 'What an unexpected pleasure, I was sure you would have left for Jerusalem.'

'I work in Haifa.'

Ahmed raised his eyebrows. 'In archaeology?'

'No, clerking at Police HQ.'

She lifted the house keys from their hook, and handed them over. 'Do you want to make an inspection?'

He shook his head. 'After fifteen years I can't grumble about wear and tear.'

'Then I'll just ring for a taxi. The phone won't be cut off until this afternoon.'

'I can give you a lift after I have spoken to the workers.'

'I have a couple of suitcases.'

'They will fit in the boot. Stay here in the dry. I will be back as soon as I have reassured the workers that they are not getting the sack.'

Patsy felt an illogical sense of relief. 'You are not selling the house, then?'

'No. A friend is going to rent it for the duration. After the war, I will make this my home.'

While waiting for Ahmed, Patsy took a nostalgic tour of the house.

'Where to?' Ahmed asked when he came back.

'You know that big apartment block on Stella Maris Road?'

Ahmed nodded. 'The monstrous building that disfigures the mountainside?'

He started the engine. Patsy took one last look at the house as they drove off, tying a mental label to it before storing it carefully into her cupboard of memories.

'I shall be back in Haifa in two months, helping my friend move in,' Ahmed said, 'Would you do me the honour then of accompanying me to a meal at the Mata'am Khaymat al-sheik.'

Such an unexpected invitation – and to the Mata'am Khaymat of all places, well beyond the means of her usual escorts. But what would people say, she wondered, if they found out that she was spending an evening with an Arab?

She found her tongue. 'I would love to, but - I don't know how I am fixed with my landlady yet, what time she expects me in each evening, that sort of thing.'

'I meant for luncheon, not dinner. Working girls have luncheon breaks, do they not?'

Lunch; there could be no harm in that. She could take a longer break than usual and make up for it by working late. What was the point of gaining her freedom if she did not use it?

'It would give me great pleasure.'

The car drew up smoothly in front of the flats. Ahmed carried her luggage up the stone stairs, and then took out a pocket diary. 'What is this address so I can send you an exact date nearer the time?'

'The postman doesn't call here. The police have theirs delivered to the Khayet building. My father has arranged for me to keep our Haifa mailbox. Send it to me c/o the Engineering Department, Haifa.'

He made a note. 'I will see you in April then,' and ran back down the stairs.

She knocked on the door.

Beth Raven, a slim woman in her early thirties, welcomed her into a small foyer with a broad smile. 'I've been so looking forward to your coming. You're just in time for lunch but I expect you'll want to freshen up first.'

The bathroom had hot and cold running water, just like her Aunt Helen's modern house in England.

She found her way, via a large sitting room with netted French windows opening onto a balcony, to a small dining room. Beth brought in two plates of grilled lamb chops, peas, and mashed potatoes. Patsy placed her hands together.

Beth, who had already picked up her knife and fork, looked worried. 'Oh, I am so sorry, I never asked. Are you a vegetarian?'

Patsy went hot, realising that Beth wasn't intending to say grace. She picked up her knife and fork. 'No, I love lamb. I am so sorry. I was miles away,' she searched wildly for an excuse, 'I was just wondering how far my parents had got.'

'Of course, you poor thing. You must be missing them already. You are so brave staying on without them. I do miss my mother. I stayed in England for a year after Roger was born, so Mummy could help me. Mummy dotes on Roger. She and Daddy were planning to come out next winter when Daddy retires, but I can't see this war finishing by then.'

While they ate, they talked about the war, inflation, and Patsy's job.

'I do envy you going out to work,' Beth said, 'I loved working in a typing pool before I married. I had so many friends.'

After lunch Beth showed Patsy her room, small but pleasant with a window looking out onto the open staircase and the mountainside. Patsy was finishing unpacking, when Roger clattered in. He dragged her at once into his much larger bedroom off the lounge, to show her his model train layout, which not only covered the whole of the visible floor but also extended under his bed. He was describing the finer points of his favourite Hornby engine when Bert Raven's gruff voice announced his father's return. Roger put down the engine and raced out of the room. The inspector picked up his son, big as he was, and whirled him round his head.

'Ready,' Beth announced from the kitchenette and they sat down to a high tea of ham salad and homemade Victoria sponge. Roger and his father kept up a running conversation about speedboats, swimming, and toy trains. Roger jumped down from the table after Beth had refused him a third slice of cake. 'Coming, Dad?' he demanded, and the two males disappeared into Roger's bedroom while Patsy helped Beth clear the table and wash up.

When they had finished, Beth led her into the living room. She found its modern furniture rather Spartan, the electric fire nowhere near as comforting as the roaring olivewood fire back home. No, not home, she reminded herself. This flat was as much home as anywhere else now.

Bert returned and switched on the wireless.

'It's time for me to put Roger to bed,' Beth said, 'There's some books there if you want to read one.'

Patsy could see no books but took an issue of 'Woman's Magazine' off the carved coffee table. She had never read one before. Her parents considered it too worldly to be allowed into their home, and Aunt Helen removed it from the newspaper order in the school holidays. She was engrossed in a short story when Beth reappeared and Bert strode back into his son's room.

'Bertie always reads Roger a goodnight story,' Beth explained.

A quarter of an hour later, Bert returned to the lounge. 'Just off to the club, darling. Don't wait up.'

Beth gave a sigh when Bert left; 'We've got so used to going out separately. I am really looking forward to this Friday when you sit for us.' She picked up the Palestine post and flicked to the page giving the wireless programs. 'There's a Beethoven concert on tonight. Shall we listen?'

Music was not Patsy's scene but she lied politely, 'I'd enjoy that.'

Beth placed a plateful of soft-centred boiled sweets on the coffee table and picked up a bag containing a half-knitted pullover. They chatted away throughout the concert, pausing only to unwrap sweets.

'I haven't enjoyed an evening so much for months,' Beth said when the concert finished. 'We really are lucky having such world-class performers here in Palestine. Oh, before I forget,' she pulled out a key on a string from a vase on the dresser and held it out.

Patsy took it, turned it over, puzzled. There had been no keyhole in her bedroom door. 'What's it for?'

Beth raised her eyebrows. 'The front door, of course. Tie it to your handbag. That way you'll always have it when you need it.'

Patsy squeezed the key in her fist, finding it hard to believe she was free to come and go as she pleased. 'Thank you, Beth.' Her eyes filled with tears.

'Hey,' Beth said, 'It's only a key. Now wait here while I make up your hot water bottle.'

'It's all right, I am not ill, just tired,' Patsy reassured her.

'Did I say you were ill?' Beth frowned.

'But you are making me a hot water bottle.'

Beth laughed.

Patsy lay in bed that night, cuddling her hot water bottle, comfortably content, until a disturbing thought flashed through her mind. She had shown Ahmed al-Zeid where police officers lived. That almost certainly breached security regulations.

But there are hundreds of ways Ahmed could have found out, she reassured herself. Besides the war has put a stop to all that terrorist nonsense, and Ahmed is not the sort of person to go posting bombs through people's letterboxes.

Chapter 38

Ahmed's note arrived at the beginning of April, bearing a Syrian address. Would Wednesday 17th April be convenient?

Since agreeing to the date, Patsy had become increasingly certain that there was an unwritten rule forbidding British police employees to fraternise with natives of the opposite sex. She decided to ignore it, and obtained permission from Leila to extend her lunch break, promising to make up for it by staying late in the evening.

She scuttled round the corner of the Khayet building, hoping no one was watching.

The Mata'am Khaymat-al-sheik stood in a quiet street behind a stone wall topped with trailing caper plants. Gardens shaded by date palms surrounded the building. A waiter took her coat and bowed her into a dining room where hanging carpets hid every inch of wall. Carpets covered the floor as well. The multitude of white robed waiters made no sound as they slid round proffering napkins and menus, carrying drinks and wheeling trolleys. A waiter, distinguished from the rest by a wide red cummerbund, led her to a table at the rear. Ahmed stood while the waiter pulled out her chair. 'Patsy, it is so good to see you.'

The waiter handed her a green velvet-coated folder inscribed in elegant Arabic script. She viewed it with apprehension but to her relief the menu inside was in French. She scrolled through the main courses and chose roast guinea fowl.

'Forgive my curiosity,' Ahmed said, when the waiter had departed, 'but why are you working in a police office, instead of studying archaeology. Have you lost sight of your original goals?'

While she was contemplating her answer, the waiter wheeled over an enormous hors-d'oeuvre trolley that gave no hint of wartime shortages. In between directing the waiter to place three fillets of anchovy onto her plate, she answered, 'No, I still want to read archaeology when I return to England.'

She bypassed caviar and pointed an inquiring finger to slivers of pale meat laid out in a perfect circle.

'Breasts of quails,' the waiter informed her. She accepted a portion.

'But England is not the only country with universities,' Ahmed said, 'You could have taken a suitable degree at the American University in Beirut.'

'I felt it right to do my bit for the war effort.'

'Very patriotic!' Ahmed arched an eyebrow.

Was she patriotic?' she asked herself, while selecting three varieties of olives and a transparent slice of Parma ham, such an old-fashioned word, patriotism, or so it had seemed before the war.

She decided, reluctantly, that the plate the waiter held was full, and allowed him to slide it in front of her.

The waiter served Ahmed next. She hoped that would give her time to consider her response to his comment, but Ahmed, twirling his wrist to give the man permission to choose for him, was still giving her his full attention.

She answered slowly, 'Before last September I wouldn't have said I was patriotic and I still don't believe in "my country, right or wrong" but I am sure we are on the side of right in this war, so, I suppose, that for the duration, I am patriotic.' She paused. 'It must be much harder for you, though, to be patriotic when you are torn between Syria and Palestine.'

She saw Ahmed stiffen and guessed she had put her foot in it.

'I don't regard my homeland as two countries,' he said, 'even if foreigners have drawn lines across the map.'

He picked up his fork. She looked away embarrassed and speared a large calamata olive. She risked a quick upward glance while she chewed round the stone. To her relief he gave one of his charming smiles. Her shoulders relaxed as he said, 'But let us not talk politics. I would rather discuss archaeology or palaeontology. There we have more in common.'

Throughout the meal, she listened enthralled as Ahmed enthused over Syrian prehistory.

'I wish I had applied to go on a dig in Syria before the war,' she said as she spooned the last delicious remnant of her mishmish compote.

'It is not too late. I can't find you a palaeontological dig, but I could arrange for you to join an American or Italian expedition working on Nabataean sites.'

She leaned across the table. 'Oh, if only I could but...'

The waiter interrupted placing coffee on the table. She looked at her watch. How had time run so quickly?

'Ahmed, the lunch has been wonderful but I must leave in five minutes. We have a pile of emergency regulations to type up. The amount of paper this war has generated, you wouldn't believe.'

'I would. Believe me it is the same in Syria.' He sipped his coffee. 'Would you like me to make inquiries about a dig? When do you have your next vacation?'

She shook her head. 'Holidays are something that happened before the war. I suppose though that I might be allowed a few days next autumn.' She fumbled for her bag and stood up. 'If you could find me a place then I would be really grateful. Thank you so much for the best meal I have had in my life.'

'It has been memorable for me too.'

Ahmed summoned the waiter who brought her coat. He walked her out into the street, putting her into a dither of embarrassment. He stood still. 'You would prefer me to escort you no further?' A glint of amusement showed in his eyes.

She felt herself redden. What could she say? Would telling him that she was breaching security be any less insulting than leaving him to assume she was ashamed to be seen associating with an Arab?

Ahmed laughed, but not in mockery, a gentle, understanding laugh. 'Patsy, I know how things are for you. I would like to take you for another meal though, sometime when you do not have to rush back to work. Have you sorted your regime with your landlady?'

She felt ashamed. How could he handle prejudice so deftly? She lifted her head and looked him in the face. 'I have a key to the front door, now. I can come and go as I please.'

'Then perhaps we could meet for an evening meal when I return to Haifa? Meanwhile I will look through the coming season's projects for a dig that would suit you. Are some evenings more convenient than others?'

'I can be free any night except Friday. I do my child-sitting then.'

'May I have the pleasure of your company on the first Wednesday in May?'

'That would be marvellous, and thank you once again for a wonderful lunch.'

Ahmed remained in her thoughts during the next few weeks while she and Leila spent many overtime hours typing up the frequent wartime additions to regulations.

Her evenings became crowded. As well as the overtime, she had started on an advanced secretarial course, one evening a week, at the instigation of Mrs Jones. 'This war may go on for some time, Patsy. You could be with us for longer than you think.'

Many of the women on the course she already knew, but there were others, notably a woman with flawless, creamy skin and rich chestnut hair cut by an expert, who had moved to Haifa from some kind of rural Jewish settlement – not a kibbutz, apparently. This woman, whose name was Dalia Leitner, was as beautiful as any Patsy had seen on the cinema screen. She was also, by far, the fastest and most accurate shorthand typist on the course. Patsy found it flattering that Dalia chose to sit next to her and Maftur in Edmonds, rather than with the Jewish women.

Whenever she had an evening free, though, Patsy walked up to the Technion to read books on the architecture of the mysterious four thousand year old Nabataean culture, with its tallying clay tablets and delicate glazed pottery. She was determined that before she met Ahmed again, she would know more than anyone else about the Nabataeans.

When she did meet Ahmed, he brandished a map of Syria. 'We can spread it out once the waiter has cleared the table for coffee.'

During dinner, even more magnificent than the previous lunch, Ahmed gave her details of several American and Italian projects. They discussed the finer points of each one. Patsy dithered. Should she plump for Latakia on the coast or Tel Halaf close to the border with Iraq?

Studying the map over coffee, she realised neither was close to a railway. She looked at the map's scale and gasped. 'I didn't realise Syria was so huge. Just travelling would use all my leave. How do you get around so quickly?'

'Before the war I flew my own plane but I can still manage by car.'

'Isn't there a project closer to Damascus?'

'None yet, although applications are still coming in. However, I could drive you to either Latakia or Tel Halaf, and work alongside you. I would welcome an excuse to get my hands dirty again. Just get some firm dates from your boss, and I will organise my diary around them.'

A whole week in Ahmed's company? She could think of nothing more enjoyable. If only she could take him up on the offer, but her pride placed objections.

'I cannot let you do this. I have nothing to offer in return.'

Ahmed looked serious. 'Your companionship would be payment enough.' He studied his immaculate half moon cuticles. 'Patsy, I enjoy being able to talk to you about my enthusiasms. I have few friends who share my interests.'

She basked in his approval.

'Do you think if I approached your father,' he continued, still studying his nails, 'that he would be willing to give you to me in marriage?'

It was as if he had crashed a stick against her head. She clenched her fists in anger. 'Approach my father!' she exploded as she jumped to her feet, 'Am I some sort of object that can be passed from one man to another?'

She called loudly to a waiter to fetch her coat. The waiter's look of surprise at being addressed by a woman fuelled her fury. Studiously ignoring the staring faces of other customers, she stalked to the door. She heard Ahmed breathing behind her, felt him by her side, silent until the waiter had come up with her coat and departed. Then he burst into a shouted whisper, 'I thought my suggestion might be pleasing to you. What I said was out of respect.'

She whirled round. 'Respect - you wouldn't know the meaning of the word,' and she ran down the path, out of the gate onto the pavement.

She slowed at the main road and felt tears dripping down her cheeks. Tears of anger, she told herself, as she slapped them from her face, not tears of regret.

During the next few days, her anger evaporated. As she mulled over the incident, she realised that, by his standards, Ahmed really had acted out of respect. Any Arab would consider it dishonourable to ask a woman to reveal her feelings before he had checked that his suit was acceptable to her family. She should have explained calmly that English customs were different.

A thought she didn't like nagged its way into her mind. Would she have been so angry if she had thought there was the slightest chance that her father would have welcomed Ahmed's suit?

She was ashamed of how deeply she had insulted Ahmed by walking out on him in public; particularly after all he had done to help her. She would never see or hear from him again, and that hurt even more than the lost archaeological opportunities.

Those archaeological opportunities would not have been there that autumn anyway, she realised a few weeks later, because France surrendered and a Vichy government took over Syria. The border between Palestine and Syria closed.

Despite that, she continued visiting the Technion at least twice a week. She abandoned the Nabataeans, though, in favour of the Neanderthals and gradually developed a theory, more a hunch than a theory if she were honest, about the lowest level at Megiddo.

Chapter 39

Italy entered the war in June 1940. Dumpy silver barrage balloons floated above Haifa harbour. Giza Barat's lodgers sat on benches in the cellar and became friends as they chatted while sewing blackout curtains.

News from Europe grew progressively worse. Miriam Cohen agonised over Josh, certain he had been in one of the ships sunk by U-boats. The last letters had arrived weeks before, all so heavily censored that only the salutations and endings remained legible.

Dalia's mother attempted to comfort her, 'Nu, if he was missing, Miriam, they would tell you.'

'Hah! Those British! You think they want people to know the war is going badly for them? They care for no one. They not only lose my Josh and send your son to prison for fighting Germans, but they force refugees back to sea to drown.'

Next time Dalia saw Shimon she tackled him. 'Just when are you going to find me a job where I can be of more use to refugees?'

'Normally we would be moving you on,' he admitted, 'but you're doing so well we're saving you for something really important.'

Chapter 40

Suzanna was helping Mrs Shepard defrost the fridge when the siren sounded.

Mrs Shepard sprang up. 'You carry on, Suzanna. No need to waste time in the shelter seeing it's only a practice. The Feders from the bakers' shop will be over any minute. I have to make myself presentable.'

Suzanna admired the realism achieved by the practice organisers. Even firing blanks, the ack-ack guns in the grounds next-door produced bangs far louder than any fireworks. In between, stomach-curdling whistles progressed from distant faintness to overhead shrill, before fading and ending in a dull thud. The 'All Clear' sounded as she finished the fridge.

Mrs Shepard escorted the Feders up from the cellar. They stopped by the fridge. 'If you ever decide to sell that,' Mrs Feder said, 'Let me know. It is quite impossible trying to find domestic machinery in the shops now.'

Mrs Shepard said nothing, but by her face, Suzanna realised that she was offended.

Opening the dining room door to let the Feders out, Suzanna discovered twisted shards of metal blanketing the veranda.

'Nu, the waste of ammunition,' Mrs Feder exclaimed.

An ebony tongue of cloud protruded from behind the roof and blocked out the sun. Suzanna ran through to the kitchen and opened the back door. The Northern sky had erupted in rolling, writhing masses of sooty smoke like a gigantic chip pan on fire. Behind her Mrs Shepard shrieked, 'A real air raid! Jimmy! The children!'

Suzanna heard her pick up the phone, 'Operator, CID offices... Is that you, Peter? Addy here. Is the Post Office OK, and Haifa High?'

Suzanna waited, chewing the end of her plait, worrying about the children, imagining their little bodies buried under a pile of rubble, until Mrs Shepard put down the phone with a sigh of relief.

'It's all right, Suzanna. Only two casualties in the whole raid, when a bomb hit a house near the refinery.'

Her brother's shop was near the refinery! Suzanna hugged her arms across her chest and shouted, 'What house?'

'Really, Suzanna, there is no need to yell.'

'My brother!' 'It could be his house.'

'There's still no need for hysterics.'

'Can I phone him?'

'No, I'll phone the police again to find out, better that way. Now pull yourself together, there's a good girl, and get the shrapnel cleared before the children come home and cut themselves.'

Ten minutes later Mrs Shepard still hadn't come out, and Suzanna doubled up with worry, was visualising Angelique's and Habib's bleeding bodies buried beneath collapsed counters of olives and cheese. She re-entered the house. 'What did the police say?'

'For goodness sake Suzanna, don't rush me. I have other things to do, you know.'

Suzanna burst into tears.

'All right!' Mrs Shepard snapped, 'If you are that worried I'll do it now.'

When Mrs Shepard had finished the phone call, she turned to her with a patronising smile.

'The bombed house was a good quarter of a mile from your brother's shop. Really Susanna, I do hope we are not going to have you panicking every time there is a raid.'

Chapter 41

Light gleamed through a chink in the cellar door when Suzanna arrived at Habib's shop a month after the first air raid. She ran down hoping to find Angelique in the bombproof office that Habib had created at the back of the cellar but instead saw Habib and his friend Ahmed al-Zeid. The Syrian was leaning against an olive barrel in a suit that looked as if it had cost more than she had received in wages over the past five years. She gave the pair a quick greeting and was about to leave, when her brother stopped her and handed her a piece of paper. She frowned as she read the English words aloud, 'I wandered lonely as a cloud.'

'Wordsworth,' she said.

Her brother laughed. 'A sample of Ahmed's handwriting so you'll recognise it. You did promise to let him write to me through you, remember? You're going to have to keep that promise soon. He is moving to Iraq to be with the Grand Mufti.'

'But I made it before the war, Habib, when we were fighting for Arab Independence.'

'You've stopped wanting Arab Independence?'

'No, of course not, but things are different now. For a start you have Angelique and the baby to worry about.'

'That's why we need your help. I want to keep this as far away from Angelique as possible.'

She felt herself growing angry at the smooth Syrian standing beside Habib. If the British arrested her brother as a spy, it would all be his friend's fault.

'You are complicating things just for the sake of it, and why write in English?'

'The censors will be less suspicious,' Habib said.

'No they won't,' Suzanna retorted, 'and let me tell you, the Shepards expect me to open my letters as soon as I receive them and want to know who they are from. If your friend's letter is in English they may even ask me to read aloud.'

Ahmed al-Zeid spoke for the first time since his initial courteous but brief greeting, 'Ya Suzanna, it won't matter, because I will write in code. I will write as a female cousin living in Iraq gossiping about her mother finding a husband for you in Baghdad.'

'You will not,' Suzanna said, 'Mrs Shepard knows my mother doesn't want me to marry until I have been through college.'

Habib gave a shrug. 'Don't worry your pretty little head, Sis, Ahmed and I will work out the code words.'

Suzanna was so annoyed by this time that she broke the rule about not showing one's brother up in front of his friends.

'You, Habib Hadad,' she shouted, 'can stop being a patronising donkey. Independence can wait until after the war.'

Ahmed al-Zeid gave her a gentle smile. 'Ya Suzanna I am afraid it will be too late then. We have to take advantage of the Europeans fighting amongst themselves.'

He held out his hand, Inglisi style. 'Come; let me shake the hand of a fellow patriot who puts her country before her own interests. I am truly grateful to the sister of my dearest friend.'

She shook his hand in some confusion and ran upstairs.

Chapter 42

Patsy dear,
Your father has been asked to take the Good News service in Haifa next Sunday. We plan to slip out of Sharing after Breaking of Bread and arrive in Haifa in time to have tea with the Manners. You are invited too. It will be our only chance to see you properly. Your father and I have to leave straight after the service because of the long drive back.

Patsy slammed down the letter. She didn't want to go to the Manners or the Good News service on Sunday. She valued her only day off work, which she spent at the tennis club and beach. She did though want to see her mother, so she would have to go.

She arrived at the Manners before her parents, and had to endure a half-hour inquisition on why they had not seen her recently at the Good News services. She prevaricated, saying that she had friends at the Anglican Church. That did not prevent Mrs Manners from assuring her that all the saints at the women's meeting were praying for her conversion.

Patsy sat quietly through high tea, concentrating on Mrs Manner's tartly sweet apricot flan and moist coffee sponge, while her father and Mr Manners exchanged views on the main thrust of Jeremiah's Lamentations.

At the New Covenant Hall, she saw Peter sitting next to the Shepards. Her mother noticed her surprise and whispered, 'Didn't you know, dear? Brother Monteith has given his life to the Lord. Surely, you went to his baptism?'

Patsy looked down at the floor.

'Oh, I forgot,' her mother went on, 'you worship elsewhere now, don't you?' She lowered her voice still further, 'Jim Shepard helped him come through, you know. They are working together on something very hush-hush. Wonderful how the Lord works things out, isn't it. Perhaps, Peter can persuade you to go to the hall with him when he is not on duty.'

Patsy, then, was not surprised when Peter approached her as she was leaving the Victor Khayet building a few days later, and asked if she would go to the next Good News service with him.

'You had a letter from my mother, didn't you?' she accused, 'Sorry, Peter, I don't want to be a Christian. I only went to the service to keep my mother happy.'

Peter responded, as if to Second Chosen born, 'Oh Patsy, if only you knew the joy of it.'

'Peter, I don't need Christianity.' She regretted the snap in her voice as she remembered why Peter might be anxious to believe in an afterlife and attempted to soften her answer, 'But I am glad, I really am, that you get comfort from it.'

She hurried off towards the suq. The sight of a deep green silk scarf, woven with a silver cedar pattern, eased her irritation. A scarf like that would enliven her tired pre-war dresses. She held it up to the light but almost dropped it on the dung-strewn pavement when she saw Ahmed, in an immaculate grey suit and red fez, gazing into a nearby shop. What was he doing in Palestine now the Syrian border had closed? She busied herself examining a set of wooden donkeys and sensed, rather than saw, him approach.

'Patsy?'

She straightened slowly. He stooped to bring his face closer. 'Patsy, I was so hoping to find you again. Please accept my apologies for the distress I caused you at our last meeting. I had no intention of insulting you.'

She inhaled deeply. 'No, I must apologise to you, Ahmed. I was unfair. It is just that, in our society, a man asks a woman if she will marry him before he approaches her father.'

'So we both apologise to the other,' Ahmed's face lost its gravity. 'Now we can be friends again. Come,' he waved his hands, 'let us have coffee together to cement our renewed friendship.'

Any sensible person, Patsy told herself, would invent an excuse and walk off casually. Instead she heard herself saying, 'What a good idea.'

'Where would you like to go?'

She needed to avoid British Policemen (so nowhere that served alcohol), and women from the Secretarial College (so not Edmonds). 'The milk bar on Kingsway?'

'That will be a new experience for me,' Ahmed replied.

Outside the milk bar, he said, 'Wait here while I check for a free table,' and dashed through the doorway. How strange, Patsy thought, it would have been more sensible to find a table together, and have her save it while he ordered.

Ahmed signalled through the glass that he had found a table. She entered the bar and immediately saw Maftur, at a table near the counter, surrounded by a group of giggling women.

Maftur came rushing over, drawing her fashionable scarf in front of her face like a veil. 'Patsy, you'll never guess who has just walked in,' she whispered.

Ahmed chose that point to come over. 'Patsy, our table is in the corner at the back.'

The one eye visible behind Maftur's pseudo veil widened to a circle.

Patsy looked away, knowing her face must match Ahmed's scarlet fez. 'Maftur,' she mumbled, eyes still down, 'meet Mr al-Zeid. He was my parents' landlord when we lived on Mt Carmel.'

She sensed Maftur dissolving into giggles, behind her scarf but struggled on. 'Mr al-Zeid, this is my friend Miss Naoud. We met when I was learning to type.'

Ahmed bowed his head. 'Miss Naoud, I am delighted to make your acquaintance. Any friend of Miss Quigley's is a friend of mine.'

Maftur extended her hand, western style. 'The honour is mine, Mr al-Zeid.' She managed to slip gracefully back to her group without an audible titter.

Patsy followed Ahmed to the back of the room, knowing that all the women on Maftur's table were watching her every movement. He said, 'Black or white coffee?'

The coffee here was abominable but asking for her usual milk shake would sound unsophisticated. 'White, please.'

Ahmed remained seated.

'You have to order at the counter,' she prompted. Ahmed looked significantly at the waitresses in dirndl skirts and Swiss blouses carrying trays to tables.

'You order, pay, give the table number and then the waitress brings it.'

Ahmed shook his head. 'Another widening of my horizons.' He rose and made his way to the counter.

Patsy buried her head in the menu, refusing to look at Maftur's table.

'I didn't expect to see you in Haifa until after the war,' she said when Ahmed returned.

'I'm only here to check everything is all right with the house.'

'But how did you cross the border?'

Ahmed winked, 'Ways and means. What do you British say? "Ask no questions and you'll be told no lies".'

She blinked to hear one of her mother's favourite axioms coming from his mouth. 'Where did you learn that saying?'

'In Cambridge, but not at college. I was in digs for a term. I learnt a lot from my landlady.' He pulled a face, 'Unfortunately not enough to avoid the mistake I made with you.'

The waitress arrived with their coffee. Ahmed sipped from his large cup and pulled a face. 'Disgusting. I am sorry, Patsy. I will ask them to change it?'

She shook her head. 'It's what they always serve.'

Ahmed put down his cup and rested his elbows on the table, intertwining his fingers. 'Patsy, I will make a confession. It was no accident we met today. I followed you from the Victor Khayet.'

She felt too startled to reply. Ahmed rushed on. 'Now that you have told me that I must ask you before I approach your father, may I send you a proposal of marriage?'

Send a proposal of marriage indeed! She took a deep breath determined not to go off half-cocked this time. 'Ahmed,' she said calmly, 'Even if I were to accept your marriage proposal, I still could not marry you. You are right to ask me before you ask my father, but until I am twenty-one, I must have my father's permission before I can marry, and he will refuse.'

Ahmed frowned. 'Then what is the point of asking you first if the matter is in your father's hands?'

'That is the British custom. First, you must ask me. Then, if I say yes, you must ask my father. Even if I say yes he can still say no.'

'Why are you sure your father will refuse. Muslims and Christians are both people of the book. Only Arab Christians do not accept this.'

Only Arab Christians and Second Chosen, she thought. 'Christians believe in monogamy,' she improvised, 'My father wouldn't let me marry someone who could have more than one wife.'

Ahmed nodded as if he had expected her to bring up that point. His answer sounded well rehearsed. 'Patsy, it is true that we who follow Islam are permitted to take up to four wives, but the custom is old-fashioned. I would promise your father to take no other wife if that was your wish.'

'My wish?' She heard her indignation, and forced herself to let Ahmed continue.

'It would certainly not be my wish to have more than one wife. It is a great expense and can often create a disruptive household. If, however, your career made it inconvenient for you to have children, you might wish...'

'I most certainly would not...' She left that sentence unfinished. 'I must go now. My landlady is expecting me back for dinner.'

'So I will write my proposal to you, not to your father?'

'Yes, but I can tell you now, I can't accept it.'

'You will read it though?'

'Yes, I will read it.'

I shouldn't have agreed to let him write, she told herself, as she walked up the mountain, but all the same, she looked forward to receiving the letter. Anticipation added spice to her daily visit to the Post Office.

When it eventually arrived, she tore it open and settled on a seat in the Post Office Hall.

I, Ahmed al-Zeid, second son of Abu Mohamed al-Zeid, present myself as a suitor for your hand.

As the land longs for water at the end of the summer drought,

As the traveller in the desert longs for the oasis,

As the night longs for the moon,

So do I long for your beauty and wit.

If you consent to marry me I, pledge that, as part of my dowry, I will pay for you to study those courses you have set your heart on. It is my earnest desire that we may afterwards work together to reveal to the world the treasures that belong to Syria.

We will run a household in the twentieth century western style, as far as it does not conflict with the way of Islam, and you will be free to practice all your Christian rites. Should Allah grant us children, however, we must bring them up in the way of Islam.

In the attached document, I set out my worldly possessions. You will see that I am able to keep you in the style to which you are accustomed.

I am a man of honour. As such, I would be unhappy to marry you without the consent of your father while you are a minor under British law. If you cannot gain his consent, I am willing to wait for you until you are free. However should the Germans prove the winners of this present war, with your consent I will marry you at once to afford you protection.

You will require time to think over this proposal. I shall be away on business for a while. I hope to be in a position to contact you early next year. My heart is always yours and, Imshallah; I will be your loving husband,

Ahmed al-Zeid

She folded the letter and replaced it in its envelope, shut her eyes and dreamt of entering the fantasy world this letter suggested. No more being bullied by her father, no more worrying about whether to remain reliant on him for her post-war university course, and as a bonus, a magnificent husband.

Back in the flat, she set fantasies aside and picked up pen and paper to write back politely refusing the offer. However, when she started to address the envelope she realised Ahmed had neglected to include his address. She could carry on dreaming.

Chapter 43

The Shepards had their noisiest row to date after the monthly Spinneys' bill arrived at the end of July. Susanna could hear them going at it hammer and tongs in their bedroom across the veranda. She was glad the girl's bedroom led off the other side of the dining room so they could hear nothing. She lay in bed sure that Mr Shepard was going to murder his wife.

Next morning though Mrs Shepard came into the kitchen seemingly unharmed, apart from a black eye.

'Get everything out of the refrigerator, Suzanna, and clean it out. I am going to have to sell it. How the government expects us to live after pegging salaries for the duration while doing nothing about inflation, I can't think.'

The next Saturday the Feders came over to look at the refrigerator.

From the kitchen, Suzanna heard Mrs Feder confide to Mrs Shepard, 'Of course before the war I would never have considered buying second-hand but now you just can't get new.'

Then Mr Feder, 'It's not in the best condition.'

Evie's voice piped up, 'It's only the ice box that doesn't get cold enough.'

'Eve,' Mrs Shepard said, 'Go back into the garden and play with Clare.'

A short while later Suzanna watched Mr Shepard load the refrigerator into Mr Feder's bakery van.

Mrs Shepard came into the kitchen, slumped onto the kitchen chair and burst into tears.

'Whoever would have thought the government would allow a British family to sink so low.'

The Shepards were not the only ones short of money. Bus fares went up. Suzanna took to walking down the mountain on Saturday evenings.

Habib was cross. 'I will write to Mr Shepard and ask him to pay you more.'

'They haven't any more to give me,' she said.

'They will have to find it,' he replied, 'I will go to see them next Monday.'

After his visit, Habib told Suzanna that Mr Shepard would give her one of the rapidly breeding rabbits each month. Habib said he would buy it from her. Unfortunately for Suzanna, part of the deal Habib and Mr Shepard made was that she would carry the rabbit out of the house alive so Evie and Clare would think she was taking it to a good home.

A week later carrying the first rabbit, Suzanna struggled to the bus stop but the bus driver refused to let her on. 'You're not using a fellahin bus now, girl. We maintain standards of hygiene, here.'

She returned to the Shepards and asked if she could use the telephone to let her brother know she would be late again.

Mr Shepard's conscience must have pricked him, because he fetched an ancient suitcase from the glory hole next to the cellar, half filled it with shredded newspaper, and used his drill to bore air holes.

With the rabbit in the locked case, Suzanna had no difficulty boarding the next bus, but had trouble again outside the bus station when she struggled through a protest march against the government's decision to deport illegal immigrants to Mauritius. Marchers barged into her and her suitcase as if she did not exist. She could not understand the fuss they were making. Surely, refugees should be grateful that the British were taking them so far from the Nazis.

She entered the shop to find both Angelique and Habib downstairs. Angelique shouted, 'Al ham du lillah. You've come. We have wonderful news, Suzanna. Belle mere is coming to stay here.'

Suzanna stood still for a moment; slow to take it in. Her mother leaving the sanatorium at last, coming to Haifa, not returning to Jaffa? Then she put down the suitcase and ran over to embrace Angelique.

'Thank you, thank you for having her. I was really upset when Um told me she was determined to return to work as soon as she left the sanatorium.'

****

Early rains had already hazed the mountain green when Aunt Melia brought Suzanna's mother from Safad.

Aunt Melia bounded out of the car but her mother cautiously balanced one foot on the ground before trusting the other to follow, and then pulled herself upright using the car door.

When Suzanna hugged her mother, she realised just how little flesh covered her mother's ribcage. A long convalescence would be needed here but, after the first excited hugs all round, her mother told Habib, 'I'm only staying until I find a job. Then I'll look for lodgings of my own.'

'Nonsense, Wadia,' Aunt Melia started, but Angelique intervened, 'Of course, Belle mere, we know that, but you will give us a month's undivided attention first, won't you?'

Suzanna received the wink that had so often preceded mischief when she and Angelique were at school.

'How will you persuade my mother to stay when the month ends?' Suzanna whispered in the kitchen a little later.

'You'll just have to wait and see,' Angelique teased.

****

The next Saturday evening, a beaming Angelique ran down the aisles of glistening olives and pickled peppers. 'Habib,' she called 'will you take over the shop while I make Suzanna a cup of tea down in the office? Belle mere is having a nap; we don't want to disturb her.'

'Guess what?' Angelique burst out after shutting the thick wooden door to the cellar. 'I've been to the doctor – and you know what?'

'Oh, Angelique,' Suzanna flung her arms around her friend. 'I'm so glad.' Then she dropped her arms. 'Have you told Um, yet?'

'Have I told Belle Mere?' Angelique exclaimed, 'Of course! I'd have left going to the doctor for another month or so otherwise.'

'Has Habib found Um new lodgings?'

Angelique flapped a hand in horror. 'Suzanna what are you saying? Find somewhere else for Belle Mere? What do you think we are? Your mother is no longer infectious, you know. I went into all that with the doctor before we invited her. No, what I wanted to tell you, before we went upstairs, is that I exaggerated a little to her about what the doctor said to me.' Angelique gave her mischievous smile. 'I told your mother that the doctor had said I needed another woman on hand all the time I was pregnant in case anything went wrong. Your mother is bound to take you aside to tell you I am having difficulties, but there is nothing wrong with me. I only told her that to make sure she stays.'

Suzanna flung her hands up in the air. 'Oh, Angelique, you are wonderful. You deserve every happiness.'

As they drank their tea, she hoped that the prospect of fatherhood would put an end to Habib's childish spy games.

Chapter 44

Dalia had received a note asking her to meet Shimon for coffee.

'We've found a more interesting job for you,' Shimon told her. 'Go down to Excel after work tomorrow.'

She felt so excited she found difficulty staying in her seat. 'What is it?'

'You'll have to wait until you see Max. I don't know anything about it, except that we'll be using you at last.'

'This post,' Max said when she arrived, 'it's a key one, shorthand typist at police HQ. Here are the forms.'

At Police HQ! Dalia's euphoria evaporated. She knew she had no chance of getting in there while her brother was still in prison, but she filled in the forms all the same.

When she had finished, Max said, 'Once your application is in, the police will go through your life with a fine comb. Being born in Germany will go against you, but on the other hand, your whole family has taken out Palestinian nationality and has been living on a politically moderate moshav for the last six years. Now is there anything else you know that the British will regard as suspicious.'

Max would know already so she had better be honest. 'M-my brother, Uri - he was arrested with the 43. He's still in prison.'

Max waved that aside. 'We know that, of course, but have reason to believe it will not bother them too much. Anything else?'

She took a deep breath. 'My grandfather, on my father's side, is German, not a Jew. He's not a Nazi though,' she added quickly.

Max frowned. 'That doesn't show up in our records.'

He tapped his nose with his pencil for a few seconds, and then seemed to make up his mind. 'If it's not in our records, it's unlikely to be in theirs. We'll risk it. Now as to this job, if you get it, keep your eyes open. Pass on anything you learn to Shimon. One thing I'd better warn you about, - the British will ask you to swear to the Official Secrets Act.'

'But I can't...'

Max broke in, his tone brusque, 'Come, you've broken promises before without a second thought.'

'I-I never-have.'

'Oi?' Max raised an eyebrow. 'So Shimon Mabovitch asks you to keep everything about Aliyah Beth secret. And the day after he recruited you, who was it blabbed to her brother?'

Dalia burst into indignant self-defence, 'Uri is in Hagana.'

'Nu! You decide for yourself when you keep and break promises. So fine, that is all you do now. Anything not the concern of Aliyah Beth you keep to yourself - anything that can help rescue just one refugee you damn well let us know about.'

He handed her a piece of paper. 'Memorise that number then destroy it. If you have urgent information for Shimon, phone and ask for a meeting. Your message will be passed on.'

She hurried from the agency, bubbling with excitement, despite common sense insisting that she wouldn't get this job.

In the middle of November, she received a letter summoning her to Northern Palestine Police HQ, in the Khayet buildings.

Part 3

Exchanging Cheeps

Chapter 45

An angry crowd blocked Dalia's way. Fighting an instinctive urge to join the demonstrators protesting at the detention of two boatloads of refugees, she pushed her way through to the Khayet building.

An Arab constable escorted her to an office labelled 'Superintendent'.

A balding man, with too many wrinkles for his upright posture, sat behind a cluttered desk. He looked up from the folder he was studying, took off his glasses to peer at her and put them on again to pick up a set of papers she recognised as her application. He glanced at it in an offhand fashion, and then offered her the job almost absent-mindedly. He turned his attention back to his folder. Without lifting his eyes, he raised his hand, recited the Official Secrets Act mechanically, and asked her to swear to abide by it.

Her voice vibrated oddly, as she took the oath, but he didn't seem to notice.

A police officer entered the room with a bulging file and stood beside her. The superintendent transferred his attention to the newcomer. 'Yes, Inspector?'

'Sir, the refugee data.'

Dalia tried to look as if she were not listening, but peeped sideways at the reporting officer. She had seen him at the beach club in swimming trunks. In uniform now, she recognised him as the sergeant who had visited Bereishit three years previously.

'The thing is, Sir, the medical authorities need this information. The CMO has asked for a copy. I've sifted out the most sensitive material. Can the rest be typed up in the general office? I know they're overwhelmed but the MO says it's urgent.'

The superintendent held out a hand. The inspector passed over a large bundle of papers. The superintendent flicked through them, pulled a face, and held them uncertainly. Then his face cleared and he passed the bundle on to Dalia. 'You may as well start work at once Miss –err,' he paused and looked down at her application, 'Miss Leitner. Inspector Monteith will show you the ropes.'

She gave a gasp. 'But I haven't resigned from my present job.'

The superintendent shrugged. 'Our need is greater than theirs. Don't worry, I'll see that they send you any pay they owe.'

Bewildered and clutching the papers, she followed Inspector Monteith down a dark corridor into a room labelled 'General Office'. Her stomach insisted that she had suffered some kind of shock.

Compared to the enormous, crowded room at the export firm this office was minute. It held only two women, one of whom was Patsy Quigley. Patsy smiled reassuringly.

The other woman stood. 'My name is Leila Boutaji. I am the office supervisor. I am pleased to meet you, Miss Leitner.'

Miss Boutaji led her to a desk furnished with a turn of the century typewriter. She glanced back at Inspector Monteith. 'I see you have brought your work with you.'

The inspector bent over her as she seated herself at her new desk and spread out the papers. 'This is a list of refugees we're holding with their medical notes. We need surnames in alphabetical order, with place of former residence and medical details on the right hand side, all in triplicate. Here's a list of recognised abbreviations. If possible, keep each record on one line...'

As he continued, she became increasingly conscious of his powerful masculine smell combined, in an exciting way, with the oily odour of Brylcreem. Only when he had straightened did she dare glance up at his face. He had smooth tanned skin, sensual fleshy lips, and soft, blue eyes - the countenance of a John Barrymore, with perhaps just a dash of a Douglas Fairbanks. She forced her gaze away and fixed it on a waste paper bin packed with screwed up carbon flimsies. Something clicked in her mind; the solution to smuggling out information.

Inspector Monteith was still speaking, 'Sounds complicated, I know, but you'll find it obvious once you start. I'm working in Inspector Sutton's room this afternoon. Bring the list there when you've finished.'

Once the inspector had left, the two women came over.

'Welcome again', Miss Boutaji said, 'Please call me Leila and I hope you will allow me to call you Dalia. You already know Patsy. It was she who persuaded Mrs Jones, the superintendent's secretary that you were as good as your application.'

'Was I the only applicant?'

Leila laughed. 'No, we had over fifty but security turned down the rest. They would have removed your name, too, if it hadn't been for Patsy.' She looked at her watch. 'As boss lady I declare it lunchtime.'

While typing up the list of refugees after lunch Dalia tucked each used flimsy beneath a blank page at the bottom of her work. When finished she asked Leila the way to Inspector Sutton's office.

'If he is there, don't let him give you any more work,' Leila warned, 'He'll want it finished ten minutes before he's handed it over and then complain that it's been done wrong. Tell him Miss Boutaji has already piled your desk high.'

On the way to Inspector Sutton's office, Dalia stopped at the Ladies' toilet. She secreted the flimsies down the front of her knickers, sadly aware that the carbon would ruin a good set of underwear. She promised herself that when she returned to her lodgings she'd make a pouch from leftover blackout material.

Inspector Sutton was not in his office, only Inspector Monteith and a civilian in a crumpled suit peering at sheets of paper through thick glasses. Inspector Monteith gave her a welcoming smile, scanned her work, looked up, and smiled again. 'Wonderful, Miss Leitner. I don't know how you've managed it so quickly.'

Chapter 46

From her bedroom window, Dalia looked down on the docks. Toy police cars herded refugees, the size of ants, onto the quay where the newly renamed Patria was waiting to take them aboard. Out in the bay, a police launch shepherded a ramshackle paddle steamer - yet another boatload of intercepted refugees, another Aliyah Beth failure.

She picked up her bag and hurried to the Khayet building where Leila had already sorted her share of that morning's work. As she removed the cover from her typewriter, the door opened and Mrs Jones looked round.

'Miss Boutaji, Miss Quigley's father has been taken ill. We shall have to manage without her for two or three days. Do your best. I know you will.'

Leila picked up Patsy's pile and ruffled through it. She held up two documents stamped 'Secret'.

Dalia kept her face impassive, although her innards were in a state of turmoil. Leila waved the documents about before reaching a decision. 'These came from Inspector Sutton. I am in no mood to tangle with him. They are only marked Secret, not Top Secret. We'll get on with them, do one each.'

Dalia felt her adrenaline level rise still higher. At last a real secret document. Deliberately she typed up three or four routine pieces of correspondence before reaching for the stamped document. Glancing through it, she experienced anti-climax. The report, although horrifying, contained nothing useful, just the information that during the previous night fifteen people had died on board the ship she had watched enter harbour. It also gave particulars of the other passengers, soon to be on their way to Athlit. She saw that the tiny paddle steamer had carried 1880 passengers. No wonder typhus had broken out. Inspector Sutton came in with another pile of papers. 'These can wait until lunchtime but I want the lists I handed in earlier by eleven, ladies.'

'We're short-staffed, Inspector,' Leila told him, 'Miss Quigley is away.'

'Then you two will have to work harder to make up.'

He slammed the door behind him, but an ear-splitting, earth-shaking explosion from outside the building drowned the crash. Papers went flying. Dalia and Leila scuttled under their desks and waited for the air raid siren and ack-ack guns. Footsteps tramped down the corridor. All went quiet. Still no siren. They crawled out and retrieved the papers.

The superintendent entered the room, his face grave. 'Ladies, that noise just now, the ship taking refugees to Mauritius has capsized.'

The image of a sky-blotting, overturning liner, discharging clouds of refugees into the water, filled Dalia's mind. She was barely conscious of the superintendent continuing, 'I've sent our men to join in rescue operations, and have signed dock passes for you both. The Red Crescent is setting up a relief tent.'

Dalia walked the short distance to the docks with Leila beside her in silence, wondering what more she could have done to prevent this tragedy. If only Hagana had acted on her information and fought to free the refugees while they were still in the detention centre. She showed her pass at the dock gates. Soldiers let them through.

The Patria was a giant autumn leaf floating on the water with blobs swarming over and round it. As Dalia came closer, the blobs resolved into men in bathing suits using drills, and divers, in more fearsome gear holding up limp bundles. The sound of pneumatic drills drowned all else.

The canteen was at the back of the quay. The organiser, a well-padded British matron welcomed them into her oasis of peace.

'I need someone behind a counter,' she told Leila. 'And you,' she said to Dalia, 'look pretty sturdy. You can be our water carrier.'

On her journeys to and from the pump, Dalia watched boats bringing in bodies. Soldiers rushed some to medical tents on stretchers but laid out other blanket-covered forms in rows on the stone slabs of the quay. Dalia hurried past them, her face averted.

At one point, while on the way to the makeshift hospital with two buckets of water, standing still, resting her arms, Dalia noticed a man who could be Inspector Monteith, on the hull of the Patria passing a child-shaped bundle to men on a tug.

Searchlights allowed rescue work to continue after dark.

'What a target we'd make in an air raid,' Leila commented when Dalia brought full pails into the canteen, but thankfully, the night sky remained silent.

Arms near to breaking point, Dalia continued to ferry water hour after hour. On one trip she found Inspector Monteith sitting on the slabbed ground; his head flung back against a wall, his chin dark with unshaved stubble, a look of despair on his face.

She lowered her buckets. 'Are you all right?'

He stared at the stars as he answered, his words almost a moan, 'It's the children – we were too late.'

His words pierced her. She wanted to sit down beside him and burst into tears at the futility of it all but she had no time to wallow in guilt and despair. She picked up her pails, hurried on, filled them, and returned to the field kitchen. Leila, behind an urn, urged a cup of tea on her.

'There's someone outside who needs one even more,' Dalia said, 'Can you sweeten it well.'

'No problem,' Leila replied, 'The NAAFI doesn't seem to have heard of sugar shortages.'

The inspector was still sitting where she had left him. She shook his shoulder and forced the mug into his hands. 'You must drink it.'

He took a sip of the treacly brew, then gulped it, and handed her the mug with a tremulous smile. 'Thank you,' but he remained slumped on the floor.

'Inspector Monteith,' she started tentatively, then carried on firmly as if addressing a new Hagana recruit after a hard exercise, 'you shouldn't be sitting round here in wet clothes. Go home and change.'

The inspector rose, gave a mock salute. 'Orders received and understood, ma'am.' He headed for the exit.

It was 2 am before Dalia returned to her digs, and then she dreamt of heavy buckets dragging her down into filthy, dark green water full of children glaring with accusing eyes.

****

Suzanna too was having a bad night. She had spent over an hour praying to the Holy Mother for the people on the Patria. Even though they were Jews, with no right to be in Palestine, she hadn't wanted them to be hurt, especially not mothers and little children.

A horrible thought occurred to her after she turned off her light. Could that friend of Habib's have instigated this tragedy, and, if so, had he involved Habib?

Chapter 47

The constable acting as Patsy's chauffeur in her dash to Jerusalem had taken to heart the superintendent's order to drive as fast as possible. He chose the coastal road and then the Seven Sisters, belting along in excess of fifty miles an hour, horn blaring, forcing camels and donkeys off the road, and overtaking long lines of slow-moving military convoys for furlongs at a time.

In Jerusalem, a Jewish protest march threatened to hold them up. She saw the slogan 'British Murderers' on banners blocking the road and wondered what the moan was about this time. The constable hooted his horn and drove straight through. To her relief the marchers gave way.

The driver dropped her outside the hospital gates and she hurried in ignoring the flower-sellers – there would be time for that later, she hoped.

'What exactly is wrong with my father?' she asked the sister in charge.

'They suspect grumbling appendicitis, dear. The doctor will take a good look round when they get him on the table, but they don't think it's anything more serious.' The sister pointed to a side room. 'That's where he is. You have a quick word with him while I let theatre staff know they can take him down.'

Patsy peered through a pane of glass before entering. Her mother, face drawn and lacking colour, was reading aloud, one hand holding her bible, the other resting on her father's arm. Her father had his eyes closed; sweat covered his forehead, his face was cuttlefish grey. Her mother stopped reading when Patsy went in and gave a welcoming smile. Her father opened his eyes.

'Ann,' his whisper faint, tremulous, 'will you leave my daughter alone with me for a few minutes, please?'

Patsy wanted to scream, 'Please, don't go, Um Pat,' but could only watch as her mother put down the open bible, withdrew her hand from her father, stood up, and stretched her back. When the door closed, her father beckoned Patsy forward feebly. She forced herself towards him. His hand shot out and seized her wrist in a grip that belied previous signs of weakness.

'Patsy, I may not come through this operation,' the grip on her wrist tightened. 'Forgive me, Patsy for what I have done to you.' The grip was so hard now it hurt, but her father's voice remained pathetically weak, 'Please Patsy, I feel the Lord calling me home. I cannot face him without your forgiveness.'

'Father, of course I forgive you. I have told you over and over again.'

'Then kiss me to show you mean it.'

She hesitated; but what if he were to die? Could she live with herself? She bent down and pecked him on the forehead.

'Patsy if you truly forgive me, give your life to the Lord.'

That was going too far. She remained silent. His whisper shrilled to a shriek. 'Please, Patsy.'

She had to quieten him before her mother returned. 'Father, if the Lord wants me converted then it will happen.'

'Lord, I have sinned,' her father's voice rose still further, 'but please remove this punishment from me.'

Patsy kept her gaze on the window that revealed nothing but a clear blue autumn sky. Orderlies, pulling in a trolley, cut short her ordeal. Her father let go her wrist, took up the bible, and put on a saintly smile.

Her mother returned while the two men were transferring her father.

'Ann, praise the lord that we have the certainty of our Saviour's redemption,' her father chanted, 'If the Lord calls me home, we will meet on the other side.'

He then faced Patsy again. 'Please, Patsy.'

She was not playing his game. 'You'll be back in the ward in no time, father.'

Standing next to her mother, she watched the trolley roll through the theatre doors.

'Oh Patsy, I am so glad you are here,' her mother said. 'Let us pray.'

This, Patsy realised, was not the time to point out the absurdity of attempting to change the mind of an omniscient deity, nor an occasion to flaunt her agnosticism. She sank into a slough of hypocrisy and made an outward show of joining her mother in prayer.

Her father survived his operation. In a twentieth-century hospital, a successful appendicitis operation scarcely warranted the status of miracle, but her mother insisted on attributing her father's recovery purely to the power of prayer. Having supported her mother in prayer for her father's survival Patsy could scarcely refuse to join in thanksgiving.

'Please stay for another couple of days,' her mother pleaded afterwards.

So the next day Patsy was once again at the hospital with her mother. She was cutting the ends of some red carnations that she had bought, while her mother read aloud from the bible. The doctor entered and asked her mother for a word in private. Her father seized the opportunity.

'Those flowers, Patsy, why did you choose scarlet?'

The truth was she had snatched up the first bunch to hand, but it seemed somewhat uncouth to admit to that. While she was searching for a smoother answer her father intoned, '"Yea, though your sins be as scarlet, they shall be as white as snow; though they be red like crimson, they shall be as wool". Oh Patsy, why can't you forgive me? The Lord has forgiven me. You are right, though. My sins remain with you. The sins of the fathers shall be visited upon the children and they shall be cast into utter darkness. Patsy, I don't want you cast into the eternal fires to pay the price of my wrongdoing. Please accept the Lord as your saviour and be cleansed.'

Patsy pressed her lips together, jammed the flowers back into the vase, and headed for the door. 'I am going to make us all a nice pot of tea.'

'Don't worry too much about your father's depression,' her mother told her when she saw her off at the bus station. 'The doctor says it's quite normal after an operation. He should be back to his old self by Christmas. I am so glad you were here, though. I would have found it hard dealing with your father's misery if I had had to do it alone.'

Chapter 48

Dalia walked wearily to work the morning after the Patria disaster, her arms and back stiff and sore. An enormous crowd surrounded the police HQ chanting anti-police slogans and waving banners. This time she had no urge to join the protesters. No one who had seen policemen climbing off the Patria, exhausted after hours of rescue work, would lay the blame at their door - but who were the real culprits?

The British Government? If they had intended to capsize the Patria, why waste money making the boat seaworthy before taking refugees on board?

The Arabs? But they wanted the Jews deported.

Hagana? Had someone assumed, as she would, that if you blew a hole in the bottom of the Patria it would sink gently upright onto the shallow harbour bed?

****

The Saturday after the Patria capsized, Suzanna stepped off the bus determined to ask her brother about his friend's role in the tragedy. Dusk had fallen. Jews surged into the street, blocking traffic, hoisting banners proclaiming,

MURDERERS WILL NOT DRIVE US FROM THE PROMISED LAND

The glances they directed at her were now hostile rather than indifferent, the shoves actively aggressive.

She was almost relieved to see Habib striding to meet her, although not looking forward to confronting him with her question.

'Wretched people!' Before we know it, we'll be a minority in our own country. Are you all right, Suzanna? You must ask Mrs Shepard to let you phone before you leave. Then I can meet you at the bus stop.'

She plunged in. 'Habib, was your friend, Ahmed al-Zeid, responsible for what happened to the Patria?'

Habib stopped mid-stride and viewed her with astonishment. 'My brother Ahmed!' he exclaimed, 'No! Never. He has no quarrel with Jews. He fights the British government, and anyone else imposing western notions of nation states and monarchies on Arab countries, but he claims there is living room in Palestine for all the children of Abraham, regardless of the way they choose to worship the one true God. I cannot follow his reasoning, but then I never went to college.'

'Have you any idea of who did blow up the Patria?' Suzanna asked. 'Was it another of the Mufti's bands?'

'No,' Habib answered, 'They would have boasted about it. My guess is it was the Jews themselves. Their leaders are evil devils.'

Suzanna relaxed. If Habib's friend had been responsible for the senseless killing of women and children, she would have had to refuse to be a go-between, however much that would have upset her brother. She wondered when and if they would start making use of her.

****

Mr Shepard brought her the first letter bearing an Iraqi stamp the next Monday evening. Her whole body tensed when she recognised Ahmed al-Zeid's handwriting.

Mrs Shepard asked, 'Who's writing to you from Iraq then?'

Suzanna made a performance of tearing open the envelope, pulling out the letter, skimming through it and saying casually, 'It's from a cousin who married an Iraqi last month. She seems lonely, poor thing. She has never been away from home before.'

She tucked the letter into the pocket of her apron and later hid it under her mattress. It remained uncomfortably in her thoughts until she delivered it to Habib the following Saturday.

****

Beth was full of the Patria when Patsy returned to the flat.

'So many children drowned, Patsy, and two British policemen as well. Who could have done something so dreadful?'

Patsy was ashamed. Immersed in her own affairs, she had ignored this tragedy. She determined to put her own problems into a global perspective and think of others more, a hard resolution to keep when her mother phoned.

Her family were not in the habit of making expensive long distance telephone calls merely to chat, so she knew her mother must be at the end of her tether when it was clear that she had no pressing business to communicate.

'Your father's depression, dear, it's getting worse not better. I can't understand it and the doctors can't explain it. I shall be so glad to see you at Christmas.'

Patsy lay in bed afterwards unable to sleep; for the first time in her life, not looking forward to Christmas. An awful thought occurred. Life would be so much easier now if her father had died on the operating table. She stretched out rigid, hating herself. What sort of person wished their father dead?

She sat up, switched on her bedside lamp, took out the letter from Ahmed, and fantasised about spending her life married to him and never having to see her father again.

Chapter 49

Patsy was typing up a report on a man arrested while attempting to smuggle two bags of rice into Syria, when Peter Monteith entered the office. Instead of a bundle of papers, he carried a bunch of yellow carnations.

She waited for him to sympathise with her on her father's illness, but instead he walked over to Dalia's desk and laid the flowers there. She watched his lips murmur something infuriatingly inaudible. Could he possibly be dating an unbeliever? Had he left the Second Chosen? She joined Leila in gently ribbing Dalia as soon as he had left.

****

Dalia took the carnations with her when she went to meet Shimon. He eyed the flowers in their expensive florists' gift-wrap and raised his eyebrows.

In provocative mood, after the baiting her colleagues had given her, Dalia shrugged. 'Just a present from my new boyfriend, a British police officer.'

Infuriatingly Shimon appeared unperturbed. 'My, but you've done well, little cousin. You will soon be our most effective agent.'

She wanted to throw the coffee pot at him but instead hurled a question. 'And what has happened to the information I have already passed on? Did Hagana use it to capsize the Patria and kill those children?'

Shimon seemed glad of an excuse to quarrel. 'That balagan occurred in spite of your information, Madam, not because of it.' He paused, then spat out; 'You're showing your origins, Dalia Leitner. Nu, I have been treating you like a sabra, and you're nothing but a displaced German Jew.'

He jumped up, flung money on the tab, and walked out.

The next two evenings Dalia kept to her room trying to forget her misery by writing stories. She was typing a paragraph, where the despised newcomer heroine rides across the desert with blazing guns to rescue her lover from a marauding band of Bedouin, when Giza banged on the bedroom door. 'Dalia, telephone.'

She rushed downstairs, willing it to be Shimon.

'My mother's sent you a cake,' - the code for an emergency meeting.

She forced words through excited lips, 'I'll fetch it right away.'

She almost danced down the road, but when she reached the cafe, Shimon was at his most professional. 'That other boat, the one in quarantine,' he asked, without preamble, 'what do you know about it?'

'The passengers are to be kept in Athlit until the authorities find another boat.'

Shimon nodded but said nothing. She noticed a peculiar gleam in his eyes and fidgeted, uncomfortable.

'Aren't you going to congratulate me?' he asked at last.

Congratulate him? What on? She opened her eyes wide. 'Uri? You haven't managed to free...?'

Shimon's expression changed. 'Sadly, no.'

Another silence, then his lip twisted to one side. 'Nu, you obviously don't keep in contact with your family as efficiently as with the British police? You have not received a phone call from your mother, yet? Mine phoned her straight away.'

'What are you talking about?'

'My engagement.'

Her stomach lurched. 'Engagement?' Then, 'When did it happen?'

Shimon laughed. 'You make it sound like a nasty accident. Yael has done me the honour of accepting my proposal.'

From deep inside she found the strength to fake a smile. 'Congratulations, and who is this Yael?'

Whoever she was, she wanted to boil her in hot oil before throwing her from the top of a cliff.

'The sabra my mother has been nagging me to marry ever since I left Technion. You will come to my engagement party, won't you? Your parents are driving down.'

'Of course.'

She would make sure that plague, dysentery or influenza incapacitated her first, preferably all three. She managed to add the appropriate words. 'Well, I hope you will both be very happy,' then glanced pointedly at her watch. 'If there is no more business, I'll be on my way. I do have a social life of my own.'

'How could I forget? However, there is something. Hagana are pulling me out of Aliyah Beth. You will have a new agent, Aaron Schmidt. I need to fill you in on your cover story before he contacts you. Are you free Thursday evening? I'll take you to a concert and supply you with the details.'

Since it was Aliyah Beth business, she nodded curtly. 'Right, let me know the time and place,' and walked off.

Chapter 50

Patsy and Beth were listening to a live Dvorak concert on the wireless.

'I do envy you having parents so near that you can spend Christmas with them,' Beth said.

'I'll only have two days,' Patsy replied and refrained from adding, thank goodness. 'Which reminds me,' she continued, 'Do you want me to sit for you New Year's Eve?' She would have no compunction in turning down an invitation she had received, if Beth needed her.

'That's sweet of you, but Bertie's men have decided to see the year in at that nightclub on Mt Carmel. He has to keep an eye on his squad, you know. He's promised to make it up to me later, and we'll certainly book you for that. You don't know how grateful I am to you already; not only for allowing Bertie and me an evening out every week, but for keeping me company so many evenings, and passing on the gossip. I don't feel nearly so cut off now as I did. It was really horrible after all my friends sailed for South Africa.'

'Why didn't you go with them?'

'Bertie wanted me to go. Said he would be happier if he wasn't constantly worrying about me and the boy, but when I looked at South Africa on the globe and saw I'd be even further from my parents than I am here, I felt I would never see them again, and besides...'

Beth stopped, picked up her knitting, began counting stitches, then looked up, and said cheerfully, 'Time to put on the kettle.'

****

In the concert hall, Dalia immersed herself in the exuberance and nostalgia of Dvorak's music and tried to forget that Shimon was in the seat next to her.

In the interval, he took her to a secluded corner of the bar.

'The cover story,' he said, as he set down two glasses of chilled wine and leaned towards her, 'is that your new agent Aaron Schmidt is trying to buy your orange grove, but you don't want to sell. His code for setting up a meeting will be 'I have a new proposition.' You will meet him in the same café you met me. Your emergency telephone number will remain the same.'

When the concert ended they left the building together. Outside on the pavement, as they said their farewells, Shimon placed his hands on her shoulders and looked into her eyes. 'As an engaged man I shouldn't be saying this, but I wish things had turned out differently. We have so much in common.'

He kissed the top of her head, dropped his hands, and walked off.

Chapter 51

'Miss Leitner, I was wondering...'

Inspector Monteith, in mufti, dark gabardine over grey flannels, accosted Dalia after work. Waiting for him to finish his sentence, she watched his face turn pomegranate red. Her own breathing quickened.

'That is, - would you care to accompany me to the cinema tomorrow evening? We would, I mean, there is a repeat showing of "The Story of Louis Pasteur." I missed it first time round.'

'Thank you, Inspector Monteith,' she began, 'I have seen it already.' Then the part of her, that belonged to Aliyah Beth, brushed aside common sense and another voice from deep inside whispered, here's how to show that rat Shimon Mabovitch that I can do without him, so she continued in a rush, 'but it is really worth seeing again.'

'What time shall I meet you, Miss Leitner? Would it be more convenient to have a meal beforehand?'

'That would be easier,' she said, conveniently overlooking the early supper that Giza Barat cheerfully laid on for anyone needing it.

She entered her digs, fizzing with guilty excitement. Running upstairs, she began to worry. Supposing the inspector ordered something non-kosher like pork or prawns or, just as bad, mixed dairy and meat dishes in the same meal? By the time she had hung up her coat, she was wondering what her mother would say. Perhaps best not to tell her, but she wouldn't put it past Giza to warn her.

En route to supper, she found a letter addressed to her on the hall table. She recognised Shimon's handwriting and ripped it open only to find a brief note saying that the man interested in buying her orange groves had been called away on business, and would be out of Haifa until January.

She had the note in her hand when she asked Giza for a late key for the following evening.

Giza Barat looked pointedly at the letter.

'From my cousin,' Dalia told her.

Giza looked reassured.

****

Dalia rushed home after work. She was straightening her stocking seams for the fourteenth time when Giza knocked on her door. 'Your cousin is here.'

Shimon? Now? With Inspector Monteith due any minute? Could he have come to tell her his engagement was a joke? She rushed downstairs but jolted to a halt when she saw Inspector Monteith staring up in admiration. 'Whew, Miss Leitner you look wonderful.'

She clenched her fists and forced a smile.

The inspector took her by the arm. 'I've booked in at a kosher restaurant just in case you were worried.'

Giza came through the hall and gave him an approving look. 'Give my love to your mother,' she said in Hebrew.

The inspector looked puzzled but replied readily enough in Hebrew, 'I will.' Outside, he asked, 'What did your landlady mean?'

'Ah, just an old Jewish greeting,' Dalia replied. She flung back her shoulders. Forget Shimon, she told herself, just enjoy the evening.

In the restaurant, renowned for the excellence of its cellar, Inspector Monteith waved the wine list away. 'Orange juice?' he asked.

So, no attempt to get her drunk as a prelude to seduction?

'No, not orange juice, 7-up, please.'

The inspector ordered fresh orange juice for himself. 'One of Palestine's greatest luxuries,' he said, lifting his glass with its frothy cap.

Dalia gave a wry smile. 'I am sick of oranges. We can't export them because of this war, so my parents send me back to Haifa with a sack every week.'

'Your parents grow oranges? I thought they were refugees.'

That led to her explaining how her father, a successful architect, had turned to farming when they left Germany. Throughout the hors d'oeuvre of pickled herring, she enlarged on her family's way of life but when the waiter brought their beef braised with onions she asked, 'What made you come to Palestine, Peter?' and wondered at what point in their conversation they had become on first name terms.

'Jobs were difficult to find during the depression. Anyway I've always wanted to travel.'

'Do you ever think of going home?'

'I did once.' Peter's fingers knotted his napkin. 'When I met a girl, on furlough.'

'What was she like?'

He smiled then, as if pleased that she had asked. 'The sweetest girl you could imagine. Her name was Penelope. She was an actress.' He pulled the knot out of his napkin, tugged the ends as far apart as they would go. 'My parents disapproved of her job, and my mother made no attempt to hide her feelings.' He crumpled the napkin in one hand. 'Oh Dalia, I have wanted to talk about Penelope for so long. It's something you can't talk about to a chap. You don't mind my talking about her, do you?'

Since this Penelope was obviously not still around, she said, 'No, please go on.'

'Penelope and I became engaged despite my mother's disapproval. I started applying for jobs in England, but when my mother said she wouldn't come to our wedding, Penelope suggested that I return to Palestine without her.' He dropped the napkin on the table and gripped his hands together. 'She promised to join me out here in six months, hoping that would give her time to persuade my parents to come out for a spring wedding, then took a short contract with a touring company.'

He went silent once more.

'What happened?'

'Penelope got soaked walking through a storm back to unheated digs, caught pneumonia, and didn't pull through.' He lowered his gaze to his lap.

Dalia had been expecting to commiserate with him on a 'Dear John' letter. His answer, as sad as it was unexpected, hit her hard. She searched for a suitable response.

Peter spoke again, 'You know, Dalia, for a long time I felt nothing was worthwhile. Then I met a civilian, Jim Shepard. It altered my whole life. I became Born Again in the Blood of the Lamb.'

'So you're more settled now?' She felt her cheeks burn as she heard the vapid words, but Peter's face softened. He smiled. 'Yes, I know the joy of the Lord.' He paused. The smile became lop-sided. 'There is one drawback. Second Chosen women are great matchmakers. I like talking to girls, just talking, they are so understanding, but I can't chat to a British girl without seeing wedding bells in her mother's eyes. That is why I felt I could ask you out, Dalia. You're not only kind, but being Jewish, your parents won't want you to marry me.'

Dalia clenched her fists, then forcing herself back into Aliyah Beth mode, smiled sweetly, gazed at Peter's beautiful full-lipped face and listened as if enraptured, not that she learnt anything useful to take back to Aliyah Beth.

After the film, Peter walked her back to her digs, took her hand, and shook it gently. 'Thank you for coming with me this evening, Dalia. I haven't enjoyed an evening out like this since...' He stopped, then asked, 'Do you think we could do it again next week?'

Could a good Aliyah Beth agent pass up that offer? Her anger at his assumption about her parents did not abate though. Her father could not object to her dating Peter when his own mother had married a gentile. The more she brooded, the more Peter's remark presented a challenge. She determined to make him see her as a full-blooded attractive woman and aimed at persuading him to invite her to the New Year Party on Mount Carmel.

She didn't mind in the least when Patsy, two places behind them in the cinema queue the following week, waved at them.

****

Patsy had been surprised to see Dalia and Peter together in the cinema queue. After Leila told had her of Dalia's encounter with Peter at the docks, she had assumed the flowers were just a polite thank you, and had dismissed station gossip that Peter and Dalia were dating. Now she wasn't so sure.

While sorting new files onto the knitting needles, during her daily stint in the superintendent's office, she wondered how smoothly an affair like that would go. A new girlfriend could only do Peter good, but the Second Chosen would make Peter's life hell if they discovered he was going out with an unbeliever, and Dalia could easily get hurt in the ensuing emotional tug of war.

The superintendent interrupted her thoughts. 'Miss Quigley, I need to speak to you?' He beckoned her over and pointed to a chair in front of his desk. When she was seated, he continued, 'I am about to do something that goes very much against the grain but, I can assure you, I am only acting for the safety of the realm.'

Patsy felt a thumping in her chest, her throat tightened, as she wondered who had seen her meeting with Ahmed. Worse still, had someone ferreted through her bag and read his proposal?

'Sir?' She had difficulty getting out even that one word.

The superintendent's face became a darker shade of red. 'Miss Quigley, in your considered opinion has a relationship developed between Miss Leitner and Inspector Monteith?'

So this was not about her, but she found it difficult to believe that the superintendent was asking her to snitch on a colleague. She kept her mouth closed, and stared at the floor.

The superintendent waited, and then said, 'Very well, Miss Quigley, I shall take your silence as an affirmative.'

****

Dalia felt she was fighting a losing battle. In the ice cream break, she had concentrated on subtly nudging Peter to the point of asking her to the New Year party but he had remained infuriatingly unresponsive. Now, taking her back to her digs, he was silent. She wondered if he was worrying about the effect of station gossip on his career.

When they reached her digs, Peter shook her hand as usual and thanked her for a pleasant evening. She turned to go in, and fiddled in her bag for her key. Suddenly Peter was touching her, pulling her towards him, turning her round and kissing her hard on the lips. Her body stiffened in surprise. Before she had recovered sufficiently to respond properly, he had released her, apologising profusely, his face almost purple with embarrassment, and then he loped off.

She stared after him, puzzled. Even if she hadn't responded as quickly as she would have done if she had had warning, she hadn't exactly fought him off, so why had he run away?

She groped her way upstairs, too shaken to hunt for the light switch, her body now aroused and screaming that she wanted Peter.

Chapter 52

2.30pm on Christmas Eve. Slightly bemused, Dalia watched British police officers pour into the Office, waving bottles of Gold Star and local wine. Someone pressed a glass of luke-warm white wine into her hand, while another police officer hung mistletoe from the light bulb. Dalia watched him drag Patsy under it and kiss her to a chorus of cheers. She finished her wine and someone immediately refilled her glass. Someone else took her by the hand, and begged her to go to the party on Carmel with him. She drank her wine while listening.

Peter entered the room. Ignoring the man by her, he seized her wrist and steered her through the door. Overcome by surprise, she made no resistance.

'Dalia,' Peter's words spurted like steam from an overheated radiator, 'I am so ashamed about last night. If only you weren't so beautiful. I promise - nothing like that will happen - ever again. Please don't stop going to the pictures with me. I need you.'

She exploded with anger. 'Your needs, your feelings!' she shouted.

Peter let go of her arm and stepped back a pace. She placed her glass on a ledge beneath a notice board and put her hands on her hips. 'Don't my feelings matter?'

Peter looked startled. 'I'm trying to apologise...'

She broke him off. 'For the wrong thing. It's not proprieties I'm talking about, Peter; it's my feelings.'

She could see he did not understand, and stamped her foot.

'Your feelings?' Peter tried tentatively.

'Yes!' Dalia yelled, 'I have feelings too.'

She beat her fists on her chest.

Peter said slowly, 'You mean - you feel something for me?'

She flushed. Peter came forward, flung his arms round her, and kissed her. She had the sense to return his kiss this time but to her annoyance, once again he released her without warning. He placed his hands on the sides of his head.

'No, Dalia,' his voice almost a moan, 'this isn't the path the Lord has chosen. The Lord owns my life now, Dalia. I can't be unequally yoked.'

'Who said anything about yoking?' she retorted, 'I'm only nineteen. Let's just enjoy ourselves.'

He gazed with horrified eyes. 'Oh, Dalia, I am already corrupting you,' then he looked down at the floor. 'Dalia, the Lord has brought us together for his own purposes. If you are the woman He has chosen for me, He will find a way. Meanwhile, I promise to control the lusts of the flesh, but please, remain my friend.'

She had had enough of this. 'Peter, someone has just asked me to go to the New Year's Party on Carmel. I haven't given him an answer him yet. Do you want to take me?'

'Dalia, Second Chosen don't do things like that.'

She turned and walked back to the office.

'Dalia,' Peter pleaded from behind her, 'Don't go, please. We will go out to dinner instead.'

He seized her arm.

'H-hmm,' a cough behind had them springing apart. Inspector Sutton stood there, back straighter than ever, chin tilted high. 'Inspector Monteith, there is an urgent matter I must discuss with you.'

Dalia escaped back to the typing room, forcing herself not to cry. She could almost smell Leila and Patsy's curiosity.

'So is Inspector Monteith taking you to the Carmel party?' Leila whispered.

She snapped, 'No,' then clasped her hands together and took a deep breath, before continuing in a calmer tone, 'Apparently his religion does not allow him to go to nightclubs.'

Patsy was sympathetic. 'I am afraid the Second Chosen have their claws well and truly into Peter, Dalia. Just make sure they don't get you, too.'

'They won't,' she answered, and scanned the room for the young man who had been asking her to the dance, but he was no longer there.

She collected her coat and went outside to clear her head and wait for her father. It was raining but getting wet was preferable to company.

Chapter 53

The bus was an express, taking people to Midnight Mass in Bethlehem but Patsy had persuaded the driver to let her off outside the station in Jerusalem.

She spent the first part of the journey staring out at pouring rain and resenting having to leave the office party early. As they climbed the Seven Sisters Road, the rain cleared, her mood changed. Before long, she was singing carols with the other passengers.

When the bus stopped in Jerusalem, Christmas sentimentality had worked its magic. The weather up here was crisp and cold. She walked to the German Colony under a sky blazing with stars, breathing frosty air and her feet cracked on ice-frilled puddles. Her mother, hovering close to the pavement, under an arched gateway, decorated with conifer foliage and silver paper stars, flung her arms round her. 'Oh Patsy, it's so good to see you.'

Inside the house, a Christmas tree, adorned with all the baubles she remembered from childhood, took up almost half the floor space. Smells of baking and traditional Christmas Eve giblet soup drifted in from the kitchen.

How much harsher her childhood would have been, Patsy reflected, if her parents had been consistent in their beliefs and practices. Throughout childhood, she had enjoyed Christmas dinners, Christmas trees, and Christmas presents, accepting without question that she should not mention these in the presence of Armenian and Arab Saints who fulminated against heathen western practices at every Sharing during December.

She had never dared question her parents about their paradoxical behaviour. If she had, she was certain her father would have stripped the tree, thrown the turkey into the dustbin, and confessed the error of his ways in loud prayer.

Nostalgia overwhelmed her so she even managed to submit graciously to her father's kiss. She didn't relent enough, though, to indulge him with his favourite nickname 'Abu Pat'.

'How are you keeping, father?'

Her mother answered for him, 'He went back to work far too soon, Patsy. He'll have a breakdown if he doesn't ease off. I keep telling him.'

'Can't slack off,' her father retorted, 'there's a war on. Good roads are the key to military success.'

'Well, you won't be much use to the war effort, dead,' her mother flung back, before retreating to the kitchen to fetch bowls of soup and a platter of hot bread rolls.

****

For the second year running, the Leitners and the Cohens combined forces for Hanukah so Dalia stood in the Cohen's kitchen rolling pastry and cutting it with the special Hanukah cutters her mother had inherited from her grandmother, feeling, as she did so, that she was reshaping her life and pressing it back into family mode.

Her mother, so much happier now the British had moved Uri to a farm prison and allowed her to visit more frequently, babbled on as she diced vegetables. 'Nu, this hard labour our boys are doing at that research station, Uri says the work is easier than here, plus he's picked up so many useful tips yet. He will try them on our fields when the government sees fit to release him.'

'Ai-ee,' she continued, turning to Miriam Cohen and Ruth, 'if only we could hear from your Josh.'

A gust of cold air and a loud shalom interrupted the conversation, and there was Josh himself in the kitchen sporting sergeant's stripes on his arm and sunburn on his face. Miriam gave an amazed shriek and hung round his neck weeping. 'Where have you been? Why didn't you write?'

'You didn't get my letter? My unit's being sent to the desert so I've got this leave.' He sat down on a chair. 'You don't know how good it feels to be home.'

His mother sat him down with a cup of coffee and a gigantic wedge of coffee cake, then put him through the third degree about his treatment by the army.

'Yes,' Josh replied, 'we were allowed to keep Seder. No, we weren't forced to eat pork. Yes, they did give us enough blankets.' He did admit to disappointment with the Pioneering Corps. 'We weren't proper soldiers; they only trained us for non-combatant duties, like a bunch of conchies.'

'Did you go to France?'

'Yes...'

'Ai-ee I knew it. I told you, Trudi. When they had that Dunkirk thing, I said my son is there. Such a close bond I have. I knew it.'

'My luck turned in England,' Josh said, 'they let me join the Commandos.'

'Ai-ee,' his mother looked as if she was going to faint, 'they are deliberately trying to kill you, because you are a good Jewish boy?'

'Nu, Miriam!' Dalia watched her mother lay a hand on her friend's shoulder, 'Leave your boy be. He is here and alive. Your

Ruth will be here soon. See, the sun is low in the sky already and we have not cleared away.'

Just before dusk, Dalia stood next to her mother in the living room, watching Ruth proudly holding her brother's menorah, while Rav Cohen chanted traditional Hanukah prayers and blessings. The table in front of them, covered in white damask, gleamed with polished glasses and cutlery.

The aroma of vegetable soup and traditional potato latkes, part of every Hanukah Dalia could remember wafted in from the kitchen. Her thoughts turned to Uri. Two years since she had held his menorah at Hanukah, nearly nine years still to go before his release.

****

British Christmas again. Suzanna carried in the large olive logs set aside for this day, swept yesterday's ashes from the hearth, and lit the fire with the help of dried orange peel. She switched on the Christmas tree lights. The lounge looked properly festive and she felt a glow of satisfaction.

Before pumping the day's water, she went back to her room to ask the Holy Mother to keep the Shepards from quarrelling in front of the children for just this one day.

Her prayers worked. Evie and Clare shouted with joy and surprise as they unwrapped the homemade presents created with care.

Just once, when the children were at the bottom of the garden, noisily following a trail Mr Shepard had marked out with sticks and boiled sweets, Mrs Shepard wiped her eyes and whispered, 'How Renshaw would have loved this.'

Overall, though, it had not been so hard to pretend to be happy this year.

Chapter 54

Boxing Day opened wet and blustery. Patsy spent a lazy morning reading and chatting in front of the fire.

While her father was taking an afternoon nap, the sky cleared. Her mother looked up from her novel. 'Do you fancy doing some sketching, Patsy? I've been taking driving lessons recently. We could go down to Rachael's Tomb. I have a spare pad and charcoal, if you need them.'

They drove up the Bethlehem Road at a stately 25 miles an hour, parked on the verge and scrambled over a low drystone wall, carrying their easels.

Her mother picked as her subject a particularly gnarled olive tree beneath which a tethered goat bleated and strained at its rope. Patsy opted for the simpler lines of the white domed building featured on the most common of the Palestinian stamps. It was something she could post on to Tim if she did it well. She shared a rock with her mother and they chatted companionably as they worked. Her mother confided how worried she still was about her father's bouts of depression.

'He was like this once before when I lost your baby brother, do you remember, dear?'

Did she remember? Patsy hoped her face did not reveal the depth of her memory. She prevaricated, 'Um Pat, you were in hospital most of the time I was home.'

'So I was. That's why I have such a dim memory of you in Haifa that summer. It must have been lonely for you, what with your father being at work all day, and up at the hospital all evening. No wonder you refused to come home for the summer after that.'

Patsy's charcoal snapped as she attempted the curved roof of the sepulchre.

'I don't suppose you noticed anything unusual in your father's behaviour then?' Her mother went on, 'Such a proud man, he would take good care to keep up appearances.'

Patsy kept her eyes on her drawing.

'I didn't want to worry you at the time, after all you were still only a child and it wasn't the sort of thing you put in letters, but your father had a complete break down after you left. It was almost six months before he returned to normal. I don't want that to happen again. I just wish he would take things easy.'

Patsy forced a response, 'What does the doctor say?'

'That he should not have gone back to work so soon, but we all know that, and of course your father refuses to follow his advice.

Says there will be plenty of time to sit back once we have won the war.' Her mother looked at her watch, 'Talking of time, we had better get back.'

After tea, her father asked Patsy to bring her drawing into his study so he could comment on it. Her mother looked so relieved to see her father displaying an interest that she couldn't very well refuse.

Her father shut the study door behind them, complaining loudly of draughts and held her picture to the light. He exclaimed, 'A whited sepulchre, beautiful outside but full of corruption within. That's why you drew it, isn't it, because that's what you think of me, a whited sepulchre?' He screwed the drawing into a ball and threw it on the floor. Patsy walked out of the room without commenting.

****

Dalia spent most of the day after Hanukah helping her father repair the cattle shed roof, damaged in the previous night's storm. She managed a few minutes alone with Ruth just before returning to Haifa and confided some of the tangled details of her involvement with Inspector Monteith, but realised, while talking, that, without any mention of Aliyah Beth, she couldn't explain properly.

Hearing only half the story, Ruth adopted a robust approach. 'You've done your best to ditch him. If he doesn't take the hint, drop him harder. Like your mother would say, he is only getting in the way of you finding a good Jewish boy.'

Dalia knew that already. What she needed was something that would stiffen her will power next time she saw Peter.

It turned out to be easier than she thought. She found him standing on the pavement when she jumped out of her father's car clutching her weekly sack of oranges.

'Dalia,' he said, 'I had to see you. I have an apology to make. I know I promised to take you out to dinner on New Year's Eve, but I can't. Jim, the friend I told you about, had to go abroad unexpectedly. He has asked me to spend New Year with his family. After all he and his wife have done for me, I couldn't say no.'

Dalia dug her nails into her palms, and worked at keeping her voice level. 'That's all right, Peter, I have made my own arrangements. I hope you enjoy yourself.' She inserted her key into the lock of the lodging house door.

From behind, she heard Peter say, 'I'd enjoy myself so much more with you, Dalia.'

She turned the key. 'Goodnight, Peter.'

****

Despite the spectacular storms of the previous night, the continuing cold wind, and sharp showers, Suzanna heard Mr Shepard bullying his family into the traditional Boxing Day ramble.

'Clare's not strong enough,' Mrs Shepard argued.

'Then she needs toughening up.'

'Can I stay behind too?' Evie asked.

'No. What's the matter with this family? No guts the lot of you.'

These British and their mad traditions, Suzanna reflected, as she stood on the veranda waving them all goodbye. She planned to sit by the fire in the lounge knitting baby bootees and reading her English set books.

The telephone rang. She ran inside. The caller asked for Mr Shepard.

'You'll have to ring back tonight,' she said, 'He's just left on a long walk.'

'Then run and fetch him back. Tell him its Colonel Forster here and it's urgent.'

'I'll try.'

She raced outside. The Shepards had only walked as far as the gate. Clare had fallen over and Mrs Shepard was trying to comfort her while haranguing her husband. Suzanna delivered the message.

Mrs Shepard, originally so set against the expedition, called to her husband, already halfway down the path, 'Jimmy, don't go back. They have no right to call you up on Boxing Day. You're a civilian.'

Mr Shepard, flung over his shoulder, 'Sorry, my dear. There's a war on, remember.'

Mrs Shepard, with Clare held close, leant against the gate, lips pressed together, eyes narrowed in anger. Evie pulled a book out of her rucksack, settled against a tree trunk. Suzanna didn't dare return to the house in case Mrs Shepard suspected her of eavesdropping. She wished she had put on a coat.

Mr Shepard returned. 'Addy, they are sending a car to pick me up in a few minutes. Carry on without me.'

Mrs Shepard drew herself erect. 'I most certainly will not, Jimmy, my boy. War or no war, they should have left you alone on Boxing Day.' She handed her rucksack to Suzanna. 'Put that away for me. Come on children, we're going back.'

That was the end of Suzanna's quiet day. Mrs Shepard had her cleaning out cupboards and polishing surfaces until late in the evening. She retired exhausted to her cubicle.

While saying her prayers, she heard Mr Shepard return, and Mrs Shepard initiate a shouting match but she was so tired even their noisy quarrel couldn't keep her awake.

****

A piercing scream woke Suzanna. She parted her curtains, saw a light in the girls' bedroom, and without waiting to sling on her dressing gown, ran across.

Evie stood in the middle of the bedroom, blood dripping from her finger. Clare sat on her bed wailing.

'What happened?'

'A mouse bit my finger,' Evie said between sobs.

A mouse? Mice carried rabies, or so Suzanna's mother had claimed. She dropped onto her knees and sucked at Evie's finger, spitting the blood onto the mound of cake crumbs that had appeared mysteriously at the foot of Evie's bed. Clare stopped keening to stare in fascination. Suzanna sucked and spat repeatedly. In between, she shouted, 'Clare, get your mother, quickly.'

She heard Clare, on the veranda, thumping on her parents' bedroom door. Mr Shepard entered as she was spitting on the floor for the fifth time.

'I got bitten by a mouse, Daddy,' Evie explained almost proudly now.

Suzanna applied her mouth to the finger once more.

'Well done, Suzanna,' Mr Shepard said.

Mrs Shepard came in armed with iodine and took over Evie's finger. 'Go and get your dressing gown on, Suzanna, and then fetch a mop.'

'That settles it, Jimmy,' Suzanna heard Mrs Shepard say on her return, 'While you are away, the girls and I sleep in the lounge.'

So another tiring day, this time spent heaving furniture from one room to another. When Suzanna asked why they were changing rooms, Mrs Shepard explained that she needed to be in the main building to hear the phone.

'Every minute will count if the Germans invade. There will be no one here but me to take responsibility.'

'And what will happen to me?' Suzanna asked.

'If you have any sense, you'll run to your brother's. You'll be safer there.'

The huge Christmas tree would not fit into the smaller room so Mrs Shepard ordered the tearful children to remove the decorations and pack them away.

By late evening, the former lounge was a bleak dormitory and Mr and Mrs Shepard's old bedroom transformed into a snug lounge.

Chapter 55

The new lodger, Golda, who Dalia already knew from secretarial school, was the only one of her fellow lodgers going out that New Year's Eve. The rest were wary of drunken soldiers on the streets.

At breakfast the day before New Year's Eve, Giza surprised everyone by announcing that she would play the piano for an impromptu concert the next evening, so long as everyone agreed to put on a turn.

'I wish I could be with you,' Golda said, 'I would enjoy an evening like that far more than the party I'm going to.'

'Nu, why don't you drop that party and stay in then,' Giza suggested.

'Go on, you're a free woman,' one of the other lodgers put in.

'I wish I were.'

'Hey, who was it at Edmonds kept telling us we should run our own lives,' Dalia said.

'This is different,' Golda said, 'I wish I could explain.' She folded her napkin and left the table.

After supper, next evening, the rest of them improvised a stage from dining room tables and set out chairs in a semi-circle.

Most of the acts were light popular songs, but Dalia, plumped up with many cushions, collaborated with the most petite woman in the house to perform a Laurel and Hardy-like skit featuring Fat Hermann Goring and Hitler discussing the failures of their friend Mussolini. She had created it the day before in her lunch hour with enthusiastic help from Leila and Patsy, and was gratified to find her audience choking with laughter.

At midnight, Giza treated them to a small glass of precious pre-war cherry brandy. They drank it, holding up V for victory fingers, and then they conga'd through the house.

When at last she tumbled into bed, Dalia assured herself that she had enjoyed the evening far more than she would have done eating a staid restaurant meal with Peter, so why was she suddenly crying?

****

New Year's Eve, and Patsy sat, one of a group of eight, under the pine trees of the open-air nightclub with only moonlight and cigarette ends for illumination. She pulled her shawl round her in the chilly air and kept a wider than strictly necessary space between herself and the police constable, Douglas, who had invited her. Bottles of Gold Star littered the table, none of them belonging to Patsy. She didn't like beer. Her first glass of warm, vinegary white wine had tasted so awful that she had been drinking Orangino all evening and was consequently experiencing the bored superiority of the sober. She envied Leila with her large family party at a group of tables further away and Dalia who was taking part in an impromptu concert at her digs.

The women, Douglas's three mates had brought with them, were draped over their partners. Patsy had been surprised to find Golda one of them and found it difficult to equate her current tartish behaviour with the dignified woman she knew from the get-togethers at Edmonds. It wasn't as if Golda was drunk either. Patsy had noticed her surreptitiously tipping the contents of her beer bottles onto the grass.

The men had reached the stage of outdoing each other with the coarseness of their lavatory humour. Douglas was obviously regretting inviting a stuck-up bint like herself to the party, but she could not bring herself to join in the puerile conversation. She contrasted these loutish men to Tim. Even at eighteen, she reflected, Tim had been more mature. She wondered where he was now. It was ages since she had heard from him. If only his regiment had been posted to Palestine they could have had fun together tonight, dancing on the polished circle in front of the bar and making proper conversation.

'Care to dance,' Douglas interrupted her thoughts.

She looked at him surprised but on the dance floor realised he was not as drunk as she had assumed.

'I am sorry about my mates,' he said, 'They're not usually as bad as that. I suppose it is their way of reacting to the Patria. Those two British policemen who drowned were pals of ours.'

Once again, Patsy felt ashamed of her own self-absorption.

****

Mrs Shepard was holding a small New Year Party. 'For the children's sake,' she explained to Suzanna.

Inspector Monteith would be there and another police officer, an Inspector Sutton, who often taught musical little Clare to play hymns on the piano, and another friend of Mr Shepard, a Lieutenant McIntyre, Mickey Mouse, as Evie called him because of the stories he told.

Suzanna and the children had adorned the battered food trolley with decorations removed from the Christmas tree, but what could they put on it that would make a special feast? Suzanna placed the remaining half of the Christmas cake in the middle and used the remnants of the last jar of mincemeat to make a dozen mince pies but could find only pickled cucumbers and marmite for sandwich fillers. With difficulty, she persuaded Mrs Shepard to open the tin of salmon stored in the 'emergencies only' cupboard, but felt that still wasn't enough for a special occasion.

She need not have worried. Inspector Monteith brought a tin of ham from the NAAFI, Inspector Sutton arrived with a box of chocolates, and Lieutenant McIntyre presented a beribboned carton of petit fours from Feder's bakery.

At 11 o'clock, Suzanna proudly wheeled the splendid trolley across the veranda to the room that was now the lounge.

An excited Evie ran over to hug her. 'Mickey Mouse brought a paper donkey with him, and we've been sticking its tail on.'

Mrs Shepard sat on the piano stool, eyes sparkling. Suzanna could not remember her mistress looking so happy since Renshaw had died.

'Suzanna, you can stay with us until midnight. We will be singing hymns after eating. I know how much you enjoy hymns.'

Suzanna was so surprised that she didn't know how to respond, especially when Mrs Shepard put an arm round her shoulders and explained to the three men, with the sweetest of smiles, 'Suzanna is like another daughter to me, you must understand. Now, where can you sit, my dear?' she looked round the small room now crammed with the bulky lounge furniture, 'Peter, will you shift up a little to make space?'

Suzanna squashed herself into the corner of the settee where there was just room for her to sit without touching the inspector, but she could feel the warmth of his body crossing the few inches between them. Even through the cloying aroma of Brylcreem, she could smell his masculinity. She sat nibbling at a sandwich and sipping a cup of tea until everyone had finished.

Mrs Shepard waved her down when she started up to clear away. 'Eve will take out the trolley,' she said and made her way to the piano, pushed against the back wall. She sang the words of a hymn, while her hands moved over the keys.

The men and little Clare joined in, but Evie, who, as Mrs Shepard so often said, had a voice like a crow, squirmed on a pouffe, just opening, and closing her mouth silently. Suzanna sympathised. She too was finding it difficult to sing. Her chest had become tight as she thought ahead to midnight and the British custom of clasping hands for Auld Lang Syne. She would have to hold Inspector Monteith's hand. The idea made her knees shake.

At five to twelve, Mrs Shepard left the piano stool and switched on the wireless. Suzanna huddled back into the corner of the settee. Then Evie darted up and dragged her to the other side of the room. So Suzanna welcomed in 1941 holding hands with Evie and Clare as was proper, but when she got to bed she couldn't help wondering what it would have been like holding Inspector Monteith's hand.

Chapter 56

When Patsy returned to work in the New Year, the sight of a gaunt, middle-aged stranger sitting at her desk in the Superintendent's Office aroused her territorial instincts. What right had he, to sit on *her* chair reading cards removed from Operation Knitting Needle without consulting her?

Mrs Jones introduced him. 'This is Sergeant Pinner from CID, Miss Quigley. From now on he will be responsible for collating information for Operation Knitting Needle.'

Sergeant Pinner looked up, 'I will be grateful for your help later, Miss Quigley, but for the moment please leave me to familiarise myself with the work.'

Patsy moved across the floor to Mrs Jones desk before her anger became too obvious. 'Mrs Jones, what's happened to Inspector Monteith?'

'Transferred to the anti-drug squad, Miss Quigley, up near the Syrian border. It's on the bulletin board downstairs.'

Later, en route to the Typing Office, Patsy stopped at the bulletin board where men, in from the last shift, were placing bets on whether Inspector Monteith's transfer would end his fling with a Jewish girl.

So Dalia was the reason for Peter's transfer, Patsy thought, and all for nothing, since Dalia had already lost interest in him. She stifled her guilt about that interview with the superintendent by concentrating on her work, and at lunchtime let off steam by grumbling about the churlish behaviour of Sergeant Pinner.

During the following weeks, she missed having Peter around. Even if he had changed out of all recognition since his fiancée's death, he had been the last member of her fun-loving pre-war crowd still living in Haifa.

Reflecting on all the changes she had experienced since the war started, she realised with a jolt of surprise, that Beth was now her only local British friend. If she were to go completely crazy and accept Ahmed's proposal, how much social life would she really lose?

****

How unlike Shimon could you get, Dalia thought, when she met Aaron Schmidt, a stocky middle-aged man in jacket and pressed trousers, entrepreneur written all over him.

Aaron listened to her report and then said, 'Not much there, Dalia. However, from what Shimon tells me, you are about to infiltrate the British Community. We have reason to believe that Inspector Monteith is an important player in British plans in the event of a German invasion.'

Dalia shook her head. 'Inspector Monteith has been transferred from Jewish Affairs and is now working on drug smuggling. I have heard nothing from him since his transfer and understand that the authorities are actively discouraging his friendship with me.'

She refrained from adding that she had done some discouraging of her own.

'You must work at resuming contact,' Aaron ordered, 'The connection is too important to be let go lightly.'

'Very well,' she replied, but did not mean it.

****

Suzanna was struggling with an essay on Shakespeare's use of rhyme, one from a long list Mrs Shepard had prepared for her the previous autumn when they had discussed that year's curriculum. Her last three essays remained unmarked. Mrs Shepard had told her that, with a war on, she would not be able to help her so much with her work, but that didn't stop her finding time to instruct Inspector Monteith in bible studies.

Not that Suzanna was complaining about the inspector's frequent visits; in fact she lived for them. Whenever Inspector Monteith spoke to her (admittedly not often, just a greeting on arrival or a thank you when she removed a used plate or cup), Suzanna experienced the same peculiar feeling at the base of her stomach, as she often did at the pictures, almost as if she wanted to wee. Sometimes she lay in bed imagining the inspector's arms round her, his lips, those wonderful lips coming down over hers. Her imagination went beyond what she had seen in the pictures, to wicked things no one had ever thought of before. She even imagined his hands, straying down her front, touching her breasts, and she shuddered, knowing there was evil inside her. Night after night, she lay in bed forcing her thoughts onto other things. She concentrated on doubling from the number two, but never passed beyond 8,378,608 before Inspector Monteith crept back into her thoughts, so that she had to start the doubling all over again.

Bringing afternoon tea into the lounge, during a bible study session, became the highlight of her life. She returned to the kitchen each time trembling. If only she had someone she could talk to about her feelings, but she would scandalise both Angelique and her mother if she were to admit how a man, and a British policeman at that, affected her.

Once, when Mrs Shepard was suffering a migraine, Inspector Monteith marched into the kitchen. She was so scared to be alone in the same room as a man that, at first, she did not take in what he was saying.

'May I have a glass of water for Mrs Shepard, please?'

She just stared.

He explained, 'To take with her aspirins.'

The message percolated; she moved to the heavy terra cotta pitcher, but Inspector Monteith was already lifting it for her onto the marble worktop. In doing so, he brushed against her sleeve.

She experienced movement at the pit of her stomach and knew her face had turned bright red. To make matters worse she could see the inspector had noticed her confusion. He was blushing too, apologising profusely, before stepping back to allow her space. The scoop quivered in her hand, as she filled a glass tumbler.

That night she played over the scene repeatedly. The way he had blushed after touching her, she was sure that he was as much in love with her as she was with him.

The next day she found, on the floor under a sofa, a snapshot of the inspector playing word games with the girls on the veranda. She took it back to her room and hid it in a drawer. Sometimes she took it out and kissed it as if it were a holy icon.

****

Dalia found life dreary after New Year until the evening Giza summoned her to the phone. 'Your mother.'

She raced downstairs terrified something had happened to her father. He was getting old now, well over fifty. Old people often had accidents on farms. By the time she picked up the phone, her heart was thumping.

'Dalia, my Dalia,' her mother shouted, 'Guess what. Our Uri is home. The British have let out all our boys. Saturday - we're having a party. You must tell Ruth at once.'

Dalia rushed round to the Nurses' Home only to find Uri had already phoned.

'Isn't it wonderful,' Ruth trotted around her room, unable to sit still, 'He's borrowing your father's car tomorrow. We're going to choose our engagement ring. We'll pick you up after work and take you back to Bereishit.'

Next afternoon outside the Khayet building, a broadly grinning Uri bounded out of the Austin 7. A radiant Ruth sat in the car holding out a left hand decorated with a gold and diamond ring.

Dalia close to tears, although sublimely happy, hugged Uri on the pavement, indifferent to the stares of passing policemen. When she stepped into the car, she hugged Ruth and duly admired the ring.

Halfway to Bereishit, though, she raised her eyebrows when Ruth slid the new ring off her finger and handed it back to Uri, who placed it in a box.

'Uri has to ask my father's permission before we can be really engaged,' Ruth reminded her.

Dalia's stomach gave a little twist. Had she really, as Shimon had accused, been mixing with the British so much she was getting to think like them?

Back home, her mother and Miriam had next evening's engagement party well and truly organised, and were almost ready to light the Shabbat candles. It was the happiest Shabbat Dalia could remember.

As soon as Shabbat finished on Saturday, Dalia and all the other women of the moshav went into frenzy. An hour later her mother stood back in the synagogue, that doubled as a community hall, surveying the tables covered in coffee, chocolate, and vanilla gateaux, 'Nu, you'd never think there was a war on,' she whispered happily.

Her duty done, Dalia snatched a few minutes with her brother and father, while Ruth went off to change into a party frock. She listened to Uri describing the new farming techniques he had learnt in prison. If it were not for Aliyah Beth, she thought, she too would be helping put those techniques into practice. She felt sad knowing that she was already too old to attend the women's farm college where so many of her school friends had gone.

She was catching up with gossip when Rav Cohen summoned Ruth and Uri to the platform. The babble died down. Dalia gazed round at her ex-classmates, as they held up their glasses to toast the couple. They all flaunted boyfriends and engagement rings. Two couples even had wedding rings. Everyone must be wondering what was wrong with her.

As soon as the speeches were over, she left the room. Outside bright stars shone with hardly a flicker. She shivered in her party frock. A cow mooed in one of the byres. In all the excitement, had anyone remembered to milk the animals? She walked briskly across the green.

Inside the cowshed, staring at cows that needed no attention (her father must have seen to them while she was helping with the food), she felt lonelier than she had ever been. In the past, Ruth would have come running after her when she left the synagogue, but not tonight, of course, and perhaps never again.

She gave herself a mental shake - what sort of friend was she - moping like this on Ruth's special night? She returned to join in the horas, forcing a smile broader than anyone else's, kicking her legs higher - but all the time thinking – if only I could speak to Ruth about Peter.

****

Suzanna was putting the children to bed after Evie's birthday party. Clare fell asleep even before she had finished helping her into her nightdress but Evie burst into tears in the middle of her prayers.

Suzanna picked her up and put her on her lap, 'What's the matter, Evie? Didn't you enjoy the party?'

'It was lovely, Suzanna,' Evie managed between sobs, 'But I wanted Daddy to have been here when I got back.'

'Your Baba won't be gone for long,' Suzanna comforted, 'It's not like he's a soldier being sent to foreign countries.'

'But he is,' Evie wailed, 'He's gone right out of Palestine.'

'Only to Cairo, I expect.' Suzanna guessed, while wiping Evie's tear-stained face, 'He often goes there. No need to worry.'

'He's not gone to Cairo.'

Suzanna frowned. 'Where then?'

Evie looked down, 'Daddy said I wasn't to tell.'

'All right then, you needn't,' Suzanna replied, in her best matter of fact voice, although conscious that Habib might consider the information useful.

Evie screwed up her face. 'I don't suppose he meant you.'

'I don't suppose so, either,' Suzanna lied.

Evie whispered in her ear. 'He's gone to Constantinople to put telephones down the chimneys of German generals.'

'How do you know?'

'He told me before he went. He said it was an important secret so he wouldn't be able to draw pictures of it in his letters but I could think of him running across rooftops like a squirrel and laugh, but I don't want to laugh any more. He said he would be back by my birthday and he hasn't.'

Only after she had gone to bed herself did it occur to Suzanna to question why her devious employer had told his daughter about the telephones and the Germans in the first place.

Chapter 57

Suzanna opened the lounge door quietly in case Mrs Shepard and Inspector Monteith were praying. As she entered carrying the tea tray, she overheard Mrs Shepard saying, 'Peter, you must pray to the Lord that he will help you put this girl out of your mind.'

Suzanna squeezed the handles of the tray until her knuckles hurt. What did Mrs Shepard have against her marrying the inspector? She would make the inspector a good wife. How dared her mistress interfere?

As she advanced into the room, she had difficulty preventing herself throwing the tray at her mistress, a restraint made more difficult when Mrs Shepard gave the inspector that warning look she used whenever the children burst into the kitchen, interrupting an adult discussion. She banged the tray onto the tea table uttering no apology for the spilt milk.

Back in the kitchen, she gave real vent to her feelings. She threw a saucepan against the pump so hard that it bounced off and knocked over a colander of shelled peas. While retrieving the peas, she calmed down enough to realise the positive side of the overheard conversation. Inspector Monteith really did love her. It was not all imagination.

From then on Suzanna pleaded with the Holy Mother every night to help Inspector Monteith resist Mrs Shepard's arguments. 'And please send him quickly to my uncle with his proposal.'

****

Dalia was helping her mother in the kitchen when Uri came in after spending the morning with Ruth who was home for a week. Looking rather apprehensive, he announced that he was joining up.

Her mother predictably sprang up and raced round the room, punching the air with her fists. 'Ai-ee. A crazy boy I have for a son. This is what they British do to you in prison? They turn you mad?'

Dalia ran next door out of it. As she had expected, Uri had told Ruth his decision before announcing it to his family.

Ruth defended her fiancé. 'He is doing it for Eretz Israel, Dalia. The Agency asked him to join a special unit. He won't be just a non-combatant like poor Josh when he started out. I am so proud of Uri, putting his duty before his own grievances.'

Despite her protestations, Dalia noticed Ruth's eyes were red.

'My mother, of course, is furious,' Ruth added.

'She can't be as angry as mine,' Dalia assured her.

'Dalia,' a tense Miriam Cohen put her head round Ruth's bedroom door, 'Your father is ready to take you back. Perhaps you can make him talk sense into that Uri of yours?'

Ruth raised her eyebrows. 'Nu, you're going earlier than usual.'

Dalia gave a wry smile. 'I imagine Abba wants some peace.'

On the way to Haifa, her father talked of everything except Uri's decision to enlist. Dalia stood waving to him when he had dropped her off, and hoped her mother had calmed down before he returned home.

About an hour later Giza knocked on her bedroom door. 'Your cousin is downstairs and wants to speak to you.'

She raced down but, as she should have guessed, she found Peter standing in the hall.

'I have been so wanting to see you, Dalia, but I couldn't get over. I have had to keep an eye on Addy Shepard in between chasing hashish smugglers.'

'I would have thought hashish smuggling was the least of British worries,' she snapped, and instantly realised two things. One, she had lost an opportunity to spout the speech prepared against this eventuality, and two, Peter had her by the elbow and was steering her through the door.

'With the Axis having recruited the regular smugglers as couriers, my new work is very much part of the war effort,' Peter replied.

'Where are we going?' she asked, 'It's nearly Giza's locking up time.'

'To a café. I won't keep you long, but I have to talk to you.'

'Make it the nearest café, then.'

They crossed the road to the local café half full with men engrossed in chess.

Dalia waited until they had sat down before starting on her prepared speech. 'Peter, I have been thinking hard about this. We should stop seeing each other.'

Peter pulled back in his chair, a hurt look in his eyes. 'But why?'

'For one thing you have no time for me, if you have to see Mrs Shepard so often.'

Peter's forehead creased, 'Oh Dalia, you don't understand.' He checked the empty tables round them, then lowered his voice, 'Listen, this is all supposed to be a bit hush-hush, so don't tell anyone. Jim went to Sofia on some sort of special mission, and Addy has not heard from him since. It's only her faith that is keeping her going.'

She was working out whether this snippet of information was relevant to Aliyah Beth, when Peter snatched up her hand and gazed into her eyes. Her mind told her she should pull away.

'Dalia, I've been missing you so much. I want you more than anything in the world. If only we could be married.'

'Peter,' she began her resolve shattering, 'perhaps...'

'I am being torn apart, Dalia, I want so much to marry you, but I can't until you find the Lord.'

Suddenly it was easy to snatch back her hand. She rested her chin on it, looked away while she talked. 'I cannot become a Christian, Peter. I would marry you, though, if you promised that our children would be brought up Jews.'

'But I can't be unequally yoked,' Peter jerked out the words, 'I've been saved.'

She drew a deep breath. 'Then, as I said, we must stop seeing each other.'

She rose to her feet.

'No,' Peter sank his head into his hands. 'The Lord is planning to join us. You must not fight it.'

'I can, Peter.'

She walked out of the door, proud of the strength she had displayed. It didn't make her any happier though.

Chapter 58

Dalia and her mother were sitting on the porch, enjoying the spring sunshine.

'Dalia,' her mother said, 'something important, I must tell you. I have discovered a way to get your grandparents out of Germany, but I am not telling your father until the matter is certain.'

'You've heard from them, Eema?'

Her mother shook her head. 'Nu, how could I? But Zamora Weiss from number 18, the one who went back to Berlin just before the war, when her mother was dying...'

'What about her?'

'She is coming back.'

'From Germany? With this war on?'

'Her daughter, Hedla, told me. Ai-ee. Great secret, it's supposed to be, but if the British can do it for Zamora Weiss then they can do it for Albert's parents. I thought, I must tell my daughter. She will find a way to get back the grandparents she loves.'

Dalia clenched her fists. If Eema knew she belonged to Aliyah Beth then the whole world knew.

She tested, 'Why me, Eema?'

Her mother raised her eyebrows. 'Who else in this family works for the police?'

Dalia relaxed. She should have known the way her mother's mind worked.

'So?'

'You will know who to talk to.'

'About what exactly, Eema?'

'Hedla said, and this is hush-hush, you must repeat it to no one, the British government are planning to exchange some of those German Templars they interned, for Jews in Germany and Poland.'

'Eema, if it's supposed to be dead secret, how can I ask the police?'

'You are clever, Dalia. You will find a way, when it is your own grandparents you are trying to help.'

Dalia sighed. 'I'll do my best, but I can't promise and please don't tell anyone else. If it's secret there's probably a good reason for it.'

At first, she dismissed it as one of her mother's crackpot ideas but the thought of doing something to get her grandparents out of Germany grew on her. She tried Aaron Schmidt. 'There's this rumour I've heard...'

Aaron listened, his plump, well-manicured hands clasped together as she floundered, trying to give facts, without mentioning sources. She finished, 'Is there any chance of getting my grandparents out by this route.'

He placed a finger on his cheek and held his chin. 'Neither grandparent has a Palestinian passport?'

'No, but my father has, and the rest of our family.'

Aaron shook his head. 'Good enough before the war, but not now. The British admit no one with a German passport. Until the war ends, there is no chance of your grandparents getting out. In Aliyah Beth we are concentrating on Youth Aliyah.'

Dalia clenched her fists. 'Why? Because old people are not worth saving?'

Aaron laid both his hands flat on the table. 'Because only the young can survive the journey's hazards.'

'From what I've heard,' Dalia retorted, 'The odds of survival for the elderly are equally slim if they stay put.'

Aaron's eyes looked sad. 'My brother is in Germany. I can do nothing for him.'

Chapter 59

Patsy's father was writing almost daily, long, abject letters apologising for his sins, begging her to accept Christ as her saviour so he could be truly forgiven. She rarely read beyond the first two lines before ripping the pages.

If only there was a letter from Ahmed! She had begun to worry. Had he already written? Had a censor intercepted his letter and passed it on to the government. Had the authorities in their turn handed it over to her father? But her father would have seized on something like that. She ought to have read each of his letters to the end.

Ahmed's letter, bearing an Iraqi stamp, arrived in early March, more a note than a letter.

Dear Patsy, I will be waiting at the milk bar when you finish work on Thursday 13th March. I hope you can make it.
With highest regards, Ahmed

No return address again, so she had no option but to go. Before she went though, she ought to know more about the proposal that she would be turning down. The only person she could think of who could help was Maftur. At the next reunion of the women from the Secretarial College she whispered, 'Maftur, I need to talk to you alone.'

Maftur, her face a study in curiosity, moved to another table, 'What is it?'

'You know when you saw me with Ahmed al-Zeid at the milk bar?'

'Ye-es?'

'You're going to find this hard to believe, but he took me there to ask permission to write a letter of proposal. I said he could, because I was curious to see what he would say but I told him I wouldn't be able to accept.'

'Did he write?'

Patsy nodded.

'Oh,' Maftur's teeth gnawed her upper lip, 'Then that is serious. What is in the letter?'

Patsy pulled it out of her purse and handed it over. Her stomach fluttered when she saw Maftur frown, but when she reached the end Maftur said, 'Patsy, this is wonderful. It means his parents have consented to the marriage already. They trust his judgement. Praise Allah, my father did not know he was so tolerant of the British, or I would have been forced to marry him, but you two will be perfect together, all this archaeology you have in common.'

Patsy risked the question that had been troubling her. 'Your father considered Ahmed anti-British?'

'I suppose it is all right to say, now the Troubles are over and the British have other things to worry about, but when his parents first approached mine, Ahmed al-Zeid was leading a band sabotaging the oil pipe in the Jezreel Valley. Of course, in the Troubles most idealistic young men did something like that, but somehow, my father got it into his head that Ahmed was not just fighting the British, but was also negotiating with the Germans. My father didn't want a son-in-law who would endanger his business connections, so he broke off negotiations, with the excuse that in these modern times he thought it right to allow his daughter to choose her own husband. So behold, everything is working out as you would say, like a fairy tale, with everyone happy in the end.'

'No, Maftur, it is not a happy-ever-after ending. I cannot marry Ahmed, much as I respect and admire him, at least not until I am twenty-one, and I don't think he will wait that long for me despite what he writes.'

'You are right. His parents will put pressure on him to break off negotiations if difficulties are prolonged, but why can you not marry him now?'

'My father wouldn't let me.'

'Why not? Ahmed al-Zeid is an outstanding prospect. His family is well respected and rich. The only reason I did not want him was because of my Ismail.'

'But Ahmed is Muslim and my father is Christian.'

Maftur raised her eyebrows, 'But your father is not an Arab Christian. Muslim men in Beirut often marry European wives.'

'Yes,' Patsy agreed, 'but I don't expect those wives had fathers like mine.'

'Perhaps something will make your father change his mind or perhaps Ahmed al-Zeid will face his parents out and wait until you are twenty-one.'

'You think a marriage like that could work?'

'Of course. Ahmed al-Zeid is ideal for you.'

'I wouldn't be a slave to his mother, or something?'

Maftur laughed, 'The al-Zeid women are in a class of their own, Patsy. They will urge you to follow your own career.'

While Maftur was talking, Patsy saw Leila walk into the coffee shop. Leila waved to her younger sister, Michelle who had at last bowed to pressure and joined the secretarial school. Leila held her hand upright, brandishing a large emerald engagement ring.

'Maftur, turn round,' Patsy exclaimed, 'Look at Leila.'

****

Suzanna gave Habib the latest letter from Ahmed al-Zeid. She was moving to the stairs when he exclaimed, 'Holy George, just listen to this. My brother Ahmed has fallen for a British woman.'

'A British woman! I thought he supported the Germans?'

'Ahmed al-Zeid probably keeps love and war in separate compartments.'

He frowned and it was obvious that he found it difficult to decode the letter.

'The idiot,' he muttered at last, 'He's smuggling himself into Palestine. He wants to stay with us. Doesn't he realise how much the British have tightened security.' He folded the letter and replaced it in the envelope.

Suzanna walked away again, but he held up a hand beckoning her back. 'It seems Ahmed al-Zeid is interested in your wandering employer. He wants you to look through any papers that Mr Shepard has left behind and check for references to Iraq.'

Suzanna drew herself up, realising even as she did so, that she was aping Mrs Shepard. 'Habib, before the war I was happy to support the fight for independence, but I am not happy to side with Germans.'

'Ahmed al-Zeid is my blood brother, Suzanna. If he asks me to do him a favour then I will do it. I hoped, as my sister, you would support me.'

Suzanna thought of Evie's trusting little face, her body snuggling up to her as she confided her secrets. She thought of her own position in the Shepard household. 'I am sorry, Habib, you will have to do him this favour on your own. I cannot spy on my employers while I am eating their bread and salt.'

She stumped upstairs, and then felt guilty because in an hour or so she would be eating Habib's bread and salt. After that there was no chance of private conversation.

Chapter 60

In the Post Office, Patsy tore open an envelope hoping it would contain better news of her father.

Her mother's normally neat handwriting scrawled over the page, the content unusually brief. Patsy managed to decipher the gist of the first four sentences before staggering to a seat by a marble pillar. She started again from the beginning.

Patsy dear,
I don't know what to say. It can't be true but if it is, why didn't you tell me at the time? It came as such a shock. Your father getting up in Sharing, making this confession, in front of everyone. Something he said had happened when I was in hospital all those years ago. I know it can't be true but he has been going on about it, asking me to forgive him. Please tell me it is not true. I don't know what to think. You must not come up here, not while your father is in this state - I don't think I can face it yet. Please write and tell me it is not true,
Your loving mother

She envisaged her mother in Jerusalem, shut up with her father, subjected to those long hours of apologies and demands for forgiveness that she knew so well. Sorrow for her mother and shame for herself, battled for supremacy.

Her thoughts changed tack. Her father had confessed, in public? He could go to prison. It would serve him right, of course, but where would that leave her mother? And could her mother ever be her friend again?

She jumped up and made her way to a café round the corner, shivering although the day was warm. She ordered a mug of hot chocolate, and wrapped her hands round it. She must be sensible, think things through.

No one could bring charges without her testimony. She must write a letter of denial that her mother could show the police, if necessary.

She finished her drink and felt ravenously hungry but could not face sitting at the same table as Beth and Bert this evening. With gossip spreading like lightening, Bert would know about her father's confession.

Next day would be soon enough to tell Beth that her father had had a nervous breakdown, and was spreading ridiculous stories.

She needed food now, lots of starchy comforting food with something sticky and sweet to follow, and took herself to a small Arabic restaurant she had often visited in the company of young police constables. It was still early, no one else at the tables. The waiter, an elderly man in a far from clean white apron, who had fawned on her previously when accompanied by a man, affected not to see her. After ten minutes of watching him lounge by the wall, refusing to meet her eye, she called him over, and ordered stuffed vine leaves in tomato sauce.

A soldier and his girl came in. The waiter sprinted across the room to take their order. He hovered round them, putting out a jug of water, carrying clean glasses, fetching a cruet, until their meal was ready. He served their meal and then went back to lounging against the wall.

Patsy summoned him again to ask how long her vine leaves would be. He shrugged, went into the kitchen, and fetched them out. They were almost cold. She felt the couple staring as she ate. She left without the sticky honey pastry she had promised herself, and bought a bar of chocolate from the confectioners instead. She ate it on the street, stuffing it into her mouth, chewing fiercely down on it, not caring who was watching.

The sun had set; searchlights played across the sky, forming circles on layers of cloud, bouncing off fat barrage balloons tethered to the docks. People would pay good money to watch such a show in peacetime, she thought, but her mind would not remain diverted long. It kept asking, how could her father have done this to his family? She banged her hands together in a loud clap then looked round in embarrassment. Luckily, no one was walking behind her.

Inside the flat, she made her apologies to Beth for missing dinner, pleaded a headache, and went straight to her room.

She re-read her mother's letter, tried to imagine that she was innocent and her father's confession a mere delusion. She took out her writing pad and unscrewed her fountain pen.

> *Dearest Um Pat,*
> *I can't make head or tail of your last letter. What is it I must tell you is not true? What did Daddy say in Sharing that has upset you so much? Why don't you want to see me? What have I done?*
> *Your loving but mystified daughter,*
> *Patsy*

That will do for the police she thought. She hoped her mother would believe it.

From the way Bert stared next morning, Patsy was sure that he had heard and believed the rumours. At work, she watched everyone. Both Mrs Jones and the superintendent seemed more distant. Dalia and Leila, though, acted normally.

In the evening after Bert had gone out, she told Beth her father had had a nervous breakdown. 'The embarrassing thing is that he suffers from obscene delusions and of course, people believe his awful stories. I can't look anyone in the face. Has your Bert said anything?'

'No, but your father's a civilian so he probably doesn't know him. What exactly has your father been saying?'

'I can't bring myself to tell you, Beth. It's too horrible. But if you hear people gossiping you will tell them none of it's true, won't you?'

'Of course. But, my dear, how beastly for you.'

'You will tell me if you hear anything?'

'Yes, but I am sure people will realise that it is part of his breakdown.'

Back in her room, before turning out the light, Patsy took out Ahmed's letter, read it for the umpteenth time, and reached a decision. She would not only meet Ahmed but also accept his proposal and try to persuade him to elope. That might prove difficult given his sense of honour. On the other hand, it could appeal to the romantic side of his nature.

****

Ahmed al-Zeid was having supper at Habib's that Saturday. All this secrecy and drama over his letters, Suzanna thought, and yet he could stay here openly whenever he felt like it? He treated espionage as a game.

She had hoped that, since he was Muslim, Angelique and her mother would serve the men separately, but her mother set cushions for all on the floor as usual. After her refusal to spy on Mr Shepard, she felt embarrassed eating at the same table as Ahmed al-Zeid. She kept her gaze fixed on her plate while eating the succulent veal Angelique had cooked in her guest's honour.

Half way through the meal, when both Angelique and her mother had slipped out into the kitchen to bring in second helpings, he whispered, 'Ya Suzanna, I respect your refusal to look through Mr Shepard's papers. You are right. It is dishonourable to spy on the people whose bread you eat.'

Angelique returned and conversation became general, but now Suzanna could enjoy both veal and conversation.

'If I may, Um Habib and Angelique,' Ahmed al-Zeid said, 'I would like to stay here again on Thursday when I have finished my business.' He lifted his head and gave a smile that was almost shy.

'I ought not to be telling you this, perhaps, but it is filling my thoughts. Imshallah, when I return I will be able to tell you that I am unofficially betrothed.'

'Why unofficially?' her mother queried.

'Um Habib, the girl I love is British and nineteen. Until she is twenty-one, she has to have her father's consent to marry. I can ask his permission only when she tells me that she is willing to marry me. Such is the British custom. If she says "Yes" and he says "No", we will be unofficially betrothed until she is twenty-one. My British friends tell me that this is not dishonourable.'

'You have British friends, want to marry a British woman, and yet plot to throw the British out of Palestine?' Suzanna exclaimed.

Ahmed al-Zeid placed his fingers together and gazed down at the tablecloth.

'Ya Suzanna, my friendships, my love, my politics, are all based on my need for freedom. I want the freedom to choose my friends; I want the freedom to choose my wife and I want the freedom to help define my country.'

'But no one is stopping you saying Syria is your country,' Angelique put in.

Her mother-in-law gave a wry smile, 'Ah, you young ones.'

'Ya Angelique,' Ahmed al-Zeid said, 'Haifa and the whole of Galilee are Syria and we, the Arab people, should be governing it as part of a United Arabia.'

'That is what the British promised,' Habib agreed.

'The British broke their promise,' Ahmed al-Zeid said, 'they partitioned the land, forced kings upon us, made pacts with the French and kept large areas under their own rule. Ya um Habib,' he appealed to her mother, 'you saw this happen when Habib was little.' Suzanna watched her mother nod her assent.

'So, Ya Angelique, all we are asking is that the British keep their promise and hand back our lands.'

Chapter 61

Ahmed was not in the milk bar when Patsy arrived, deliberately two minutes late. She placed her scarf on a table at the back of the room and went to the counter to order coffee for two.

The coffee arrived but Patsy was still alone. She poured a single cup and sipped it slowly, glancing up between each sip. Half an hour later, she poured herself a second. She sipped this one as slowly as the first, even though it was cold. She continued to gaze at the door.

After two hours and several more cups of coffee, she made her way home.

****

For the first time in weeks, Mrs Shepard had found time to go through Suzanna's work. Suzanna looked on in dismay as her mistress slashed a red pencil across every page.

'Suzanna, this is disappointing,' Mrs Shepard said at last. 'And I have too much to do at the hospital to give you the extra tuition you need if you are to pass matriculation this year.'

'But I've done all the exercises you set. I will do them again if you explain where I have gone wrong.'

Mrs Shepard gave a sigh of exasperation. 'Suzanna, don't you realise there's a war on? We all have to make sacrifices. Anyway, even if you were to take the exam and pass it, there is no way you are going to get to England this year or the next. We're in for a long haul.'

'I don't have to go to England. I could go to university in Beirut.'

Mrs Shepard compressed her lips. 'You are not listening, Suzanna. I said that my war work will leave me no time to give you extra tuition.'

Suzanna could not believe that, after all her years of drudgery, Mrs Shepard was reneging on her side of the bargain. Only the prospect of not seeing Inspector Monteith ever again prevented her from handing in her notice on the spot. She snatched up her exercise books and stalked to her cubicle. There she threw the books on the floor and buried her face in her hands. Why was Inspector Monteith taking so long to ask her family if he could marry her?

Looking up, she caught sight of her alarm clock and realised it was time to catch her bus.

At the bus station, Habib rushed towards her. 'Have you another letter?'

She experienced a surge of irritation. 'It is less than a week since you saw your friend.'

'He did not return on Thursday night.'

'The woman probably turned him down and he felt too ashamed.'

'He would regard that as discourteous to Angelique, and Ahmed al-Zeid is never discourteous.'

At the entrance to the bus station, they stopped to let a donkey leading a chain of camels pass. Suzanna turned to face her brother. 'Why are you so worried about your friend?'

Habib stared at the camels and said in a low voice, 'I am afraid he may have got himself arrested.'

Suzanna shook her head. 'You would have heard. His solicitor would have sent a message.'

'I have spoken to his solicitor. He has not heard from him.'

'There you are then. Your friend has not been arrested.'

Habib frowned. 'If the police know my brother Ahmed is spying for the Axis, they may be holding him in secret, hoping to catch his accomplices. Suzanna, when you go back, keep an ear open when your employers' police friends come calling.'

Suzanna agreed to that without hesitation. It was quite different from searching through Mr Shepard's papers for political reasons. Anyway, if Mrs Shepard would not let her sit matriculation, why should she remain loyal to the British?

****

'Your cousin is here asking for you,' Giza announced.

Dalia breathed in hard. 'Shimon?'

'No, not Shimon, your other cousin. Prepare for bad news. He is looking upset.'

Dalia walked downstairs slowly, determined to be firm, whatever Peter had to say. She was unprepared for his ashen face, his red eyelids, and his shaking hands, but did her best to harden her heart.

She stopped on the bottom stair. 'Well? What brings you here?'

'Please,' Peter muttered, 'I have to talk to someone. I'll go mad if I don't. It is nothing to do with you and me. Please, come and have coffee so I can talk to you.'

'Why not take your troubles to Mrs Shepard?'

'Dalia, I can't. If you let me tell you what's wrong, then you'll understand.'

His face had the hurt expression of a child. Instinct urged her to run up and comfort him. She resisted, but could not bring herself to send him packing in his current state. Curiosity, too, tugged. Just what was it he could not tell his friend's wife?

She knew she was acting foolishly, when she said, 'Wait. I'll get my coat.'

Upstairs putting on makeup and brushing her hair, Dalia tried to rationalise her behaviour, persuading herself she was doing this for Aliyah Beth.

Peter led her to a café where high seats created private booths. He peered round on either side to make sure the adjacent booths were empty before bursting out, 'Dalia, last week I murdered two men.'

'You did what?' She put her hand to her mouth.

'My squad - we killed two Arabs.'

She shook her head. Peter was a policeman. Killing Arabs came with his job. Why this fuss? 'Surely you can take that to Mrs Shepard.'

'I can't, Dalia.'

'Why not?'

'These Arabs were spies - only doing for the Axis what Jim is doing for the Allies, and Addy hasn't heard from Jim for weeks.'

The Aliyah Beth portion of Dalia's mind noted the confirmation that Jim Shepard was a British spy but the emotional part could no longer remain objective. Her tone softened. 'Peter, tell me what happened?'

The story juddered out. 'We've been shadowing this hashish smuggler. Weeks now. A man owning a few donkeys, a minor German agent.' Peter pushed his hair back. 'That afternoon. We didn't expect it. He met the Mufti's top man. We surrounded them. They flung down their pistols. I went in with the handcuffs -' Peter clenched his fists. 'The first smuggler pulled a knife. I fired my revolver at his hand, but my squad shot both men. They only did it to protect me. I am to blame. I was in charge.'

'So what do the authorities say?'

'We didn't tell them. We didn't take the bodies back. Muslims have to be buried before nightfall. We couldn't get the bodies to Haifa before dark. Another thing. I recognised the second man. A member of a powerful Syrian family. All hell would be let loose.' Peter paused. 'I ordered my men to bury them under a pile of stones there where we had shot them.'

'L'Azazel!' Dalia shouted. She could not believe she was hearing this. 'All bodies, even those of your worst enemies, should be treated with respect.'

Peter placed his head between his palms and kept his eyes on the table. 'We tried. We buried them facing east, but I couldn't do other things like washing all blood off and dressing them in a shroud. One of my men said they would consider they had died martyrs, so washing them didn't matter, their blood would smell like perfume in paradise. I went along with that. It simplified my problem. I shouldn't have, should I?'

Peter seized her hand, which was lying on the table. 'The Muslims among my men said prayers. I tried to pray too, but the words sounded so wrong after we had just killed them.'

They sat in silence. After a while, Peter pressed her hand hard, 'Dalia I am glad you have listened to me and that we are friends once more.'

He looked so vulnerable, with his red-rimmed eyes, she could not bring herself to say they weren't.

****

'Patsy dear, you've obviously got a touch of flu. I'll put some blankets on the sun bed and you can rest on the balcony. I'll phone the super and let him know.'

Patsy knew all that was wrong with her was spending the last few nights sobbing into her pillow, but gratefully accepted Beth's diagnosis. Propped up on pillows, gazing out at the calm blue of the bay, she brooded about Ahmed.

High in the clear sky a glider trailed a banner. She watched four small puffballs of cloud cluster round it, followed by four dull bangs from ack-ack guns hidden in the orange groves, and made the transition from sorrow to anger. Ahmed should have told her face-to-face that he no longer wanted to marry her, whatever the reason, whether he had heard rumours of her father's confession, whether his family had turned against a foreign marriage, or, whether he had simply obtained all the information he needed from her. She didn't know with whom she was angrier, Ahmed or her father.

Beth brought a bowl of beef soup.

'I'm just popping down to the Post Office to pick up mail. If you give me your key I'll see if you have any.'

'Beth, you're an angel. I am expecting a letter.' Hoping for a letter, she should have said.

The warmth of the soup relaxed her and she fell asleep. When she woke, Beth was sitting beside her, reading a magazine.

'Your letter,' Beth said and passed it over.

Patsy almost tore it from her hand, but it was not from Ahmed. She did not recognise the writing. She opened the letter slowly, conscious of the effort of moving arms that lacked energy.

Dear Patricia,

If only I could call you my sister in the lord. We are all praying for you here in the gathering of Saints and trust you will soon find how good it is to lay your burdens on the Lord.

Yea, though your sins be scarlet yet, hallelujah, through his blood they may be washed as white as snow. All you need do is repent and give your life to the Lord.

We would be happy, dear child, if you would join us for afternoon tea next Sunday and afterwards accompany us to the New Covenant Hall where I pray you will receive the Lord's blessing and hear his call.

Yours, in the sure knowledge of salvation,
Emmeline Manners

Patsy closed her eyes and imagined those women's afternoon meetings. So Mrs Manners hoped to parade a prize sinner in front of them? Not bloody likely.

'You didn't like that letter, did you?' Beth commented. Patsy opened her eyes to find she had screwed it into a ball.

'Oh Beth, I don't know what to do. I have to get out of Palestine. I suppose I could volunteer as a nurse, although I hate the thought of being bossed about by ward sisters.'

Beth laughed. 'I can't see nursing suiting you, but why leave Palestine?'

'People are taking my father's confessions at face value.'

'That will pass over. Please don't go, Patsy. I shall miss you too much. I can't tell you how much happier I have been since you came to live here.'

That made her feel slightly better. 'I've enjoyed staying with you too, Beth. Until this trouble with my father, despite the war, these past months have been the happiest in my life since I was little.'

Chapter 62

Mrs Shepard pushed a pin into the thick plaits beneath her navy straw hat. 'It's been so long since I heard from Jimmy, Suzanna. If he were still alive, he would have got a message through by this time. We must prepare ourselves for bad news. The Lord giveth and the Lord taketh away. Blessed be the name of the Lord.'

Mrs Shepard, Suzanna reflected, must have great faith in the afterlife to bear up so well.

'It's the uncertainty that's so difficult,' her mistress continued, 'I'll call in at the Post Office, just in case. While I am out, I want you to give the dining area a thorough clean. Inspector Sutton is coming to dinner tonight. It's his birthday so I thought we should make it a bit special for him after he has been so good to the children. He has been just like another father.'

'He gets on better with Clare than Evie,' Suzanna remarked.

'Nonsense,' Mrs Shepard snapped, 'Both children adore him.'

Suzanna knew better than to continue the discussion.

A happy thought occurred once Mrs Shepard had left – when Inspector Monteith had a birthday, Mrs Shepard might arrange a party for him, too.

The phone rang. Suzanna answered it and nearly dropped the receiver when she heard Mr Shepard's voice.

'Mrs Shepard's just left,' she stammered, when he asked to speak to his wife, 'I will run and see if she is still at the bus stop. Shall I take your number?'

'No,' Mr Shepard said, 'I'm coming straight home. When you get back from chasing my wife, will you heat water for a bath?'

Suzanna raced off and caught up with Mrs Shepard who had obviously stopped to chat en route and was still in the back lane. She delivered her message. Poor Mrs Shepard turned pale, too shocked to show her joy, all she said was, 'Jimmy, he's back really?'

'Yes. He will not be long. He asked me to heat water for his bath.'

'I'll have to nip to the shops to buy some coffee.'

'We have coffee,' Suzanna reassured her.

'Not fresh enough, Jimmy will want fresh coffee.' Mrs Shepard hurried off.

The bath water was only luke-warm and Mrs Shepard had not yet returned, when a Post Office van dropped an incredibly dirty and evil smelling Mr Shepard off at the front gate.

He looked disappointed when Suzanna met him. 'You could not catch up with my wife?'

'I delivered your message but Mrs Shepard has gone to buy you fresh coffee.'

Mr Shepard shook his head. 'I'd rather have my wife than coffee, but at least she is spared seeing me like this. The sooner I am in that bath the better.'

He was still in the bath when Mrs Shepard returned. He ran out of the bathroom in a dressing gown, dripping water over the floor, he threw his arms round his wife and dragged her along to the dormitory.

When they emerged, two hours later, Mr Shepard's face was glum and it was obvious that Mrs Shepard had been crying.

****

The end of April had re-painted the mountain slope above Dalia's digs from ranunculus orange to flax pink. In the harbour, the white and red paint of a hospital ship stood out from the drab camouflage of other ships. The setting sun cast a golden glow on the buildings round her. Dalia walked downhill certain that things would work out with Peter. He had not been born Second Chosen. He had all the enthusiasm of a new convert but his religion was not fundamental to his identity.

When she reached the cinema, where Peter was keeping their place in the queue, she found him in equally high spirits. 'Dalia, you won't believe this but Jim's back. We'd almost given him up. We had too little faith in our Lord.'

'Where was he?'

'All over the place, but he finished up in Greece, and returned on the last convoy from Athens.'

Dalia wondered if Aaron would be interested.

In the ice cream break, Peter confided, 'You don't know how much Jim's return means to me, having someone with whom I can really share my problems.'

So all this time, she had only been a substitute for Jim. Dalia knew she shouldn't feel disgruntled. If Peter were to finish with her, that would solve her problems.

She was not surprised when, outside the door to the lodging house, looking awkward in his embarrassment, he announced, 'There's a globe-trotting American from Hollywood speaking at the New Covenant Hall next Thursday.'

She said nothing, waiting, with a touch of malice, for his embarrassment to grow, but instead of the expected 'so I am afraid there will be no time to meet, next week,' she heard, 'Would you come with me?'

An American from Hollywood? Now that was something! And going to the New Covenant Hall would be obeying Aliyah Beth's instruction to get closer to Mr Shepard. She replied quickly, 'Yes, I would enjoy that,' despite a small voice at the back of her mind nagging 'Don't be so stupid'.

'7.30 then.' Peter paused and fixed his gaze on her bare head, 'Oh and it's one of those occasions when you wear a hat.'

A hat? A posh do, then? That meant best clothes as well. Back in her room, she ransacked her wardrobe and found a newish pair of navy court shoes, but her dresses were all past it. Her bank balance still contained emergency savings. This was that emergency.

As soon as she was confident that Peter would be out of sight she ran out of the house to the nearest public phone and dialled the Aliyah Beth contact number.

****

Dalia rushed out to the shops at lunchtime. At the milliners, she bought a cartwheel polished straw hat in navy, and at the drapers four yards of white linen material printed with navy polka dots, together with a Coat's pattern for a dress with fashionable cap sleeves. She hurried on up the street and presented the material and pattern to an Armenian dressmaker, asking to have the frock made up by next afternoon. The dressmaker insisted on measuring her, so she was late for work, but Leila forgave her when she saw the hat.

'That must have set you back a month's salary. For one of those showy Jewish weddings?'

Dalia tilted the hat back, put a finger under her chin and gave a seductive smile, 'No, but I have been invited to a posh British function.'

Leila grinned. 'No prizes for guessing who invited you.'

Dalia allowed herself a smug blush. Patsy looked up and frowned, 'Don't get too involved, Dalia. Peter is still one of the Second Chosen.'

Dalia raised her eyebrows hoping Patsy would elaborate, but Inspector Sutton chose that moment to put in an appearance and all three women became extremely busy.

'That Britisher you told me to keep an eye on,' she told Aaron when she met him at the coffee shop after work, 'He is back in the country. Next Thursday I have an opportunity to meet him.'

Aaron waxed enthusiastic. 'Dalia that is wonderful. It is vital, not just for Aliyah Beth, but for the sake of all Jews in Palestine, that we find out just what this man is up to.'

****

The Shepards were not bothering to keep their voices down.

'Addy, I've said I'm sorry. I wish I had never told you, but we promised to be honest with each other. Please give me a chance. You admitted you were tempted yourself while we were apart.'

'Yes, but I never succumbed. That is the difference. You'll have to give me time, Jim.'

It should not be Mr Shepard apologising to his wife, Suzanna thought. It was only natural for men to be unfaithful every now and then. Mrs Shepard should be apologising to her husband over that Inspector Sutton. She would never understand these Inglisi, except perhaps for their children. She looked down at Clare and Evie enjoying her homemade lemonade. If it were not for them and Inspector Monteith, she would have been looking for a new job weeks ago.

If the Germans invaded though and the Shepards left Palestine, she would have to find a new job anyway. She must study the job advertisements.

****

Patsy too was contemplating a change of job. She had written to the curator of the Cairo Museum, asking if he had any vacancies. She opened her mailbox at the Post Office, hoping for a reply. Instead, she found an envelope, stamped OHMS, carrying Tim's handwriting.

Her conscience pricked when she saw the two-month-old date at the top of his letter. It had been so long since she had received a letter from Tim that she had stopped writing to him. She felt still more ashamed when she read the opening lines.

Dearest Patsy,
Thank you so much for your amusing insights into life in Palestine. You don't know how much they cheer me up out here.

The censor had blanked out almost all the rest of the letter.

As soon as she reached home, she sat down to compose a witty reply but found herself short of interesting material. Anything important, such as her father's confession or Ahmed's disappearance, was obviously unsuitable but even jolly anecdotes about soldier's antics in town had to come out when she reread them from a censor's viewpoint. Eventually she filled the letter with a description of the sun setting over Haifa Bay as seen from the Raven's balcony.

Chapter 63

Dalia saw the admiration in Peter's eyes as he looked up, so half way down the stairs she posed to display her new dress and hat to full advantage.

'My, but you are beautiful.'

She ran on down, satisfied by the compliment, and clasped Peter's arm ready to leave. He shook his head regretfully. 'No, you need your coat.'

'But it's so warm.'

His voice turned firm. 'It will be chilly later. I don't want you catching pneumonia.'

She was about to protest further, then remembered the reason for his anxiety, so, although her old coat would ruin her appearance, she ran back to fetch it.

As she followed Peter downhill, Dalia envisaged the New Covenant Hall. It would be a miniature version of the grandiose YMCA, with an interior like that of the Christian Churches depicted on postcards, full of gilded statues, jewelled crucifixes, and suspended ostrich eggs.

Close to the drystone wall at the bottom of the Baha'i Gardens, Peter led her into a short alley, past a dilapidated Arab house, to a rusty corrugated iron building that looked like an old workshop. He stopped outside a wooden porch tagged onto the front.

'Here we are.'

'This is the New Covenant Hall?' she asked in dismay as Peter ushered her inside.

The interior of the building was scarcely less dismal than its exterior with a scuffed wooden floor, dark brown walls and curtain-free, frosted glass windows set well above eye level. The only adornments a painted, crimson banner bearing gold-brushed text in English, 'For God so loved the World that he gave his only begotten Son, that whosoever believeth in him should not perish but have everlasting life'. Beneath the banner were the familiar Ten Commandments in English translation.

A soldier stood by the door, as if on sentry duty. He handed them faded, cloth-covered books. Another soldier led them past rows of members from all three branches of the armed services. He ushered them into seats behind a cluster of drably dressed civilians who turned their heads and nodded at Peter, but stared curiously at her. Dalia opened the book the soldier had given her and discovered it contained Christian songs. She was angry with Peter for tricking her into attending a Christian service, until she realised that the misunderstanding had been hers.

Her inappropriately frivolous hat embarrassed her now. She removed the hatpin. A look of almost horror filled Peter's face. 'Put your hat back on,' he hissed.

She looked around but could see no bareheaded women, so pushed back the hatpin. 'Where are the Shepards?'

Peter pointed to the front row. 'They're counsellors. I'll introduce you after the service.'

She craned her neck forward, but a group of Ozzies in the second row obscured her view.

In front of their aisle an elderly woman in an ancient felt hat, who had been drooping in front of an upright piano, straightened her back and began to thump out Beethoven's *Pathethique*.

Two men emerged from a side door and walked onto a raised platform. One, elderly, white-moustached, and balding, she recognised as the bank manager who had interviewed her when she had opened a current account in Haifa. The other, clean-shaven, dapper in ecru linen, strutted jauntily alongside.

Her bank manager gave a long eulogy on the American, who appeared to have spent his entire life, apart from a month each year at home in Hollywood, crossing and re-crossing the Atlantic in the service of his Lord. The bank manager finished by announcing a hymn. Everyone stood. The woman at the piano pounded the keys.

Peter handed her his book, open at the correct page and took hers in exchange. The congregation sang lustily, making up in volume what it lacked in melody. It wasn't until the third repeat of the chorus 'Will you let him save you now? Will you take his loving hand, Pilot to a better land, Will you let him save you now?' that she would have felt competent to join in. She didn't though because she suspected that her parents would have considered the sentiments blasphemous.

The bank manager ordered those assembled to close their eyes. He proceeded to thank the Almighty for Saints who had returned unscathed from battle, to request the safety of the allied armed forces, listing each military front in turn. Tobruk featured prominently. He then moved on to pray for endangered civilians. Moscow and blitzed London received special attention but Baghdad, where relatives of so many Palestinians, both Arabic and Jewish, were in imminent danger, he left unmentioned. Lastly, he made an impassioned plea for many souls to be saved that night. Loud Amens and cries of 'Yes, oh Lord, yes', from the civilians in front, punctuated his prayer. These people, she thought, seemed so certain of their faith, not like most people she knew. Even Rav

Cohen admitted that no one could be sure of the existence of God, all one could believe in was the Jewish way of life.

Another hymn and then the star turn. The American's arms waved high, his voice caressed and soothed, as he painted a picture of the blissful wonders of heaven. Without warning, his mood changed and he was thundering the torments awaiting unbelievers. His body twisted, he bent low and banged the floor as he described the agonies of a fiery hell. Then he was back to cooing and sweetness as he pleaded with the audience to come forward and be saved that night, to give their lives to the Lord Jesus, the saviour promised in the Old Testament. Dalia recognised the reference he gave. Next weekend she would ask Rav Cohen about this interpretation. Perhaps Christianity was not blasphemy. Come to think of it, she had never heard Rav Cohen say it was.

While the American was still talking, soft music sounded from the rear of the hall. Five women in white stood in the back row and sang persuasively, 'Oh please say yes. Say yes. Say yes. While He so gently, so patiently knocks: oh, let Him in tonight.'

The American, continuing against the musical background, spoke tenderly of mothers, back home in England, praying for their sons' safety, he went on to wives, fiancées, sisters, fathers. He criss-crossed the platform as he talked. How wonderful the affection of one's family he said, but how much greater still the love of Jesus who had sacrificed all for their sakes. The music, in a way she could not explain, seemed to make sense of what he was saying.

The evangelist drew his oration to a close. The main lights went off leaving the only illumination at the front. The singing became slightly louder, the tune hauntingly beautiful. The American, his face floodlit from the sides, beckoned to the congregation.

From the front of the hall, just visible in the gloom, a hefty marine clambered over legs, stumbled into the aisle. Soldiers, sailors, and airmen singly, and in pairs followed, walking towards the platform as if in a daze. Peter turned his head. Even in the dim light, she detected such obvious love in his eyes that her thighs clenched. She wanted to hold him close, to shout, 'I love you too,' and to kiss him passionately. She stood up to relieve her tension. Peter rewarded her action with a wide smile. His hands urged her on. She edged out into the aisle. Her logical self, relegated to the back of her mind, muttering, 'I don't believe you're doing this.' She joined a fair-haired nurse in front of the platform.

The singing died away, the evangelist descending from the platform, spoke to every new convert individually, looking each directly in the eyes, 'Do you give your life to the Lord Jesus?'

She was last. She wanted to scream, 'No, I made a mistake. I don't know what got into me,' but staring into those large, round eyes, she found herself meekly answering, 'Yes.'

Another long prayer, the evangelist roared his thanks for those brands saved from the burning and invited the new converts to move into the back room. This should have been her cue to hightail it back to her seat but she could not face Peter's disappointment, so obediently followed the rest.

In contrast to the high emotion in the hall, the atmosphere in the back room was uncompromisingly prosaic. Army privates, playing at recruiting sergeants, sat at a trestle table, taking names and contact addresses. They rapped out a brief prayer of blessing and handed over each recruit to a counsellor who led the way to wooden chairs lining the back of the room.

Dalia had just decided to slip quietly away before she was processed, when a short slim woman, with hair braided into a bun beneath a nondescript hat, took hold of her hands and folded them between her own, then kissed her on the cheek. Despite no make-up, and a dowdy dress, the woman was beautiful.

'Praise the Lord that at last you have opened your heart to Jesus, Dalia Leitner,' the woman said, 'My name is Addy Shepard. I am a friend of Peter Monteith.'

At least one thing had gone to plan that evening. She had got in touch with Mr Shepard's wife. Aaron would be pleased. She herself would have been better pleased if Addy Shepard had been slightly less attractive.

Addy talked while leading her to the rear of the room, 'I expect you are wondering what happens now. Well, the next stage is your baptism, when you show the world that you have truly been born again, and of course from now on you will want to immerse yourself in the word of God.'

Addy chose two seats, leaving one vacant between her and a male couple. She fished into a capacious purse and brought out a book bound in soft black leather.

'Here is the Holy Word of God for you to keep. I hope you will spend at least half an hour each day reading and meditating on it. Since you are already familiar with the Old Testament, I suggest you concentrate on the New. With the Lord's grace, I will be on hand to help. Could you come to my house twice, starting tomorrow evening if possible? Peter will show you where I live.'

'Tomorrow's Friday I have to go home for Shabbat,' Dalia started, but as she spoke, the enormity of what she had done overcame her. She had given up her right to Shabbat. She had thrown away the identity she had inherited from 3000 generations. She did not dare go home just yet and tell her parents, so added quickly, 'No, it is all right, Mrs Shepard, I will phone home and leave a message asking my father not to fetch me.'

'Please call me Addy, my dear, and I am so glad you came to that decision.'

Addy stood and tapped the shoulder of a small man in thick spectacles, thumbing through a bible open on his lap, while he talked earnestly to a soldier.

'We're going back into the hall, Jim. I'll see you there.'

'That was my husband,' Addy explained as she opened the door.

Dalia turned her head. She recognised that insignificant looking man in the shabby brown striped suit, as a civilian she had seen with Peter inside Police HQ and could scarcely believe he was the famous spy who had been having the amazing adventures Peter had told her about all over the Balkans. Well, she reflected, if a spy actually looked like a spy that would defeat the purpose.

Peter strode over and seized her hand. 'Dalia,' he exclaimed, 'Oh Dalia'.

'I imagine you two want to be left alone.' Addy included them both in her radiant smile, 'I'll expect you tomorrow.'

As Addy moved off, Dalia followed Peter out of the hall, glad that they were not lingering to talk to strangers. As soon as they were out of the door, Peter threw his arms round her and hustled her into the deep shadows round the side of the building. He drew her to him and kissed her hard. She responded with enthusiasm.

'Oh, Dalia,' Peter said at last, 'I knew the Lord would find a way. Now we can get engaged.'

Although Dalia had yielded so readily and unthinkingly to his kiss, his words forced reality on her. She was not the heroine of a Hollywood romance and kisses did not change everything. She drew back, hid her face in her hands, and tried to block out Peter's presence as she thought of her mother, her father, Ruth and Uri. She would have to retract this conversion, even if it meant letting down Aliyah Beth.

Then she felt Peter's arms round her again, his face burying itself into her neck. Her body took over, creating a pulsing throb at the base of her stomach. Her mind put up a final effort to assert control, but only at the cost of tears.

'I am a Jew,' she sobbed as she pushed Peter's head away. 'I want to go on being a Jew.'

Peter stroked her hair. 'Dalia, you don't have to stop being a Jew just because you're a Christian. Jesus never stopped being a Jew.'

She could see he did not understand. She wiped her eyes and interrupted.

'Peter, Christians may allow me to remain a Jew, but Jews will not. To my parents Christianity is blasphemy.'

Peter had his hand under her chin, gently forcing her face up so he could look into her eyes. Waves of lethargy left her body limp, unable to assert itself.

'Dalia, you'll see things more clearly once you've received spiritual guidance. Come now, I'll take you home and tomorrow after work we'll go out and buy your engagement ring.'

She wanted to scream that they were not engaged but her body had a different agenda. A logical section of her mind even lent her body support. She would never again, have an opportunity to get close to Mr Shepard if she rejected Peter now. Eretz Israel was more important than any individual and she was not the only one having to do things for Eretz Israel. Look at the sacrifices Golda was making.

After Peter had dropped her at her digs, she walked down to a public telephone and left a message for Aaron.

****

Suzanna was ironing in the dining room angry that Mrs Shepard had insisted she get on with it, even though Inspector Monteith was visiting this evening. She had so wanted to make the trolley look special because she knew this was going to be **the** evening. The inspector had only been waiting for Mr Shepard to return before opening marriage negotiations.

The outside door opened. Evie raced in. 'Suzanna, you won't believe it but Inspector Monteith has brought his girlfriend with him. She looks just like a film star. She wears make-up and has the most gorgeous hat and the most beautiful engagement ring in the world. Just wait until you see her.'

Suzanna gripped the board hard. 'For St George's sake, Evie,' she said through gritted teeth, 'The lady is a new convert come to visit your mother. Inspector Monteith has no girlfriend.'

'She is his girlfriend, really and truly, Mummy says so.'

'It's not true, Evie. You've got things muddled.'

Mr Shepard opened the door. 'We've two visitors, Suzanna. Can you lay on tea and cakes, please? Come on, Evie, you can join us now. The prayer meeting is over.'

'Who are the visitors, sir?'

'Peter Monteith and his fiancée. A right good looker he has there, lucky man.'

Evie shouted, 'Suzanna, look out, you're burning Daddy's best shirt.'

Automatically Suzanna snatched up the iron, but too late and she wasn't sorry. She waited for Mr Shepard and Evie to leave the room before she flung the iron against the bathroom door. Part of the handle broke off but she was past caring. She moved through to the kitchen, her eyes burning, wiped away a tear angrily as she lit the Primus under the kettle. She dragged out the trolley, not bothering with a cloth. Before she loaded it with crockery, she set out a plate of rock cakes and spat on one - but how could she be sure the woman would choose it? To be on the safe side she spat on the lot.

Chapter 64

Saturday, and Patsy and Leila were alone.

'They are taking on my sister, Michelle, when I leave,' Leila said, 'Please keep an eye on her, Patsy. She's a bit flighty you know. I want her to settle down in this job and not upset Dalia.'

'So Mrs Jones has persuaded the superintendent to give Dalia your job?'

'Yes, he agreed they couldn't waste time vetting external candidates.'

'Dalia would still have got the job if they had advertised outside,' Patsy said, 'No one at secretarial school could touch her for speed and accuracy, and she's a natural organiser.'

'I wish the same could be said of my sister,' Leila replied. 'I wouldn't have put her on myself but my father wrote to the superintendent and I suppose it saves security having to do a lot of extra checking.'

Mrs Jones looked in. 'Miss Quigley, the superintendent wants a word.'

Patsy raised her eyebrows at Leila who shook her head. 'Nothing I know of,' she whispered.

'Miss Quigley,' the superintendent started, 'You applied for a job in a museum in Cairo a while ago. Have you heard anything?'

'They have filled the post sir.'

'You are still interested in archaeology though? You have been keeping up your studies?'

'I am an external reader at the Technion and try to get there a couple of times a week but have had no opportunity to gain practical experience.'

The superintendent stared at his desktop and fiddled with his fountain pen. 'Miss Quigley, we all appreciate your work here. I am more than satisfied with the way that you have helped Sergeant Pinner come to grips with Operation Knitting Needle.'

She wondered if the superintendent realised that input into Operation Knitting Needle had slowed to a trickle since Sergeant Pinner had taken over.

The superintendent, now leaning over his desk, went on, 'It's just, with the career you have in mind, I wondered if you would like me to keep an ear open for a suitable vacancy in Egypt. I can give you excellent references.'

Patsy clenched her fists. The story of her father's confession had achieved official status. The superintendent wanted her out.

He was smiled paternally as if expecting gratitude and she realised he was trying to help so placed her hands tidily on her lap. 'Thank you, sir, I would appreciate it.'

The superintendent sat up straight. 'Meanwhile,' he said, 'You will, of course, take on the role of office manager when Miss Boutaji leaves.'

'But Miss Leitner, her qualifications...'

'Out of the question, my dear. Top brass won't wear another foreigner in charge of the office. I had to pull strings all this year, as it was, to keep Miss Boutaji. It is either you or we'll have to bring in a British police officer from traffic, and none of them has decent typing skills. Managerial experience will look good on your CV, Miss Quigley. We'll interview both you and Miss Leitner, of course.'

Patsy left the office fuming at the injustice, and felt guilty because she couldn't fight it. The matter was out of the superintendent's hands. She was glad Dalia didn't come into the office on Saturdays. She couldn't have looked her in the eye.

****

Dalia woke from a dream that had left her sexually aroused, alarmed that Shimon not Peter had featured in it. She looked at her clock wondering why the alarm clock hadn't sounded, until she remembered it was Saturday and she had left a phone message for her parents saying that she would be spending Shabbat with friends.

She reached for her purse and took out her engagement ring. Replacing it on her finger by the window, she admired the opal's changing colours. Mrs Shepard had liked it too. 'Unusual, but it suits you,' she had said.

That reminded Dalia that at some point during their visit to the Shepards the previous evening, she and Peter had agreed to join them on a ramble to Khayet beach today and she was meeting Peter for breakfast.

She replaced the ring in her purse. She didn't want Giza telling her mother about her engagement before she did.

She fished out a dirndl skirt and white blouse. Not a particularly suitable outfit for a ramble, but close fitting shorts would scarcely ingratiate her with Addy. Footwear? Her tough walking shoes and thick socks were at Bereishit, so it was either high-heeled court shoes or sandals. Sandals invited stubbed toes but were less likely to cause a sprained ankle.

She packed her swimming costume, towel and sun cream into a haversack, pulled on her floppy tembel and slipped quietly out of the empty Sabbath digs to join Peter at an Arabic café near

Kingsway. Peter came to the door and kissed her on the cheek. 'I do love you so,' he whispered.

He had already ordered, so coffee was on the table, and the waiter immediately brought them grilled flat fish with lemon wedges and warm pita bread. As Peter unfolded his paper napkin he asked, 'Did you write to the superintendent to let him know you were taking a day of your annual leave, tomorrow?'

She nodded, while biting into the bread.

'And did you ask to have your day off changed from Saturday to Sunday in future?'

She nodded again, tears not far from her eyes as she wondered how she was going to break the news to her parents.

By the time they had finished breakfast, the sun was already warm but pleasantly so, quite different from the enervating heat of high summer. They took the bus that climbed the Stella Maris Road. Dalia pushed away the memory of roaring up it on the back of Shimon's bike. She must not think of Shimon. Peter was just as good-looking and a great deal kinder.

The Shepards, their two children and a smooth-haired terrier were waiting on the veranda but the sullen Arabic maid, who had glared fiercely the previous evening, was not with them.

Addy, dressed in a tweed skirt and sensible brogues, eyed Dalia's sandals doubtfully, 'Are you sure you'll be all right walking in those?'

Dalia nodded, although she knew she wouldn't.

Addy and Jim struggled into hefty rucksacks and picked up stout walking sticks, the two children put their arms through their haversacks. Dalia felt her eyes smart the scene reminding her so much of the carefree outings when she was little and her family had explored the forests of Bavaria.

They took the rutted lane at the rear of the house that led, sooner than she had expected, to an unspoiled section of mountain. Lush grass highlighted by tall yellow daisies made up the last float of the colourful spring parade preceding the drab march of summer. The air smelt fresh but warm. Jim Shepard let his dog off its lead and it bounded out of sight behind weathered limestone rocks, only to scamper back to check on its owner's continued existence. The children raced ahead. Jim and Addy strode on purposively.

Peter took her hand and they lagged behind to steal a surreptitious kiss behind a large rock. Peter tugged her down to green but dry ground. She took a deep breath and relaxed, keeping her engagement ring prominently on display to reassure Peter that he was entitled to a certain amount of lasciviousness with a fiancée.

'I could stay here with you all day,' Peter said as he lay above her, propping his weight on his elbows, and kissing her neck, while his hands slipped over her breasts.

The sensations thrilled her and she longed to go further, but this was hardly the time. 'I think the Shepards might notice our absence,' she whispered.

Peter released her reluctantly, and, to her relief, without signs of Second Chosen guilt. They hurried to catch up with the others who were standing at the tip of the mountain spur.

'Jim and I often wander here in the evening to enjoy the view,' Addy said.

Dalia gazed at the promontory to the south bearing the picturesque ruins of an ancient castle. Who would guess that, close by, lay a modern concentration camp imprisoning Jewish refugees?

She looked down the steep, craggy slope to the emerald strip of citrus trees separating the Carmel range from the white-rimmed sea. Deceptively peaceful those citrus groves, but she knew they hid army camps and ack-ack guns. She tried to pick out her own property at el-Tirah and wondered if British soldiers were hiding beneath her orange trees. If so, was her manager charging them rent? It would provide a useful source of income now oranges were worthless. She must ask her father about it. Memory jolted into place. Would her parents still be talking to her?

'That's our route,' Jim said, pointing to a narrow path twisting its way through thorn bushes. Dalia surveyed her flimsy sandals.

'There's a proper road on the next spur,' Peter said, 'That goat track's not safe.'

'Nonsense, Peter,' Jim contradicted, 'Addy and I have scrambled down here more times than you've had hot dinners.'

Without waiting for an answer, he jumped down three feet of rock. Addy, Evie, and Clare followed close behind. Dalia watched the children bump down on their bottoms using thorn bushes as brakes.

Peter's face had lost its earlier good humour but he held out his hand to help her down.

She slipped and slithered despite Peter's help, kicking stones that ricocheted down the slope. Only the zigzag nature of the path prevented the stones injuring those in front.

Dalia saw the Shepards, now well ahead, stop where the path temporarily widened to a grassy sward. She noticed Jim and Addy pull out handkerchiefs and hold them to their noses, Clare was hiding her head in her mother's skirt, and Evie had clapped her hands over her face. The terrier, high on the rocks over a small gorge, lifted his head skywards and howled.

As she and Peter drew closer, a terrible smell hit her, like the stench of forgotten meat. A grey sweetness caught the back of her throat.

Jim took his handkerchief from his nose long enough to shout, 'Come here, Dandy,' but the dog maintained its post, howling yet more loudly.

Jim gave a piercing whistle and the animal jumped slowly, reluctantly down the rocks, whining all the way, its tail between its legs. Dalia wanted to move on, but Peter put his arm round her restraining her. She noticed his arm was trembling.

Jim put the dog on its lead but it strained forward, whining, trying to drag its master up the rocks.

'Where is that smell coming from?' Addy asked, 'Jackals and hyenas should have finished off anything before it reached that state of decay.'

Peter stared down at the ground and muttered, 'We killed a couple of smugglers round here.'

Dalia stiffened. So this, she thought, was where it had happened, that incident that had so upset Peter in March.

'You left the bodies unburied?' Jim looked shocked.

Peter shook his head, 'No. We piled a stone cairn above each body. Nothing could have dug them out.'

Jim handed the dog's lead to Addy, and climbed the rocks. Clare was still hiding her face in Addy's skirt. Evie had wandered off towards the gorge.

'Evie!' Addy yelled, 'Wait for your father. You don't want to see anything you shouldn't.'

Evie scuttled back and clutched Dalia's hand.

Addy looks accusingly at Peter, 'Shouldn't you have taken the bodies to Haifa?'

Dalia clenched her fists. What had it to do with Addy? But she bit her tongue.

She could tell Peter was trying hard to appear nonchalant when he shrugged, but his short, jerky sentences betrayed tension. 'They were Muslim. My men said we should bury them. Before dusk. Identification would have been a lengthy process. They weren't Palestinians.'

Jim shouted from the top of the rocks, 'Peter, didn't you bury them before you piled on those stones?'

Peter muttered, 'We'd no spades.'

Jim climbed down again, 'You kept jackals out all right, but you left chinks for the flies. If you couldn't dig, you should have found a cave.' He wiped a band of sweat from under his hat. 'Nothing you can do about it now, short of pouring a few sacks of concrete over the lot.'

Addy thumped the ground with her stick. 'Jimmy, hurry up and move on. This is no place for children.' She marched forward, her back rigid with disapproval, Clare still clinging to her skirt.

Dalia, feeling an illogical need to explain, withdrew her arm from Peter, let go Evie's hand and strode forward. 'Addy, Peter didn't want those men killed.'

Addy gave her a hard stare. 'With hashish smugglers it's a case of kill or be killed. You'll have to learn to live with that, my girl, if you're going to marry a British policeman.'

Behind her Peter protested, 'Police are supposed to protect people not shoot them, Addy.'

****

Suzanna had not gone out onto the veranda to wave everyone off, not with that Miss Leitner clinging brazenly to Inspector Monteith, and them not even married, just engaged.

She scanned the list of tasks Mrs Shepard had left on the draining board but was in no hurry to start. When enough time had passed to make it unlikely anyone would run back, she made herself a cup of tea and some toast. She brought out the newspaper that she had hidden in her cubicle and sat in the dining room as if she owned the house, re-reading an article about government training grants for health care nurses.

She took some of Mrs Shepard's best writing paper from the desk in the lounge and wrote a letter, heading it with her brother's address, then walked down to the main road to post it.

****

The cool changing-hut on Khayet Beach smelled of seaweed. Dalia sat in her bathing costume on the sand-sprinkled seat, her arms huddled round her thighs. She thought she had known all there was to know about death and violence but that scene half way down the mountain had brought home the reality of human mortality. She knew how unsettling Peter would have found this morning's episode. She wanted to comfort him and, if she were honest, wanted him to comfort her.

Outside the door Evie called, 'Miss Leitner, we're going into the water now, Mummy says we'll see you down there. Please hurry. It will be more fun with you.'

She stood up, folded her clothes and opened the door. Peter was standing outside. She flung her arms round him. He kissed her gently and then drew her, not towards the sea, but to the rear of the bathing station. She leaned back against the hut as he bent towards her and kissed her harder, his tongue exploring her mouth, his hands slipping down her bathing costume straps to expose her breasts. This is what she wanted, needed. 'Oh, Peter,' she whispered. He moved his head down from her lips, past her neck still kissing her until his mouth fastened on her right nipple. Intense pleasure surged through her body. She arched herself against the throbbing mass imprisoned in Peter's swimming trunks. Sliding her hands down the length of his body, she closed her fingers around the cord of his trunks, drawing him towards her.

'Peter, Dalia, where the heck have you got to? The children are all waiting for you.'

Jim's voice from somewhere close.

Peter pulled away, and Dalia hastily pulled up her straps.

'Oh, Dalia,' Peter whispered. He stepped back a pace. 'Oh my darling, I do so want you. Go on down to the sea with Jim, dearest. I'll see you there.' He turned and hurried off towards the fence separating the site from undisturbed sand dunes.

Dalia took a deep breath, straightened her costume and attempted to step sedately between the huts.

'Peter is feeling sick after that experience on the mountain,' she told Jim, 'He needs a little while before he joins everyone.'

'The idiot should have thought of that, two months ago,' Jim replied.

Walking across the sand Dalia found she was shaking with excitement, and could still feel the thrill of Peter's mouth on her body. She flushed to think how far they might have gone if Jim hadn't called them. She knew now, without a doubt, that she loved Peter, and the way things were going they should marry as soon as they could.

****

Half an hour before Suzanna was due to catch her bus, Evie came back alone, bursting through the kitchen door in tears and flinging her haversack on the floor.

Suzanna knelt down and put her arms round her, 'What is the matter, Evie, where are the others?'

'Mummy's caught the bus into Haifa with Clare and Miss Leitner. Daddy said I had to go home with him because I'm not a cissy.'

'But where's your father?'

'With Inspector Monteith at the bottom of the lane. Daddy said I had to run home and ask you to put the kettle on.'

'But why have you been crying?'

Evie merely pushed her head more firmly against her.

'Didn't you enjoy the seaside?'

She heard a muffled reply, 'Suzanna, it was lovely, but I hated the smell.'

'Smell?'

Evie raised her head. 'From when Inspector Monteith buried real dead people under piles of rocks.'

'You found dead people and Inspector Monteith buried them?'

Evie shook her head vigorously. 'No, Suzanna, Inspector Monteith buried the people a long time ago and they were smelling. He told Daddy they were hashish smugglers.'

'Why did he bury them?'

'Because he killed them.'

'Evie, policemen don't go round killing hashish smugglers. They arrest them and take them to prison.'

'Suzanna, it's true. Inspector Monteith told Daddy all about it on his way home. He said they would get tied up in red tape if he took them back.'

Evie burst into tears again. Suzanna automatically soothed her hair while thinking. She knew that Ahmed al-Zeid's group used hashish smugglers to deliver their messages. Could he be...?

Evie lifted her head again. 'I wanted to go home on the bus with Mummy, Suzanna. I didn't want to walk home with Daddy and Inspector Monteith and smell the bodies again. I don't ever want to walk to Khayet Beach again.'

'Perhaps your Baba will choose another path next time.'

'But Suzanna, you can't go any other way, except if you go all the way round to the next bit of mountain to the road and Daddy doesn't like walking on proper roads. All the paths down the mountain go to that place because it's only a thin bit of mountain. There's wadis on both sides.'

Habib would be able to pinpoint the location from that description, Suzanna thought, as she filled the kettle. She looked at the clock and hoped Mr Shepard would arrive soon or she was going to miss her bus, but she couldn't leave an eight year old on her own in that state.

Ten minutes later, she phoned Angelique to say she was catching the later bus. Angelique told her Habib had already left to meet her.

Mrs Shepard and Claire arrived home before Mr Shepard.

'That husband of mine, He hasn't the sense he was born with,' Mrs Shepard said by way of apology, 'All the same, Suzanna, there was no need for you to stay. The Lord would have protected Evie.'

****

After listening to a long grumble about being kept waiting for so long at the bus station, Suzanna told Habib what she had learnt.

'You were right to stay and listen to the child,' he conceded, 'I pray it is not Ahmed, but in my heart I am sure it is. Only yesterday, someone called into the shop saying that the Grand Mufti needed him in Baghdad urgently and asked if I knew where he was. No one has heard from him. I will collect some of Ahmed's friends and investigate.'

Chapter 65

Dalia did not intend to repeat Thursday's sartorial mistake. After breakfast on Sunday, she changed out of her office clothes, removed her make-up, and dressed in her dowdiest clothes; then waited in her room until it was time to meet Peter. She slipped downstairs and closed the front door gently behind her.

Peter, waiting outside, hooked her arm into his. 'The two of us going to Sharing together!' He gave a satisfied sigh. 'I have been waiting for this moment for so long.'

She wished they were off to the beach or somewhere else where they could continue what they had been doing yesterday before Jim had interrupted them, but said nothing, just kissed him on the cheek.

They reached the hall. Outside, clusters of people in elegant clothes stood round chatting. Jim came rushing over, 'Dalia, would you mind if I take Peter off?'

She did mind but, without waiting for her reply, Jim led Peter round the side of the building. People threw her curious glances and she was conscious yet again of her inappropriate attire. She went into the hall, looking for Mrs Shepard, but the chairs were now arranged in a number of small circles, and occupied by groups of children, so she went back.

No one talked to her. The heat radiating from the hall's corrugated iron wall grew uncomfortable. She moved into the shade of a fig tree growing in a dry-stone wall. A pair of bulbuls, pecking at ripening apricots beyond the wall, reminded her of Bereishit, and by association, her parents. She worried yet again about her parents' reaction to her conversion. It was all very well telling herself that her grandmother had married a gentile but at least her grandmother had brought up her father as a Jew.

Peter and Jim returned. Peter's cheeks glowed angry red. Jim looked sad. He said, 'The Spiritual Guides want to see you, Dalia.'

She clutched Peter's arm but he shook his head, 'They insist on seeing you alone, sweetheart. I'll wait here.'

Curiosity more than anything made her follow Jim through a door at the rear of the hall. She found herself in the room where she had met Addy on Thursday but the furniture had been re-arranged. A group of men, in best suits sat in a semicircle, bibles on their laps, facing a single empty chair. She recognised Inspector Sutton next to Mr Manners in the centre. Jim Shepard slipped into a seat at the side.

Mr Manners waved her to the lone chair. She realised then that she was in an interview situation and regretted more than ever her shabby dress.

Mr Manners addressed her formally, 'Miss Leitner, you came forward on Thursday to give your heart to the Lord, for which we give praise.' He paused. The other men chorused Amens. 'We live in dangerous times for those who have cut themselves off from God's love, so recently we have adopted the practice of receiving converts on active military service into fellowship as soon as they come forward.' His voice changed to a tone she imagined him using to a customer who had neglected to arrange an overdraft. 'However, you, Miss Leitner, are not on active service and you are no brand to be plucked from the burning. As a member of the First Chosen you already have a contract with the Almighty, but are at liberty to move on to the new when you understand the differences.'

'Such being the case, it is the opinion of the Spiritual Guides assembled here that you should receive adequate instruction in the New Testament before we receive you into fellowship. Our Sister in the Lord, Adelina Shepard, will provide this.' Mr Manners paused and glanced at Inspector Sutton. 'There is one other matter. Until you are baptised and received into the fellowship of Saints you must understand that it would not be proper for our brother in Christ, Peter Monteith, to enter into a state of holy matrimony with you.'

Dalia sat up straight and tilted her chin. How dared these pompous men interfere with her private life? Before she could frame an indignant response, Jim Shepard had stood and was facing the others, 'Dear Brothers in Christ, the Lord has commanded me to speak on this matter. This young soul,' he glanced at Dalia and gave her a brief smile, 'made a courageous decision on Thursday when she let the Lord into her heart. She forsook the ways of her parents and friends, a sacrifice many of us have not been called on to make.' He looked hard at Inspector Sutton who flushed and averted his eyes. 'Being a babe in faith,' Jim continued, 'she should be treated as we treat our young children of the flesh, and although she may not participate in Sharing, I say she should be allowed to sit with us in companionship.'

A serious looking man with a tidy toothbrush moustache, called out, in a heavy Arabic accent, 'Amen, Brother Shepard. The Lord our God is a merciful God. He tempers the wind to the shorn lamb.'

Mr Manners drew himself up even straighter and stared the man down. Jim resumed his seat and Inspector Sutton rose.

'Brethren in Christ, we agreed after much prayer that we needed to test this young person's faith. We did not take that decision lightly. Our brother Shepard must search his heart to discover why he is in conflict with the rest of the saints gathered here.'

'Amen to that,' Mr Manners intoned. 'Now let us pray again.'

The men knelt on the rough, wooden boards. Jim motioned to her to follow suit. She hesitated, intending to walk out but remembering Aliyah Beth needed her to be close to Jim, obediently dropped to her knees. She cursed under her breath when she heard a gentle zing and felt a ladder in one stocking run from knee to thigh.

On the other side of the wooden partition children sang, *'One door, the Lordly one, and yet the sides are two. We're on the inside, but where are you?'*

If she was an insider for Peter, she thought, she could stomach being an outsider for other Second Chosen.

Mr Manner's lengthy prayer finished. Jim stepped forward and escorted her back.

'I'm sorry, Peter,' he apologised. 'I couldn't swing it. Len persuaded everyone that Dalia only converted to marry you.'

Peter tucked her arm into his reassuringly, 'We both know that's not true, Sweetheart.'

Dalia hoped Jim would blame the heat for her flushed face.

Evie and Clare skipped over from the hall. Jim waved them away. Dalia watched them droop over to the bus stop. A bus drew up.

'Dalia,' Jim said, 'I am afraid you are going to have to sit on the bench at the back during Sharing.'

Peter glared at him. 'Then I will sit with her.'

Dalia felt confused, unsure of why the issue of where she sat seemed so important and gazed round her. She saw Addy step off the bus on the main road dressed in dark patterned silk with a fetching saxe-blue couturier hat. Evie and Clare ran over to their mother and clung to her hands. Mr Manners approached her. Addy bent down and said something to the children. They let go of her hands and walked slowly over to their father.

Peter took her arm again and they went into the hall. Fewer people present this morning, mostly civilians, the men in well-pressed suits, the women in expensive dresses and pretty hats. The chairs had been re-arranged yet again, this time into two concentric circles surrounding a table that held a still life arrangement of earthenware jug, silver chalice and cottage loaf on a wooden platter.

Peter led her to a bench at the back and sat beside her while Jim and his children settled in the inner circle. Addy joined her family. She saw Jim say something to his wife. Addy turned and waved. A man in the outer circle stood and, in broken English, asked everyone to join him in prayer. For the next hour and a half, men from both circles chose hymns, stood with open bibles to ramble on about pomegranates on the bottom of priests' robes and prophets burning dung; more men prayed. Other men shouted Hallelujah and Amen at frequent intervals. The women listened and joined in the singing.

Halfway through the service Mr Manners walked to the central table and broke the loaf of bread with his fingers before passing the plate to a man in the front row. The plate passed from hand to hand. The adults, both men and women, took a crumb and ate it. Jim left his seat when the plate reached him, and brought it over to Peter. The two men each took a crumb. Jim returned to his place and passed the plate on. The last person to receive the bread returned it to the table. Mr Manners then poured wine from the jug into the chalice. That too went the rounds, everyone taking a sip, Jim again leaving the circle to bring the chalice over to Peter.

Mr Manners gave out notices about women's meetings and forthcoming baptisms after which the program resumed its previous impromptu style. It ended with Mr Manners intoning a blessing.

On the final Amen, Peter sprang from the bench and dragged her outside.

'I'm not going to that hall ever again,' Dalia stated as soon as they were outside. Peter took both her hands, 'Of course you're angry, Sweetheart, and so am I. You needn't attend Sharing until you are baptised, but evening evangelical services are different. Like Thursday's Service, but not on such a grand scale. Mrs Shepard has invited us to supper tonight, so we have to go.'

He put his arm round her and kissed her hair.

She had to keep in touch with Jim Shepard, so gave in. 'OK! But no Sharing again, you promise?'

'Not until the Spiritual Guides let you sit in fellowship.'

'What about our wedding?'

'That will be the hardest part, but the Lord will give me the strength to contain myself. I will not give way to my baser instincts again as I did yesterday.'

She wanted to say 'Do I have to restrain my baser instincts too?' but without the boost of alcohol felt too embarrassed to voice her thoughts aloud.

Chapter 66

Patsy saw the notice on the bulletin board inviting people already on the payroll to apply for the position of office manager. She felt tempted to do nothing about it, but the vision of a ham-fisted British Constable in charge was more than she could bear. What should she tell Dalia, though? Claim to be applying just to get interview practice? Why did war have to make things so unfair?

She arrived in the office close behind Dalia, who immediately shot her left arm into the air and flourished an engagement ring with a stone that shimmered pink and pearl.

'Oh, that's beautiful,' Leila exclaimed, 'I have never seen an opal in an engagement ring before, but it's really lovely.'

'Peter could think of nothing beyond a straightforward diamond,' Dalia replied, 'but I picked this out. The assistant gave a great spiel, that opals were unlucky unless they were your birthstone. Luckily, Peter overheard. He treated the woman to a sermon on superstition and insisted I had it.'

Patsy grinned as she took her place at her desk. 'For once the Second Chosen have their use, but watch your step, Dalia. They'll take over your life if you let them.'

Dalia flushed, paused at Patsy's desk on her way to her own, and whispered so only she could hear, 'I got converted on Thursday.'

Patsy was too staggered to reply.

Leila called over. 'You'll still be applying for my job, won't you?'

'It won't be worth it,' Dalia replied, 'I'll be leaving as soon as Peter and I are married.'

Patsy experienced a wave of relief that receded to reveal a fresh anxiety. Dalis'a conversation gave her access to Second Chosen gossip. The office would no longer be a haven. The sooner she found herself a job in Egypt the better.

****

Mrs Shepard was working at the hospital. Evie answered the phone, a new skill, exercised with pride. 'Suzanna, it's for you. Your brother says he wants to speak to you.'

Something had to be very wrong if Habib was phoning her at work so Suzanna told Evie to take Clare into the garden. Her hand shook as she picked up the receiver. 'Um?' she almost whispered.

'No, our mother's OK,' Habib said.

Suzanna's relief made her feel dizzy. Habib's voice altered. 'But you know those bodies you told me about?' He paused and she heard a sob as he said, 'One was Ahmed.'

She reminded herself that Ahmed al-Zeid had been Habib's best friend so moderated the relief in her voice. 'Ya Habib, I am so sorry.'

Habib rushed on, 'Suzanna, you do not know what it was like. I could only identify Ahmed because of his watch. Can you imagine that? And I had to do it on my own.'

'On your own? You said you were taking friends.'

'Yes, but they were Muslim. They helped remove the top layers of stones, and left me to uncover the bodies. Said they were not allowed to touch them. It was all right for me. Then they kept asking me to check things like - were the bodies facing east and how were they dressed and then they decided it didn't matter what they were dressed like because they were martyrs. It was horrible; they kept shouting unimportant things at me while I was looking at the awful thing that had been my friend.' She heard the break in his voice, 'My blood brother, and I could not bear to touch him.'

Suzanna gripped the receiver hard. If she had known how identifying the bodies would affect Habib, she would never have told him where they were.

'What upsets me most, Suzanna,' Habib continued, 'I can't talk to Angelique about exacting revenge. I wish I could. She is clever; she would know the best way.'

'Habib,' Suzanna shrieked. She took a breath and lowered her tone, 'It's not your job to plan revenge. Your job is to keep your household calm while Angelique is carrying your baby. Ahmed enjoyed taking risks. He would have appreciated you making the effort to find out what happened to him but that is the end of your responsibility.'

'What *is* the matter with you?' Habib's shout had her jerking the receiver from her ear. 'I have to avenge him. He was my blood brother. I will kill his murderer, Suzanna, you can count on that. I may let his other friends help, but I will be the one doing the killing.'

'No, Habib. Think of Angelique and the baby.'

'You don't understand about blood brothers, Suzanna.'

****

At the Hadassah hospital, Dalia sat in an armchair intended for patients' relatives. Ruth had only a ten-minute break so Dalia announced her engagement without preamble and showed Ruth a studio portrait of Peter.

Ruth studied it closely, 'He looks sensitive, your Peter, and very handsome, but are you sure about this, Dalia? You, of all people, marrying a gentile?'

Dalia returned her friend's gaze without flinching and said, 'Yes,' with her chin high, but knew she was lying.

Ruth gave her a hug. 'Then Dalia, I am so happy for you. When are you planning to marry?'

'Not until September.'

'Oh Dalia, I am going to Egypt at the end of July! I hope I can get leave to come up.'

'You'll have to. You're my chief bridesmaid.' Then she remembered, 'But you may not want to be. Things are a bit more complicated than I told you.'

'With you they would be,' Ruth sighed, and settled back into her chair. 'Your Peter is in the middle of a divorce, I suppose?'

'No,' Dalia stared ahead at the corridor's white wall tiles. The smell of carbolic was strong. 'You may think it's worse though.' She gritted her teeth and came out with it. 'He's a fundamentalist Christian, Ruth.' She looked down at the black and white floor tiles, 'and this is the bit you'll hate. We can only marry because I converted.'

Ruth sat up straight, her face a mask of disbelief, 'Ai-ee! You! You've converted - to Christianity!'

'Yes.'

'But why? Just so you can marry this Peter?'

Dalia wished she knew the answer. 'Ruth, I can't explain what happened.' She felt her fingers dig into the flesh of her forearm in her frustration, 'One minute I was sitting on a chair listening to this weird American preacher; the next I was walking down the aisle being saved.'

Ruth shook her head. 'I've heard of that happening, but,' she added comfortingly, 'the conversion wears off once people remember who they are.'

'Ruth, if it does wear off, I lose Peter.'

Ruth bit her upper lip, 'Dalia, only you can decide, but one thing I know. This will really hurt your parents and Uri.'

'Don't I know it! How I am going to break it to my mother?'

Ruth frowned. 'You could hang on without saying anything for a while. Sometimes things resolve themselves.'

'Well, let me put it this way, how am I going to explain not coming home for Shabbat? I've had to change my day off to Sunday.'

A stern looking sister poked her head round the door leading into the ward. 'Nurse Cohen, you are needed, now.'

Ruth shrugged helplessly and stood up. 'Oh Dalia, you have got yourself into a pretty pickle. You can use me as an alibi any time you like, but I can't really see that working for long.'

'Nurse Cohen!' the sister barked.

Ruth scuttled off and Dalia was alone in the white tiled corridor.

Chapter 67

This was one of Patsy's Roger-sitting evenings. It entailed kneeling on the floor, racing engines, and reminded her of playing trains with the loving father of her childhood.

'Never mind,' Roger consoled after her fourth crash, 'You're almost as good as my Dad, now.'

She was picking up her derailed engine, when the phone rang. She answered. It was her mother, and to her relief, speaking normally.

'Patsy dear, your father is going back into hospital for tests for a week, so I thought I would snatch the opportunity to visit Haifa on Saturday and spend Sunday in Nazareth with Nelly Barker. You remember her, don't you, the head of the Anglican girl's school? Are you up to seeing me?'

'But of course I want to see you Um Pat.'

'Oh Patsy, I am so glad. You don't know how ashamed I am for keeping you away, but quite honestly, I didn't know whether I was coming or going. The psychiatrist has explained it to me now, how common all these delusions are. He has given me a book by Freud to read, not that I can make head nor tail of it but it is comforting to know that this sort of thing happens quite often. What time do you finish on a Saturday? I hope the flap over Rommel crossing into Egypt hasn't given you too much overtime?'

'I generally work until seven now, but on a Saturday I can arrange to leave at four if I have something special on.'

'Good. I'll meet you outside the police station and we'll have tea at Grizzly's. Then I'll treat you to dinner at the hotel I've booked into, not the tennis club one. I couldn't face that. So many people don't understand about your father's delusions. I'm staying in a little Jewish place on Kingsway, more convenient for seeing you, as it turns out. On a Saturday they don't serve an evening meal until after dark, of course, but you won't mind, will you? Oh, I nearly forgot. Would you like to come to Nazareth with me on the Sunday to see Nelly Barker? I'm going to Morning Service at the Anglican Church with her and Nelly says you are very welcome to have lunch with us afterwards. I'm catching the afternoon bus back to Jerusalem. You'll be all right on the bus back to Haifa by yourself, won't you?'

'Um Pat, I am twenty, remember.'

'Of course, dear, I keep forgetting. How time flies. I'll see you Saturday then after work.'

Patsy put down the phone, and breathed out hard. A fraction of the iceberg in her stomach disintegrated. Thank goodness for that psychiatrist, although she had a feeling that her mother might have deliberately misunderstood what he was trying to tell her.

****

Dalia's mother punched the air repeatedly as she strode round the kitchen, letting fly a long tirade punctuated with the refrain, 'Ai-ee. We should never have allowed you to work in Haifa.'

Dalia had not yet told her mother the worst, only that she had brought Peter home to speak to her father. She kept as still as she could. Usually that worked and her mother calmed down as fast as she had exploded.

Eventually her mother stopped pacing, and challenged, 'So, do you love this man?'

Dalia dared not answer aloud, just nodded.

'And you have settled on a date for the wedding?'

'Next September.'

Her mother, picking up paper and pencil from the sideboard, abruptly transformed herself from tragedy queen to efficient organiser.

'We will have everyone from Bereishit of course, that's 80,' she declared, 'And then you will want your class from school and their husbands and fiancés, say another sixty. Then there's the Rehovot group, another 30. Now how many people do you think this Peter of yours will want to bring?' She did not wait for an answer. 'Not to worry, say fifty, but that can be changed later. No need to order the marquees yet.'

'Stop, Eema, we cannot do it that way.'

Her mother looked up, frowning, 'Of course we can. Everyone will contribute like they did for Uri's engagement.'

'Eema,' Dalia began, but burst into tears before she could continue.

'What is it, darling?'

'Oh, Eema' she tried again, and became conscious of her mother's eyes measuring her waist-line, 'No, Eema, It's not what you're thinking. It's just...I don't know how to tell you. We are not getting married in Bereishit.'

'You are planning to marry in England? Ai-ee, you think the war will be over by September?'

'No Eema, not England, Haifa. We have to marry in the New Covenant Hall where Peter worships.'

Her mother moved into tolerant mode. She waved her hands, 'No matter. We will still have the reception in Bereishit.' Then she narrowed her eyes and looked suspicious, 'You say you have to marry where he worships? You have told this Peter of yours, I hope, that all my grandchildren will be Jewish?'

The moment she had been dreading had arrived. Dalia looked down at the flagstones and said, almost in a whisper, 'No Eema, they won't be.'

'Oh, yes they will. You leave it to me, my girl. I will soon put him right.'

'It's not like that, Eema.'

Her mother cut in, 'Dalia, we will say no more on this subject until I have spoken to your Peter.' She busied herself at the stove.

Obedience now would be cowardice, but Dalia had no stomach for heroics.

Peter and her father returned, Peter's face grave.

Her father put an arm round her mother's shoulders. 'Trudi, the four of us must talk before Shabbat.' He drew her mother gently away from the stove and settled her in a chair. Dalia sat down and motioned Peter into the chair beside her.

Her father was the last to sit. He placed his hands flat on the table, looking from one face to the other as if about to chair a committee.

'Trudi,' he said at last, 'Dalia has informed you that Peter came tonight to seek my permission to marry her? She has told you the complications?'

'About not being married from here...' Her father looked at her mother steadily. She faltered, cupped her chin with one hand. 'There's more?'

'Yes, Trudi, there's more. Dalia has converted to Christianity.'

Her mother gave a screech. 'Ai-ee! Dalia, tell him he has got this wrong.'

Dalia wanted to race out of the room. She wanted to hug Eema and reassure her. She wanted to cling to Peter. She wanted to rush to her father and sit on his knee as she used to when little. She wanted to do all these things at the same time, but none were appropriate.

Her father waited, impassive, looking as if he expected her to say something.

'I am sorry, Eema,' Dalia pushed her words through a constricted throat, 'but it is true.'

Eema jumped up, held her head high, and blazed, 'Then you are no longer my daughter.' She pushed her, 'Get out of my house.'

Her father stood, put both arms round his wife. 'Trudi, I know our Dalia. She is a true Jew however much, for the moment, she may imagine herself to be Christian. Dalia,' he said softly, 'You should have discussed this with us before making a decision that will affect our grandchildren.'

He stroked her mother's hair as she sobbed into his jacket. Then he looked at Peter. 'Peter, I believe it is only because my daughter loves you that she has taken this step. If you love her, as you say you do, would you still marry her if she were to retract that conversion? Would you still marry her if you had to bring up your children in the Jewish tradition? If not, it seems to me that you are asking her to love you more than you love her. You told me that you pray before you make any decision. Then I ask you to pray over this matter and if you love my daughter less than she loves you, I ask you not to marry her.'

Peter looked her father in the eye, 'Sir, I cannot love any human being more than I love my Lord but there is no living human I love more than your daughter. I have faith that she too loves my Lord more than she does me.'

Abba continued stroking her mother's hair.

Dalia shouted, 'I am going to marry Peter, Abba. No one can stop me.' She took hold of Peter's hand and pulled him outside.

While Peter was cranking the starting handle of the ancient Morris he had borrowed from a friend, her father came out and leaned through the window. 'Dalia, your mother is more upset perhaps than you might have expected. Some of it is not your fault. Ever since Shimon Mabovitch broke off his engagement, she and Aunt Elsa have been matchmaking. She will lose face.'

Dalia's eyes widened, her back stiffened. Why hadn't someone told her that Shimon was no longer engaged? But why should they? What business was it of hers that he had broken off his engagement?

Her father continued, 'Dalia, if you intend to go through with this marriage, then it would be better if you stay away from Bereishit until after your wedding. Before the wedding, there will be nothing but trouble between you and your mother. You will say things to each other that neither will forgive. When she can no longer change things, then your mother will come round and accept Peter as her son-in-law.'

The engine started and Peter jumped into the driving seat. Her father kept one hand on the window and lifted the other. He spoke to both her and Peter, 'I cannot let you get married without my blessing, so you have it, for what it is worth to you.'

He stepped back and returned to the house without looking back. Dalia burst into tears.

Peter drove out of the moshav and stopped the car a mile or so further on. He handed her his handkerchief, 'My poor darling, what a terrible evening you have had.' He pulled the ring out of his pocket. 'At least your father gave us his blessing so now you can wear this again.'

She shook her head. 'Not just now, Peter, please.'

****

Still shaken by the news she'd heard on Miss Barker's wireless in Nazareth, Patsy walked slowly up the steps leading to Beth's flat. Ovear one thousand people dead in London, another 600 buried under rubble; Westminster Abbey, the Tower of London and the Royal Mint, all hit. Would there be anything left of the England she knew?

Peter came out of his flat and approached her. 'Patsy, may I have a word?'

She followed him into his flat for the first time since that awful night he had received the telegram.

'Patsy, I am being exiled to Beersheba, just when Dalia really needs me. She's getting culture shock right, left and centre, her mother disowning her, the Second Chosen being over-cautious about accepting her into fellowship and she hasn't a clue about ordinary British customs. Could you keep a friendly eye on her while I am away?'

'Why me?'

'You're British, you work with her, you're the same age, and you understand the Second Chosen.'

'But I don't belong to them, Peter.'

Peter screwed his face, 'Under the circumstances that might even be an advantage. I could cheerfully murder the spiritual guides myself. Addy Shepard is being a brick but Dalia needs someone her own age to talk to. What I would like you to do, Patsy is put Dalia right on things like what to wear, and the kind of small talk that British women of your age indulge in.'

****

Patsy invited Dalia to coffee after work. They talked of the wedding dress, wedding cake, and bridesmaids.

'Clare and Evie will be flower girls, Patsy, and my best friend Ruth has agreed to be my chief bridesmaid, if she can get leave. Would you be a bridesmaid too?'

Patsy considered this. 'No,' she decided eventually, 'I am flattered but the Second Chosen won't allow it because I haven't been converted.'

Dalia stared. 'But why do you have to be converted? You were born Christian.'

Patsy sipped her coffee slowly to cover her own surprise, and then asked, 'Dalia, what does "being converted" mean to you?'

Dalia spoke as if stating the obvious, 'To change from being a Jew to being a Christian.'

'That is not what conversion means to the Second Chosen,' Patsy told her, 'they believe no one is born Christian. They don't count people from other churches as Christians unless they have been baptised by total immersion when grown up.'

Dalia looked confused. 'Then what is conversion?'

'I was hoping you could tell me, Dalia. Ever since I was five, I have wanted to know. Until I was nine, I took it for granted that I would be converted when I was old enough, even though I didn't understand what conversion was. By the time I was twelve I was afraid that I never would be converted, but when I reached thirteen, I became convinced that no one ever really converted, they just faked it. That theory works fine for people who have been brought up Second Chosen, but it doesn't explain why people like you and Peter get up from their seats and go down to the front. Why did you do that?'

Dalia laughed, a not very happy laugh Patsy thought. 'I don't know either, so that makes two of us.'

Patsy noticed Dalia's knuckles showing white as they clutched the tabletop.

'Staying with Second Chosen theology,' Dalia said, 'where does it leave me, with Ruth, coming all the way up from Alexandria to be my bridesmaid, if the spiritual guides won't let her?'

'The Second Chosen may allow you a Jewish bridesmaid since Jews don't need to convert. You will have to speak to Addy about it.'

'If Jews don't need to convert why can't Second Chosen marry Jews?'

Patsy sat still for a few seconds as she thought that one out. 'I guess the Second Chosen regard the new contract between God and themselves as bringing more responsibilities. Both partners in a Second Chosen marriage have a duty to bring up their children so they will convert when old enough. My father feels humiliated because I haven't converted. My mother is more relaxed about it.'

She remembered sitting beside her mother and Nellie Barker at the Anglican service in Nazareth. Her mother fitted in so well. She was glad she and her mother were still friends. Poor Dalia, having her mother disown her because of her conversion.

'Your mother,' she said to Dalia, 'Do you think she'll relent and come to the wedding?'

'I'm inviting my parents to the registry office ceremony. I hope my father will persuade my mother to come.'

****

'Keep your voice down,' Suzanna pleaded, 'you never know who is listening.'

While escorting her to the bus stop, Habib was rehearsing his plan to avenge his friend. Suzanna was by no means certain that Ahmed al-Zeid needed avenging. He had known the risks he was taking. In her opinion, the biggest crime Inspector Monteith had committed was making a fool of himself over that Leitner woman, but even for that, she didn't want him dead.

'Habib, from what I have heard, Inspector Monteith didn't kill your friend. It was his squad.'

'Suzanna, the squad were only following orders. We don't exact revenge on Arab policemen if they have to kill another Arab in the course of their duties. There would be no Arab policemen if we did. The British planned this murder. The British must pay. When will Inspector Monteith visit the Shepards next?'

'For St George's sake, Habib, even if I agreed with you about avenging Ahmed, charging up to the Shepards' house, and shooting Inspector Monteith there, is not the best way to set about it. You have Angelique and our mother to think of.' Not to mention other people, she thought. What would it do to the Shepard children if they witnessed the killing? 'You should leave revenge to your friend's family.'

'His family and Syrian comrades are concentrating on tracing the British woman who betrayed him. His other Palestinian comrades are assisting them. They all feel she is most to blame. They are leaving it to me to kill Inspector Monteith although they will assist me set up my trap.'

'Well, you can't kill him where I work. You'll get me into trouble.'

'If you don't want me to kill him at the Shepards' house, suggest somewhere more suitable.'

'I'll think about it,' she prevaricated, and jumped on to her bus.

Back home, she found Mrs Shepard in a foul mood.

'Jimmy has been called away again,' her employer informed her as soon as she stepped indoors, 'Inspector Monteith has been transferred to Beersheba, Lieutenant McIntyre has been posted to Cairo, and Inspector Sutton is on his way to Singapore. We women are going to have to manage on our own until the powers that be see fit to send my husband back.'

Suzanna wished Mrs Shepard had not told her where the police had posted Inspector Monteith, but was thankful it was at the other end of Palestine.

****

Addy knitted, while she talked, a baby's matinee jacket in fluffy white. She laughed when Dalia asked if she was pregnant.

'No, not for me. Suzanna's sister-in-law is expecting a baby soon.' She counted the stitches on her needle before looking up again. 'Peter told me that changing your rest day has made things awkward at your lodgings. You are very welcome to stay here overnight on Fridays, and on Saturday's too come to that, especially now Jimmy is away. We could use those evenings to help you catch up on scripture study.'

Dalia knew she ought to be grateful but resented the way Addy was taking over her life.

'Of course there's your other problem,' Addy continued, not giving her time to respond, 'Peter told me how you feel about attending Sharing while those pig-headed men on the Guidance Council are barring you from fellowship. Jimmy and I prayed it over before he flew off. While Peter is in Beersheba, it might be an idea if you have Sunday lunch with us. Sunday is Suzanna's day off, of course, so you could make yourself useful keeping an eye on the dinner while the children and I are at Sharing.'

It took Dalia a few minutes to realise the opportunity Addy had laid open.

'Hunt through every room of the Shepards' house.' Aaron had instructed at their last meeting, 'Find out where Jim Shepard keeps his papers. We have already searched his office.'

She had comforted herself then that she wouldn't get a chance to obey that order, but a good Aliyah Beth member couldn't let slip an opportunity thrust upon her.

Chapter 68

Patsy's first day as office manager. With the help of two constables, she manoeuvred Leila's large desk so that she could sit with her back against the wall. As she sat and sorted documents marked secret from the rest, she felt a new sense of responsibility, as if, at last, she was a real grown-up.

Most of the work that she reserved for herself stemmed from the revolt in Iraq. A top-secret report from Mr Shepard, suggested that British Intelligence should ask several Jewish terrorists, recently released from prison, to use their skills against the Iraqi rebels. She hoped the superintendent would allow her to add that item to the knitting needles. It was hopeless waiting for Sergeant Pinner.

She and Dalia were both hard at work when Leila's sister Michelle arrived. Remembering Leila's warning about Michelle's skills she handed her a pile of easy documents but, at the end of the morning, was dismayed to discover just how badly Michelle had typed them. The office was going to be more difficult to run than she had anticipated.

****

Sunday morning, after Addy and the children had left for Sharing, Dalia discovered Jim's papers spilling out of a folder in the Shepards' communal bedroom, a hotch-potch of diagrams, handwritten memos, and typewritten documents. She concentrated on text. The bulk concerned British plans for Palestine in the event of a German invasion. Those, she thought, would interest Aaron most.

When she spoke to him, though, he displayed more curiosity about the diagrams.

'I did not understand them,' she apologised.

Aaron waved a hand. 'No matter, I will have to bring in a photographer and communications expert anyway. When can you let us in?'

She had not anticipated that. It was one thing to look around the house, quite another to allow strangers in. Her conscience pricked as she thought about Addy's kindness, but there was no way she could back out now.

'Sunday morning is the only time. The Shepard family go to chapel then and it is the maid's day off.'

Chapter 69

Saturday evening and Suzanna was even more pleased than usual to be starting her day off. That scheming Miss Leitner had been at the Shepards since Friday evening, sleeping in the children's old room only a metre or so from her own cubicle.

Her brother's house was in turmoil when she arrived; the baby on its way. Angelique's mother had taken charge of her daughter and the midwife. Her own mother ruled the kitchen; Habib had escaped to a coffeehouse.

Suzanna huddled herself into a corner stuffing cocoa tins with cotton wool, as instructed by the midwife, unsure what this had to do with the coming baby but glad to be of use.

The baby, a healthy six-pound boy, arrived just before midnight. No long debate about the baby's name. The eldest son of a Christian Hadad was always George.

'If only Ahmed were alive to call me Abu George,' Habib said when she fetched him from the coffee shop.

She had to wait her turn to see the baby, so tiny, so beautiful and the image of Habib. The smell of him made her want to pick him up and hug him and cry. That awful Miss Leitner no longer seemed so important.

In the morning with her mother still in charge of the kitchen and Angelique's mother fussing over the baby, Suzanna felt surplus to requirements. She thought of the viyella nightdress she had made for the baby and the matinee jacket Mrs Shepard had knitted. She would have time to nip back to the Shepards and fetch them before lunch.

Suzanna couldn't remember when she had last been at the Shepards on a Sunday morning. She unlocked the back door with the key she kept in her bag and sniffed the aroma of roast beef as she let herself into the kitchen.

****

Dalia had locked the back door. She was standing on the veranda with the dining room door open behind her while Aaron and his colleagues worked in the dormitory. To her horror, she heard the hinges of the back door squeak open. She felt in her pocket. The key was still there. As a warning to Aaron, she called loudly, 'Who's there?' and moved cautiously inside.

****

When she heard the shout, Suzanna clapped a hand across her mouth to muffle a scream. She watched the door handle turn, too terrified to move. She almost fainted with relief when it opened to reveal the Leitner woman. Her relief turned to anger when the woman had the cheek to ask, 'What are you doing here?'

'I might ask you the same question,' Suzanna retorted.

Miss Leitner turned up her arrogant nose, 'Mrs Shepard invited me to stay overnight, and left me in charge until she returns from Sharing. She said nothing about you coming.'

'If it's any business of yours, which it isn't, I'm collecting the presents for my brother's new baby.' Suzanna moved forward until she was almost touching her opponent. 'Let me pass.'

Miss Leitner took her time stepping aside, then marched in front and leaned against the door leading into the family bedroom while Suzanna retrieved the baby gown from her cubicle.

She turned towards the bedroom but Miss Leitner did not budge. 'You have what you wanted, now leave.'

This really was too much. Suzanna glared at the other woman. 'I have to take Mrs Shepard's present as well. You may watch me collect it if you think me a thief.'

Miss Leitner opened the door reluctantly. Suzanna stooped to collect the matinee jacket wrapped in tissue paper from the sewing box beneath the table Mr Shepard used as a desk. As she stretched up, she noticed that his papers were arranged more neatly than usual. Mrs Shepard must have done some much needed tidying up. Mr Shepard hated anyone touching his work. She hoped he wouldn't be angry when he returned.

She mulled over the incident on the bus back to Habib's. It occurred to her that it could have been that Leitner woman, who had tampered with Mr Shepard's papers. The more she thought about it, the more convinced she became.

She considered mentioning her suspicions to Mrs Shepard but was certain her mistress would not believe her. There must be some way she could show up the woman for the underhand, scheming cow that she was.

The opportunity presented itself a week later when Mrs Shepard brought an extra bag of dirty clothes into the washhouse. 'I told Dalia we would do a bit of washing for her.'

Suzanna shook the contents out of the bag and put on one side an almost clean handkerchief reeking of the vile Lily of the Valley perfume Miss Leitner used to seduce Inspector Monteith.

When no one was looking, she dropped the handkerchief into Mr Shepard's folder.

Chapter 70

The hot weather had set in. Both Dalia and Michelle were sensible enough to stay indoors during their lunch hours but Patsy felt impelled to continue the trips to the Post Office that she had been making ever since Ahmed had stood her up.

On this day, her box still contained no explanatory letter from Ahmed, only a letter bearing her mother's handwriting. Patsy wiped the sweat from her face while she read it.

Dear Patsy,
Your father is back at work! He shouldn't be, of course. The doctor said he should convalesce for at least another month and if it had been peacetime, he would have recommended early retirement on medical grounds. The Spiritual Guides here in Jerusalem have been less than helpful about your father's troubles, and I am sorry to say your father is very much at odds with them. For the time being, we are attending the Anglican Church.
My doctor has insisted I take a break.

No surprise that. Her mother must be at the end of her tether. Goodness knows what she had to endure each evening after her father had come home. The current heat would make matters even worse.

Mrs McKinnon from the Scottish Church has offered to lend me her apartment in Safad. Would your superintendent let you take a few days' leave so we could spend some time together, just the two of us?

Patsy finished reading the letter and placed it in her purse. She had leave due but dared not abandon the office for a whole week. She would ask the superintendent for four days.

****

On the first day of her break, a cool breeze blowing across her face, Patsy lounged on the wooden balcony of an apartment in the older part of Safad, by her side a stack of green Penguin detective novels borrowed from the soldiers' rest home in Jerusalem, in her hand a glass of freshly squeezed orange juice. Three thousand feet below, curving beneath the tawny flanks of the Golem heights, the Sea of Galilee sparkled blue.

'I can't believe I am doing this,' her mother said as she picked up a novel. 'Having a holiday without your father. I couldn't have done it if Cook hadn't promised to keep an eye on him and ring the doctor if he has a relapse.'

****

Dalia sat mechanically typing, excited by the note Peter had left on her desk.

Dalia darling,
I've driven all the way from Beersheba and it's nearly dawn now. When I've finished this, I am going to the flat to sleep. I know you said you are having to do overtime all this week but could you phone me this afternoon to let me know what time you are finishing and I'll meet you and take you out to dinner.
Yours in the love of our Lord,
Peter

Tonight, Dalia thought, she would tell him about the full-dress civil ceremony that she and Addy were planning. She couldn't get over how sympathetic Addy had been after the Spiritual Guides had refused to let Ruth be part of the religious ceremony.

The telephone rang on Patsy's vacant desk. She left Michelle to answer it.

'For you, Dalia,' Michelle had her hand over the receiver, 'A man.'

'Peter?'

'No, someone else.'

Dalia rose from her typewriter, her stomach suddenly queasy. Who, apart from Peter or Addy, would ring her at work? Certainly no one from Aliyah Beth. An emergency? Something had happened to Peter, Uri, her parents?

'Hello.'

'Jim Shepard here.'

Instant relief. Probably just something to do with her baptism.

'I need to speak to you urgently.' Jim's voice sounded distant, not the ingratiating tone he usually used with her, 'I can't talk over the phone. Meet me in the café opposite the Post Office at 12.30.' He hung up.

What was the matter with Jim? What had he to say so secret that he couldn't tell her on the phone? Surely, the spiritual guides had already done their worst.

Conscious of Michelle's curious gaze, she said casually, 'A friend of Peter's. Wants to meet me at lunchtime; about the wedding, I guess.'

After that, she couldn't concentrate on her work. Her eyelids felt bloated, her mouth dry. Suppose the Spiritual Guides were postponing her baptism? Peter would insist on changing the wedding date. Only that morning she had posted invitations to the civil ceremony to both her parents and Ruth. Ruth had already applied for leave. Well, she would tell Peter there was no reason to change the date for the civil ceremony even if he postponed the religious one.

****

Peering through the café window Dalia could see Jim inside, stiff-backed, his lips pressed hard together. Walking through the café entrance she felt as if she were entering the principal's study after being caught truanting.

Instead of a conventional greeting, as she seated herself opposite him, Jim mouthed, 'Mossad el Aliyah Beth?'

She felt the blood drain from her stiffening face and wished she still carried a powder compact to hide behind.

'What are you talking about?'

The waiter arrived and took their order. Jim drew a handkerchief from his top pocket and wiped first his glasses and then his forehead. When the waitress had left, he said wearily, 'Stop the nonsense.' He drew a paper bag from his jacket pocket, held it out to her, 'You won't deny this is yours?'

She looked inside and saw the embroidered handkerchief that she had left amongst other clothes Addy had kindly offered to launder. It still gave out whiffs of Lily of the Valley, indicating Addy hadn't yet washed it. What, though, had it to do with Aliyah Beth?

She stared at Jim, wondering what he wanted her to say. He stared back as if the handkerchief explained everything. Seconds dragged on to minutes. The waitress brought their coffee. She picked up her cup; sipped gingerly at the hot liquid, determined that Jim should make the next move.

'You left it in my briefcase,' he said at last, 'I have investigated your background thoroughly since.'

Now she was well and truly confused. She had not bought this handkerchief until after she had searched through Jim's papers.

'Dalia, I'm giving you the chance to resign,' Jim ground out, 'to leave Haifa without ruining Peter's career. If you've any feeling at all for him that is the least you can do.'

He stood up leaving his coffee untouched. 'That's all I have to say.'

She wanted to scream, shout, and burst into tears. Instead, she sat in the café, finishing her coffee, thinking, now it was too late, of what she should have said, if only to learn how much he had found out.

She gazed round the crowded cafe. Any of the people here could be spying on her at Jim's orders. Contacting either Aaron or Max immediately was out of the question.

She made her way back to work, sought out Mrs Jones, pleaded a severe headache, and caught the bus to the top of Mt. Carmel. She sat on a seat in Allenby Park, deserted at this the hottest time of the day, sobbing while flies buzzed round the outside of her head and everything whirled inside.

When a young mother with a pram sat on the seat beside her, she stood up and found herself walking automatically towards the Shepards' house.

****

Suzanna was sitting under the locust tree, shelling peas when Miss Leitner walked past, without so much as a good afternoon. Insect bites covered the woman's face and her eyes were puffy red. She went through the back door as if a permanent resident.

Suzanna hurried into the kitchen after her but the Jewish woman had already moved on into the dining room, leaving the inner door ajar.

Suzanna sat at the kitchen table with the peas, positioning herself carefully. Through the partially open door, she could see Mrs Shepard leaning over a dress pattern pinned to the bridesmaids' material.

'Dalia,' her mistress was saying without lifting her eyes from her work, 'would you mind if we have today's session in here so I can finish cutting out this dress? It won't be done in time if I don't get a move on.'

Suzanna could not see Miss Leitner from where she was sitting but heard the stammer in her voice, 'I-if you don't mind, Addy, I need to talk to you in private.'

Mrs Shepard rolled up the material with the pattern still stuck to it and said, 'Eve, ask Suzanna to fetch a tray of tea into the lounge.'

Suzanna gave a smile of satisfaction. Inspector Monteith had almost certainly had the scales removed from his eyes and ditched the Leitner woman.

****

After the three quietest, most relaxing days Patsy had ever spent, she and her mother took a taxi and picnic meal to Tiberias, and hired a boat. The boatman had warned that he would have to take them back before dark so he could go fishing, but they

- 326 -

persuaded him to stay while the sun, setting over the Galilean hills, cast a golden path across the water.

Patsy trailed her fingers through the water while her mother talked about Jesus calling the fishermen. She was working out how to respond to the inevitable closing sentence, without hurting her mother's feelings. The anticipated sentence arrived at last, 'Patsy, I wish you would listen to the Lord's call, as those fishermen did.'

She responded with a question, 'Um Pat, how old were you when you were converted?'

'Well, dear, as far back as I can remember I have always felt my life belonged to the Lord. I went forward at a Good News service when I was fourteen but that was really only to confirm publicly what I had known in my heart since I was tiny. If you want to know about sudden conversion then you will have to speak to your father. He was a real sinner at university – but you must have heard his testimony many times when you were little. No? Perhaps he gave it most often before you were born.'

Her mother's hand was in the water now and Patsy watched the bubbling vee-shaped trail it created.

'Can you tell me about his conversion?'

Her mother smiled, 'My brother, your Uncle Stephen, brought him home from university. They were planning to see some plays in London and I guess our house was cheaper than a hostel. Your father asked me to go to the theatre with him, but of course, I couldn't go with an unbeliever, so I suggested, that if he were free that evening, why not come to the New Covenant meeting instead. My friends all prayed that he would be saved, and the Lord heard our prayers. He went forward that night and was baptised before the university vacation ended.'

'His parents were Church of Ireland, weren't they? How did they take it?'

'His father had died by then, but his mother told me when she came over for the wedding that she was so relieved one of her sons had finished sowing his wild oats, she didn't care what church he took up with so long as it wasn't Papist.'

The sun sank behind the hills leaving a faint glow in the sky. The boatman rowed back to shore.

****

Dalia had decided that she must confess everything, or nearly everything, to Addy. In the privacy of the Shepard's living room, she explained that she belonged to an organisation whose sole purpose was to help Jews escape from the Nazis and settle in the Promised Land.

'That's not wrong, is it?'

'My dear, of course not. The Lord has called you to do this work, so how can it be wrong? You sound just like the Scarlet Pimpernel.'

Dalia felt a wave of relief. She had Addy on her side. She took a deep breath. 'Jim doesn't see it your way.'

'No,' Addy answered, 'He wouldn't. His undercover work seems more important to him nowadays than the bible.'

'Undercover work?'

Addy clapped her hand to her mouth, 'Forget what I've said. Let's concentrate on your difficulties. We must pray this through.' She settled on her knees.

Dalia had endured enough instruction by now to know the drill, but all she could come up with tonight was a heartfelt 'Help me, Lord'.

'Better sometimes just to listen than to speak,' Addy comforted so they spent another ten minutes or so kneeling in silence.

'We'd better go to the Good Book for guidance,' Addy said at last. She opened her bible at random and resumed her place on the settee. 'The Lord has guided us to Ephesians 1,' she said.

Dalia had not brought her bible. While Addy was fetching a spare copy from the bookshelf, Jim came in. He stopped at the door and glared. 'Addy, I am taking the dog for a walk,' he announced and went straight out.

Dalia and Addy went through both the first and second epistles to the Ephesians, each reading alternate verses. None of it seemed pertinent; although, Addy claimed, the reference to the Commonwealth of Israel was significant.

It had been a mistake, coming here, Dalia told herself but it was already growing dark by the time she escaped. She walked down the main road and slipped behind houses to the unspoiled hillside that sloped steeply to the lower leg of the Stella Maris Road.

Cicadas, oblivious of her misery, scraped a continuous high-pitched chorus. The moon, like a divine searchlight, silvered the blacked out buildings of down town Haifa. In the foreground, the apartment block, where Peter lived, loomed tall against a backdrop of corrugated sea. Dalia remembered that Peter had asked her to phone after work. She had to see him if only to find out what Jim had told him.

She sat on a patch of sweet smelling thyme, plucked two weed leaves already slightly damp with dew, and placed them on her swollen eyelids. Slowly she counted to 500 before removing them, then stood, and made her way gingerly in her office court shoes down a goat track, conscious of thorn bushes shredding her stockings and pulling threads from her dress.

She knocked on Peter's door. He shouted something in Arabic from the other side.

'It's Dalia,' she called.

The door opened wide and Peter enveloped her in his arms, took her into the living room, and seated her on a sofa.

'My poor dear darling, whatever is the matter? Why didn't you phone?'

Coherence was a problem but after a while, Peter interrupted gently, 'You're telling me that you've been reporting to Mossad Aliyah Beth and Jim has had a go at you?'

Dalia found it impossible to speak. Peter hugged her again, 'But, darling, I guessed about you and Aliyah Beth. I *am* a detective, you know! But some of us in the British Police are not entirely heartless. We ignore refugees entering illegally unless our bosses insist we take action. What I can't understand is why the deuce is Jim making this fuss?'

Reluctantly, and only because she was sure that Jim would tell him anyway, she confessed to reading his papers. She omitted the bit about letting in Aaron and his companions.

'Well, that was a bit naughty, but darling, it is not as if you were selling information to the Germans.' He kissed her hair. 'I can see that you may have to give up your job, but that won't matter. You will be leaving when we marry anyway.'

She looked up at him in a daze. 'You still want to marry me?'

'Of course, sweetheart.' Then he let her go. His face contorted. 'Oh Dalia, I have just thought - if Jim talks to the authorities I won't be allowed to marry you. I must speak to him.'

'Peter, will they send me to prison?'

'It won't get as far as that but...'

The telephone rang. Peter walked out into the hall, leaving the door open.

'It's Jim,' he called back.

Dalia felt sick. Jim would turn Peter against her.

****

Suzanna was in her cubicle wishing she had been able to listen in on what that woman had told Mrs Shepard this afternoon. She was confident Inspector Monteith had dumped her, but it would be nice to know for certain.

She heard Mr Shepard's footsteps and listened to him lifting the receiver to give the operator a number. She placed her eye to a chink between two curtains and saw Mrs Shepard place a hand on her husband's shoulder. Mr Shepard said into the phone, 'Hello, Peter. Jim here. Has Dalia spoken to you since she left our house?'

Suzanna clutched the curtain waiting. At last, he asked the important question, 'You're not still intending to get married?'

She could hardly breathe. If only she could hear the other side of the conversation. Mr Shepard put his hand over the mouthpiece. Even though he was whispering, being so close, she could hear him clearly, 'Addy, Peter says Dalia's there now. She's told him everything. The wedding's still on.'

'Thank goodness for that,' Mrs Shepard exclaimed.

Angry tears blurred Suzanna's view. How could Inspector Monteith sink so low as to marry a spy? How could Mrs Shepard condone it?

Mr Shepard was speaking again, 'What about the security risk?'

Another silence then Mr Shepard shouted angrily, 'Clearance be blowed. I have new evidence. I have to do my duty.'

Mr Shepard, at least, seemed prepared to do something about Miss Leitner's spying. Unfortunately, his voice grew calmer.

'I can't do that, Peter. She'd be laying all of us wide open. The only way I can keep quiet is if she resigns.'

How could Mr Shepard even consider keeping quiet?

He gave an exasperated sigh. 'No complicated excuses needed, Peter. Dalia can just say she needs time to get ready for the wedding.'

Another silence then, 'Yes, I can see that is a problem. Hang on. I'll put Addy on.'

Suzanna blinked her eyes clear as she continued to peer through the curtains. Mr Shepard had his hand once more over the mouthpiece. 'Addy, I think you'd better sort the next bit.'

Mrs Shepard took over the phone and listened.

'Wait a moment,' she said eventually, 'I want to ask Jimmy something.' Now it was Mrs Shepard's turn to put her hand over the receiver. 'Dalia will have to come and stay with us, until the wedding, that is.'

Mr Shepard exploded, 'Not with my paperwork all over the place!' Mrs Shepard retorted, 'You could try keeping your papers at the office where they belong for a change. It will only be for a few weeks. Without work, Dalia can't afford lodgings, and she can't stay with her parents because they don't want her to marry Peter. Can you think of another solution?'

Prison would be a good idea, Suzanna thought, but Mr Shepard remained silent.

Mrs Shepard lifted her hand off the mouthpiece. 'Jimmy and I would love you to stay with us until the wedding, Dalia, dear. It'll make things easier all round getting everything arranged.'

Suzanna could not believe she was hearing this.

Mrs Shepard handed the telephone back to her husband who listened intently.

'We could get away with it, Peter,' he said eventually, 'but remember both our jobs are on the line if anything comes out.'

Suzanna was so disgusted she almost forgot to pray before she went to bed.

Chapter 71

Patsy returned to an office in chaos. In her absence, Dalia had taken two days off and had come in this morning, looking like death warmed up. She knew she ought to send her home but as she watched Michelle screw up a third attempt at a document, realised that she couldn't afford to.

She would have to say something to Mrs Jones about Michelle – see if she could get the superintendent to order her to retake the basic typing course. Michelle though was not the sort to do anything in her own time. The woman must be driving her parents insane, out every night, so different from her staid sister. The war had certainly changed the outlook of the younger generation.

Hark at her! Patsy laughed, middle-aged before she was twenty, even. With Michelle the way she was, though, she must make sure that Dalia knew that wartime regulations allowed her to carry on working after marriage. Perhaps Mrs Jones could persuade the superintendent to post Peter back to Haifa.

Patsy stopped worrying and concentrated on her typing until 6 o'clock, when Michelle grabbed her hat and left the office at a run. Dalia came over and held out a letter, 'Patsy, this is my resignation. I won't be coming back next week. I know I forfeit a month's wages, but Peter is insistent.'

Patsy sank back against her chair. 'You can't do this to us, Dalia, not when we have work stacked to the ceiling. Why the sudden decision? Are you moving to Beersheba?'

'No. The Second Chosen have decided I need more preparation for my baptism.'

The Second Chosen! She might have guessed they would have had a hand in this.

'I don't want to go into details,' Dalia continued. 'It is all so complicated. Believe me I would rather be working here. I will have to lodge with members of the Second Chosen, who have no room for my things. I have to move most of my stuff up to Peter's flat, but my landlady is enforcing the No Men Upstairs rule. That means I have to bring everything down to street level by myself.'

Even if Dalia was making life difficult for her, she was still a friend, so Patsy offered, 'Can I help?'

'Oh Patsy, would you? My typewriter worries me most. It's so heavy and I don't want to drop it.'

'You're in a mess, there's no two ways about it,' Mrs Jones agreed after Patsy had consulted her about the situation in the typing office, 'and you don't know the worst, my dear. The army are requisitioning our spare equipment. Typewriters are at the top of their list. If we don't place a body behind the third typewriter in your office, they'll take it. Then we won't be able to appoint anyone. Let's beard the superintendent together after lunch.'

Patsy was grateful for Mrs Jones' support. When she asked the superintendent for a few minutes of his time, he put his fingers together, invited them both to sit down and heard them out.

When they had finished he said, 'Place an advert in the papers straight away, Mrs Jones. I will alert security to give priority to applications for the typing post. In the meantime, I'll order the station sergeant to place a constable in the typing office every day, and one in here as well, until the army has forgotten us. I hate to do it when we are so short of manpower but this is an emergency.

My men won't be much good to you I am afraid, Miss Quigley. They are all one-finger typists. Meanwhile I will have to withdraw you from the Egyptian market.'

'Of course, sir, but I hope you put me back when we are at full strength.'

She couldn't see that happening until the end of the war though.

****

Dalia was desperate. Addy had been sticking to her like a tick. The only time she had to herself was a half hour meditation period, the only writing paper, the notebook Addy had given her for bible study. Mr Shepard had expressly forbidden her to write to anyone, so how could she contact Aaron to let him know what had happened?

An idea occurred to her one morning when she and Addy passed the XL job agency on their way to the Armenian dressmaker who was remodelling her second-hand wedding dress.

During her next meditation period, she tore a page from the notebook, wrote a brief note to Aaron, and placed it in her purse.

The next time they went for a fitting, she limped for a while before stopping by the agency door. 'Wait a moment please, Addy. I have a stone in my shoe.'

She placed one hand on the door while slipping her shoe off, and giving it an ostentatious shake. At the same time, she surreptitiously slipped her note through the letterbox.

Suzanna was in the kitchen making rock cakes, when Mrs Shepard and that Miss Leitner returned from a shopping trip.

'Fetch a pot of tea into the lounge, Suzanna. Dalia and I are absolutely parched. It's been murder trying to fit everything in this morning, but worth it. We've at last found gloves and a veil to go with the dress.'

Suzanna managed to keep all expression off her face until Mrs Shepard had left the kitchen, and then banged her hands against the wall. Why should Mrs Shepard treat that lying, conniving Leitner woman like an honoured guest, while she was just a skivvy? She had a good mind to report the woman to the police.

That evening, she filled in the government form but could not post it because she needed to put in the names of two referees. Mrs Shepard ought to be one, but could she depend on her mistress providing a good reference? After all, if she left, who else would Mrs Shepard find to work for so little pay? Mrs Quigley should be a referee too unless she was angry with her for rejecting the scholarships she had set up.

She hid the papers in her desk, took out a clean sheet of paper, and wrote to Aunt Melia.

Chapter 72

Patsy hadn't been able to face Maftur after Ahmed had failed to show up at the milk bar, but she didn't want that disaster to end their friendship. She forced herself to attend a gathering of the secretarial group. If Maftur asked how the assignation had turned out, she would claim that she had changed her mind about meeting Ahmed.

Maftur jumped up and came running over when she arrived at Edmonds. 'Patsy,' she whispered in her ear as she hugged her, 'I am so glad to see you. We must talk.' She drew her over to the far end of the room. 'First I must tell you that I do not believe what people are saying about you.'

Patsy had been so certain only the British would have heard the gossip. She burst out, 'Not you too, Maftur!'

Maftur, looking nervously back at the other women, whispered, 'Quiet, please, Patsy.'

'But how did you hear of it?'

'Through my brother.'

'Your brother? Does your brother know my father?'

'Your father? What has your father to do with it?'

'To do with what?'

'Ahmed al-Zeid.'

'Maftur, you can forget what I told you about Ahmed. I decided not to turn up for the meeting.'

Maftur stood back and stared. Her expression showed suspicion tinged with pity. 'Patsy, about Ahmed al-Zeid? You do not know?'

'Know what?'

Maftur closed her eyes, 'I thought you would know.'

Patsy steeled herself to answer coolly, 'If he is marrying someone else that is no concern of mine.'

Maftur gave a backward jerk of her head, 'No.'

Patsy felt a tiny flame of hope but Maftur doused it.

'Ahmed is dead, Patsy.'

'Dead?' Patsy sank heavily into a chair. The room grew dark. 'When?'

Maftur sat beside her, her voice low, 'They say it happened the day he was due to meet a British woman.'

So all that time that she had been waiting for him, Ahmed had been dead, and she had been cursing him instead of mourning.

'How did he die?'

'A British policeman killed him.'

'Why?'

'They say Ahmed was so desperate to travel to Palestine to meet a British woman in Haifa, that he asked to take a special message from the Grand Mufti to an Axis agent here, even though he knew how dangerous this was. The police killed him in an ambush.'

Ahmed not only dead, but killed in an attempt to meet her? Patsy wanted to scream the café down. In her struggle to control herself, she latched onto Maftur's opening statement, 'You said that you don't believe what people are saying about me. What are they saying?'

Maftur twisted the end of her scarf round her little finger. 'Well, it's not about you as such, because they don't know you are the woman Ahmed al-Zeid was planning to meet, and I haven't told anyone.' She unwound the scarf. 'They are saying that the woman Ahmed al-Zeid wanted to marry was a British spy, who deliberately enticed him into Palestine so the police could kill him.'

Patsy folded her arms and dropped her chin. Staring into her lap she whispered, 'Maftur, what they are saying is not true. I lied to you just now about not going to meet Ahmed.' She suppressed a sob. 'I did go, but he didn't turn up. I thought he had stood me up.' Her fingernails dug into her kneecaps. 'I was going to say yes to his proposal.'

She mustn't cry here, she told herself, not here in public.

She felt Maftur put her arm round her shoulders, 'I believe you, Patsy, but I am not the one you have to convince. Ahmed's friends have vowed vengeance. You must leave Palestine before they find out that you are the one Ahmed al-Zeid.'

Patsy stood, kissed Maftur on the cheek and left the café, too grief stricken over Ahmed's death to take in Maftur's warning. Only later as she lay in bed did she begin to worry about her own safety, but she couldn't just flee and leave the typing office in the lurch. Now that Dalia had left she was the only capable person there. Clumsy police officers seconded to the spare typewriter only served to distract Michelle's attention even further from her work. She wished she had someone with whom she could talk things over.

'Something's worrying you,' Beth said next evening when they sat with their feet up listening to a concert, 'Don't tell me your father has had a relapse?'

'No, my mother says he is on the mend.' Patsy rubbed her fingers along the cut moquette of the settee. 'Beth, if I tell you something will you promise not to pass it on?'

'Of course.'

Patsy poured it all out.

Her proposal from Ahmed ('How romantic, just like a film I saw when I was little.').

Ahmed's death (Beth took her hand at that, 'Oh you poor old thing – how dreadful.').

Her present danger ('Oh no, Patsy what will you do? You must tell the police –Oh yes. I can see why you can't.').

Her need to leave Palestine ('What about the WRENS? Can you volunteer for the WRENS from Palestine? You can join the ATS but I don't think they would suit you.').

The situation in the office that prevented her from leaving her job.

At that, Beth sat up. 'Wait, at last something I think I can help with. You know Shirley Peeps on the floor above, the one who moved in last month from Jaffa, whose husband is in Traffic and has a daughter Roger's age? I've made friends with her. We were discussing only the other day how to make some extra money, with inflation being what it is. We are both trained typists but can't go out to work because we need to be at home for our children when they are ill or on holiday. Do you think the police would let us share a job? If they did we could take turns looking after the children.'

'Oh Beth, the Police are so desperate for British typists I am sure they would consider it. Why don't you try the idea out on Mrs Jones.'

'I'll phone Shirl now and put it to Bertie tonight. Our finances are desperate, especially if you're thinking of leaving and we can't count on your rent money. He's bound to agree. If everything is all right with Shirl and Bert, I'll speak to Mrs Jones tomorrow.'

By the end of the week, Patsy had not just two part-time workers but four. Shirley Peeps had recruited two of her friends, both experienced office workers.

'It makes me feel alive again being out at work,' Beth told her. 'The others all say the same.'

****

Suzanna was up to her elbows in greasy water and worrying. For once, she was not looking forward to her day off. She was sure her mother would be cross about her change of career plans and she didn't want to see Habib.

The previous Saturday Habib had been bitter. Nothing she had said could deter him from planning his revenge although he refused to tell her the details. She thought back to his parting remark, 'It won't be long now. Everything is in hand, but no thanks to you, Suzanna.'

Her only consolation was that Beersheba was a long way off and she hadn't told him Inspector Monteith was intending to come up to Haifa for Miss Leitner's baptism.

Mrs Shepard poked her head round the door, 'Phone for you, Suzanna.'

Suzanna's wet hands flew to her face. 'Habib?'

'No, your Aunt Melia. She wants to check arrangements for Saturday.'

Suzanna took the receiver, her hands still shaking.

Aunt Melia came straight to the point; 'I received your letter. I phoned Mrs Quigley. She has invited us to lunch on Sunday. You had better warn Mrs Shepard that you will be home later than usual.'

'Have you talked to my mother about my application?'

'A great deal. I've been with her in Haifa since Wednesday while Angelique is in Nazareth visiting her family. Your mother agrees that you will make a very good nurse and is proud you have made a decision for yourself. She says she was about to suggest you leave the Shepards anyway, since it seems certain the Germans will invade Palestine. So, Chick, you need have no worries on that score.'

'Thank you so much, Aunt Melia.'

'It's a pleasure, Chick. I'll pick you up from Mt Carmel on Saturday evening and drive you back to Jenin. We'll set off to Jerusalem early Sunday morning. I'll drop you off at the Shepards on the way back and spend the night with your mother in Haifa. She'll be looking after the shop until Habib comes back.'

'Has Habib gone to Nazareth with Angelique?'

'No, he is spending Saturday and Sunday camping with a few friends.'

Suzanna came away from the phone torn between pleasure at her mother's response to her application and anxiety over what Habib was up to - had he gone to Beersheba? She wondered what his reaction would be if he found out that she had known all along that Inspector Monteith would be in Haifa on Saturday and Sunday.

Chapter 73

The time had passed slowly, but now it was less than a week to her wedding. Dalia was refusing to think about her baptism the next day. She would be unable to go through with it, if she did. Instead, she concentrated on the picnic lunch that would precede it. The picnic had to be special since it was not only her baptism but also Addy's birthday.

While Addy whirred away on the sewing machine in the next room, she set Jim and the two girls on to creating wafer thin sandwiches with mint and cucumber filling. At sunset, she slipped across the road to Feders' Bakery.

Waiting for Mrs Feder to open up, she gazed at a brochure in the window, showing the wedding cake she had chosen because it was so similar to the one in her mother's treasured wedding photographs.So many family members in her mother's photographs! She wouldn't have many in hers, but at least her parents had agreed to come to the civil ceremony, and Addy, bless her, had promised to invite them to the reception at her house afterwards.

The birthday cake, Peter's present to Addy, was almost as magnificent in its pink and white way, as the glorious silvered centrepiece she would be collecting the following week. She sneaked the birthday cake into the kitchen where Jim and the children duly admired it.

'I hope Peter makes it to the baptism,' Jim said, as they packed the picnic into a hamper.

'So long as he's here next Saturday, that's the important thing,' Dalia replied.

Jim's face changed. He looked sternly at his daughters, 'Evie, Clare, get to bed now. We grown-ups need to pray.'

Dalia had a horrible feeling that she had said something out of place, but couldn't think what.

As they crossed the veranda to the lounge, Jim asked, 'Is your wedding really of more consequence to you than your baptism, Dalia?'

He waited for her to reply, but her mouth felt paralysed. He continued, 'Are you really sure that you have given your life to the Lord?'

'Yes,' she almost shouted, forcing the words through frozen jaws; but she knew that she was unsure about the baptism, unsure about Peter, unsure about everything. Her life was rolling down hill out of control, and she was refusing to apply a brake, because stopping would be more painful than rolling on.

Addy joined them. They were falling to their knees in prayer when Evie flung open the door, wearing an air of self-importance above her pyjamas. 'Superintendent Fielding is on the phone, Daddy. He says he has bad news, and it's very serious.'

Jim followed Evie out of the room. Dalia and Addy stared at each other.

'This is it, Dalia. The invasion,' Addy said. 'We'll have to get you evacuated with us. I'll tell the authorities you are the children's nanny.'

'No,' Dalia said, 'I am staying in Palestine. I have to look after my parents.'

'Peter should be your first concern now, dear. You must forsake all others.'

'But I can't forsake my parents!'

Even if they have forsaken me, she thought.

'The bible tells us...' Addy didn't finish her sentence. Jim had returned, his face pale, both hands gripping his bible. 'Dalia, you are going to have to be brave.'

'Peter?' she screeched, just before her hand slapped against her teeth. 'He's been killed?' she whispered through open fingers.

'No-o,' Jim answered slowly. 'But he has been very, very badly wounded.' He paused. 'He's been shot in the stomach.'

Jim was talking as if on the other side of glass. 'I've ordered a taxi for you and Addy.'

She followed Addy out of the room to get her coat. Why wasn't she crying? The worst thing that had happened in her life and she was not crying.

Addy prayed in the taxi, all the way to the hospital, but Dalia could not join in. A vision of Peter lying on waste ground, blood and entrails mixing with dust and weeds left no room for prayer.

Peter lay between sheets only marginally whiter than his face. She hid her face in his bedcovers.

'He's full of morphine,' a nurse told her. 'Don't worry if he doesn't recognise you.'

Dalia placed a hand on Peter's chest and continued to kneel, not praying, just trying to pour the excess of her own life into Peter.

'Penelope,' Peter called out, 'Penelope darling, you've come.'

She pressed her forehead into the white bedcover. 'Peter,' she whispered, 'It's Dalia; Dalia here waiting for you.'

A nurse tapped her gently on the shoulder. 'We're taking him to theatre now, dear.'

Porters wheeled the bed out of the room, down a long corridor.

'No further,' a nurse restrained her gently.

Dalia stood staring at closing double doors until a nurse led her back to Addy.

'I've phoned Jim to let him know what's happening,' Addy said, her knitting needles clicking. 'He'll come down tomorrow when he has parked the children at Sunday school.'

She put down her needles. 'Let us pray.'

Dalia closed her eyes and listened to Addy pleading for Peter's life, but still couldn't pray herself.

Eventually Addy stopped and resumed her knitting.

They waited. Outside the window, black night gave way to grey sky over a leaden sea. Then crests of waves glowed orange. Dalia hoped they were messengers of hope. The sun rose from behind the mountain. The sea turned blue. A nurse brought cups of tea.

A British doctor entered the room, asked to speak to Addy outside.

Addy returned, a handkerchief pressed to her eyes.

'He's passed into glory,' Addy whispered, 'The Lord giveth, and the Lord taketh away. Blessed be the name of the Lord.'

Everything still now, except she felt her lips moving. 'Where's Peter. I want to see him.'

A nurse stood in front of her, white overall filling the world. Dalia concentrated on the white, her lips still moving. The nurse put out her hand. She walked behind the white into white, to a white Peter on a white bed. She knelt, pressed her head on his chest, her throbbing temple melding into his still chest. If she stayed long enough, they would become one. His heart would beat again.

Someone joined them, someone in white. 'He's mine,' she told Penelope and flung her arms round Peter to hasten the melding process. From behind, she felt Shimon tugging her back. She struggled to stay in place, tightening her arms round Peter, keeping the all-important contact between her head and his chest.

Something pricked her arm.

Part 4

Cracking Open

Chapter 74

Suzanna swept the chopped beef into the soup pan and stared in horror at her bloodstained hands. The Holy Mother was telling her that she was as guilty as her brother. She rushed to her room, pulled out her stolen photo of Inspector Monteith, placed it in front of her icon, and prayed for his soul. She prayed for her brother too, asking the Holy Mother to forgive him and protect him from the authorities. She tried to pray for her own forgiveness but knew those prayers were floating to a deserted part of heaven.

****

Oh, poor Dalia, Patsy thought, when Bert Raven brought the news that Peter Monteith had been fatally wounded, how will she cope? Grief for Peter mingled with pity for Dalia.

'How did it happen?' Beth asked.

'He received a tip off and rushed his men to a wadi near the Syrian border. The assassin was hiding behind rocks. CID think it was a personal attack, although no one knows why.'

Patsy froze behind her desk, her eyes shut. Fragments of knowledge - drug squad - hashish smugglers - Axis agents, knitted together into a recognisable pattern. Why had she never wondered before which British Policeman had shot Ahmed?

'Patsy, are you all right?'

She opened her eyes, to see Beth watching her, concern in her eyes.

'Yes, Beth, I'm sorry. It's just that Peter was one of the first friends I made when I came back to Palestine. Did they get the assassin, Bert?'

'No, he ran off. They brought the dogs in but the trail ended at the main road. I would say he had an accomplice waiting with a car.'

So the assassin was still at large and she was the next target.

Chapter 75

The Cathedral was already full, except for seats in the front row holding reserved notices. Patsy noticed Dalia was not there yet as she slid into the space Beth and Bert had saved for her. She hoped Dalia's parents were supporting her, however much they had disapproved of the intended marriage. She squashed up still closer to Beth when Aileen arrived, visibly pregnant.

'Where's Mick?' Patsy whispered.

'He's a pall bearer.'

Patsy turned her head and saw Jim and Addy Shepard in a rear row. Dalia sat between them, a gauze veil drawn over her face.

'Why isn't Dalia in the front row?' she exclaimed indignantly.

'Mick sent a telegram to Peter's parents, so he did,' Aileen replied. 'He asked about funeral arrangements, saying he thought Peter would have wanted the service at the New Covenant Hall and telling them his fiancée was taking his death very badly. They sent a reply saying they knew nothing about Peter joining the Second Chosen, or about any fiancée. They asked for a cathedral service and left it to the superintendent to send out invitations.'

Patsy sat back fuming, not for Peter's sake. There was nothing left of Peter to care, but why had the super snubbed Dalia? All right, she could understand him being chary of her as a CID officer's wife, but now that Peter was dead, he could at least have shown some common humanity.

****

Dalia watched British policemen place a large box, covered in a police flag, on a trestle inside this building that resembled Barclays Bank.

'Where's Peter?' she asked Addy.

'Sh,' Mr Shepard said.

'Peter's in glory,' Addy whispered, 'Only his body is in that box.'

The ceremony that followed was confusing. People prayed, kneeling as if at Mrs Shepard's house, except they had comfortable cushions for their knees. The prayers sounded like English versions of Jewish prayers, not the rhythmless ramblings of the Second Chosen. People sang hymns as if they were in the Second Chosen Hall but also chanted responses reminiscent of the synagogue service.

The Police took the box outside and lifted it into a van.

Now they were outside Khayet Beach, the sun blazing down. Beyond the wall in front was the spot where Peter had so nearly made love to her. Behind loomed the mountain, where two smugglers lay buried under piles of stones.

Close to her was a deep damp pit.

The policemen lowered the box to the bottom of the pit. A single trumpet wailed a forlorn tune. Peter was down there in the pit, about to marry Penelope. The treacherous ring on her hand sparkled with joy. She pulled it off and flung it away. It landed in the pit. She had given the ring to Penelope and had to get it back. She ran forward but Penelope barred the way. She lifted her arm and hit Penelope as hard as she could. Penelope fell back and rose again as Patsy.

'Dalia,' Patsy said, 'I am so sorry.'

'Miss Quigley,' Addy said at her side, 'I am afraid only true believers can offer comfort to Dalia in her hour of sorrow. Dalia dear, it is time we went home.'

Chapter 76

Patsy returned from the cemetery to the office, her neck and shoulders tense after imagining an assassin behind each eucalyptus tree, a bullet drilling through her head, a dagger slicing her spine. Her arm hurt where Dalia had thumped her.

She reminded herself that Dalia was in a worse state and that Peter would have wanted her to help Dalia. Should she ignore Addy Shepard and contact Dalia? Addy was right, though. What comfort could she give Dalia if she did not believe in life after death?

Without enthusiasm, she picked up the bundle of work Mrs Jones had put together the night before, and noted a request to give priority to the catalogue itemising the contents of Peter's flat.

'The auctioneers are hounding us,' Mrs Jones had scribbled.

Not a task vital to the war effort. She would hand it to Michelle. Even if Michelle made a hash of it no great harm would be done. She remembered Dalia had left some things in Peter's flat. Had she removed them? Patsy glanced down the list. A typewriter originally included, had been crossed off. So Dalia had taken it back.

Mrs Jones came in, 'Miss Quigley, the superintendent wants a word.'

She passed the list to Michelle and the more important work to Shirley Peeps.

'A sad occasion, Miss Quigley, but I think we did Inspector Monteith proud,' the superintendent greeted her. 'It will show the lads that we honour sacrifices made in the line of duty.'

He leaned back in his chair, steepling his hands. 'But life must go on. Mrs Jones tells me you have done wonders training your Mum's Army and that I am free to release you to this outfit in Cairo that has been bending my ear. Do you still want to go?'

'Want'– not quite a word she would have used for this loosening of her spine, the instant disappearance of the background headache, so permanent she had become used to it. 'I am ready for the change sir.'

'Good. We'll be sorry to lose you, of course, but in this case, I think their need is actually more important than ours. No need to drag things out. I have looked up your records and we owe you three days leave. You might as well take them before I inform Major Forsythe that you are free to travel – give you a chance to visit your parents, launder your clothes, eh?'

'What does the new job entail, sir?'

The superintendent tapped his nose. 'It's Hush-hush, Miss Quigley! You will be told on arrival.'

****

Suzanna kept looking at the forms and changing her mind. Applying felt too much like trying to run away from the mess she had created. On the other hand, if she did get in, it might be possible to make amends for her part in Inspector Monteith's death by learning to save lives.

The Saturday after Inspector Monteith died and just before the application had to be in, she asked Mrs Shepard if she would be a referee.

Her mistress stood with her hands on her hips, her lips curling. 'So you are deserting the sinking ship, are you Suzanna? Well, let me tell you, the British have come off worst in many battles but so far have never lost a war.'

Suzanna forced a conciliatory smile, took a deep breath, and spouted her rehearsed argument. 'It's not about the war, Mrs Shepard. When I went to visit Mrs Quigley, we prayed about what I should do. Mrs Quigley said that since I am not taking matriculation this year, I could serve the Lord better by helping sick and blind village children. She is giving me a good reference. My training with you makes me particularly suitable, she said. She told me to tell you she would be delighted if you would phone her and have a chat.'

Mrs Shepard's lip uncurled. She picked up the phone. 'I'll have a word with Ann and see what all this is about.'

After speaking to Mrs Quigley, Mrs Shepard turned conciliatory, and said that of course she would write a good reference.

Suzanna completed the form well before she was due to catch her bus.

Before she left, she carried a tray with beef broth to Miss Leitner. She could not be angry with her any more. The poor woman had been crying non-stop since Inspector Monteith had died and had eaten nothing. Suzanna realised Miss Leitner had loved the inspector better than she had.

She succeeded in coaxing Miss Leitner into taking half a bowl of soup.

On the way to the bus stop, she posted the form and sat on the bus worrying, unsure of how to face her brother.

Her emotions whirled as she walked over to Habib. He stepped beside her without saying a word until they were well away from

- 352 -

the bus station. Then he stopped. By this time, Suzanna's heart was pounding with both anger and anxiety.

'It's done now,' Habib said, 'I know you don't approve, but I had to do it. The others are still looking for the girl but that is their affair. My part is finished. Let us say no more about it.'

That was probably the only way to deal with it, Suzanna thought, but it didn't seem right.

****

The blur was timeless. Dalia was conscious of Addy and the Arab maid telling her to eat. When her bladder urged she shuffled to the toilet but the blur obscured the intervals of lucidity.

Now, though, someone was shaking her, shouting. She forced open inflamed eyes. An elongated Addy stared down.

'Dalia, it's important you pull yourself together and listen.'

She hauled herself out of the blur and saw a real Addy, sitting on a real bed. Addy handed her a handkerchief. She blew her sore nose, placed her hands on her inflamed eyes, and crept them up to lank and greasy curls. 'I need to wash my hair.'

'Dalia, listen. You left some things in Peter's flat? Do you know where he put his will?'

'A will?' What was Addy talking about?

'A will, a legal document, Dalia. Pull yourself together, girl.'

She knew nothing of any will and told Addy that, hoping she would leave her alone, but Addy continued to sit there, talking and jamming back hairpins that refused to stay put. Why did Addy wear her hair up if her hairpins would not stay in place?

'Dalia, I am certain Peter made a will recently, leaving everything to you. Jimmy advised him to, but the police insist they haven't seen it.'

There popped another hairpin. When Addy jabbed it in, hairpins on the other side of her head turned into miniature croquet hoops.

"The police only have the will Peter lodged with the superintendent when he first joined the force. Unless we find the new one, the police will auction everything in his flat and send the proceeds to his parents. We need to get down to the flat at once. Even if we cannot find the will, you need to retrieve your things.'

Her things? She remembered Peter putting her typewriter on a table. 'I must save my typewriter.'

'A typewriter will be heavy,' Addy gave a sigh. 'But if you insist we'll try.'

'I must wash my hair.'

- 353 -

'I'll put on a saucepan of water. When the water's hot enough I'll help you wash it, but we can't take too long.'

Dalia's hair was still damp when she and Addy left the house, but the hot sun had dried it by the time they reached the bus stop. The key Peter had given her was in her pocket, something he had handled. Her fingers caressed the smooth metal as she sat on the bus. It made Peter seem less absent. She drew the key out of her pocket when they mounted the steps to Peter's flat, but there was a padlock on the front door. The key turned dead and heavy in her palm.

Addy sighed. 'We'll have to call in at Police HQ.'

Rather than waiting in the sun for a bus, they walked into town, taking advantage of the shade cast by tall buildings. Dalia's legs would hardly hold her up when they reached the Khayet building. She thought ruefully of the long hikes the girl she had once been had undertaken.

The Arabic sergeant at the front desk was a stranger who refused to let either of them further .than the reception area. Addy, in her most haughty British voice, demanded to speak to the superintendent. The sergeant ordered another policeman to usher Addy through, but Dalia found herself left behind.

Addy eventually returned, but without a key to the padlock.

'Dalia, have you any receipts? The superintendent will only let you take your stuff back if you can provide him with receipts.'

'My parents bought my typewriter in Germany back in 1932. I don't think my mother will have the receipt.'

Addy placed her hands on her cheekbones, 'Oh, your typewriter? I am afraid I have bad news on that score. The army has requisitioned it. Apparently, there's an acute shortage of typewriters. If you have a receipt you will receive the money, the superintendent says.'

Dalia looked at Addy in disbelief. Her typewriter? The British had stolen her typewriter? First, they sent Peter off to be killed and now they had taken her typewriter? She slumped back on a raffia chair, tried to sink into the blur again but Addy stood over her.

'The rest of the stuff is still there, Dalia. Even though it has been catalogued ready for the auctioneers, the police will let you have anything that belongs to you, just so long as you produce a receipt.'

'My name is in some of my books,' Dalia muttered. Books she could replace, but not the typewriter.

'I'll go back and ask about the books,' Addy promised.

'Eema and Abba will know...' But Addy had already left.

Where were Eema and Abba? Why had they not contacted her? They must have heard about Peter. It would have been on the wireless, in the paper. Why hadn't they come for her? She slipped back into the blur until Addy pulled her out of it.

'Sorry to be so long, Dalia. The superintendent insisted I stop for a cup of tea. He did try to help, Dalia, he really did. He telephoned through to the legal department in Jerusalem but they say a name on the flysheet is insufficient evidence. They need receipts.'

'It doesn't matter.'

Nothing mattered now.

Chapter 77

Patsy stood on the platform at Lydda watching her train arrive, amazed to see Beth leaning out of a window.

'I've bagged you a seat,' Beth shouted, 'I cleared your PO box like you asked, and thought I'd deliver the post myself.'

Patsy jumped into the carriage, placed her bag on the seat, and hugged her friend, 'You are a dear, but how are you getting back?'

'Mick's taking me when he comes off shift. Aileen's delighted I could come. She hated the idea of you leaving Palestine without a proper send off, but the midwife said no way could she come in her condition.'

Patsy glanced down at her post – an OHMS envelope - Tim's writing.

She asked, 'How's everyone at the office?'

'Big news my dear. Michelle is engaged to Sergeant Hadad from CID. Did you ever meet him?'

Patsy tore her letter open as she replied, 'No, but he was in Peter's squad the night he was killed, wasn't he? I only hope marriage is more in Michelle's line than typing.'

She glanced through the first few lines of Tim's letter.

'Oh Beth, It was good of you to bring this. You know I told you about the boyfriend, I had in England? He says he's coming to Palestine on his next leave and will look me up. I must drop him a note to say I'm on my way out of Palestine. Can you post it for me?' She took a card from her bag.

'Of course but if your Tim says he is coming to Palestine on leave, the odds are he's stationed in Egypt.'

Patsy used her suitcase as a desk as she listened to Beth.

'When you find out where you are staying in Cairo, you must send him a proper letter, giving him your new address.'

Patsy thought about that. She excavated through layers of guilt and grief, back to the schoolgirl who had left England in 1938.

'No! I am no longer the flapper he knew and I can't begin to guess how much war has changed him. I don't think it would be sensible to see him again.'

'Of course it will. It's always good to meet someone you know in a strange city. It doesn't have to be romance.'

The guard blew his whistle. They had a quick hug and Beth jumped off the moving train.

Habib took the monthly rabbit out to the back to wring its neck while Angelique placed a government stamped letter into Suzanna's hand.

Suzanna's throat tightened. She found it difficult to breathe.

'Open it,' Angelique insisted, 'It's too thick to be a rejection.'

Suzanna forced herself to slit the envelope and read the covering letter.

'I am in,' she yelled, 'I am in.'

She hugged Angelique, who took her hands and danced with her round the olives and cheeses. An old woman entered the shop.

'My sister-in-law is going to be a community nurse,' Angelique shouted. The old woman clapped in time to their steps until Angelique stopped to serve her.

When the shop was empty again Angelique said, 'I bet you can't wait to see Mrs Shepard's face when you tell her you're leaving, and she realises that from now on she'll have to do her own dirty work.'

'I can't think how she'll manage,' Suzanna replied with a grin.

****

Dalia's thoughts were wandering. Addy had thrust a bible into her hands and insisted on a prayer session. Prayers? What good could prayers do? Peter was dead and buried. She knew that. Prayers would not bring Peter back from Penelope. She shouldn't be here. She should be home in Bereishit. Why had Abba and Eema deserted her?

When Jim came home, Addy broke off the session. Dalia headed for her room expecting Suzanna to fetch her supper as she had done ever since Peter died, but tonight Addy insisted she sit down at table for a proper meal.

Throughout the lengthy grace, Dalia told herself that she should have returned home. The Amen came at last. Dalia picked up her fork and tried to spear a bouncing piece of India rubber masquerading as beef.

'What can I do now?'

She did not realise she had spoken aloud until Jim replied, 'We're about to sort something out.'

Addy glared at her husband before saying, 'Jimmy and I have had an idea, dear, but we didn't intend to speak about it just yet.'

Jim grunted. 'No reason to delay,'

For some reason Addy's face reddened. 'Dalia,' she almost whispered, 'Did you know Suzanna has handed in her notice?'

Why was Addy embarrassed unless Suzanna was leaving because of the extra work she had caused?

'I'm going to be stuck with running this house by myself,' Addy rushed on, plucking dog hairs from her skirt. 'Jimmy and I,' Addy stopped, and examined her skirt even more closely. 'Well, until you find yourself a proper job that is, Jimmy and I were wondering if we could make you a small allowance in return for you helping me about the house.'

It took a minute to sink in. They were planning to turn her into the domestic drudge they had had in Suzanna. She needed air. She stood up, walked over to the only window in that large room, and opened it, but because of the blackout, the exterior shutters were closed.

'Only the sort of things you would do for your own mother,' Addy pleaded.

Her own mother? If only she were back in Bereishit. She closed the window and faced the Shepards. Addy was gazing down at her shoes, looking sad. Dalia recalled Addy standing up for her when Jim had found out about her spying. Addy was now the only person in the world who cared about her, so she answered, 'Just for the time being, until I get myself sorted.'

Addy leapt up and kissed her exuberantly. 'You won't be plunged in at the deep end,' she promised, 'Suzanna will show you how we do things, while she works out her notice.'

****

A short while ago, Suzanna would have revelled in the situation. Hoity-toity Miss Leitner, having to learn from her, having to descend to first name usage, but now she could take no pleasure in the Jewish woman's fall. She did her best to be kind and gradually found Dalia thawing. Before long, they were enjoying each other's company.

As they sat together, peeling potatoes the day before she left, Suzanna told Dalia how much she was looking forward to her new career.

'What exactly will you be doing when you start?'

'I'm on a pre-nursing course attached to a rural nurse at Al-Lajjun...' Suzanna noticed Dalia's questioning look. 'Yes, I know, it's an odd name. My Aunt Melia says it goes back to the time the Romans had a camp there, and it should really be al-legion. It's about half way between Haifa and Jenin but there's a really good bus service.'

'How did you get the job?'

'I answered a government advert for a nursing course, but I don't start that until I am eighteen. My Aunt Melia wangled me the position at al-Lejjun, through the Women's Movement. My Aunt

Julie, who is my real guardian doesn't like the idea of me having a career, all she wants me to do is get married. So Aunt Melia told Aunt Julie that the son of one of her doctor friends was teaching at the village school for a year before going on to university. Aunt Julie was suspicious at first because Aunt Melia isn't in favour of arranged marriages but Aunt Melia replied that although she would never force a mule to drink, she didn't mind leading it to the oasis. That's when Aunt Julie let me go.'

Dalia laughed then, the first time since the inspector had died. Suzanna thought it was good to see her laugh then realised she had been talking about herself for too long, so asked, 'Have you ever been out to work before?'

'Yes, I was a typist at the Police HQ.'

'Is that where...?' She hesitated. She had been intending to continue – where you met Inspector Monteith - but substituted 'where Leila Boutaji worked before she married?'

Dalia looked surprised. 'You know Leila?'

'She was a bridesmaid at my brother's wedding. I will be seeing her again in November. Her sister is marrying a cousin of mine and I've been invited.'

'Her sister? Not Michelle Boutaji?'

'Yes, that's the one.'

'I never thought Michelle would settle down so quickly. Who is she marrying?'

'Another relative of mine - Sergeant Hadad in the CID. Do you know him?'

Dalia shook her head. 'No, typists were discouraged from mixing with the police. I only got to know Peter because I brought him tea while he was rescuing refugees from the Patria.' Dalia bit her lip. Her knuckles turned white on the paring knife.

Suzanna was angry with herself for reminding Dalia about Inspector Monteith, and once again, guilt over her part in his death swept through her.

Dalia went on speaking, obviously determined to make an effort at normality, 'Come to think of it, there was a Sergeant Hadad in Peter's last squad. I wonder if it is the same man.' She paused. Suzanna waited for the tears to fall, but Dalia picked up another potato and began gouging the eyes out. 'So Michelle will be leaving? Patsy Quigley will have a job finding a replacement.'

Now it was Suzanna's turn to grip her knife hard. The potato she was holding in the other hand snapped in half. Mt Etna erupted in her stomach 'Patsy Quigley? My Mrs Quigley's daughter? I didn't know she worked at Haifa Police Headquarters?'

Dalia appeared to notice nothing amiss.

'That's right. She's the office manager now – a good one too. I expect she will be at Michelle's wedding. Please give her my regards and tell her I will be pleased to see her whenever she has the time.'

Suzanna put the knife down, stood up, and busied herself getting saucepans from the other end of the kitchen. Miss Quigley - the treacherous girl Habib's friends were hunting? She couldn't believe that of a daughter of Mrs Quigley. It had to be a mistake. She must find out what really happened. But how could she set about it without making people suspect that Habib had something to do with Inspector Monteith's death.

Sergeant Hadad held the information she wanted. She could understand that he had kept quiet about the incident out of loyalty to his chief while Inspector Monteith was alive. Now that the inspector was dead though, he might enjoy boasting about his role in breaking up a spy gang especially if he didn't think his story would spread beyond their Christian community.

One thing she had to consider before she poked her nose further into this business. What if she found out that Miss Quigley was guilty?

She thought long and hard for several days after she had left the Shepards. In the end, she decided that if she discovered Miss Quigley had lured Ahmed al-Zeid to his death, she would not tell Habib. There had been enough killing already.

Chapter 78

Dalia woke sweating from a nightmare – Penelope, all in white, pointing to red anemones sprouting from the wound in Peter's side as he hung crucified; Penelope shouting, 'See what you have done!'

Damp sheets twisted round her legs as she tossed and turned, terrified of dropping back to sleep. Slowly she untangled the dream's message. Peter had had to die to atone for her false conversion. His soul would suffer in Gehenna until she returned to her people. She spent the next two days going mechanically through domestic tasks while she allowed herself to accept that Peter had always been in love with Penelope.

Three days later she woke clearer-headed than she had been for weeks, as if her mind had resolved its problems while she slept. She lay in bed, reviewing her life, trying to find some gain from her time in Haifa.

The main benefit, she decided, was that she had learned about the way the mandate worked, useful knowledge in any post-war struggle for independence. That stage in her life, though, was now over. She could revert to her earlier ambition.

In this new positive frame of mind, she realised that staying on at school, instead of leaving early to attend the women's farming college, had its own advantages. She had the qualifications to take an agricultural degree course. She would have to find a well-paid job first, of course, to save for tuition fees.

She tackled Addy while they were cooking breakfast, 'Addy, I am so grateful for the way you have looked after me, when I needed it so much, but I feel I can manage on my own now. Tomorrow I am going to Tel Aviv to try for a proper job.'

Addy argued that she should stay in Haifa until she was certain of employment but Dalia stuck to her decision.

'I will miss you,' Addy said at last. 'I will give you a good reference, of course, and Jimmy will write you a letter of introduction to the Saints in Jaffa. If things don't work out, you must come back here. You will be constantly in our prayers.'

A letter of introduction was something she could do without, but she didn't want to hurt Addy, so said nothing.

Next morning Dalia picked up her packed bag, stared hard at the studio portrait of Peter on the windowsill, and turned her back on it.

She endured Addy's parting shots, 'We'll be praying for you, Dalia. I know you'll pull through this, and we'll all come to your baptism in Jaffa.'

At the bus stop, she tore up the letter of introduction and placed it in the used ticket bin. She was not a Christian, she told herself and never had been.

Her first port of call was her bank. To her amazement, her account showed a large positive balance. Studying the details, she saw her orange groves at el-Tirah, worthless since the outbreak of war, had made a huge profit. She recalled reading that someone at the Hebrew University had invented a way of producing fuel from orange juice, but had not realised the implications.

Finding a seat in the marbled hall, she assessed the changed circumstances. She could apply to the Hebrew University straight away. She rushed to the Post Office and sent a telegram to the university giving Poste Restante, Jerusalem as her address, then walked back to the bank.

She wrote a cheque to the Shepards, more than enough to repay them for all they had spent on her, drew out cash for a month's living expenses and the bus fare to Jerusalem. While the cashier was counting her money, another clerk handed her two letters. 'Miss Leitner, the manager said we should give you these when you next came in.'

Letters from Mr Manners? Setting new dates for her baptism, no doubt. She was about to throw them unread into a trash bin but something made her look at the envelopes. Ruth's handwriting, her mother's writing. She tore her mother's letter open first. The date was three weeks old.

Dalia darling,
We're going mad with worry. We heard the terrible news about your Peter. We have tried and tried to get in touch with you but Giza has no idea of where you have gone. Then we heard that you were staying with a British family, but no one, neither the Post Office, nor the police, will give us their address so I am taking this note into your bank as Ruth suggested. Please forgive my nagging ways and come home. We all love you so much.

How could she have been so stupid? Of course, the British would not let any Jew know Jim's address; even the wedding invitation had only named the registry office.

She rushed to the counter and pleaded with one of the bank staff to let her use their telephone. She left a message with the nurse at Bereishit asking her mother to phone the bank. While waiting, trying to stop her feet bouncing on the floor, she opened the letter from Ruth.

Dearest Dalia,

Uri and I are so sorry about your Peter. We came up to look for you. Where are you? Your parents are desperate to find you. I spoke to the brother of one of the nurses I knew at Haifa who works at your bank, and he explained the situation to the manager who gave permission for our letters to be kept in your bank file. Please write as soon as you get them.

A bank clerk approached. Her mother was on the telephone asking to speak to her.

'Ai-ee, Dalia,' her mother started, and she could hear her panting, she must have run all the way across the common, 'you wait right there. Your father is already on his way to collect you. The Romanians are killing a calf. Now tell me which portion you want me to cook first. Miriam is busy baking already.'

The same Eema as always. Dalia's throat constricted. She couldn't reply.

'Dalia, my love, please forgive me. I have been nearly dead with worry. Nu, say you are all right. Please say you are all right.'

'I am all right now, Eema,' she managed.

'Good, you stay right there. I must get back to the cooking. I will roast the legs. I must pick some marjoram.'

Dalia commandeered one of the comfortable bank chairs in front of a writing desk and concentrated on gaining control, but lost out when her father arrived. She clung to his neck, laughing and crying at the same time.

'Hush,' her father soothed as he led her out to the car. 'You are back with us now. This is all over.' Once he was driving, he kept up a stream of conversation, news of Josh, Ruth and Uri, and a description of the harvest until she calmed down.

She told him then about her decision to study at the university.

'Nu, your mother and I will drive you to Jerusalem tomorrow,' her father said, 'the Romanians can cope with the farm for a week. We will stay at a hotel until you settle in. We will buy your study materials, sort out your clothes if you have to start lectures straight away. We will make sure we know where you are staying before we leave, so we do not lose touch again.'

****

In Jenin Suzanna found herself subjected to a barrage of questions after her first week working with Community nurse, Um Jusef.

'It's the best thing I ever did, changing jobs,' she told family and friends as they enjoyed the autumn sunlight in Aunt Julie's courtyard. 'Rural nursing is so worthwhile. I hadn't realised how many children go blind because there is no one to treat them when their eyes get infected, or how many babies die of dehydration because their mothers don't understand what to do when they are ill.'

After she had satisfied everyone about the most minute details of the Muslim family with whom she was lodging, the talk turned to the wedding of Cousin Sergeant Philip Hadad to Cousin Michelle Boutaji.

Suzanna seized her opportunity. 'Michelle's older sister told me that the Sergeant once caught two spies, after senior British police had set a trap using a beautiful British woman. Does anyone know anything about this?'

'No, I never heard that,' her aunt replied, but Suzanna could tell her curiosity had been aroused.

No one else knew anything either but Suzanna was sure the telephone gossip lines would soon be buzzing and eventually her aunt would learn every detail.

The gossip line was even speedier than she had expected. On her next visit to Jenin, her Aunt said, 'About Sergeant Hadad and those spies, Suzanna, you were wrong. Whoever dreamt up beautiful women trapping them has been seeing too many Hollywood films. Your Cousin Jalna had it straight from the sergeant's mother that the senior police had nothing to do with it. The sergeant and his boss, Inspector Monteith, the one who was murdered a few weeks ago, they spent weeks tracking one spy until he met the other one. It was all good solid police work. The senior British did nothing to help them.'

Suzanna felt a surge of relief. She had accomplished the first stage of her mission. Now how was she going to persuade her mule-headed brother to tell Ahmed al-Zeid's other friends, after he had declared the subject closed?

She sounded Habib out when he and Angelique brought baby George up to Jenin

'That British girl,' she said, 'the one your friends were after, have they found her yet?' A stupid question, she knew, everyone would be gossiping if a British woman had been assassinated but she could think of no other way to introduce the subject.

Habib shrugged. 'I saw one of Ahmed's friends, Ismail Shawwa, at Cousin Leila's wedding. He told me that they were on her tail, almost certain who she is. But I've heard nothing since. I told you I have done my part. From now on, I just want to mind my shop and keep out of trouble for the sake of Angelique, George. Have you seen him rolling over by himself yet?'

Suzanna admitted she had, and that baby George was quite the cleverest baby ever known but plucked up the courage to pursue the conversation she had initiated.

'I am sorry to return to a subject you find distasteful, but from something Aunt Julie told me, and she got it from cousin Jalna who heard it from Sergeant Hadad...' To her surprise, Habib listened quietly while she told him what she had learnt.

'I will check with Aunt Julie,' he said, 'and if it's true, I will see what I can do. It would be a waste if Ahmed's friends got themselves executed for killing a woman who had nothing to do with the ambush.'

A couple of weeks later, when she was visiting Angelique in Haifa, he told her, 'You were right. There was no woman involved in the ambush. I will tell Ahmed's friends. Please do not speak to me on the subject again.'

Suzanna went to Sergeant Hadad's wedding, satisfied that she had done all she could to ensure the safety of Mrs Quigley's daughter, but grew increasingly anxious when the woman did not put in an appearance. She was sure Michelle would have invited her if they worked in the same office. Suppose Habib had not passed the message on, and his friends had found out that Miss Quigley was the person they were hunting? They could have ambushed her on her way to the wedding.

She tugged at Leila's sleeve, when she came round carrying sweetmeats. 'Is Miss Quigley expected?'

'Oh no, hadn't you heard? Patsy left Palestine in October. Everything in the typing office has completely changed. The wives of British policemen are managing it now.'

Suzanna was so relieved she almost forgot to respond, but just in time managed a polite, 'Do you miss the office?'

'Not a bit! Life in Tiberias is too much fun, so different from home. I just love the neighbours. They are Jewish would you believe, but in Tiberias everyone mixes. We seem to party every evening. I work as my husband's receptionist in the day, so I meet even more people. But how about you? Do you like your new job? I hear there is a certain young man singing your praises.'

Suzanna felt herself turn red and was glad when Leila moved on with the sweetmeats so she didn't have to answer. How people gossiped. The young teacher had not even spoken to her directly on the only occasion she and Nurse Um Josef had made a routine visit to his school to look at hair and eyes. She would like to get to know him better though. Everyone in the village thought so highly of him.

She looked round to see who else was there that she knew, and noticed a tall, elegant, and unusually beautiful woman heading her way. 'Suzanna, I have been looking for you,' the woman told her. 'I am Maftur Shawwa. Do you remember me? You came to my wedding with your brother. I am so glad you are here. I wanted to thank you for what you have done.'

'Thank me?' How could she have helped this sophisticated woman? Especially when she hardly knew her. Maftur obviously saw her confusion because she leant closer, and looking round, whispered, 'Yes, for clearing Patsy.'

Suzanna felt scared for her brother's sake. 'You know about that?'

'Of course. I wish we had found out sooner though, I was so hoping Patsy could come to my wedding. Have you told Patsy yet?'

'No. I wasn't sure Habib had passed on the message. Do you think I should?'

'Best not to put it into writing, but if we don't tell her, Patsy will be terrified every time she visits her parents. Perhaps you could find out from her mother when she will be visiting next and tell her then.'

'I'll try,' Suzanna said.

Chapter 79

Patsy entered the office.

The major waited until she was seated, and had tucked her skirt straight, before saying, 'I have to break some very bad news. I received a telegram from Jerusalem a few minutes ago. I can't say how sorry I am to tell you that your father passed away suddenly...'

****

Jerusalem March 5th 1942

'You remember little Suzanna Khader, don't you, Patsy?' Ann Quigley stretched her arms, taking a break from the pile of sympathy letters.

'That orphan you found a job for with the Shepards? The one aiming to go to Missionary College in England?'

'Yes. She changed her mind though, and decided to go into Rural Nursing, enjoying it too, so perhaps she made a wise choice. Such a sweet letter even though she never knew your father. She's invited me to visit her at Al-Lajjun.'

Patsy tried to place the name. 'Al-Lajjun?'

'A village near the crossroads by Megiddo. I think I'll go. I'd like to get out of Jerusalem if only for a day, but don't fancy driving all that way. I'll take a taxi. Would you like to come with me, have a good prowl round Megiddo while I visit Suzanna.'

Patsy hesitated. She knew her mother needed her company. After all, it was only because of that, she was still here in Palestine risking an assassin's bullet every time she left the house. Wandering round next to an Arab village though, with her mother broadcasting her presence, would be pure lunacy. What plausible excuse could she give? She saw the look in her mother's eyes and knew she wouldn't find one.

After she had agreed to go, she tried to dwell on the positive aspects. Apart from comforting her mother, she wanted to re-visit Megiddo. Ever since her peculiar experience in Wad' el-Mughara, she had promised herself that she would explore the lowest level there. She wished though that Tim could have been there with her.

She thought a lot about Tim in the next two days and the conversations they had had when he was on leave last. She could tell him so many things that she couldn't talk about to anyone else.

He hadn't laughed when she had described those weird feelings she had experienced while climbing up to the cave at Wad' el-Mughara, and had even encouraged her to undertake an experiment. If only she had been able to say yes when he had asked her to get some leave sorted so they could tackle Megiddo together. She could have faced the danger of assassination so much better in his company, but she couldn't risk his life as well as well as her own. It was bad enough that she was already partly responsible for two men's deaths.

****

Getting out of the taxi at the crossroads by Megiddo, Patsy glanced warily to left and right. She gazed behind her, studying the tallest of the roadside rocks, hunting for shadows. When she turned back, her mother was standing with her back to the Tel, staring at the lush spring greenery of the Jezreel Valley.

'Armageddon,' her mother said, sweeping her hands to encompass the panorama, 'Seamus was convinced that the Germans would come through here and initiate the world's last battle.'

Despite maggots of fear wriggling down her spine, her mother's words filled Patsy with frustration. She could be based in Palestine helping prepare against German invasion, if only she were free of the men hunting her down.

Beside her, her mother whispered, 'I can't believe he is dead, Patsy.'

'I can't either, Um Pat. I had no idea he was that ill.'

'No one did, dear. It was all so quick. There he was, eating his steak and kidney pie one minute and the next he was lying with his face in the gravy and his spirit gone to glory.'

This was the first time her mother had talked about the moment of her father's death, up to now she had concentrated on the funeral, its organisation, the service, and the mourners.

She gave her mother's shoulders a comforting squeeze, feeling guilty at her relief that her father had not prolonged his dying. How would she and her mother have felt about each other now if her father had rambled full deathbed confessions in the presence of them both? She closed her eyes to blot out the nightmare scenario.

As she and her mother set off up the broad dirt track, she glanced round frequently, still conscious of the foolhardiness of her excursion.

'I wish you would join me in Cairo, mother. You're going to be lonely here.'

'Lonely? No,' her mother shook her head. 'The Lord has been kind to me. I have so many friends from the Anglican and Scottish churches who helped me through that difficult patch last year. I can do my bit for the war effort in Jerusalem. I would be like a fish out of water in Cairo. I've applied for a job at the government hospital. The matron is desperate for qualified staff. I'm only forty-four, Patsy. I know that is ancient to you, but I have half a lifetime ahead of me.'

'I didn't know you were qualified?'

'Oh, yes. I kept your father waiting until I'd finished. I need to refresh, of course, but the matron says she'll soon have my skills polished up.'

'Haven't you ever wanted to go back to work before?'

'Well, dear, when you went off to boarding school, I did suggest it, but your father wouldn't hear of it, said people would think we couldn't live on his salary; there was plenty of voluntary work, he said. He was right, too. I have been able to help people like Suzanna Khader, for instance. I wouldn't have had time for that, if I had been out at work.'

'Why did you and father pack me off to boarding school, Um Pat? There are good convent schools here that take non-Catholics.'

Things would have been so different, she thought, if she hadn't been sent away.

For the first time since his death, she remembered the Abu Pat whom she had loved before going to England, the father who told her exciting stories about road building through the ages, who played fun games like Crusaders versus Saracens. She was sure the father, who had died, only came into being because she had grown up during those first two years she was away without giving him time to get used to it.

'I really wanted you to stay,' her mother replied, 'but your father said no daughter of his was going to a papist school. "It's bad enough them stealing my country," he said, "they're not going to steal my daughter as well." It was a good thing, too in a way that he insisted. If you had stayed, you wouldn't have known where you belonged.'

'I don't know going to boarding School helped me belong anywhere. Palestine will always be my real home.'

'In that case I can expect to see you here quite often?'

Still wrestling with ambivalent feelings towards her father, Patsy had no room in her head for inventing plausible excuses, so didn't answer.

They walked in silence through the excavated tombs at the foot of the mound while Patsy tried to put herself in her father's place. If she had been the one who had wrecked their loving relationship, how would she have dealt with it? For a moment, she experienced her father's agony, so painful she nearly cried out. Oh Abu Pat, she thought, I do forgive you. I really do; but she knew the forgiveness was for her own sake. Her father no longer existed to need it.

They reached a point where the path divided.

'I'll meet you by Solomon's Gate about twenty minutes before our taxi is due,' her mother said, before taking the path that led to Al-Lajjun.

Patsy climbed the Tel, taking no notice of her surroundings, her mind still in a whirl. She stood still when she reached the top, and worked at shutting all thoughts of her father out of her mind, before looking round.

In 1939, the place had been bustling with labourers and archaeologists. Deserted, it looked very different. She hunted for the entrance she wanted. Once she had located it, she peered down into endless darkness. The bottomless pit, Dr Guy had called it, while excavating the shaft that pierced twenty strata, and 6000 years of human history. She knew she was mad to contemplate going down alone and imagined herself with a broken leg deep inside the Tel unable to climb back, while her mother sent search parties round the surrounding countryside. She wished she had told her mother what she intended to do but hadn't wanted to worry her.

At least there were modern steps down. She switched on her flashlight and examined the top ones. They seemed sound and dry. If American technology was all people said, the stairs should be safe. She made a cautious descent, keeping one hand on the damp rock wall, holding her flashlight with the other, trying not to think of the distance she would fall, if she slipped. At the foot of the first set of steps, she found another flight and descended a further thirty-five feet. She circled her torch and saw that she had reached the entrance to the 165-foot long, seven-foot high tunnel. Dr Guy had told her about it, but had refused to show her. She stepped cautiously along this magnificent piece of Bronze Age engineering, her echoing footsteps reminding her of the whole weight of the Tel above.

She reached her goal, the underground cave at the end. If her theory was correct, it had once been home to Neanderthals. She shivered and wished she had brought a coat.

Standing by the spring-fed pool inside, she felt a sense of awe, but underground water always affected her that way. The awe bore no relation to that other weird feeling she wanted to explore.

Sitting on the packed earth floor, her back against the damp rocky wall, she switched off her torch, closed her eyes to shut out the total blackness, and tried to concentrate on Neanderthals, but her mind wandered. She kept wanting Tim to be there with her, and wishing that her relationship with him would go just a little further than the platonic friendship she had insisted on when they had first met again in Cairo. Except, with all the secrets she had to keep, she knew she didn't deserve to be loved. She wasn't counting Operation Goliath, of course, that was an official secret, it wasn't cheating to keep that from Tim, but Ahmed and her father, they were different. She could perhaps bring herself to tell Tim about Ahmed, and why his friends were hunting her, but she could never tell him about her father.

Less than five minutes of the twenty she had promised herself had passed, when rapidly approaching footsteps, shouts and laughter ruined her experiment. Beams of light wavered towards her, and a group of young people packed in front of her. When the cave was full, an elderly man stood beside the pool and began to lecture in Hebrew.

Pushing her way through the students, she thought that it didn't really matter about the experiment. One day she would carry it out properly with Tim beside her. She switched on her torch, and started up the tunnel. She had not gone far when she heard footsteps running behind her. Instinctively she too started to run. She should have been on her guard, she told herself. She knew Ahmed had been a student at the Technion, so why had she assumed all the students in the cave were Jewish. She should have waited and returned with them, protected by their numbers. This tunnel was uphill work. Her desk job had left her out of condition. The footsteps were closing in on her unprotected back. She panted, short of breath, her legs aching. Her assailant was really close now. She swivelled round, thrust her torch in front of her at head height, hoping to dazzle, while swinging her bag to deflect a knife thrust.

'Patsy,' a familiar voice called, 'It is you, Patsy, isn't it?'

She dipped her torch and stilled the arm holding the bag. Her body sagged in relief. 'Dalia!' she said between pants, 'What are you doing here?'

'Patsy, I really want to talk to you, but I ought to be at this lecture. Are you going to be on the Tel long?'

'About another hour.'

'Good, can I see you on the surface in about twenty minutes?'

'Yes, I'll be waiting.'

'Shalom.'

Patsy watched Dalia turn and run back down the tunnel, then walked sedately until she reached the steps and climbed them slowly.

Her sense of relief evaporated when she emerged into the open. An assassin stalking her could be hiding anywhere among the ruins. She could do nothing about it, so, she kept her fears at bay by concentrating on Solomon's stables. She examined closely the mangers, the postholes, and the stalls. Definitely stables, not a pagan temple as the first archaeologists to work on the site had argued. If only Tim could be with her, so they could talk about the structures together. She immersed herself so thoroughly in the site that it seemed no time at all before she heard the students making their noisy way up the stairs.

Dalia strode towards her. If she had not agreed to meet her Patsy would never have recognised this bronzed muscular woman clad in blue shorts and shirt, so unlike the elegant office worker she had known in Haifa.

'I didn't know you were interested in archaeology, Dalia.'

'I am not, but I am interested in water storage. Today's ramble is part of my arid farming course.'

They walked across the Tel as they talked.

'So you are a student now?' Patsy commented.

'In agriculture with a view to farming in the Negev. Much more my sort of thing than sitting on my bottom typing all day. What are you doing? I heard you had moved to Egypt.'

'Still sitting on my bottom, I am afraid, but at a desk in Cairo.'

Even while they chatted, Patsy was storing Dalia on a mental index for Operation Goliath. She would need to get her address so someone from the team could contact her.

'It's lovely seeing you, Dalia,' she tried, 'and I do hope we can meet up again soon, perhaps go for a cup of coffee.' If only we could, she thought. She tore a page from her notebook and scribbled on it. Here's where you can contact me. May I have your address?'

Dalia pulled her own notebook from her bag. 'I'll be away on fieldwork soon, so I'll give you both addresses.'

While Dalia was writing, Patsy looked across to Al-Lajjun on the gently sloping hillside opposite and was surprised to see a minaret. She hadn't realised her mother's protégée worked in a Muslim village. Her trip here had been even more foolhardy than she had realised.

Movement on the path leading to the Tel caught her eye. Her mother was walking beside a young woman, probably one of the village mukhtar's wives showing her the way.

She pointed her mother out to Dalia.

'I think I've seen your mother before, but I've never spoken to her. Nu, isn't that Suzanna Khader beside her.'

'No, that's a grown up, Suzanna's only little.'

'How long since you've seen her? She was growing fast last year in Jerusalem.'

They watched the two women reach the foot of the Tel.

'Yes, that's definitely Suzanna,' Dalia decided, 'but she's had her hair cut.'

'I didn't know you knew her?'

'It's a long story.'

'Of course. You were staying with the Shepards after...' Patsy's voice trailed off as she remembered the scene at the funeral.

Dalia was silent for a moment, staring at the ground, then she said, 'Addy was very kind to me when I desperately needed kindness, but as you warned me, the Second Chosen can get quite suffocating.' She banged her hands together as if crushing a memory, then leaned over the edge of the Tel and shouted 'Shalom, Suzanna!'

'Saida, Dalia,' Suzanna shouted up, 'I am so happy to see you,' but to Patsy's ear, the reply contained more surprise than pleasure.

Dalia didn't seem to notice. She darted down the path. Patsy followed more slowly. By the time she had reached her mother, Dalia and Susanna were hugging each other and exclaiming how well the other looked. Her mother was slightly in front now.

'Patsy,' her mother greeted her, 'Suzanna asked to meet you.' She glanced backwards. 'Who is that other girl?' she whispered. 'I've seen her before somewhere, haven't I?'

'Probably,' Patsy whispered back, 'Her name's Dalia Leitner. We worked in the same office.'

She watched Suzanna say something to Dalia, break free, and come over. 'I don't know whether you remember me,' Suzanna said, 'You came to tea sometimes when I was working for Mrs Shepard.'

'Of course I remember you,' Patsy said, 'but I didn't expect you to be so grown-up and tall.'

From the corner of her eye, she noticed Dalia walking back up the Tel. She hoped she wouldn't just leave.

Suzanna looked awkward, more like the young girl Patsy had envisaged.

'Miss Quigley, I asked your mother if we could have a word alone. Maftur said I had to tell you something personally, if I saw you. It's sort of private.'

Her mother suddenly took an intense interest in a small clump of blue flowers growing beside the path. 'I'll just go and ask Dalia if she knows what these are called,' she said, and went off briskly.

Patsy could feel her chest vibrating but forced a smile. 'When did you see Maftur?' She fell in step beside Suzanna who was walking downhill in the opposite direction from Dalia and her mother. She could see Suzanna struggling to speak, almost as if she was inventing the answer.

'At a cousin's wedding about a month ago.' She paused, and then went on in a rush. 'Maftur said I was to tell you, Ahmed's friends know that Ahmed's death wasn't planned beforehand and the woman they had suspected of betraying him is innocent.'

'Innocent?' Patsy repeated. She frowned. She wanted more than that. Surely Maftur had expanded on that message. 'Did she say the woman was now safe?'

'Yes,' Suzanna spoke more quickly, more confidently, 'she said that, too. She said the men who had been looking for the woman had gone back to Syria.'

The sun went dark and then redoubled its intensity. Patsy felt the bulls-eye between her shoulder blades fade, and the tenseness in her shoulders loosen. Smiling was easy now.

'Suzanna, that is the best news anyone has ever given me. Please will you say thank you very much to Maftur.' She wanted to say more, so much more, as every muscle in her body became supple again, but she couldn't think what to say, didn't even know if Suzanna was aware of the meaning of the message she had brought. Instead, she just stared at Suzanna in silence willing her to receive her gratitude. She saw Suzanna smile uncertainly, shuffling her feet. They turned and made their way back up the Tel.

Everything was different now, Patsy thought. Plans whirled in her head. She was free to visit Palestine and her mother, whenever the opportunity arose. She could play an active role in Operation Goliath, recruit Dalia herself. Perhaps she could add Suzanna to her list. She must find out her political views. Suzanna could be especially useful if she was working in a Muslim village. And what about Maftur? Now the danger was over she could get in touch with her again. If the Germans invaded, someone with clerical skills could be invaluable. As soon as she returned home that evening, she would phone Cairo. Ask if there were any errands she could do in Palestine before she went back.

They reached the top of the Tel. Abu Pat and Dalia were side by side, looking over the plain. As they drew nearer, she heard Dalia telling her mother about improved wheat varieties for arid regions. Her mother was managing to look interested.

Dalia stopped talking, whirled round, and came forward to hug them again.

'The two of you, both in one day!'

Patsy said, 'Yes, and we are all a lot more grown-up now.'

Just as well, she thought looking over the fields of Armageddon and thinking of Rommel's seeming invincibility. They were all going to have to be very grown up, if they were going to survive the next few years.

Glossary of Terms

Abba - Hebrew for father

Aliya - (Sometimes transliterated Aliyah) used mostly in the phrase 'to make aliya' - to emigrate to the homeland of Israel (Eretz Israel) as Zionist Jews called Palestine.

Aliyah Beth - (also known as Ha'apala) a Hebrew term used for the immigration by Jews to Palestine in violation of British restrictions against such immigration.

Axis – the European countries on the same side as Germany.

B'Seder - Hebrew for OK

Bobkesh - goat shit - used to mean 'rubbish'

Chutzpah - Yiddish for 'cheekiness, impertinence'

Dirndl – a skirt easily made from a single straight piece of material by gathering the material and sewing to a wait band at the top.

Effendi – a middle/upper class city dwelling but often land owning Arabic male. Like 'sir' in English often used as a term of respect.

Eema - Hebrew for mother

Fellah - singular of fellahin - roughly equivalent to the English peasant.

Fez - (Turkish) or Tarboosh (Egyptian) In Palestine booth terms were in use - a felt cap (usually red) for a man; shaped like a flat-topped cone with a tassel usually black

Garagenik - Someone who works in a garage

Gehenna – the Hebrew equivalent of Hell

Grand Mufti - Haj Amin al-Husseini was born in Jerusalem in 1893, he went on to serve in the Ottoman Army during World War I. The British appointed him Mufti of Jerusalemby in 1921 because they thought he would be easy to influence. He was however anti-British and Anti-Jewish and soon became the most prominent Arab figure in Palestinian politics. He was dismissed from his position and exiled following riots in 1936 but continued his extremist activities from abroad. In WW2 he helped Hitler recruit Muslims from Yugoslavia into the SS.

Hagana – (Sometimes transliterated Haganah) An underground Jewish organisation which, until after World War 2, favoured passive resistance to the British but actively supported the British during WW2.

Hanukah – (often transliterated Chanukah, Hannuka or Channukah) Festival of Lights, a Jewish festival that occasionally coincides with the Christian Christmas.

Irgun - An underground Jewish organisation which favoured active defiance of the British but agreed to support the British during WW2.

Keffiya - a male head dress kept in place by an iqal. In Palestine before 1938 this was usually worn by fellaheen and Bedouin, and was most commonly white. Variations in colours throughout the Arabic countries tended to be tribal although he Arab Legion in Transjordan wore a chequered one as part of their uniform. Nowadays in the west bank the colour of keffiyas tends to be political although Christian Arabs in Nazareth still wear white keffiyahs Before 1938 townspeople would have worn red tarbooshes made popular in Egypt or turbans, common throughout the Ottoman Empire. In 1938 the Grand Mufti ordered all Palestinian Arabs to wear keffiyas as most of the activists wanted by police were fellaheen who stuck out in urban surroundings. Women were told to wear black scarves, commonly worn by rural Muslim women. Up to that time, urban Arab women would have worn western style hats and rural Christian Arab women would have worn white scarves.

Kibbutz - a Jewish settlement where all property is held in common and the children are reared by the community not the family.

Kibbutznik - a resident of a kibbutz

Kibitzn - Yiddish for complaining

Matric – abbreviation for matriculation. A qualification to undertake a university degree course. In England, at this period, fifteen year olds in grammar schools gained matriculation exemption if they passed five subjects with credit (including English, maths and one foreign language) in the school certificate examination.

Menorah – The traditional Jewish Menorah has seven candle holders but the Hanukah menorah (also called hanukiya) has nine.

Moshav - a Jewish settlement whose members own and husband their own land but plan crop rotation and sales co-operatively.

NAAFI - The Navy, Army and Air Force Institutes is a non-profit retaining organisation created by the British government to run recreational establishments needed by the Armed Forces, and to sell goods to servicemen and their families. In Palestine the British Police were entitled to use the NAAFI. In wartime Palestine the NAAFI sold goods that that were unobtainable by civilians and it sold them at pre-war prices.

Nu - an interjection with multiple meanings, often analogous to "well?" or "so?

Po - euphemism for chamber pot

Sabra - a Jew born in Palestine

Second Chosen - a fictional fundamentalist Christian sect based on an amalgam of several real evangelical sects.

Shabbat – Hebrew for Sabbath

Shalom – a Hebrew greeting meaning 'Peace'.

Simchat Torah – a Jewish holiday

Suq - a Middle East market

Tobruk – a town on the Libyan coast with a useful harbour. Rommel needed to control Tobruk before he could invade Egypt.

The Stern Gang - An underground Jewish organisation that continued to resist the British throughout WW2.

Um - Arabic for mother

Wadi - a dry river bed generally creating a ravine near its source.

Wrens – a nick name for members of the Womens Royal Navy Service.

We hope you enjoyed reading this book;

Please do feel free to get in touch and let us know your comments.
reviews@discoveredauthors.co.uk

Undiscovered Authors is a national writing competition searching out literary talent.

www.undiscoveredauthors.co.uk

This new initiative from Discovered Authors aims to help exciting, original works by talented authors get the bookshelf space and readership they deserve.

Please turn the page to find out more about our Undiscovered Authors winning titles to be published in 2006 and to learn more about our other authors and browse our online bookshelves please visit:

www.discoveredauthors.co.uk

Discovered Authors
50 Albemarle Street
Mayfair, London
W1S 4BD

Other Undiscovered Authors competition winning titles published in 2006 include:

The Tale of Findo Gask by Huw Thomas
National Winner of the 2005 Undiscovered Authors Fiction Competition.
The Tale of Findo Gask tells the story of a thief, born in a ditch, raised in slums and educated by the underworld. An unregistered child with no official identity, Findo begins to steal in order to survive, but his exploits soon become more audacious...
This is not a crime novel, but the story of an unconventional life; of alienation, love and a desperate search for acceptance.
National Winner of the 2005 Undiscovered Authors Competition.

Sentinel by Tony O'Reilly
Ireland National Winner for Undiscovered Authors 2005 Fiction Competition
After a viral artificial intelligence is accidentally created, a chain of events begin to unfold which promise to bring chaos to society. Spanning the Middle East, France, Spain and Ireland, Sentinel follows the journey of three strangers as they join together in a last desperate attempt to fight the seemingly unstoppable life force... but the final confrontation leads to a truth more terrifying and far-reaching than they could ever have thought possible.
Winner of the Undiscovered Authors 2005 National prize for Ireland.

Laughing Star by Jo Nisbet
National Winner of the 2005 Undiscovered Authors Non-Fiction Competition.
Laughing Star is an autobiographical account of a mother's personal journey dealing with children who suffer from Attention Deficit Hyperactive Disorder (ADHD). When fourteen year old Emily becomes so out of control, sending her to Brat Camp becomes her mother's last and only resort.
Jo Nisbet, a counseling Psychologist, began to write Laughing Star as a means of catharsis to download her experiences after a challenging and confusing time.
Regional Surrey winner of the 2005 Undiscovered Authors competition.

All Discovered Authors titles are available to buy at
www.amazon.co.uk and all good bookshops.